Praise for *Don't Tell Ima*

"I want to commend you for your bringing the issue of marital abuse to the public forum... I wish you success in this endeavor and pray that the content and message of the book become only fiction in the future."

— *Rabbi Zev Leff*
Rav, Moshav Mattisyahu

This book surfaces an important discussion about domestic violence, and that is not limited to physical abuse, but accurately portrays domestic violence by its central dynamic of power and control and includes many forms of abuse including financial, emotional/psychological, spiritual, sexual, and verbal abuse. Understanding this, and that no one should feel alone or trapped, is an important step forward as we join to support all victims of abuse in all communities.

— *Dr. Shoshannah D. Frydman*
Executive Director, Shalom Task Force

Congratulations on a very important contribution to the literature of Jewish life... As someone who deals with divorce and its trauma in my professional life, I found the book very informative on the "gut" level. I found the characters including the children very credible... I feel this manuscript (is) very important for the training of marriage and family therapists.

— *Rabbi Moshe Brody*
Marriage counselor

Lisa Barness has written an extremely important work. Emotional abuse is a huge problem... I hope this book will bring a bit of comfort to the many victims, who are usually doubly victimized by not having their pain validated and are chastised for even speaking out and "complaining" and not being able to "suffer silently" or "fix" the abuser.

— Dr. Miriam Adahan
Co-author, I Thought It Would Be Different

❖

Don't Tell Ima is one woman's courageous tale of tragedy and rebuilding in the face of terrible abuse and atrocities. I was extremely moved by the story and its underlying message of *emunah* and hope, even in the darkest times. May it be a source of *chizzuk* for anyone who has experienced this trauma.

— Avigail Rosenberg
Editor, Healing from the Break

❖

Lisa Barness, with unusual courage, wisdom, and eloquence, tells the story of her marriage and the abuse she and her children suffered at the hands of a man who presented himself as the epitome of Torah values and behavior. She carefully and painstakingly describes the road she traveled from the young naïve *kallah* who believed in the righteousness and commitment of her husband the *tzaddik*, to the mature mother who had to learn how to interpret her experiences and discoveries, and then to extricate herself and her children from the web of lies and secrets that threatened them.

Therapists, rabbis, communal leaders and educators will all learn from the story of Lisa's marriage and growth. All readers will gain greater appreciation of the terrible price we pay for allowing criminal behavior in the name of religious values to be conducted in an atmosphere of deceit and secrecy.

— Rabbi Chaim Tabasky
Torah educator and narrative therapist

DON'T TELL IMA

A Novel

Lisa Barness

ISBN: 978-965-7041-03-1 (paperback)
ISBN: 978-965-7041-04-8 (ebook)

Although this novel is based on a true story, all of the names and details of the characters are fictional.

Publishing services were provided by JewishSelfPublishing. The content of the book is the sole responsibility of the author, who plays the role of the publisher, and does not necessarily reflect the opinions of JewishSelfPublishing.

www.jewishselfpublishing.com
info@jewishselfpublishing.com
(800) 613-9430

The author can be contacted at donttellima@gmail.com.

We sincerely hope you enjoy reading this book. The author would be very gratified if you would show your support by posting a nice review on Amazon.

ONE

GOD OF THE UNIVERSE, *does everyone have to repeat the same mistakes, suffer the same torment? Can't anyone learn from the experiences of others?* A chill went up my spine, tingling through my arms. Sitting on the bamboo garden chair, I observed the sunset's thin red-orange waves blending into the last pink remnants of light.

Is this some existential plan that each generation has to repeat mistakes — and then attempt to correct them?

I felt agonizing frustration mounting in my chest. My kids had suffered, and I was unable to defend them. When I finally understood what had happened and fought the dragon, we talked freely about the signs of abuse and bad character traits. But still, they had suffered.

Does my daughter have to repeat the torment I escaped?

I did not notice soon enough. And now she can't hear me.

I can't believe this. No. No. NO!

My child, heart of my heart. I held her endlessly after birth. I gazed for hours into her eyes, those deep, beautiful wells into her soul. Her first smile shone in my arms, reflecting my joy.

Whenever she saw me, she crawled, toddled, and later ran into my arms. Only with me would she be immediately calm, laying her head onto my shoulder like a baby bird nesting. I felt close to and loved all my children, but this daughter and I had somehow forged a special relationship.

Today those blue eyes are angry and defiant.

1

Why are we so incapable of shielding our children from harm?

"Ima," my daughter insists fiercely, "I know what I'm doing. Stop seeing abusive people everywhere."

She doesn't listen to anything. She doesn't hear.

I must think. The wrong words will push her farther away.

Leaning back into the garden chair, I am inundated with powerful memories of my earlier years. I hardly recognize that woman now, but I need to remember. Perhaps from the memories of my previous life I will learn what to say to my precious Ariella today.

Two

1962

WHEN HE WAS EIGHT and I was five, my brother began to imitate my father's humiliating attitude toward my mother, only with me as the victim. I don't remember clearly, but I guess Mom's attempts to stop him from attacking me were as futile as her efforts to stop her husband from embarrassing her.

It could be that when she sighed, she was including within it her own pain the verbal and physical assaults — or conversely, the stifling, absolute silence and disregard that I suffered. If so, she never let me know it. I assumed the guilt for my brother's volatile anger, my father's cold aloofness, and my mom's inability to come to my defense.

I was glad that my baby sister seemed somehow untouched by the melancholy that permeated our home. Yet, it seemed to emphasize that *there must be something wrong in me that offends them.*

I tucked myself away in my bedroom, separated by the swinging door that divided the house into two — them and me. There I created a fantasy life in a safe, impenetrable world. In school I was invisible, unless the kids needed someone to bully. I remained a good student and was quiet, so the teachers did not need to pay me much attention.

Leaving home as soon as I could, I stumbled and fumbled through a maze of confusion, ill-advised lifestyles, and misconceptions. With rare exceptions, no one offered help or seemed to care, until I met Efraim.

THREE

1976

I SAT SPELLBOUND AT THE edge of the shul's red, velvety cushioned chair to catch Efraim Baumen's compelling voice. Speaking softly into the microphone, he offered a Kabbalistic view of marriage. "The *neshama* is whole and pure, complete in every way. When the soul agrees to come into this world, it splits, like an atom, into two parts." As he detailed the longing of each half of the soul searching to find completion with its other half, I found myself staring at this gifted speaker and feeling drawn toward him.

The silence in the large auditorium, where young men and women sat separately, emphasized the electric charge of his words. His long, slender fingers held the notes that he barely referred to as he looked into the approving faces of the crowd. With a shiver of jealousy, I realized many young women were leaning forward to catch every word. "Our *tikkun* (rectification) and completion in this world occurs as we seek and find our other half, embedded in a finite body."

He continued, "This choice is already known in heaven and is announced forty days before the souls are conceived into their respective wombs."

Was I imagining that he was looking at me as he spoke?

"When husband and wife merit, the Divine Presence resides in their midst. We can all agree that sharing life together with a loyal partner and having children are important elements of the marital relationship, yet there is another deeper level. According to the *Zohar*, husband and wife are in essence one soul, half of which is clothed in the husband's body, while the other half is clothed in the wife's. That means that each one alone contains only half a soul. Only when a man and a woman unite do they possess one whole and complete soul." Pausing momentarily, he added, "This may explain why even those who say they'll wait to wed seem to be always looking for someone. The sense of imcompletion just doesn't let up."

Looking around, I noticed quite a few smiles.

He continued, "For some reason, God decided that for many years, from the moment of birth until the marriage, the two halves of the soul remain apart. They may be in different countries, living very different lifestyles, or they can be the next door neighbors. Only when the proper moment arrives will they find each other and marry. And that," he paused again, "is when the two half souls once again merge and unite."

I could not resist nodding in agreement with every word.

Swept away in his gripping imagery, I nearly missed his closing words.

"This, then, is the inner dimension of married life. Although they remain two distinct personalities and bodies, when they marry, the husband's and wife's respective half-souls unify and merge into one singular entity. It is in this new reality that a person feels whole. In marriage the man and woman find what they have always felt was missing."

A sea of movement threatened to engulf me. Amid applause, the crowd of young modern Orthodox Jewish singles was rising to their feet. In a moment, Efraim, adjusting the *kippa* on his jet black, wavy hair, was surrounded by the enthusiastic audience now mingling near the podium. With charming bashfulness, he glanced down as members of the audience complimented him. My cheeks were burning, and I hoped the flush was not as visible as it felt.

Efraim merged into the crowd, shaking hands with the young men. As he approached me, he stopped and turned.

The move came unexpectedly and the close proximity of his handsome, high-cheeked features so near me sent a tremor through my whole body.

"Hi, Shifra," he said. I was surprised he remembered my name. We had met very briefly one Shabbat morning at the 'singles' Kiddush.

"You spoke well," I mumbled, wishing I'd dressed in a more co-ordinated fashion.

He half-closed his eyes and grinned. "See you later," and he winked as he was drawn into the crowd.

The pounding in my chest only eased after I was bundled in my winter coat and scarf, as I walked slowly into the biting wintry night, not feeling the harsh cold.

On the short walk home, I imagined Efraim accompanying me, whispering secrets of the *neshama* longing for its soulmate.

"How was it?" asked my studious roommate. Glenda looked up briefly from her voluminous reference books. She spent every second studying for her medical exams. "Life," she had already informed me, "will be renewed after I pass the tests."

"It was nice," I answered as I walked into the bathroom to check on my reflection. *Why did I cut my hair so short? I look like a pixie.* There was not much I could do about it now.

Nearing the mirror, I pulled at my cheeks. Was that a pimple or a red mark from the stinging cold?

My thoughts raced. Since I learned about Judaism and moved into this Orthodox community, I met more young Jewish singles than I ever knew existed. Many gathered at the weekly evening programs on topics from *halacha* to the esoteric. Tonight's lecture was meant to encourage the shy or lazy to commit to finding their *bashert* and begin their families. Efraim, a single *ba'al teshuva*, was a popular speaker. He was known in his yeshiva and the community for countless acts of kindness and for his charismatic influence on non-religious Jews. I didn't know more, but looking in the mirror, I blushed again. "See you later, Shifra," he had said. That was all I needed to know.

Even before I became religious, I was never drawn to romantic novels. Yet no doubt a romance writer might well describe my feelings tonight. I felt as though I'd known Efraim forever and couldn't wait to see him again. Was he thinking about me? Next time I'd be sure to dress in a better matching outfit.

FOUR

"**C**AN YOU GET THE phone?" my roommate Glenda called from the shower. "My mom's supposed to call."

"No problem." I followed the loud ringing as I reached across the table where books, Xeroxed papers, files, and Glenda's notebooks were all stacked neatly. Finishing the last of the Shabbat leftovers, I gulped some honeyed sweet potatoes as I lifted the receiver.

"Hello."

"Hi," responded a soft-spoken male voice. "Is Shifra there?"

His voice was smooth and soft as butter.

Grabbing a crumpled but clean napkin, I wiped the last remnants of the sweet orange vegetable from my lips and slowed my breathing. "That's me."

"Hey, how are you doing?"

I hope he didn't hear me gasp. "I'm OK, *baruch Hashem*. And you?"

"I'm good, thank God. Have a minute to talk?"

Efraim, you can have all the time you want. I pushed my dinner away. Spilling some chicken gravy, I absorbed it quickly with a napkin before it spoiled Glenda's notes. "Sure."

I accidentally kicked over the bottle of water that Glenda had insisted we keep on the floor so it wouldn't spill on her numerous pages of biology notes. Her notes were dry, but I wondered if I would have caused the puddle on the floor if the bottle had been on the table. Throwing a *shmatte* over the water, I listened.

"We're having a Shabbaton at Ohel Sarah, our new shelter for

7

homeless women. In a month, we're bringing girls from different high schools to meet the Ohel Sarah residents."

"OK," I said.

"Some of the teens are religious and some are on the way. It'll be amazing."

"How does it work?" I tried to keep my voice nonchalant. I didn't know much about Ohel Sarah or what Efraim wanted.

"A young couple is running the show. It will be great," he chuckled. "Not everyone is so pleased with our little rehabilitation center in their neighborhood." More seriously, he added, "There are several goals. One is to offer an opportunity to be compassionate toward the less fortunate. We want the girls to see how this is an essential facet of Judaism. Another is to try to integrate the lonely women in the shelter with their neighbors."

"Wow, amazing," I said enthusiastically, but feeling like it was way over my head. *What does he want me, a recent baalat teshuva, to do?*

Glenda walked into the room wearing her light-blue bathrobe and a bath towel wrapped into a graceful turban balanced steadily on her head. "Is that my mom?" she reached for the phone.

Raising my eyebrows, I pulled the receiver away, as my finger wagged *no*. I whispered Efraim Baumen was on the line.

He continued to explain, "We need to call the high school girls. I'll give you the names and numbers of the locals to invite them. And I have a list of topics for the advisors to choose from to prepare their discussion groups." Efraim chuckled again. "Come to think of it, maybe you should have started two months ago."

"I was just wondering the same," I replied, overwhelmed, but undaunted, "but I think I can do it."

Glenda furrowed her eyebrows, noticing the small gravy stain on her otherwise pristine notes. I winced and mouthed an apology as I jotted the time and place of the Shabbat program onto my calendar, agreeing to meet Efraim to get the phone numbers.

"Should I bring the lists over now?" he asked.

Surveying our apartment's casual appearance, I told him I was busy but would be happy to meet in a couple of hours.

"How about 9:00 tonight? Is that OK?"

Again, covering the mouthpiece, I asked Glenda with the sign language we had developed between us if she had time to help me straighten up. Shaking her head, she indicated a big exam that she'd be studying for all evening. It was already 7:00 p.m.

"Let's say 9:30," I countered.

"Great, see you then. *Shalom*, Shifra."

Glenda motioned that she was going to get dinner ready. "Oh, he hung up already."

I laughed, realizing that I had lingered before replacing the receiver. "He wants me to make phone calls for his Shabbaton next month."

"Nice way to meet more friends too," she commented. "Maybe a *shidduch*?" she teased.

"Really, Glenda, I'm just making some phone calls."

"Right," she winked.

While she went to brush her hair, the food she was reheating for dinner started to burn.

Turning the flame off, I faced a sink full of the dishes we hadn't yet washed from Shabbat. In an effort to meet new community members, I had invited a few young people. Glenda preferred small meals so she wouldn't have to spend her precious study time on preparations and clean up, so I agreed to do most of that.

"I'm spending my parents' life savings on medical school," she commented responsibly. "How can I ask them to buy food for all my friends too?"

I rolled up my sleeves and started cleaning.

"Hi," said the good-looking young man when Glenda opened the door.

"Hi, come in. Shifra will be right out." Glenda let Efraim in, leaving the door slightly open.

He nodded and smiled shyly. "Would you like something to drink?" Glenda asked.

"No thanks. Hey, what's your name?"

"I'm Glenda, Shifra's roommate," she said before returning to her newly reorganized study space. Noticing the sopping wet rag on the floor, she quickly scooped it up and hurried to the bathroom to wring it out.

In the bedroom, I brushed my hair, sorry again that I had cut it so short. But it really doesn't look so bad, I convinced myself, buttoning up a clean blouse.

"Hi, Efraim, how are you?" I was glad we were meeting on my personal and freshly spotless home turf.

The phone rang and Glenda answered.

"Mom, hi. How are you? Just a second, I'll go into the other room to talk." She smiled at me, as Efraim looked up.

Efraim sat down, fluffed one pillow under his arm and leaned back onto another. His long legs pushed forward until his knees pressed into the coffee table, laden with fruit and drink.

"Here, you don't have to suffer." I reached forward to move the table.

"In Sodom, knee squishing would probably be considered an elevated form of hospitality," he mocked. He laughed at his own joke about the biblical community that hated guests and tortured the ones who did appear.

"We've come a long way since then. You can sit on a comfortable couch as your knees get crushed," I joked back.

When I heard the muffled sound of a ringing phone, I realized Glenda was finished on the phone and would study in her bedroom. I made a mental note to thank her for her consideration.

"Shif," she called out, "it's Anna. She wants to know if she can eat here on Shabbat."

"Sure, tell her that's great — and if she wants, she can sleep over too," I returned. "Thanks. And Glenda, if anyone else calls, please tell them I'll call back tomorrow."

"No problem. I'm turning off the ringer then. Goodnight." The bedroom door closed.

With the palms of his hands pressing onto his legs, Efraim leaned forward. "It's only Sunday and you already have plans for Shabbat?" he asked curiously.

"I like to have guests. I enjoy cooking and baking for them and..."
I looked up to see him nodding encouragingly.

"And I heard when you start to learn Torah, you feel like a child in
first grade. The Chassidim say when you learn *aleph* and *beit*, you can
teach someone else *aleph*. I'm up to *beit*. After all the Torah classes,
I have something to share," I rambled. "Anyway, I grew up in a home
without guests, and I want to have lots of them."

"I like your enthusiasm." He leaned back again. "It's a good character trait." All of a sudden, I felt shy. Reaching across the small table
to fill the cups with hot tea from the thermos, I changed the topic.

"How did you get involved with the homeless and set up a shelter?"

"It's a pretty selfish reason. I hated that people were living on the
street." He shuddered. "When I first came to yeshiva, I used to stop
and talk to this guy who lived on a bench a couple of blocks away.
There he was in his tattered, smelly clothes and I wanted to find out
how he got there."

I visualized Efraim scrutinizing this destitute man.

"He always kept his hand on his shopping cart like he was protecting his life's treasures. I thought he was mentally disturbed at
first, that he probably never had much of a life." Efraim shook his
head. "Boy, was I wrong. It took months of prying, but when he saw
that I came consistently, he started to trust me."

Efraim's mouth turned up into a boyish grin. "I guess the food I
sneaked to him out of the yeshiva cafeteria wasn't so bad after all,
hmm."

Efraim told me about the young man's wealthy parents, his wife
who died tragically in childbirth, and the severely handicapped baby
he tried to raise alone. His parents insisted he give his daughter up for
adoption, but he couldn't. When they refused to help any longer, and
he finally agreed to give her over to an institution, something snapped
inside. Efraim snapped his fingers loudly to emphasize his words. "It
was such an effort to get him to say anything about his personal life.
Then he finally confided that he had an M.A. in engineering, but he
started drifting from job to job, each one more degrading. It wasn't
long before he couldn't pay rent. He just put some pictures of his

wife and a few other belongings into a shopping cart and went to the streets." Efraim grew silent. "It broke my heart."

I felt like crying. "It's a tragic story."

"Yeah. When he finally showed me his wedding picture, he started crying, and so did I." Efraim paused. "They looked like a happy, loving couple." Efraim stood up to pace, as he continued. "He told me no one ever talked to him anymore. He felt as if he had become invisible, and he liked it that way. He didn't feel there was anything to live for. He refused to speak to his family. And they either didn't look for him, or if they did, they couldn't find him." Efraim lifted his hands, fingers spread wide, palms up. "How could they?"

"What happened?"

"He considered suicide several times, but in his words, he couldn't get that right either."

"*Baruch Hashem.* There are some things it's good not to be successful at." My thoughts flashed back to my own childhood sadness. I shuddered to think of this young man.

"Would you believe he told me he didn't know if he had a name?" Efraim's voice broke into my ruminations. "Then he said he did have one, but couldn't remember it." Efraim returned to the couch. "Wow, it was like pulling teeth until he finally recalled the name he had seen on an old electric bill that had found its way into his shopping cart years earlier. Somehow it surfaced, reminding him of his identity. Brother, until he let me see it. Unbelievable how protective he was. Like he was becoming visible again and the transformation was extremely painful to him."

Efraim's eyes narrowed as he began to stare, as though replaying the scene as it happened. Afterward, he spoke with the reborn Alan for hours trying to convince him to contact his family.

"'No, no, no!' Alan kept yelling. Like I was hurting him, killing him. It was frightening. The next time I went to his bench, he wasn't there. I searched the neighborhood. I was afraid he might kill himself." Efraim gulped air. He relived the moment.

"I debated going to the police, but figured that if they found him, they'd insist on knowing his name and would try to track down his family. He would think I had betrayed him." Efraim shook his head. "I couldn't do it. I knew if he would meet his family, it would have to be in his own time."

The doorbell rang. Excusing myself, I gave some change to a man collecting *tzedaka* for a poor family.

"You know, I never told anyone this part before." As he looked into my eyes, I felt he was entrusting me with a deeply personal secret. "I passed by that bench several times a day, feeling guilty that I'd pushed him too far."

He paused, his forehead wrinkled and his jaws clenched. I noticed a dimple on his chin.

"One day he was there, barely recognizable, but there. He told me he never sat *shiva*."

I was perplexed.

"Don't you get it?" he said, "Don't you see what just happened?"

"Wha...?" I didn't get it.

"He's Jewish! I didn't know he was Jewish. He was telling me that he's a *Yid* — and he knows something about tradition." Efraim snapped his fingers and jumped up. "I'll bet that's why he didn't commit suicide. I'm sure." He talked more to himself than to me as he stood and paced.

"Remember — he barely told me his name. We never got to discuss religion."

I sat, nodding in amazement.

"Wow. And where was he all this time?"

"You won't believe this." Efraim began wringing his hands together. "He told me that after we spoke, he began to cry and he couldn't stop. He went to live at a building site not far from there. He said it was so noisy, no one heard him bawling."

I was in shock. An image of my own tearstained childhood face appeared in my mind's eye. But my refuge was my small bedroom, separated from the other members of my family by a swinging door, them and me. Pulling the quilt over my head to suffocate the sound, I cried out my isolation. I felt great compassion for this man, Alan, suffering in solitude, surrounded by machinery and the hard stone and steel of a deafening building zone. And I was drawn closer to thoughtful and compassionate Efraim who exhibited extraordinary patience.

"Do you get it, Shifra?" Efraim stopping walking, and waved his hands. "He finally could mourn. Years after his beloved wife died, he gave himself permission to feel the pain. He chose not to cut his beard because he needed to sit a long overdue *shiva*."

I felt that I almost knew Alan. And this young, sensitive man across from me had, literally, given him back his life.

I shook my head, amazed. "Did he work things out with his family? What happened to him?"

"He made a lot of progress, but it was slow. He agreed to come to learn in the yeshiva's *ba'al teshuva* program a couple of hours a day. He began to wear normal clothes and to eat regular meals in the cafeteria, and he even received special permission to stay in the dorm. After he lived for a few months with a name, sleeping in a bed, and feeling supported by the guys at the yeshiva, he started to come alive. Like a person awakening from a coma, he began to express an interest in everything."

I felt I was a privileged witness to a miracle that resembled a resurrection of the dead. *And if so, was this the Messiah sitting across from me?*

"This is the most amazing part," he said, glancing at his watch. "Wow. It's after midnight and I haven't given you the numbers yet."

"But don't stop now. The suspense is too great. What happened to Alan?"

"I'll tell you quickly now and give you more details another time," he looked at me shyly, "if that's OK."

"That's fine, on both counts," I agreed.

"My *rav* is an incredible *talmid chacham* and has an amazing ability for solving complex interpersonal dilemmas. After I introduced them, he became close with Alan."

Drawn into the mystical world of *Chassidut* that opened before me, I sat enraptured in the drama.

"My *rav*'s compassion, compared to most people, is like a major forest fire as opposed to a miniature birthday candle burning. After a while," Efraim chuckled graciously, "I know I said I'll make this short. Anyway, Alan agreed we could help him contact his parents and mediate a get-together with them. My *rav*, Rabbi David, would be present to help keep things calm, if necessary. It turns out that..."

Despite the late hour, Efraim talked on. I was entranced, though my eyes were having difficulty remaining open. The details became fuzzy, but I understood that Alan's parents tried to find him for years. They hired private investigators, but the trail always went cold. With no rental contract, no driver's license renewal, no voter registration, nothing that implied a normal life, they feared he was dead. But after spending tens of thousands of dollars, they did not turn up a death certificate either.

The tears that fell when parents and son were reunited with the help of Rabbi David and Efraim were immeasurable. They had all suffered excruciating pain. Efraim's *rav* was moved by their poignant expressions of grief. When the weeping ebbed, he recommended they say a thanksgiving prayer. Alan and his parents were willing to do that, but they wanted to do something else to express their gratitude.

Efraim went on as my uncontrollable yawns grew.

"They decided to start a home for the homeless based on an idea that I had formulated. They bought this cottage, worked through a web of bureaucracy to get the appropriate licenses, and hired a trained staff."

I fought sleep.

"Alan insisted that I would be in charge."

My head dropped.

"Wow! It's really late, Shifra." Efraim stood. "Thanks for listening. I guess it's been on my mind."

Half asleep, I walked him to the door.

"I'll call you with those phone numbers tomorrow, OK? Good night and really, thanks a lot."

It was nearly 3:30 a.m. when — exhausted in an exhilarating way — I went into the bedroom.

Glenda, who just finished studying, opened one sleepless eye.

"What was that all about?"

"I'm going to get involved with his project. It's really exciting."

"But Shif, you hardly have breathing space. Remember your work, studies, Torah classes, and your lavish Shabbat meals. This will be major. Do you have a team?"

"You're more organized than I ever will be, even in your sleep." I started to giggle.

"What's so funny?" Glenda asked, flipping off the lamp.

"I don't think he ever actually asked me to do it. It's like he assumed I would, and," slipping down under the quilt, I said, "I am really happy to do it."

I could tell Glenda was agitated. Allotting precious time was something she took very seriously.

Tucked under my cozy feather covers, I tumbled into sleep, thinking, *How can he be so good? And how can someone so good care about a loser like me?*

FIVE

WHEN EFRAIM FINISHED HIS narrative and finally left Shifra's apartment in the early morning hours, he felt exhilarated. His exaggerated heroic efforts on Alan's behalf echoed in his mind as he straightened his nearly six-foot frame, accentuating his triumph. *She seemed really impressed.*

Swelling with pride, Efraim's broad shoulders swung back as he took the elevator in Shifra's building. *That was good.* Sweeping the black hair off his high forehead, he pushed it confidently to the side.

He savored the rush of adrenalin flooding his veins, warming and energizing him. *That was really fantastic!* He imagined her admiring look, her believing eyes. Thunderous applause. *To strengthen people's faith and commitment to Judaism, you have to create a vision. Does Shifra appreciate what I did for her?* He stepped out of the apartment building into the freezing night air.

Not everyone can do what I can. He pulled his hood over his head, tied the cord at his chin. He pushed against the wind.

Efraim noted the stragglers hurrying to find shelter from the biting cold. He approached one bedraggled form to ask if he had a place to sleep the night. The man stared at him, lifting his hands defensively and rushed off. Efraim called after him, but the figure disappeared in the dark.

Wearily, his thoughts floated through the many changes in his life these last two years since becoming a *ba'al teshuva*. In his youth, his unremitting daydream was to rescue the endangered from the criminally minded. He had not decided if he would become a lawyer

17

or a police detective. Now that vision was converted to one of saving souls. *Why is this generation so set on self-destruction?* After his rabbis taught him the underlying principles and values of life, he often asked this question.

As he walked to his yeshiva dorm, Efraim recalled when his dad held great hopes for his brilliant progeny, the youngest of his children. His father expected Efraim would follow in his footsteps to become a surgeon, or at least a medical professional. Efraim would not listen. That was not his calling. Pulling on his warm leather gloves, he wiped snowflakes from his cheeks.

When he began to keep Shabbat, Efraim and his father had intensely debated its purpose in the modern world until his dad acquiesced. They bought Efraim his own dishes. Over time, their home became Sabbath observant and kosher. Efraim gritted his teeth, remembering their long, sometimes shrill diatribes over his future. In the end, Efraim's domineering dad reluctantly accepted his son's equally bull-headed decision to become a rabbi. Efraim was determined to bring Jews closer to Hashem and Torah.

Deep in the warm pockets of his fleece jacket, his fists clenched tightly. *I will reach the most unlikely candidates for repentance. I, Efraim Baumen, will bring the lost souls of* Am Yisrael *back to the fold.* He thought to add the *b'li neder* that customarily accompanies an intended oath. He had learned that one is meant to take promises seriously and breaking a sworn statement is anathema to Jewish law. A short phrase, *b'li neder* neutralized the word's status, making it more of a possibility than a promise. *But, to this I swear, without compromise.*

He headed several blocks east to the empty park, not far from the yeshiva and stopped at the bench where he first met Alan. Standing under the glaring street lamp, he pulled out from his large black satchel the magazine he'd purchased earlier today. *If I want to counsel guys who are dealing with repulsive low-life issues,* he told himself, catching his breath as he ogled the forbidden pictures, *I need to understand what drives them.*

He repeated his need to understand in order to help, as his breathing became shallow and he felt warm perspiration break out on his forehead. He felt his blood rushing, his adrenalin speeding. *I have to be able to see this and not be devastated by it*, he persuaded himself. *Why do religious guys want to destroy their pure souls on cheap lure?* he tried asking himself, mesmerized. He licked his lips, feeling his heart race. After many minutes of commanding his will to obey, he closed the magazine. He considered shredding the impure pages or burning them. But he had to push himself; he had to be able to discuss or see anything and remain holy, no matter what. He scratched his fingers over the colorful, life-like pictures, folded the magazine, and pushed it down into the bottom of his bag of holy teachings and outreach pamphlets.

Walking into the back door of the dark, silent yeshiva dormitory, he went straight to the bathroom to throw water on his face and the back of his neck. He splashed the coldness over his eyes, but couldn't wash away the images. He glided stealthily to his dorm room, quietly passing the dorm counselor's open door. He took a cold shower until his teeth chattered and he shook violently.

I must be able to help save guys who sell their souls to Satan, he insisted to himself. Wearing warm flannel pajamas, he still trembled.

Efraim's thoughts roamed once more to his formative years. Throughout his public elementary and high school years, he volunteered every free moment to assist the poor, handicapped, and homeless. He gave away his allowance and his salary from summer and part-time jobs. He convinced fellow classmates and friends to help out. Whatever he became involved in, he did so with all his heart and soul.

At twenty, Efraim Baumen, the recent returnee to Judaism, was committed to rising to the highest levels of holiness to return Jewish pride to *Am Yisrael*. He was ready to sacrifice himself and do whatever was necessary to save tortured Jewish souls.

In his latest endeavor, Efraim decided not to take counsel with his *rav*. He told no one of his decision to forfeit his own world-to-come for his fellow Jews. He shared this monumental decision only with his roommate and closest friend, Rafi. He was confident that only his lifelong comrade could understand what inner drive motivated

Efraim to damage his own soul with his righteous fervor and love for his fellow Jews.

Rafi had awoken early. When Efraim returned, Rafi sat near the portable heater, wrapped in a fleece bathrobe and wool socks, poring over his *mishnayot*. When Efraim, still shaking, sat on the edge of his bed, Rafi closed his book. He turned the small radiator toward his friend. "You need this more than I do." He got up to boil water on the small electric burner. Rafi gathered some scattered books and papers, mostly Efraim's, while preparing the tea.

In those minutes Efraim vocalized his dream and mission.

Rafi sweetened the tea and placed the cup in front of his good friend. "It's dangerous. You're taking upon yourself too difficult a test. If you fail, you could lose everything."

"Rafi, it's your dream too. Admit it. Since we were little, we wanted to do stuff that no one else dared. We wanted to make a difference in a way that few others could." Efraim felt his vigor return.

Rafi did not try to talk him out of his inspired scheme. He knew from past experience that once Efraim decided to do something, he turned a deaf ear to anyone who disagreed. Instead, as he fingered the vile pages that Efraim pulled from his bag, he allowed himself to understand the astuteness of his best friend's daring.

Efraim reminded Rafi of the story of the Chassidic Rebbe, Reb Nachman of Breslov. Efraim had his own self-serving interpretation, which allowed him to do anything. "When the prince went crazy, thinking he was a turkey..."

"Some say a rooster," Rafi interrupted, well aware of where this was going.

Efraim continued, "The prince would remove his clothing, sit under the table and grab at crumbs or bones that fell for his meal. None of the royal doctors could identify his troubles or offer a cure."

Rafi continued, "One day a wise sage approached the grieving king, offering his help. 'I will try to heal him.'

The despondent king had nothing to lose, so he agreed.

Efraim recreated the conversation. "The sage did everything the prince did. As they sat together on the floor, the prince asked the sage, 'Who are you? What are you doing here?'"

Efraim sat on the floor to emphasize the drama. Using different voices, he portrayed the conversation between the disparate characters.

"What are you doing here?" the sage asked.

"I am a turkey," said the prince.

"I'm also a turkey," answered the sage.

This went on for some time, until they became good friends.

Knowing what would come next, Rafi threw Efraim a shirt. The prince asked him, "What's going on?"

Deepening his sagacious voice, Efraim asked, "Do you think that a turkey can't wear a shirt? Why, you can wear one and still be a turkey." So they both put on a shirt.

"Or was that a rooster?" Rafi laughed, as he threw a pair of pants to the star of the show.

"The prince was perplexed when the sage pulled on the pants, explaining that you can still be a turkey and wear pants. After a while, the prince did likewise. In time, they sat at the table where regular food was brought on plates."

Efraim's eyes glazed at the story's climax. "See, you can still be a turkey, and sit at the table and eat good food." Step by step, the sage demonstrated what a turkey could do and still, remarkably, remain a turkey. Eventually he became a prince again.

Rafi did not want to be left out of this grand conclusion. "And so, the sage had gone to the level of the prince's madness, lifted him up, and made him whole." Rafi summarized Efraim's perception of life, "Sometimes you have to go to the level of the sinner in order to elevate him."

They pledged that no price was too high for the good of the Jewish nation.

Efraim's vision of the future began to take on a new form when he grasped that he had a natural gift for design. What he had once considered imaginative doodling throughout his high school years was now taking more form and structure. He found himself creating innovative blueprints for homes, apartment buildings, and offices. At the same time that he had become drawn to Judaism and things of the spirit, his architectural urges turned toward Jewish structures, like shuls and yeshivas.

He resolved his longing to learn Torah with his architectural talents by attending college by day and continuing his yeshiva studies at night. And he persisted in talking to people in a compelling way to teach them about Judaism. He especially wanted to influence those who, like Alan, were in a bad situation.

Even as an undergrad, Efraim achieved a good name for his architectural projects. During one of our increasingly frequent conversations, he described his latest ideas:

"Using the contrasts offered by sun and shadows, I designed a fine stained-glass skylight with doves encircling a Star of David. The delicate details of olive tree leaves held in the beak of each snow-white dove are highly defined in the midday sun. With a recessed light, it is elegantly beautiful at night. I planned for a slight eastern angle so that early risers for morning prayers could enjoy the colorful scene."

For the next three years, Efraim and I would continue to work closely together, planning special Shabbat programs and projects for Ohel Sarah while caring for the women there. I was completing my college credits in social work, while working in an insurance agency.

Efraim's best friend, Rafi, who was considering a public defender position after law school, was like a brother to him. They consulted closely on everything. We became a close-knit trio.

Six

THE NEXT EVENING, I enthusiastically told Glenda about Efraim's soul-saving adventure. I couldn't comment enough about how wonderful he was.

My practical, no-nonsense roommate confronted me as I swept the floor. "You know what they say about 'too good to be true,' right?"

"No, who is 'they,' and what do 'they' say?" I responded dreamily.

"The influential and often wise 'they' say that if you think something is too good to be true, then it probably is."

"It is what? I lost you."

"Snap out of your fantasy world, Shif." Glenda's snapping fingers appeared in front of me. "If you think it's too good to be true, it probably is too good to be true!"

I only half listened. "Not this time, Glenda. He's a *tzaddik*. Even his rabbis say so."

"OK, but he's human, right?"

"So? What are you talking about?" I swept some large dust balls from under the side table.

"So tell me something that's not OK. Some area he needs to improve on." Glenda pushed. "Just one."

I pushed the broom under the fridge and pulled out some loose change and a shopping receipt.

"I'm thinking. Wait a minute. I know," I answered brightly. "He needs to learn how to choose a girl. Why should a guy who can spend time with almost anyone choose me?" Stopping to consider the point, I commented, "Take Sandy. I saw her trying to catch his attention at

23

the class he gave. She's from a normal, religious, well-to-do family. And she has a wonderful, outgoing personality. But he came to talk to me." I snapped my fingers. "That's his problem."

Glenda glared. "Stop it, Shifra. First of all, he wants you to run a program. Don't start thinking he asked you to marry him." She was flustered. "Listen. Before you get carried away or hurt, you have to think of two things he needs to work on. They don't have to be major, but you have to keep your wits about you."

"OK." I shrugged my shoulders and faked a military salute. "Yes, ma'am, and I'll report back to you as soon as possible."

Glenda wasn't finished. "I'll give you some ideas. For one thing, my friend, he inconsiderately kept you up until 3:30 in the morning. Did he ask if you need to be up early? Did he notice your exhaustion? Your needs?"

Her comments took me by surprise. I was unable to see any wrong in Efraim, and she had no difficulty pointing it out.

"Did he ask if you have time for this project, or did he just get you excited and then dump the whole thing on your lap?"

"OK, he wanted to share an amazing real-life event that happened, and he didn't take the time into consideration," I admitted. "Does that make him a bad guy?"

She went on, "Shifra, listen, Does he expect you to make all of those phone calls alone? It's not like you know all those people. You have to introduce yourself to each one, explain the project, what's expected of them, and so on." Glenda warmed up some soup left from Shabbat as she dissected Efraim's personality. "And he came to give you the phone numbers but never got around to it because he wanted to tell you this story. Doesn't that sound a little irresponsible to you?"

"What's the big deal?" I answered. "Not everyone is as efficient and logical as you. Some of us just say what's on our minds without keeping our eyes on the minute hand."

Glenda was adamant. "And don't put yourself down. You're a great girl." She handed me a pen and a blank sheet of paper. "Two things he needs to work on. OK?"

"OK." I shrugged, not taking her seriously.

SEVEN

EFRAIM CALLED ME OFTEN to review a resident's situation or to share a success story. Whenever the phone rang after midnight, Glenda cringed. She no longer worried that the late-night ringing brought bad news.

"But it's not normal to call at midnight," she insisted.

"It's his only free time," I said in appeasement. "I'll turn the ringer down."

"What about you?" she questioned. "You also wake up early. He's disturbing your sleep."

"I don't mind. I'm glad to be a part of his efforts for *Am Yisrael*."

I was pleased that aside from his best friend Rafi, I was his closest confidant.

Everyone knew Efraim. His classmates called him "the "*tzaddik*," "*Eliyahu haNavi*," the "forerunner of the Messiah," a "*gutte*." Efraim was always ready to help a friend, or a stranger — Efraim, saver of lost souls.

Rafi once told me that any yeshiva student with a problem knew to come to their room and Efraim often stayed awake through the night to help him solve his issues.

My concerned and ever realistic roommate lifted her nose from the books enough to inquire, "So, *nu*? Did he ask you out yet?"

I explained we were a team. I didn't need to date him to know him. I watched his kindhearted attitude toward the homeless and troubled classmates. I respected his tireless patience.

In response to Glenda's prodding, I had to admit that neither of

26

us was practical with time or money management or goal setting. I never planned farther than the day, and even that was hit or miss.

If I needed help or was going through some minor crisis, Efraim was there. That was enough for me.

When the phone rang at midnight, Glenda shrugged her shoulders. "It's for you," she said without hesitation.

"We have a new tenant at the home. Can you go to meet her and assess her needs?" Although there was a part-time social worker on the premises, Efraim liked to hear firsthand, meaning from me, what was needed.

"Sure." My response was enthusiastic. "I'll go tomorrow."

The first time I met Stella, she sat in a sofa chair in the Ohel Sarah living room, laughing. Her wavy, dark hair was twisted into a bun. She was heavyset with a ghost-like complexion, but it was her eyes that frightened me. I wasn't sure if she was crazy or in denial.

Stella was very eager to tell her story. She was laid off from a high-paying legal secretarial position in an unexpected office downsizing. Until then, she had lived lavishly on her "plastic card collection," as she called it. "When the pink slip landed on my desk, my world caved in. I could no longer make the monthly payments on my car, home entertainment center, or the twenty-one-day cruise to Spain I had always wanted and finally enjoyed. The landlord sympathized, but he let me know he also had bills to pay. 'Stella,' he told me, 'you have until the end of the month.'"

She shook her head as though not believing what happened to her. "Here I was living in a fancy high-rise, with a doorman and an Olympic swimming pool out back, but I didn't have change to take a bus." Her rambling subsided. I sat silently, hearing her pain, with tears glistening in my eyes. When she saw my concern, she allowed herself to cry. "I worked for twelve years in that office. And in one day, they threw me out like an old newspaper." She took the package of tissues I offered her.

Stella told me she'd been out of touch with her family for years. "And my so-called friends dropped me as though poverty was contagious." She looked away, frowning, her eyes empty of feeling.

I nodded, sensing her pain. "How did you find out about Ohel Sarah?"

"The one person I felt I could turn to is my cousin, who happens to live in this neighborhood. We enjoy getting together occasionally. She keeps me updated about my family." Stella paused, seeming lost in some memories. I hoped she would share more. Maybe her family would want to help, but right now the disillusionment seemed too raw. Hopefully, later on, Stella would attempt reconciliation.

She returned from her reverie. "So my cousin told me about this place and gave me the number. I called, and here I am, at your doorstep."

Several days later, Stella came down with a high fever and I went to care for her.

Through her troubled night's sleep, I spoon-fed her tea with honey and sips of chicken soup. Sitting at her bedside, I washed her face and held the bucket for her to vomit into. Toward morning, I must have dozed off. The upchucking came fast and she leaned over the bed, throwing up on the floor. Jarred from sleep, I washed her face and gave her some water to rinse her mouth. I found a rag to clean the mess. Rolling up the filthy rag, I went to find a plastic bag to contain the reeking stench. Suddenly, I sensed someone watching me, and in a quick glance, noticed Efraim turning and walking away quickly. He returned in a minute and handed me a garbage bag. "Good job, Shifra."

A few days later, Rafi told me that my willingness to do whatever was needed really made an impression on Efraim. Rafi smiled approvingly. "I've never seen him look so happy."

Glenda, on the other hand, was becoming really concerned. She asked what I knew about his family and his background. "Have you ever gone out and just talked about each other? What are his parents and siblings like? What does he know about you and your family? Does he have hobbies? What makes him angry and what does he do with his frustration when things don't work out as he plans?"

"Glenda," I laughed. "The guy's a *tzaddik*. I'm not doing a lab experiment on mice. For three years we've been deeply involved in very challenging projects. I've never seen him get angry." Shaking my head at her exaggerated practicality, I suggested, "Ask anyone, Glenda. He's a *tzaddik*."

We ran very successful Shabbat programs. Local families were coming to know "our women" and were treating them less as lepers. Our open educational approach was paying off. Several of the families who joined us for the third meal had each "adopted" one resident. Each family agreed to invite her "adoptee" to come for at least one Shabbat a month and to call or visit an additional time.

On Saturday night, after thanking the volunteer counselors and assistants and checking that the cleanup crew had been thorough, I hugged the Ohel Sarah women with whom I became very close.

As I turned to go, Efraim asked if I could wait a moment. Of course I could. We walked out of the air-conditioned home into the warm spring evening. The sprinklers had automatically turned on at the end of Shabbat. The recently mowed grass was glistening in the moonlight. Colorful groupings of red begonias, purple-streaked pansies, and orange marigolds lined the path to the house and dotted the lawn, releasing their pleasant scents.

The spreading lavender bushes on either side of the stairs leading to the front door had provided the *Havdala* spice this evening. It was my idea to plant them near the entrance as a welcome to the troubled women who live here. I bent to pluck a light-purple sprig. Rolling it between my fingers to release a stronger scent, I inhaled deeply.

Efraim bent his face toward my hand, taking a deep whiff of the lavender. "Beautiful," he said bashfully.

"Yes, it is." I agreed.

We walked quietly for a few minutes, which surprised me. Typically, Efraim would review an event, turning over what was or could have been. We'd discuss who needed extra care and who was doing well.

The sky was dotted with twinkling stars, and the full moon lit the heavens and earth. I noticed the manicured hedges surrounding the fancy homes of this attractive suburban neighborhood. Two cars nestled in most of the driveways. Extravagant lawn furniture dotted the well-trimmed grass. I was lost in thought, trying to balance this image with Ohel Sarah, the home of the homeless.

After walking a couple of blocks in atypical silence, Efraim cleared his throat.

"Will you marry me?"

Although this was the moment I was waiting for, an image of Glenda flashed in my mind.

Have you ever just talked to each other about yourselves?

He's a tzaddik, Glenda. You just don't know him, I answered her telepathically.

"Yes, Efraim," I answered, and the world suddenly became a wonderful and perfect place.

EIGHT

IN A WHIRLWIND OF wedding plans, Efraim and I never sat and talked about ourselves or our life together. There were Shabbatot to organize, a wedding hall to find, and somewhere in between, we met each other's families.

Dr. David Baumen was a well-renowned and respected surgeon. He was thorough in his preliminary findings and decisive in his prognosis. After our first meeting, I sensed I had been sized up — or down — and tossed out like a bursting appendix.

Efraim's mom, Janet, was kind and soft-spoken, but she did not say much. Her husband left little space for her to insert a word. He spoke for both of them. My background, schooling (or lack thereof), cultural circles, my parents' small appliance service shop, and their financial status were nonstarters.

I learned that Efraim was equally stubborn. I had never seen him stare down and demand as he did that day. Part of me was redeemed. I was someone worth fighting for.

The two men stepped into the garden, looking like they were set to do battle, while Janet showed me around their lovely home. She told me not to worry. "Their bark is worse than their bite."

I sensed she wanted me to relax, but I was not comforted.

"Look at these, Shifra." She pulled out an old photo album and we looked at little Efraim playing with his older siblings, wearing a Purim costume, wiping jam on the dog.

I asked if Efraim got along well with his brothers and sisters. She nodded. "They're all very close. And they do lots of things together."

I wondered why I had never met them.

"Are they involved with any of Efraim's outreach projects?" I asked.

"Sometimes. Everyone's so busy, you know."

Actually, I knew very little about them, and wondered when we might meet.

I was concerned about the conversation between Efraim and his father. As we toured the house, I noticed Mr. Baumen's war medals, scholastic honors certificates, and framed medical licenses filled the hallway walls. Efraim's mom pointed to a picture of her uniformed husband. The young soldier saluted the American president as he received a citation of honor.

"I'm really proud of him," she said. "He's my hero."

I understood her but wondered if he would be my friend or foe.

The two men returned clearly not of one mind or one heart. Both were red in the face, and Efraim's eyes held a tension I'd never seen.

"We'll be going now," Efraim said tersely.

His father nodded slowly, his mouth rigid. He was uncharacteristically silent as we walked out by ourselves. Janet Baumen stood next to her husband.

Efraim whispered for me to keep walking.

As we turned the corner, our steps slowed. "What happened? What did he say?"

"It doesn't matter," Efraim said, gritting his teeth. "According to Jewish law, a man can marry whoever he wants."

"But maybe we can talk some more. It's only the first time we really had a chance to talk. Your mom seemed happy about us."

"She's nice to everyone, but her opinion will be whatever dad says. She never disagrees."

I stared straight ahead. "Maybe he'll listen to ..."

"Hey, my dad doesn't listen. He decides. And it's done."

I felt confused. During the years we'd worked together, I had seen Efraim's parents several times at some of our special events. Though we spoke only a few words, they knew I was working with their son. His father would tell some jokes and set everyone at ease. Janet would laugh comfortably.

I would comment on some wonderful thing their son had done, and they would nod knowingly. Everything appeared fine. *Couldn't they guess that we might fall in love?*

Meeting my parents was not much better. My dad, who was feeling unwell, asked a few questions about Efraim's goals. My mom served hot drinks, smiling nervously. When Efraim said he wanted to marry me, Dad shrugged and said, "If that's what Shifra wants." He smiled wanly as he used my Hebrew name, which he could not get used to.

Efraim looked content, and Mom said *mazal tov.* I was glad that my brother was not home. My younger sister walked in for a few minutes, met Efraim and gave me a hug. "Gee, sorry I have to go now. I made some plans to meet my friends. Bye."

There was no enthusiasm, no feeling of happiness or sense of involvement. I was relieved when it was over.

"Easier than my parents," Efraim whispered as we left.

My parents lack of warmth would not deter me. I had all I wanted in Efraim. Despite my disappointment about our parents' responses, I was blessed.

Efraim's father remained aloof and angry that his youngest, most promising son would neither enter medicine nor marry someone of their stature. He asserted he would not invite his many associates, colleagues, or friends.

My parents had few friends to invite. Neither of us had many relatives apart from our siblings, a few aunts and uncles and some distant cousins.

We decided on a small wedding with only our immediate families and a few friends, mostly the counselors from the home, some of Efraim's classmates, and of course, Glenda, to enhance the *simcha.* Efraim told me that Alan and the "homeless" would also join us, giving us an opportunity to bring them a real Jewish celebration.

Even Glenda had stopped asking me to elaborate on our relationship, as she chipped away some of her precious internship hours to help me shop for my wedding dress.

It bothered me that Efraim's parents refused to meet with mine before the wedding. I wanted this to be a new beginning, but nobody was taking a conciliatory step. Disheartened at the lack of concern or even basic warmth from our families, I asked Efraim if he thought we should wait a while. "Maybe if I get to know your siblings, they'll have some influence with your parents."

"No one tells me who I will marry, even if they never speak to me again. I spoke to my *rav*, who said I have the right to choose my *kalla*." I was honored by his unyielding resolution to marry me. Yet something inside of me was distressed that he could cut off his parents so unflinchingly, dispite claiming to love and respect them.

We found a small apartment, filled it with the basics, and sent out a few handwritten invitations. The time passed too quickly for me to process how fragmented I was feeling. I wanted to marry Efraim, but something stuck in my throat. Glenda's words floated in and out of my thoughts, unwanted: *Shifra, if something sounds too good to be true, it usually is.* She no longer raised questions, but even as the preparations proceeded, I asked myself, "Have we ever just talked to each other about ourselves?"

As Efraim continued with our wedding plans, I went along with him, ignoring my dilemma.

NINE

SIX WEEKS LATER, EFRAIM and I stood under the *chuppa* on the freshly mowed lawn of Ohel Sarah. Some close friends and I prepared a modest but appetizing festive meal. I wore a simple, lacy white dress that Glenda had spotted in the sales section of a local dress shop.

Efraim's parents and some of his siblings joined us for the *chuppa* but left soon after the separate dancing began. My parents remained a while longer, staying by themselves on the side. Rafi and Glenda were among our friends. Together with the residents of the home, they danced themselves into a fervor, intent on enhancing our happiness. I watched as Efraim was lifted onto his friends' shoulders.

If my beloved *chattan* was larger than life before, he now seemed unlimited, able to do anything he set his mind to, anything at all. My love for him was thorough and unquestioning.

Several couples from the yeshiva, a few shul families, and the Ohel Sarah staff and women prepared *sheva berachot*. Knowing how busy her schedule was, I asked Glenda not to make one, but she did join us. Our families chose not to celebrate with us. The week whizzed by and in no time, we were back to our community projects.

TEN

O N TISHA B'AV, WE awoke early to drive to the women's shelter. Efraim and I had prepared a special program to enhance the message of national loss. Our theme emphasized how each of us personally needed to develop our unconditional love for *Am Yisrael* in order to heal our nation's wounds. We invited some girls from a religious shelter for the mentally handicapped to join us. These girls lived together with devoted counselors who were assisting them to live independently.

"Do you think they'll get the Tisha B'Av connection?" I asked.

Unlocking the car, Efraim answered, "The only way to heal our nation's wounds is through unconditional love. Letting the homeless women from Ohel Sarah be the hosts this time will help them feel good about themselves."

Slipping into the passenger's seat, I agreed. "And the girls from the mentally handicapped shelter will benefit from being invited to share in the program. I hope we'll be able to get the message across in a way they'll understand."

"Their capable counselors will be with them, filling in any gaps we leave," he said, throwing me a newlywed smile.

Efraim's creativity in bringing together apparently disparate groups or individuals amazed me. I would not have thought of this connection, but he had a way of making everyone feel included, important, a part of something larger. He set the example that we were not better or lesser, but equal in complementing ways. Efraim revealed with his actions and deeds that every person genuinely needed each other.

Rabbi David, Efraim's *rav*, would be joining us at Ohel Sarah for today's program. He frequently complimented Efraim on his dedication and mentioned Efraim publicly at a recent yeshiva dinner.

I settled in the passenger seat and recalled the *rav* citing him as an example to illustrate the "Power of One." "One person with a vision who develops wisdom and the character of wholesome leadership really can make a difference in this often anonymous world. *Am Yisrael* needs more Efraim Baumens."

As he spoke, I looked around the room. All eyes seemed riveted on the *rav*. I noticed Rafi, sitting off to the side. His smile and slight nodding of the head confirmed his affectionate approval of Efraim's works. They really were more like brothers than close friends, always encouraging each other.

Today the *rav* told the story of one of Efraim's all-night counseling sessions. "With dedication, Efraim Baumen, himself fairly new to Jewish tradition, was capable of returning a young Jew to his roots. In the course of one night's loss of sleep, Efraim explained and refuted deceptive missionary propaganda. Overnight, a Jewish *neshama* was returned to his people. Today that young man is becoming an outstanding student in our yeshiva."

Enjoying the show of appreciation for my husband, I reflected for a moment on our lives since we had married.

"I'm expecting to cook up a storm for Shabbat for all the lost souls you discover, so go out and get 'em," I had teased, enormously proud of his reputation and accomplishments. I was pleased that my cooking and baking skills complemented our desire for an "open Jewish home" lifestyle.

Efraim did not let me down. Every week he scrounged the streets and found sad, distressed Jews who had never known their heritage or who once had but left it behind. In our home, good food accompanied encouraging conversations and a set of values in a novel way for many of our guests We watched our extended family, as they came to be known, growing in self-worth as they adopted a more ethical way of life.

We parked in the Ohel Sarah parking space just as a van of girls pulled up. The palpable warmth between the counselors and girls told me they could impart their own lessons of unconditional love.

"May this be the last time we have to fast on Tisha B'Av," I greeted our guests. *Please, Hashem, help us learn from history, and from each other, and take these teachings to heart.*

Eleven

I WAS HAPPY THAT EFRAIM and I shared the dream of living in Israel. We both knew we wanted to raise our family in a wholesome Jewish environment. We agreed that in Israel our children would learn more Torah, speak Hebrew as their mother tongue, and nurture good character traits.

After Efraim received *semicha* and his architecture degree, our plans took form. I attended an ulpan several mornings a week, and Efraim looked for someone to take over Ohel Sarah. In the end, the person responsible for the program's initiation took over. In time, Alan returned to a normal life. His tragic experiences led him to want to help others and he returned to school to do a second masters as a social worker.

Together with the fundraising backing that had gradually taken root and his parents' continued support, the place provided a home to dozens of women yearly. With their self-confidence rebuilt, retraining programs allowed many of them to go on to reestablish their lives. Others settled in for the long run.

It was harder for me to part from "our women" than from our personal families. Our parents never met or spoke again after the wedding. I still had a detached relationship with my parents. The Baumens were aloof and my parents felt snubbed and belittled.

Although Efraim's dad and I came to a quiet truce, we had not developed a warm or comfortable relationship. His mom was pleasant enough, but she maintained an emotional distance for the sake of her own marital peace.

I was actually grateful we were leaving when I was pregnant. The thought of our families coming together at a *b'rit* or *kiddush* made me queasy.

Efraim and I never discussed suitable communities. I looked up North where there were some English speakers with comparable lifestyles and levels of religious observance. There we settled on a small home with a little garden. Since Efraim was too busy tying up loose ends, I also tried to research work options for him. Our meager savings would not go far, but we were accustomed to going with the flow.

TWELVE

THE NEXT FEW YEARS went by like a whirlwind. We began to adjust to *leben* and falafel, speaking Hebrew, calculating the Israeli currency, and calling out *"rega, rega"* (wait a second) to the bus driver when our bus stop approached.

In our first year in Israel, our son Dovy was born. Although we were far from our families and were still new immigrants learning a new language, my joy was immense. My second birth to Kayla was beautiful and natural. It was one of life's perfect moments. We now had a son and a daughter, were living in Israel, and Efraim Baumen was my husband. I felt more content and whole than ever.

Still, it took a great deal of energy to concentrate on caring for our little children. With no family or support system, they kept me constantly busy.

In addition, almost immediately after making aliyah, Efraim indulged his passion for Shabbat guests. Whomever he met, he invited to our home. Before long we had ten, fifteen, or twenty guests or more every Shabbat. The cycle of shopping for Shabbat, preparing, cooking, and finding places for our company to sleep, all the while caring for a baby and a toddler, reached its crescendo by Thursday night. The cleanup lasted until Tuesday, and then it was time to start again. I felt enveloped in a vague fog of faces and names that blended into each other. In contrast, Efraim's capacity to take a personal interest in each person was mind-boggling. He absorbed names and an individual's needs immediately; his sharp mind missed nothing.

He worked in a well-known architectural firm by day, and in the evenings he volunteered with one of the *kiruv* organizations that were beginning to mushroom in Israel. From the start, he began to come home later in the evenings. There were so many lost and searching young people to reach out to. I forgot he had ever come home before midnight.

Soon enough, our home became a mini Ohel Sarah, where a guest might stay for a few days or weeks, or more, until they found a program or other living quarters. The house was small, but we both agreed that with love in our hearts, we would find room for all of our guests. We didn't talk about it much, but the assumption was made: He found and counseled them; I fed and cleaned after them.

THIRTEEN

E FRAIM AND I WAITED for the bus. I glanced at my watch impatiently, hoping to be home on time to pick up the kids from *gan*, preschool.

Efraim held a printed sheet. "Hey, look at this. There's a weird group of people trying to implement the concept of concubines today."

I shrugged, trying to shield the sun from my eyes, hoping to see the bus speeding around the corner.

"There are Ashkenazi rabbis involved," he continued, mumbling a name I could hardly hear, and had no interest in.

He looked up as our bus approached. "That's an interesting concept." Stepping up, I gave our bus ticket to the driver, who punched it twice. As we found two seats near the rear of the bus, Efraim continued, "Imagine all the lonely women who might have a chance to have a family."

He mentioned a pleasant, obese woman we had both known for many years, who had never married. "Like Betty. She may not find a husband, but as a concubine, she would be committed to one man, have children, and lead a respectable life."

I shrugged, thinking it an unlikely, hypothetical scenario. I liked Betty as a neighbor and an occasional guest. It was sad she lacked a husband, but that did not mean another woman had to share hers.

Looking out the window, I half listened as Efraim thought aloud through Jewish law, social angles, and the possibilities of helping lonely people.

He was not asking my opinion, as if he ever did. And I didn't

43

think it required a response. It was unacceptable in modern society. I listened as Efraim, in his inimitable style, talked.

As the bus approached home, I stopped hearing him. It was more urgent to plan the lunch menu, pick up the kids, and discover who needed extra attention this afternoon. My dear husband did not notice my attention had wandered as he continued his monologue. And I did not hear the enthusiasm that filled his voice with each argument and counterargument he provided.

FOURTEEN

ONE AFTERNOON, EFRAIM RETURNED home with a distraught looking young woman whom he introduced as Mona. She had recently arrived in Israel and was looking for an apartment, but in the meantime, maybe she could stay with us "for a few days."

Mona wore a short-sleeved minidress. Her long henna-painted, frizzled hair was too red. I couldn't tell from her downcast face if she was fifteen or thirty, or somewhere in between.

Efraim called me aside, "Mona ran into some hard luck. I met her in front of a pizza shop in town, sitting on her suitcase." He shrugged as he gulped a glass of juice. "She had no place to go and I couldn't just leave her there." He wiped juice from his shirt. "She needs a friendly environment to get back on her feet, just for a few days." With that, he rose, ending the conversation.

I'd heard that before and wondered how long she would really stay.

When I returned to the living room, Mona was glancing around, as though looking for something. "Hi, Mona," I offered my friendliest smile. "I'm happy to meet you."

She appeared scared. Looking down and away from me, she said nothing.

"Would you like a drink or something to eat?" I tried. Her drawn face turned away in an uncomfortable silence until Efraim returned. She told him she'd like some water. "Nice house you got, Effie." She sat down, and to me, she looked very much at home.

45

FIFTEEN

OVER THE SUMMER, MY father became ill. After he was hospitalized for more than a month, the doctors said there was nothing they could do to stop the spreading cancer. When I heard Mom's trembling voice telling me, "It's time to come," a fog lowered over me.

I needed to make plans quickly for the flight, bringing little Kayla with me, and leaving four-year-old Dovy with his *abba*. Within hours I arranged for a ticket, which mom offered to pay for. Dovy would go to friends after preschool, and of course, Efraim would stay with him in the evenings. I always kept extra food in the freezer and knew that pizza would appear when it ran out.

I packed in a daze, taking the necessary papers, even as I threw in another laundry and folded more clothes. The early morning flight would allow me time to say some prayers for dad and sleep a few hours.

When Efraim returned late that night, I was still preparing for the trip. He assured me he would get Dovy to *gan* in the mornings and be in touch with families about afternoon visits. He would remain home at nights with Dovy, and we agreed that, obviously, Mona would have to find somewhere else to stay, at least until I returned.

The trip was uneventful. After Kayla's initial excitement of being on the plane and looking out of the windows to spot clouds, she snuggled next to me and slept for much of the flight. We took a taxi to my parents' home. Waves of nostalgia did not bring a smile to my face, and the memories were better left dormant. Instead, I pointed out to Kayla the scenes of my childhood.

Dad was home in the rented hospital bed, breathing slowly and deeply. The medications were working well, and he appeared to be in little pain. I was grateful we would have some time together. I held his hand, told him about my family, and asked his forgiveness for so many times I may have let him down.

He was barely able to move, yet he nodded his head ever so slightly.

My older brother was there but refused to speak to me. And I still didn't know why. "Hey, we're older now," I tried. "Let's let it go, just for now, for Dad's sake." A wall would have been more responsive. Glaring at me, my younger sister whispered angrily, "Every time you're home, there's arguing. It's upsetting Mom. Why did you have to come?"

I gathered up Kayla and went out for a walk, and to cry. I had a ticket for ten days but had thought to stay as long as Dad was still here. Now, jolted into reality, I realized it would not be comforting to anyone.

Conversations with Mom were short and tense, as though it was too much to have us all together. Dad floated in and out of recognizing us. He slept for longer periods of time. My siblings and I scheduled sitting with him so that we would not have to speak with each other.

I asked Mom if she wanted me to remain. She shook her head, "There's not much you can do now. Go back to your husband and son." As she looked away, she seemed to be searching for something encouraging to say. "You keep praying that your dad won't suffer too much."

I held her hand and tried to hug her, but she was as unresponsive as I had remembered. "I love you, Mom. And I'll be praying for Dad — and for you — to be well." She nodded, pulled her hand away, and suggested I pack. Even cute and sweet Kayla was unable to rouse more than a brief smile. I began to pack.

The week before Rosh Hashana, I returned home.

SIXTEEN

WEARILY, I WALKED INTO my home carrying my sleeping two-year-old Kayla. A young man I'd never seen before sat in the hall speaking quietly on my phone hushing me, his finger pressed to his lips. Waving his hand, he implied that this was a private, long distance call and that I should go into the other room.

In the living room sat a twenty-something silent, despondent young man. *Another new arrival*, I sighed. He barely looked up when I entered. In response to my greeting, he nodded. He pointed to himself and mumbled what I assumed was his name before returning to his previous head-down, morose position. It sounded like Steve, but I didn't catch it, and I was too stressed to care.

After putting Kayla down on the bed in my room, I went out and dragged the suitcases, which the driver had placed on the sidewalk, inside. Taking a look around, I noticed the beds were made and the floor was clean.

I was eager to see Dovy. Efraim was well aware of my arrival time but had not bothered to be home.

Tomas, as he introduced himself, had finished with his call, and we walked into the kitchen simultaneously. This tall, heavyset fellow with tight curly black hair was dressed in a red plaid, flannel shirt and worn jeans. Notifying me in a rapid Hebrew-English-Spanish blend, with a lisp, that Efraim would be back soon, he went on to tell me his life story. Life in Argentina with his crazy family, his political persuasions, and something about a conversion, poured out in a blur. Almost as an afterthought, he asked, "Who are you?"

48

As though I need to explain my presence in my own home.

Opening the cabinet doors to take out pots and utensils, he started to prepare lunch for my family. He seemed familiar with the dairy and meat divisions, and everything else about the kitchen. Without even waiting for my response, he started to describe the ingredients of his favorite South American stew. And he was careful to mention that the beans had been checked thoroughly to ensure they were bug free.

"Light the fire," Tomas demanded, explaining that "as soon as my conversion takes place, I'll be able to do all the cooking myself. For now, though, a kosher Jew must light the stove." His thick Spanish accent blurred the words, but I held the match to the gas, feeling myself implode. All I wanted was to escape from the room.

The next time the door opened, Mona, the dispirited girl/woman with the straggly henna-painted hair, walked in with her tattered suitcase. Her torn satchel looked as battered as she did.

"You're back," she observed limply and went to the bedroom she had occupied for the past three months.

After unpacking a few articles of clothing, she parked herself in my favorite rocking chair in the living room.

I returned to my bedroom and crawled into bed beside Kayla, wearier now than from the twelve-hour nonstop plane trip with an active toddler.

By the time my family arrived, Tomas had a steaming pot of beans and rice with vegetables ready. While Dovy and I hugged and he began opening my suitcase to search for treats, Efraim went to speak with Mona. Sunken into her pitifully lonely life, she seemed to respond only to his attention. Initially, he implied she'd only stay a week or two until she found another place. When I had hinted a month later that her week was up, he asked, "What would she do if she left?" My responsibility was obvious.

I wanted to hear all about my firstborn's adventures.

"How are you? How was *gan*? Did you go to your friends?"

I wanted desperately to catch up with him and to reestablish my place in this distended family. Kayla was now awake She hugged

Dovy and they tickled each other as if there'd been no separation at all. Dovy ran to bring us his welcome home drawings. *The questions would be answered later, or not.* I wasn't so sure I wanted to know all the answers.

It seemed that Mona had been comforted from having been forced to depart her free and homey lodgings when she smiled and nodded at something Efraim was telling her. I could see that her perennially raised shoulders, a sign of her constant state of tension, had relaxed. My husband moved on to sit with the despondent Steve, still head down on the couch. Efraim had a way of whispering softly, making the listener feel worthy of a uniquely shared confidence.

I knew what Efraim said was irrelevant. Sure enough, Steve (if that was his name) perked up as my husband leaned toward him, speaking as much with his hypnotically slow-moving hands as his mouth. I noticed a glimmer of hope in Steve's darkened eyes.

When he was able to allow himself breathing space from his duties to *Am Yisrael*, Efraim came to welcome me home. He spoke quickly, not needing to use that soft caring tactic with me. I heard detailed accounts of Steve's suicide attempt, Mona's difficulty finding and remaining in one place, and Tomas' illegal entry into Israel. How could Efraim not help? Of course, "he" meant "we," and "we" in all things practical meant "me."

In the midst of my being overwhelmed, I asked about Dovy.

"Everything was fine. He ate. He's dressed in clean clothes. Tomas did all the laundry. He looks healthy, right?" As he suddenly became short of words, the topic of my elder son was shuffled away. It would be weeks before I would uncover the details as Dovy's naive comments drew me a broader picture. Relaxed, in passing conversations, Dovy admitted that he had missed many days of *gan*, eaten lots of pizza, and met some of Abba's interesting friends.

Tomas and Steve had moved into the apartment's windowless storeroom shortly after I left, while Mona had returned to her room.

"Ima," Dovy shrugged, "she had nowhere else to go." I heard his father's intonation in his innocent voice.

Word of my father's passing came only a few days after I arrived in Israel. At the *shiva,* not a few people asked me if Mona was also related. Her perennial mournful appearance had confused them. I found myself discussing her woes, at least as much as I spoke about my father, but I said little about my recent visit to see him.

No gentle hints or outright requests could get Mona to leave the house. At least the other two guys seemed to know when they were in the way, and they left. When Efraim took the kids for a walk, she would tag along with them, but never went out on her own.

Neighbors who brought food kindly included extra for Mona. Only my closest friend, Rivka, seemed to understand my need for Mona to leave. "It's taking its toll on you to have her here so long, especially now. There is a limit to how much kindness one can offer." She looked me in the eyes, and I felt her deep caring as she added, "Too much, even of a good thing, becomes unhealthy and unwise."

Soon after the *shiva* ended, I told Efraim we needed to ask Mona to leave. He retorted, "She's looking for a place all the time. As soon as she's ready, she'll move out."

"I hardly see her leave the house. How is she looking?" Before his rebuttal could come, I proposed, "Let's give her a date by which she needs to move out."

I had never seen him as irate as he was at that moment. Or had I?

My thoughts soared to our first visit to his parents. When he had discussed our marriage with his father, the same impassioned obstinacy appeared.

"She'll leave when she's ready. And you have no right to kick out a forlorn Jewish soul with nowhere to go!" He slammed his fist into his hand, staring at me as though I had wanted to do her harm.

Seventeen

ON EREV YOM KIPPUR, Efraim invited Tomas to join us on a trip to the Kotel. I sat on the bus with Kayla, and he stood beside us. Grinning broadly, he sang one of his nonsensical Spanish-English songs. I asked him to be quiet. "It's disturbing me and the other passengers. Please go sit down."

Opposite me, Efraim turned to reprimand me. "Stop bossing him around. He's an adult, not your child."

Flushing, I told him, "I don't care if he sings somewhere else, but not near me. I don't want to hear it."

People began turning their heads in our direction as Tomas sang his song even louder, and Efraim continued spouting his disapproval at me in an intimidating way. "You have no right to embarrass someone in public," Efraim was brazen enough to tell me.

I whispered back that he was embarrassing me in front of my children, who were now glued to every word.

Efraim stopped for a moment but quickly vented again in defense of our ward. "A true *bat Yisrael* has compassion for the stranger who is alone and desperate for some kindness." He lowered his voice, but it could still be heard. "You fail sadly to display that trait," he pronounced, shaking his head grimly. He appeared distressed at the thought.

I did not say anything else. The kids have heard enough. And so did anyone else sitting nearby. But the words pounded in my head: *Why shouldn't your first reaction be to defend me? I am an orphan from my parents. And I am also an adult, the mother of your children — and I have no one to defend me. Tell Tomas I'm tired and have a headache, or whatever cover-up you want! But stick up for me. I am your wife!*

Eighteen

I REASONED THAT EFRAIM MIGHT simply be exhausted. Aside from his chaotic *kiruv* counseling, he was working full time and hosting our legendary Shabbatot. In addition, for the last several months he'd been developing a stunning project which he had submitted to the annual Israeli Architectural Designers awards conference. Generous prizes were offered.

That glamorous evening was approaching, and I hoped some of the tension would diminish when it was over. *Assuming, that he receives one of the coveted awards.*

Efraim insisted I attend with him. For the first time since we were married, he demanded I buy a new dress.

The architectural award presentation was more ostentatious than I realized. Elegantly suited architects and their fashionably dressed wives or companions walked around the Jerusalem exhibition hall, holding champagne glasses, swishing the contents gently. Each one pointed out the highlights of the architectural model he had prepared.

Efraim seemed to be the youngest among them. He composed himself as he approached an impressive-looking older gentleman who was surrounded by several of the most well-known designers. Enjoying the great esteem of his companions, the gentleman appeared comfortable accepting the admiration reserved for the extremely rich and accomplished. As he emphasized his words with sophisticated and expressive gestures, the man's large gold ring and massive gold watch reflected well in the stylish, well-designed radiant lighting of the large exhibition hall.

This highly-regarded architect with the broad smile had an air of complete competence yet seemed to put everyone else at ease. Efraim exchanged a few words with him. After a mutual and friendly pat on the back, my husband glided back to me.

"That guy," he whispered excitedly, "won world-class acknowledgment for his exceptional development of wood, glass, and natural stone structure with contemporary sophistication."

"That sounds pretty impressive."

"Yeah, and he's one of the judges for this year's competition." Efraim nodded, with a faraway look.

The walls of the hall were filled with posters displaying sprawling residential homes finished in the famous Jerusalem stone, tall exclusive apartment towers of green tinted glass, and modern malls. These would be the structures of the future. One from each category would win the coveted Israeli Architectural Designer's first-place prize of $50,000. Second place for $25,000 wasn't bad either.

I would have been pleased with the $10,000 offered to the third-prize winner. Those in the fourth and fifth places would gain acknowledgment for their creativity. But I knew Efraim would be disappointed if his exceptional home design with a unique skylight placed over an indoor-outdoor garden at its epicenter, failed to win first-place.

He had hardly spoken of anything else for the last seven months as he contemplated every detail, from the outer finely-finished, color-stained Jerusalem stone wall to the hardy flora that would attractively fill the enchanted Garden of Eden and the elegant rock fountain embedded with semi-precious gems and recycled crystal-clear water from a pearl-studded water jug. It really was breathtaking. I had encouraged him to put all his best effort into it.

We took our seats as the presentation ceremony began. The judges had already chosen the winners, who would be called up to expound on the concepts and details of their projects.

The gentleman with the glimmering gold jewelry called the first two names, winners of the fourth and fifth places to a wide round of applause. He spoke briefly about the architects and their well-finished designs. The proud designers stepped up to the podium, received admiring applause, and returned to their seats.

The third-place award was presented, leaving the runner up and winner of this year's recognition of excellence. I noticed the tension on Efraim's face, realizing how urgently important to him this prize was. Everyone seemed to be sitting closer to the edge of his or her seat as the moderator announced the winner of the second-place award, Efraim Baumen.

Although he maintained his composure, I noticed joy and relief flooding onto my husband's face. He was in. Others, no doubt disappointed, applauded as he stood up, waved and winked to no one in particular as he approached the dais.

I looked around, proud of Efraim's achievements. His well-rehearsed presentation drew strong applause from his peers. I also hoped it would make him feel more content and less anxious. As I applauded proudly and smiled encouragingly at Efraim, the thought crossed my mind that now maybe he, and I, would be able to get some more sleep.

As his colleagues stood to shake his hand, or slap him warmly on the back, a broad smile lingered on his face. The rest of the evening was a whirl of congratulations, good wishes, and warm feelings.

It was only as we walked outside and hailed a taxi that his enthusiasm fell. He began to sharply criticize the judges' decision.

"They were wrong. I should have been awarded first place." He rejected my encouraging comments that he was still so young yet received second place among top international architects. "Everyone seems to believe you will rise to become a world-class architect. And I believe you will, Efraim." I tried to touch his hand, but he pulled away and was silent for the rest of the trip home.

NINETEEN

O NE MORNING, AFTER ESCORTING each of the kids to their preschool groups, Efraim came back and atypically remained at home. From the minute he reentered the house, he spoke on the phone. Whispering in a barely audible tone, he closed his eyes pensively. In his characteristic forward leaning, elbow on knee and head down position, he dispensed his much sought-after, sage advice.

I cleared the kitchen table from breakfast remains, gobbling the leftovers of two bowls of cereal and cups of juice. The mushy bananas were honey sweet in a way only a mother could love.

I patted my blossoming tummy. Having endured the traditional early months of morning, afternoon, and evening nausea, I was enjoying the middle months of this pregnancy. I loved feeling the movements of the life I carried within me.

Suddenly, I realized someone had walked in.

Not bothering to wait for anyone to answer her almost inaudible tap on the door, Mona entered.

After months of putting up with her moodiness and her low-class speech, which I was constantly censoring, I had felt a great weight lift from my heart when she left. Shortly after I'd returned from my visit to my Dad several months ago, she had finally found her own apartment. Since she moved out, she'd neither called nor visited, which was fine with me. Toward the end of her stay with us, she'd become more withdrawn or conversely, nasty, especially toward me. Efraim had encouraged me to tolerate her since, due to her neglected childhood, she'd never experienced a normal mother-daughter relationship.

"A lot of us had troubled upbringings," I'd retorted. "I do not want to be a replacement for every incompetent mom. I want to pour my efforts into our kids and," I was growing defensive at his fierce expectations that I give all my compassion to strangers, "it wouldn't hurt if you would do some of the same."

I winced momentarily as Efraim flicked his fingers into my face. "You've really become a selfish person. You used to want an open home with lots of guests, but now you complain about everyone who walks in. You lied to me. You better start acting like a decent Jewish woman."

He glared menacingly into my eyes. "You think you're such a *tzaddeket*, such a goody-goody." He screwed up his face, the contempt obvious. "You selfish pig." I could still feel that sharp slap across my psyche. It had left me sullen and wondering, indeed, when I'd changed so drastically.

Returning to the present, I attempted to restrain my frustration at Mona's unwelcome intrusion.

"Hello." I offered, keeping my voice neutral. Her shoulders slumped and she lowered her eyes, peering sideways toward Efraim, who nodded, continuing his phone conversation.

Mona was carrying a large grocery bag filled with milk, fruits, and vegetables. A loaf of whole-wheat bread peeked over the top.

"Good choice of foods," I complimented her. Only when she lowered her bags to the table did I notice her protruding belly. *What is this?* I gasped inwardly. Suddenly the food shopping made sense.

In all her months living with us, her daily diet consisted mostly of the three C's: chips, cola, and chocolate, no matter how often I urged her to eat homemade salads or vegetable dishes. Occasionally she would honor me by eating a family meal. Mostly she crammed whatever starchy side dish was offered and washed it down with her Cokes.

Mona commented lethargically that for her baby she'd eat well. *It's the least you can do.*

"Have a healthy pregnancy," I said.

"You're not angry with me?" she ventured in a childlike voice, as though awaiting my indignation. We, or rather I, spoke with her about modesty in dress, speech, and action. I encouraged her to create a different kind of life for herself. I was willing to lend a hand. That every word had fallen on deaf ears was clear, especially in her present condition. But Efraim was opposed to giving up on a Jewish *neshama*.

Too bad for the baby, my lips pressed together as I cringed within. *What can you offer him?* Noticing Efraim's glare in my direction, I suggested, "You really have to take care of yourself now."

Efraim hung up the phone and nodded solemnly, adding that we would both help in any way we could. He smiled encouragingly, seemingly glad for the opportunity to display his open-mindedness and present his wife as warm-hearted and compassionate.

The conversation died, and he rose to accompany her out the door. I asked him to stay. "We need to discuss Kayla's playgroup for next year — and sign her up soon."

Barely turning, he mumbled, "I'll be right back." He shut the door behind them. He did not return.

That evening he sauntered in for dinner. Dovy and Kayla were chattering about Pesach preparations in their preschools. Each one stood next to my growing tummy, describing the decorations and repeating the story of our freedom from slavery, so the baby could hear too. Dovy playfully pressed his mouth straight into my skirt. None of us could understand a word, but he giggled happily, too pleased with himself to care.

Shortly after dinner, it was blessed bedtime. After the final story, the last cups of water, and the very last song, the kids fell asleep.

I was still humming *Shema* as I closed the bedroom door behind me. Efraim was already pulling on his new jacket, bought by yet another grateful parent. More and more he returned from his counseling and *kiruv* sessions with clothes or other personal gifts. He now insisted on traveling by taxi nearly everywhere.

"It's an excessive expense," I told him, but he dismissed my comments as selfish.

"My time is more valuable than the *grushim* I pay for the traveling," he asserted. "And it gives a livelihood to these courageous ex-army guys."

What about our livelihood? The long overdue bills remained unpaid.

As he lifted the phone to call for this evening's driver to pick him up, I stepped in front of him. "Who's the father?" I wanted to see his eyes, but he bent to tie his shoes.

"What?" he asked, flicking his fingers toward me, as he would to an annoying gnat.

"Mona's baby. Who's the father?" Again, I moved in front of him.

"She doesn't know. She has two boyfriends." He shrugged. "Who cares? She'd never marry either of them. And they're not interested in raising her kid." He brushed past me and headed for the door.

"A baby should know his father," I snapped indignantly. "One day, he'll want to know."

Efraim repeated coolly, "It doesn't matter. She's got us to help her out." And he was gone.

Only then did I realize that I also needed to know who that man was.

TWENTY

PERHAPS BECAUSE OF MY general exhaustion and some confusion as to how Efraim was acting toward me, Yair's birth was the most difficult. I hoped that by naming him after my father, it would offer some consolation to my family, and to me.

He was cute and colicky, with a capital C. I spent many nights walking outdoors under the stars, patting his back, holding his stomach, rocking him in the baby carriage, and trying to figure out what might calm him. Baby massage with gentle oils was helpful, at least for a short while. One Yair seemed more than double the other two.

I asked Efraim to slow the stream of guests unless he wanted to take over the kitchen. For what I thought was an attempt at light humor, his eyes narrowed until I felt them penetrating me with a sharp sting. Didn't Efraim see how exhausted I was? I didn't sleep at night, and the short daytime naps were insufficient to fill in the gaps.

Several months after Yair was born, Efraim insisted we visit Mona after her difficult birth ended with a Caesarian. I placed Yair into his baby carrier, praying he wouldn't scream. Mona lay in her hospital bed swearing at the doctors and nurses, and at us.

Angry and in pain, she claimed they had "cut her open" and forbidden her to give birth naturally. She would sue them and they could all go to hell. When I entered behind Efraim, she shouted, "What's she doing here?"

"Don't touch my baby," she screamed. "You already have one!" she added as I extended my hand toward her. I stepped back as Efraim stood between us. He leaned toward her and whispered something,

61

and she stopped yelling, at least momentarily. As he stepped away, she wrapped her arms around the baby boy and drew him closer to her. She appeared terrified that I might take him.

My attempt to smile was hindered by the confusion and embarrassment she evoked in me. She did not offer to show me the baby or comment on him. All she could do was mutter about this evil hospital and how they should all drop dead. Although I could understand her disappointment about the birth, it was hard to tolerate her coarse expletives. I felt great pity for the child who would grow up in her care.

Efraim's words caught my attention. "We will help you in every way we can. We will organize the *b'rit*, and Shifra will do the catering in her own amazing style." He nodded toward me, with his charming smile. "You still have a few days until the *b'rit*, so no problem." It was an announcement, not a request.

"I'll make sure there's a *minyan* and a *mohel*," he continued.

"I don't want no *mohel* to cut up my son," she began screaming again, attracting everyone's attention.

A nurse called me to leave, which I was eager to do. Efraim remained to calm her in his own unique way.

"Are you family?" the nurse wanted to know. I explained that Mona had lived with us, and we were trying to help her. She refrained from asking about a father, as Mona had given her name alone as a parent. The concerned nurse was amazed at Efraim's patience.

"He was there when she came out of the general anesthesia and seems to be the only one who can calm her," she nodded approvingly, and I tried not to flinch. "She's very fortunate to have both of you." The nurse continued that Mona insisted she's not going to nurse. "It's barbaric," Mona had said. Maybe I could talk to her.

A strong advocate of natural, unmedicated birth and full nursing, I shook my head. "In this case, I'm not convinced that will be best for the baby." Seeing me wearing my own infant, she looked surprised. I shrugged my shoulders as Efraim peeked out of the room. "Come and give her some motherly advice," he said. "You know — about nursing and all."

I looked at both of these advocates of women's health and shook my head. "What do I know? There are lactation consultants on the staff. Send one of them to her."

Efraim fumed that I did not do more to help Mona stop her ongoing tantrums or to further her mothering skills. With perfect timing, Yair chose that moment to scream. I had never appreciated his shrieking before. Excusing myself to the nurse and offering a parting *mazal tov* to Mona, I quickly left them and the hospital. It did not bother me that my son's crying drew attention. It was a normal, gassy-baby reaction, which I would do my best to comfort. It was more tolerable than Mona's dysfunctional outbursts. The fresh air was invigorating, and even Yair quieted down more quickly than usual. I think he needed to get away from her madness too.

TWENTY-ONE

EFRAIM CONTACTED THE SAME *mohel* we used for Yair's *b'rit*. The *mohel* had joked that he had experience with fathers calling him ten or eleven months after a *b'rit* to do it again, but three months was a "new one." They had a good laugh over that.

Efraim told him Mona's address and the time and location of the *b'rit*. Neighbors, local congregants, and previous live-ins were contacted to come to this special occasion, for a woman who has no family, no finances, and no support team.

"Attending Mona's *b'rit* is a great *chessed*," he made sure to tell everyone. The day before the baby's *b'rit*, between comforting my sweet, screeching infant and caring for the others, I began the preparations for a *seudat mitzva*. Several quiches, plates of pasta, and assorted salads later, Efraim walked into the kitchen.

"She's really scared and nervous about the *b'rit*, so make sure you do your best to keep things calm," he cautioned.

"It's hard to pacify a volcano," I muttered quietly. Without looking at him, I asked, "Will the baby's father be coming to his son's *b'rit*, maybe just as one of the guests?"

Efraim did not have to think. "Forget about the father. He's out of her life, as good as dead." As he cut a slice of the still warm squash pie, he made it clear, "She has no one who will take any responsibility for her kid. No one." I continued grating the carrots for the salad, knowing there would be more.

"That's why we are going to help her in every way possible." He licked his fingers and took a cold drink. "That kid will grow up knowing he's part of a family."

I lifted my eyes to meet his. They were not the compassionate blue eyes I had once known and loved. They were icy and piercing. And they told me not to ask any more questions.

Twenty-two

EVERAL MONTHS AFTER WINNING second place at the International Architects Conference, Efraim told me he was quitting his job. "The firm doesn't appreciate my talent. They give me ridiculous projects way beneath my capabilities. And anyway," he turned away to look out the window, "this job is taking too much of my precious time." Turning toward me, he stated, "I could be saving Jewish souls."

I was stunned. "You have such a special gift. You're designing structures with lasting Jewish value. You're so creative, and this is only the beginning. Efraim, you could become a top, world-class professional."

Thinking of our many Shabbat guests, I added, "And it is mainly through your work that we are able to extend so much hospitality to so many, to say nothing of supporting our own family."

Efraim argued, "You think small. You've become so greedy. You used to be idealistic and really wanted to help people. Now you just want the money I earn." He slammed his fist into his hand.

"Listen, they don't appreciate the work I do. They are so closed into their little boxed-in minds." Looking straight at me, he added, "Just like you," before stomping out angrily.

I was confused, and concerned.

He loves design; it's part of him. It was impossible for me to understand why someone so highly praised in his profession would quit.

TWENTY-THREE

THE WORDS "OUTREACH" AND "Efraim" were practically synonymous in our part of the country. We were often approached by rabbis and counselors to have young people join us for the Sabbath, holidays, or any other time in our lively open home.

One of these young people was Simmy. When she was becoming religious, Simmy spent some of her first Shabbatot with us. Her bubbly enthusiasm for learning Torah brought her gradually to embrace a proud Jewish lifestyle.

"This is so amazing. One day in seven, we are totally elevated above time and space. Imagine! In a mostly mundane world, even a simple person like me can feel holy on Shabbat. I want to experience this connection every week for the rest of my life!" Simmy expressed her bliss.

I felt very comfortable with her and so did the kids.

"Simmy, tell us a story." Dovy, Kayla, and Yair claimed her attention when she arrived early Friday evening before the meal.

Petite with long, curly, brown hair worn in a high ponytail that reached almost to her waist, she had an incredibly creative personality.

"Once, there was a large, beautiful, white horse who was searching for her rider," I heard her begin, captivating the kids. The story was interrupted by Efraim's rousing "*Shalom Aleichem*," but she promised to continue before bedtime or on Shabbat afternoon.

Unlike many of our guests, Simmy helped clean up after the meal. Donning my apron, she rolled up her sleeves, soaped the dishes, and quickly passed each one under the water, chatting cordially the whole time.

And she never failed to compliment me. "Thank you for a beautiful Shabbat, Shifra. The food was delicious. How do you prepare for so many guests, and take care of the kids too?"

She wanted more than a simple answer; she wanted to know how she might run her own home one day.

"Thanks for being so thoughtful, Simmy. You're one special, young lady," I commented, as I walked her to the family where she would be sleeping Friday night. "The kids and I really look forward to seeing you each week," I encouraged.

As the kids ran to demonstrate their balancing proficiency on a low stone ledge, I turned to my friend. "This was my vision, Simmy. I dreamed of a home where the young or older would feel welcome, a place where they could discover a more spiritual and satisfying life. I wanted the kind of home that I would have liked to have been invited to for a Shabbat experience when I was younger.

"Usually, I enjoy all the preparations. And I think it's educational for the kids to witness and participate in this hospitality. I'm so proud that Efraim wants it too. And he has an amazing gift of teaching—straight from the heart."

I did not say that I was often lonely when Efraim spent so much time away, or that I wouldn't mind occasionally to be just with our own family for Shabbat. Instead, I shared, "But Simmy, not everyone has to have so many guests, all the time. It's OK to have a few, sometimes, and still have a beautiful Jewish home."

Simmy's enthusiasm was boundless. "I love to watch you light the candles on Friday night. When you cover your eyes, I imagine you are entering a place of single- minded devotion to Hashem." Her eyes were shining. "Everything else dims compared to the radiance of Shabbat," Simmy said as we hugged good night.

❖

Reuven, a young man who had hiked through Europe looking for answers to his philosophical quandaries, found them in a local yeshiva and began to join us for Shabbat about the same time. It turned out that he and Simmy had been friends in public high school years ago in Arizona.

Soon after their reunion in our home, they realized that their individual journeys may have taken them on different paths, but they now wanted to remain on the same one, together.

A few months later both sets of parents joined their children at a beautiful wedding ceremony in Jerusalem. Efraim received permission from the local Rabbinate to perform the marriage.

After their wedding, Simmy and Reuven moved into our neighborhood, not far from us. They met new families and invited many guests into their home. Although they came to us less frequently for Shabbat, Simmy and I remained friends, and she considered Efraim her "*rebbe.*"

TWENTY-FOUR

"MA," DOVY YELLED OUT, "Simmy's on the phone."

"I'm so excited," she said, and I heard the familiar animation in her voice.

"My seventeen-year-old cousin Lori from Texas is coming to Israel in two weeks for the first time. She's never experienced Shabbat, and she's open to hearing whatever we suggest. Maybe she can come to you for a Shabbat meal and meet your family. Then Efraim can take her around to various outreach programs." She barely paused for a breath.

"I still remember the first time Efraim took my friend and me to the Kotel Hakatan in the Old City. He made it come alive. It was the first time my Judaism meant anything to me," she reminisced.

Simmy continued, sounding pleased with her idea. "That would be great. Maybe she'll get really turned on and become a *ba'alat teshuva*."

Even after all this time, I couldn't help smiling at my friend's enthusiasm. *Sometimes Simmy talks too much, but she's a breath of fresh air.*

"You're right, anything can happen. I'll ask Efraim to plan some time for her."

"Wow, Shifra. I really appreciate that you let your husband help so many people. I don't know if I could do that yet. I want Reuven to spend his free time with me." Thoughtfully, she said, "Everything in its time, right?"

I silenced my sigh. When Efraim and I were engaged, I also wanted it. Sometimes though, I wondered if we could just do it in a little

70

more balanced manner that would allow Efraim to spend more time with the kids and me.

Talking to Simmy was like having a mini whirlwind blow through the house, I smiled to myself. *She is such a good caring person. I really enjoy her breezes.*

Two weeks later, Lori joined us for the Friday evening meal together with twenty other guests. Leading the lively singing of translated Shabbat songs, Efraim drummed on the table with his hands. He good-naturedly encouraged everyone to join in. I observed his tall, athletic appearance as he rose spontaneously to pull several young men into a circle around the long, dining-room table. Soon enough, the kids and I pushed all the couches off to the side of the room to allow more space for dancing. Efraim's life-long friend Rafi was with us to help guide some of the others to their feet. Together they kept up a lively pace.

Kayla and the female guests joined me on the side, clapping and smiling. Sometimes I would pull them into the other room to dance, but I was exhausted and hoped some foot tapping and head bobbing would suffice tonight.

Efraim, with his parted black hair falling just above his eyebrows, looked more like an energetic yeshiva student than a father of three. He belted out one of Reb Shomo Carlebach's songs that for decades had attracted youth searching for their Jewish roots.

> *Return again, return again,*
> *Return to the land of your soul.*
> *Return to what you are,*
> *Return to who you are,*
> *Return to where you are born and reborn again.*

Moving the circle of boys in the opposite direction, he continued, "Return to what you are, return to who you are, return to where you are, born and reborn again."

Lori's long, thick, braided hair swung as she shook her head to the beat, clapping to the rhythm of the lively tune. Little Kayla normally did not enjoy mingling with new guests, but Lori's enthusiasm, like her cousin Simmy's, was invigorating.

"This is so much fun," Lori nudged Kayla, running her long fingers through her new little friend's straight black hair. Her sparkling eyes glanced in every direction trying to absorb everything. *Just like her cousin.*

I went to the kitchen to bring out the main course. Lori tagged along with the kids as they came to help me carry individual servings to each guest. "I'm having so much fun," she giggled. "Do you sing and dance every Friday night? And do you always have so many guests?"

Dovy, who had ducked into the kitchen, was quick to answer, "Yep, that's how it is at the Baumen home — the center of the universe." His sly grin revealed a hint of sarcasm to me, but Lori did not pick it up. My oldest son was growing impatient with our weekly Shabbat crowds.

"This is how Shabbat is in many homes," Kayla offered shyly.

I raised my voice a bit so Lori could hear me over the animated singing. "It's a weekly opportunity for families to be together and share an inspirational experience." I relaxed and breathed in slowly. I really meant it when I said, "I love Shabbat."

During the meal, Lori became entranced whenever Efraim spoke. "Most of the ways we measure time are easy to comprehend. The solar year has 365-and-a-fraction days. The obvious lunar month has about thirty days. A twenty-four-hour day from sundown to sundown is logical. But how, and why, do we measure a week?" he asked the attentive group.

I noticed several wrinkled brows. They looked thoughtful, but shaking their heads, remained silent. "We have a seven-day week cycle in order to remember that God created the world in seven days. Even the non-Jews who call Sunday their day of rest took the weekly cycle from our Jewish sources, only changing the day of the week."

Efraim moved his hands expressively, fingers spread, palms apart.

"The number seven represents Hashem's Will in the natural world. He wants people to work — to advance the world, to buy what they need and want. But He doesn't want us to think that that is all there is." His deep blue eyes studied the faces that were glued to him.

Efraim continued, "God decided that every seven days we need to recharge our spiritual batteries. We need to remember that we are more than we can see and touch. So, He created a cycle of seven days — six are for us to build and create things in our world."

He paused as several deep breaths from the listeners punctuated Efraim's softly spoken words. "On the seventh day, we rest from our regular work and tune into our *neshamos*, our souls. On Shabbat, everyone is equal. It doesn't matter if someone has more or less money because we don't care about it. We don't use it at all. And no one has more or less honor. Each individual stands alone before God, who sees the inner person. On Shabbat, the holy day, each one of us can tap into our higher souls, that wonderful part of us that is Godly."

In the silence that followed, I noticed Lori's head nodding along with the others.

TWENTY-FIVE

THE NEXT MORNING, AFTER Dovy left for school and I returned from walking the younger kids to *gan*, I stood in the kitchen to survey the damage. My shoulders drooped in anticipation of the task ahead. Along with the stacks of dishes was the pile of soaking pots.

The stovetop was speckled where chicken soup and tomato sauce had splashed. It was time to change the tinfoil lining, and I needed to scrub the wall behind the stove. Glancing at the stained floor, I planned a major *sponje*.

Surveying the customary post-Shabbat storm, I remembered it was for a good cause. I was very proud of my husband's ability to present Torah-true Judaism in such an inspiring manner. I occasionally needed to remind myself of my daydreams that in my home everyone would feel welcome for Shabbat, a traditional meal, and learning about their spiritual heritage.

The craving for Efraim to be home more, spending time with our own next generation and with me, gnawed at me. I couldn't help wishing that Efraim could lend me a hand with the kids and at home.

It was becoming harder to restrain my frustration. *That's just not how he is.* His missions for *Am Yisrael* were the priority. But that was no longer acceptable

Efraim returned from morning prayers to pick up his stack of Torah pamphlets that were practically a part of him. He distributed them freely to anyone who would accept one.

"Good morning," I looked up from my sweeping when he walked

in. He still looked as handsome as I remembered when we first met, exuding a boyish charm.

"Where are you off to today?" I asked, sweeping another pile of litter into the garbage can.

"I'm taking Lori to Jerusalem and the Jewish Quarter and then to some outreach classes," he said between gulps of juice and a bowl of cereal.

It was about 10 a.m. when they knocked on the door. I set the broom down before I let them in.

"*Boker tov*, Simmy. Hi, Lori, come on in," I welcomed them. Wearing jeans, a short-sleeved top, and sandals, Lori reminded me of the many young girls who had come to our home, eager for adventure in the Promised Land. Some of them eventually changed their dress as they altered their outlook on life. With developing Jewish pride, more than a few gradually adapted to Jewish traditions, including more modest attire.

"Shifra, can you come too?" Lori invited.

"I'd love to Lori, but," I grinned, "look at this mess."

Waving my hand at the disorder, I added, "And I have to be here when the kids get back." With a friendly hug, she suggested, "Maybe it will work out another day."

"Sounds good to me," I agreed.

"Hey, so are you ready, Lori?" Efraim asked.

She giggled with excitement.

Simmy seemed as thrilled as her younger cousin. "She's all ready to learn about her Jewish roots, and I told her you're the best tour guide in Jerusalem, Rabbi Baumen." With a warm hug and kiss on the cheek, Simmy told Lori, "Sorry I have to run, but I need to do some errands before the baby wakes up. Thanks so much, Rabbi Baumen. See you later, Lori."

Simmy's good energy was catchy, as her cousin eagerly followed Efraim out the door.

"*Lehitraot*," I called after them. "Have fun."

TWENTY-SIX

I N THE EVENING, SIMMY called. "Lori seems to have enjoyed herself. She really felt connected at the Kotel. She told me she was quivering as she approached those ancient stones. I knew she would."

Simmy went on, "Being in Jerusalem must be making a big impression on her, because she's been really quiet and thoughtful since she came back. She said Efraim wants to take her to Kever Rachel on Wednesday. Wow! It's amazing he finds time to help so many people. I'm really excited. And Shifra," Simmy barely paused, as she changed topics, "do you have time to give me the recipe for your famous pineapple-walnut cake?"

"No problem," I laughed, "my pleasure."

All too soon, on the following Sunday, Lori would be leaving Israel. "Please join us for a Shabbat meal before you go," I invited. When she hesitated, I wondered if she felt she was taking up too much of our time. "We'd love to have you. And the kids really enjoy your company," I assured her.

Lori sat on the side with Kayla through much of the meal. I wanted to ask her what she was feeling that made her appear so subdued—her long, braided hair didn't bounce even once. Between serving and clearing, small talk with our other guests, and tending to Yair who had developed a low-grade fever, we never talked.

"Lori, we'll miss you," Efraim told her in front of all the guests. "And we hope you'll come back home to Israel soon!" He led them in singing a rousing "*Am Yisrael Chai*," a song everyone seemed to know.

TWENTY-SEVEN

WEEKS LATER, IN TOWN, I ran into Danny, the company manager of Efraim's former architectural firm. He seemed to want to avoid me, but I continued walking toward him.

Nodding his head in my direction, he began, "I'm really sorry we had to let Efraim go," he uttered hesitantly. "Shifra, I really tried to keep him on staff. He is a very gifted architect, and we expected that he would climb high up the ladder in our company."

I nodded for him to continue.

In a lower voice, Danny confessed that he spoke to Efraim a number of times. "I recognized his extraordinary creativity and need to work independently, so I did not insist he works from the office, as all other staff members did." Almost apologetically he continued, "But I had to insist that he turn in the projects."

Glancing around to see if anyone might be listening, he said, "Look, I know he's doing a lot of good work with local youth, and I tried to extend the deadlines whenever possible. I put in a good word for him with the boss more than once, but we could only make so many concessions. Our clients also have their project deadlines."

He seemed uncomfortable, as I listened in confusion. *They wanted him to stay, encouraged his success, made exceptions so that he could work more freely?* I could hardly speak. *Efraim had not quit because they didn't appreciate him, he was fired — because he wasn't producing.*

So not only was he not home in the evenings, or rather into the early morning hours, but he had not been at work, had not completed his work assignments. *At this point, he wasn't home nearly round the*

77

clock. He had begun to return only in the early mornings to send the kids off to school, and then he disappeared.

As he left, Danny suggested that perhaps, in the future, Efraim would reconsider returning to the firm. "If he does, I'll put in a good word for him."

"I appreciate that," I said sincerely. "Thanks, Danny for all your efforts."

TWENTY-EIGHT

"SHIFRA, CAN I COME over?" There was no good morning greeting, and Simmy's voice on the phone had never trembled like this before.

"Are you OK? What's wrong?" I asked.

"I'll be right there."

I gathered scattered toys and shoes into a pile. Rinsing the loosened calcium deposits from the bottom of the electric kettle, I filled it with tap water and switched it on.

A few minutes later, we sat at the edge of the familiar couch where we'd shared so much of our lives.

"Simmy, here, I prepared your favorite." I held out a cup of steaming, honey-sweetened chamomile tea.

Tucking a dangling wisp of hair under her dark blue scarf, Simmy waved the cup away and looked down. She maintained an odd silence as she rubbed her fingers over one eye and down her cheek. I had never seen this young woman at a loss for words. I observed her youthful freckles and fair skin color.

She was the mother of a gorgeous, sweet baby, but aside from a more mature look on her face, she still looked like the girl who had come to us for Shabbat just a few years earlier. As she stared past me, I fished for a clue.

"Is everyone feeling well?" No answer. "How can I help, my friend?" I was beginning to feel quite anxious. Placing my hand gently on her knee, I reminded her, "I'm here for you, honey, no matter what it is."

79

"Reuven wanted to speak with Efraim," she began. "He said it might be *lashon hara* if we told someone else about it, even you." She looked at me for the first time. "As our rabbi for so many years, we thought we should ask Efraim about this first. Maybe there's a mistake because it seems so farfetched..." Simmy's voice trailed off. "But I felt intuitively, I mean you have a daughter, and she has friends...and all your female guests, and the outreach work..." she lifted her petite hands, closing them into fists which she pounded into her thighs.

I was becoming more perplexed and concerned. "Simmy, can you just tell me what happened?"

She pulled an opened envelope bearing an American stamp from her purse. Hesitantly removing two handwritten pages and laying them on her lap, she said, "It's from my aunt..." Looking away, she added almost inaudibly, "Lori's mom."

Absentmindedly bending to scratch a piece of chewing gum from the floor, I waited.

"Will you tell me what it says, or shall I read it myself?" I asked, reaching for the letter.

Simmy laid her hand defensively on the lined pages.

"Is something wrong with Lori?"

Silence.

"Come on Simmy, let's have it."

Her deep, troubled brown eyes focused away from me and she twirled her wedding ring on her finger.

"OK." Taking a deep breath, she read:

" 'Dear Simmy,

"I hope you and Reuven and the little ones are well.

"I didn't want to call you because I needed to process what I want to tell you. I'm going to write to you in the order of things as they happened so that we can try to make sense out of this.' "

I leaned back on the couch, my mind wandering momentarily to all the chores I'd planned to do this morning. *They would wait.*

She continued. " 'At first Lori was really enthusiastic about her visit to Israel. She told us how much fun she had with you and Reuven and the babies. And she felt very comfortable that first Shabbat with your friends, the Baumens. On her first trip to the Kotel the next morning she got goose pimples. She told us she felt like it was really a spiritual awakening.'"

Tapping her foot, my good friend looked at me. "Look Shifra, we still have to talk to Efraim. Maybe Lori has a wilder imagination than I knew about."

I yanked the letter she now held toward me and skimmed down to something that could give me a clue to Simmy's apparent melancholy.

With a shiver, I nibbled at my lower lip, trying to guess where this was leading.

I read on, "After a few weeks back home, Lori started to become really quiet and introspective. She refused to go out with her friends or participate in any of the extracurricular activities that she loves. Do you remember how she loves to sing? Well, she even stopped going to her choir practice."

I peeked over the letter, to observe Simmy's slumped figure.

Lori's mom went on to describe her frustration. "I kept asking her if something was wrong, but she pulled away and wouldn't say anything. You know we were always so close. We used to discuss everything together.

"Well, last night we sat outside in the garden and finally she let me hold her. I asked if she could tell me more about her trip to Israel. And she started to shake and cry.

"Simmy, in a thousand years I didn't expect what I heard next. This is what Lori told me through her tears.

"After they left the Kotel, Rabbi Baumen took her to an apartment building somewhere in Jerusalem. He said he needed to pick something up and it would just take a few minutes. Lori said she would wait outside, but he said he wanted to show her something interesting there. So they went in an elevator to the fifth floor. Rabbi Baumen unlocked the apartment and Lori said she'd wait in the hall, but he wouldn't hear of it."

"What apartment? Why does he have a key to an apartment in Jerusalem?" I mumbled to myself as I felt my forehead crease. I tried to remember if he had mentioned such a place.

I forced myself to concentrate. "He took some papers out of a drawer in the living room, then sat down and took off his shoes. He said his feet hurt. When he stood up, he put his arms around her. Lori tried to push him off."

My mouth dropped. My chest heaved. I felt like a woman drowning, gasping for air. *Efraim? Oh God, Lori.*

The letter continued. "He started to kiss her, pushing her onto the couch. She twisted away from him and ran to the door, but it was locked. Lori told him that if he touched her again, she would scream.

"He stopped, smirked, and ran his fingers through her bangs. Just as abruptly as he began, he turned and went to put on his shoes. When he went into the bathroom, Lori considered calling the police but didn't know the number. And she had no idea where she was. He came back into the room. She said his face was contorted into a weird grimace.

" 'Nothing happened, right? Nothing happened. I know nothing happened, and you know nothing happened.' He pulled hard on her braid and pointed his finger menacingly into her face. His expression frightened her and she felt threatened."

Numbed, I looked up to see Simmy sullenly staring out the window.

Shaking her head, Simmy recollected what had happened on the following Wednesday. "The day Lori was supposed to go with Efraim to Kever Rachel, she kept asking if she could just stay home with me and play with the kids. I insisted I didn't need her help. This is a wonderful opportunity to go visit the tomb of Rachel, one of our matriarchs."

Troubled, Simmy shook her head. "I can't believe I insisted she go with him. I was so happy thinking he'll bring her closer to the Torah. She didn't indicate anything was wrong." Her voice trailed off.

I read on. "Lori was too confused to explain to you why she didn't want to tour with him. This time he drove straight to that same place. She feels really stupid about it now, but she said Rabbi Baumen seemed to take control of her. Everyone spoke so highly of him that she felt confused. Maybe she misinterpreted what had happened.

Anyway, she wasn't able to verbalize a reason not to go inside, so she agreed to go with him."

Oh God, what is this?

I read, "Again he unlocked the door and walked in. This time Lori noticed the fancy pink lace curtains and the expensive looking white couches. The floor had large white tiles with a stylish mosaic design. She stood near the door. Without warning, he pushed her against the wall and started fingering the buttons on her blouse. He tried to slip his hand inside.

"She started to scream and he covered her mouth. His intimidating look frightened her. He made another attempt to touch her, but she managed to kick him and twist away. Then he told her. 'Nothing happened. Do you hear? You're just a kid. No one will believe you. Do you hear me? No one will believe one word you say. You're just a teenage girl with a wild imagination.' Keeping his voice low while glaring angrily, she said it felt like his words were piercing her brain."

I saw that Simmy was gritting her teeth. I felt my body tense, frozen, but forced my eyes back to the page.

"She kept asking me, 'Why did he do that to me? How could he do that? And he's married. He has kids. He's a rabbi!'

"Simmy, she really starting sobbing. She's hardly even gone on a date with a boy yet! It was a shock to her, and to me. What's wrong with that man? Is he crazy? He calls himself a rabbi? How could you let her go alone with him? Did you have any idea about him?"

We both sat still as stones, nearly paralyzed.

"It's not true. It can't be true." Shocked at the idea, I maintained, "Efraim doesn't have a key to any apartment in Jerusalem. And Efraim gives his heart and soul to help Jews, not hurt them."

Simmy remained slumped on the couch, shaking her head. She picked up the letter whose words had shattered my world. "Lori is a down to earth woman. She wouldn't lie about something like this." The letter fell from her hand. "I've never known her to lie at all," she said softly.

"Simmy, I... I..." the words did not come. "Did you...? Did he...?"

"No, Shifra, never! If he'd ever tried anything with me, do you think I would have sent my cousin with him?"

My stomach turned into hard knots and I thought I might vomit. *Did I have a clue? If this is true, shouldn't I have known? Did I know but was refusing to believe it?*

Simmy didn't say another word when she left me in a fog.

I reviewed what I'd just heard, quivering nervously. I could barely imagine Efraim forcing himself on a child less than half his age. My sense of embarrassment ran parallel with my disgust. But disorientation reigned.

He's out there saving souls. Then this letter comes from Lori's mom, who's only reporting what Lori told her. I needed to hear what Efraim would say. Keeping my voice steady, I left messages with some of the counselors he worked with, asking him to return early. A few hours later he returned my call.

"Something came up and I really need to talk to you," I stated.

"Are you and the kids OK?" he asked.

"Yes. But this is important."

"I'll try to get back, Shifra, but I'm talking to this kid who left home months ago. He won't agree to see his parents. He's been living in a nonreligious kibbutz and I need to hang out with him for a while." Efraim lowered his voice. "You should see this guy. He painted his hair wild colors and has a huge ring in his nose. Whew. I hope I can get through to him. Daven for me—and him," he added before he hung up.

This is my husband the "tzaddik." I realized he was staying out later and later, but that's when he was able to work with the youth who had gone off the *derech*. I wondered about the mystery apartment he supposedly had a key to. *Whose was it?*

TWENTY-NINE

"**L**OOK IMA," DOVY CAME running into the house. "We found a puppy." A small, barely moving, brown and white mixed-breed mutt with a white patch over his eye lay very still in Dovy's arms. I had to lean close to hear him breathing.

"He was lying in the street whimpering, Ima. We couldn't just leave him there," Kayla explained.

"What happened to him?"

"Some kids were throwing rocks at him. Look." Kayla pointed to a bleeding gash on the side of what I guessed was a month-old pup.

"Kayla started to yell at them," Dovy said proudly, nodding toward his sister. "She told them to leave it alone."

"Yeah, she did." he repeated, placing the puppy tenderly on the floor atop the clean towel Kayla had brought from the linen closet.

"Who would want to hurt a little fella like this?" Kayla wondered, petting its nose gently.

"Good for you, Kayla." I was surprised, not for the first time today. It was hard to imagine my quiet one admonishing some malicious brats.

Dovy returned with a small plastic bowl filled with soapy, warm water and a washcloth.

"Ima, can you wash out the wound?" He handed me the washcloth. Down on my knees, pouring the warm liquid over the pup and dabbing at the fresh bleeding, I noticed my hands were shaking. *The kids may be thinking that I'm nervous about caring for the pup, but I'm disturbed about more than that.* Disoriented thoughts drifted through my mind.

85

"In the meantime, bring him a bowl of water," Dovy called out as Kayla walked in with a small saucer of milk. Yair splashed some of it to the floor.

What a well-coordinated team, I thought to myself as our living room turned into an emergency vet's clinic. The gentle petting accompanied by sips of nourishment seemed to be working its magic. The wound appeared clean and was not so deep.

What madness comes over someone to cause them to act so cruelly? I cuddled our newest houseguest.

Had insanity overcome Efraim? Was Lori innocent? Did Lori say what she wished had happened? Questions formed chaotically. I knew other young women had tried to get his attention. Even at our Shabbat table in my own home, I sometimes noticed a girl leaning forward to listen, to watch him, and to be noticed by him.

It seemed to be an implicit challenge of his profession: to be loving and accepting, a teacher and a guide, yet to maintain clear, respectful boundaries. Until this afternoon, I had assumed he was a winner in those ethical battles. A picture of Mona floated into my thoughts. *Maybe it is just my cowardice to assume he was a winner?*

Suddenly I reminded myself to do a quick review of the laws of proper speech. One must assume innocence until the person in question has a chance to explain his actions. We aren't supposed to believe what someone says about another without appropriate scrutiny, especially when the questioned individual's character is believed to be highly moral. The words "highly moral" echoed back at me, with wicked laughter. *Right! Highly moral. Ha, ha, ha.*

Stop it, I screamed silently. *Just stop it!*

Trying to quiet the infuriating voices, I decided to wait to speak to Efraim before forming an opinion.

The kids agreed they would take turns puppy-sitting, while the others did their homework and chores. Friends came to visit, the phone rang with requests for meals, and the technician finally came to fix the washing machine. Our present houseguest, a recent refugee from a missionary group, wanted to talk to me urgently.

"Join me in the kitchen while I prepare dinner," I offered, trying to evade my apprehensive thoughts. With a jolt, I wondered if Sandy's problem was connected to Lori's.

Twenty-year-old Sandy left college to come to Israel with a missionary group she met on her American college campus. With little knowledge of Judaism, she was easily convinced to join this proselytizing group.

As a Jew, she was considered a good catch for the born-again Christians. Less than a week after she arrived in Israel, one of our neighbors met her in Tel Aviv handing out thinly disguised missionary pamphlets and encouraging passersby to visit their missionary center.

When our neighbor ascertained that Sandy was Jewish, he called Efraim who went to meet her without delay. Within a few days of discussions and stimulating Jewish history lessons, she agreed to attend classes on Judaism in Jerusalem's Old City. Sandy sensed that her spiritual searching was finally taking the right direction and decided to learn in a girls' program for *ba'alei teshuva*. Until those classes started in a few weeks, she was staying with us.

"I need to explain to my parents why I want to learn in a religious girls' school." She shrugged her shoulders, as I continued peeling the carrots. "They think I'm crazy. First Christianity, now this. They're asking if I'll be joining an ashram in India next."

Relieved, I laughed. "Really? Do you think so?" I winked at her before suggesting some ways of explaining to her parents her transformation to her true spiritual roots. "We make mistakes in life, and then, hopefully, we learn and grow from them and make better choices. Your parents were totally against you joining a Christian group. You might remind them gently that you have discovered your spiritual nature, and you want to explore it in healthy Jewish ways."

Yair ran excitedly into the kitchen. "Ima, Puddles is walking around. He's OK."

"Puddles?" I winced. "Oh, no."

"What's wrong?" Sandy asked.

"Once they give an animal a name, it means they plan to keep it," I sighed, only half smiling.

Sandy and I conversed until dinner was ready.

The rest of the evening went by in a blur. Kids, dinner, showers, stories, and bedtime tripped over each other while Sandy went out to meet some of her new friends.

THIRTY

A T MIDNIGHT EFRAIM WAS still not back. I gave in to my exhaustion and went to bed. Dressed in his pajamas and looking like he'd slept fitfully, he woke me about 6:30 a.m. "I didn't want to wake you when I came in, but you said there was something urgent to discuss. Let's talk before the kids get up."

Yawning, I woke and washed up. He started telling me about his latest adventures, but I reminded him that this was my time.

"Right. So, what is it?" he propped the pillows behind him and leaned back to listen.

"Did something happen when Lori was here that could have upset her?"

"What are you talking about?" he shook his head, perplexed. "We went to the Kotel, some classes. We talked." He looked at me.

"Lori told her mom that something happened. That you took her to an apartment in town..." *Should I just say it straight out?*

"What? What apartment?"

"Some fancy place, in a tall building with an elevator." I scrutinized his face. "On the fifth floor. Do you have a key to an apartment in Jerusalem?"

"Right," he smirked. "I have a key to the city. It opens doors for me everywhere."

"Efraim, did you try to ... did you do something she could have misinterpreted as hurtful, like..." It hurt to say it. "Like you made a pass at her?"

He sat straight. "I knew that girl meant trouble. When we left

89

the Kotel, she held onto my arm. 'It's really exciting to be here,' she said." He mimicked her Texas accent. "I pushed her away, but she said she felt a little faint, so I brought her to a shady area and told her to rest a little. After I bought her a drink, I told her that I'd come back soon, but she asked me to stay with her."

"Did you?" I asked.

"Don't say that so accusingly. What would you have done?" He threw his hands into the air. "Yes, I learned for about half an hour. She kept asking me questions — about you, about our marriage." He looked down. "She wanted me to kiss her and I told her no. When I got up to leave, she pulled me by the arm, trying to hug me and I pushed her off. She said she would do something to break us up, but I didn't think she would take it so far. I told her to cool it. And we left."

"Why didn't you say something before? And why did you take her around a second time if she was acting like that?"

"She's a kid. Lots of girls get stupid ideas in their brains. They think because I pay them some attention that I want to be their boyfriend." He sank down again. "If I didn't talk to all the kids who want me to be their father, mother, uncle, friend, boyfriend, or lover, I wouldn't have anyone to talk to. And I wouldn't want to bore you by telling you about each one's fantasy."

He snorted. "Look, these kids are messed up. Something's missing in their lives. As soon as someone shows they care about them and gives them some good quality attention, they can be molded, guided."

He lowered himself to lie down. "It's much better for these little Jewish children that I'm the one they meet when they're so needy. There are many guys out there who would love to take advantage of them." With that, he closed his eyes and dozed.

I started my day feeling a tennis ball bouncing from his side of the net back into my court. It landed in my throat and moved to my chest. *What should I do now?*

Thirty-one

Tall, good-looking, and soft-spoken, Rafi had been Efraim's best friend for most of their thirty-some years. They always had some idea or project to develop for the betterment of the community.

As a lawyer, Rafi achieved a good name for himself in his legal defense of the downtrodden, especially Jews who appeared to have been libeled by anti-Semitism in one of its many ugly forms. Moving to Israel several years after our own aliyah, he chose to live in our neighborhood.

He was as quiet and reserved as Efraim was talkative and hyperactive. His gentle temperament and charismatic smile easily attracted people to him, especially young women. When these two community-minded guys created a *chessed* organization to work with single moms and troubled teens, the number of female volunteers far outweighed the guys.

"How are things going for you?" Rafi would often ask me in his soft, concerned, confidential manner. I found it easy to voice my feelings to him, and he appeared to be sympathetic. His presence and concern boosted my ego.

One day, he came over to wish me a happy birthday. "Do you have any plans for the day?"

Efraim, who was oblivious to adult birthday celebrations, had not mentioned any celebration.

"I'll be home," I told him, not expecting any other kind of recognition.

He left, saying he forgot something, and he'd be back.

Celebrate? Me? I thought of the housework, the kids returning from school, and the live-ins who might need me. Truthfully, it was nice that suave Rafi remembered my birthday. Returning to my chores, I hummed.

Before I finished the first pile of laundry, Rafi returned with a beautiful creamy cake with "Happy Birthday — Mazal Tov" spelled out in chocolate sprinkles and walnuts. I understood he had thoughtfully bought it at the local supermarket.

"Wow! Thanks. What an amazing surprise." I decided to cut it when the kids came home, and a lick of the icing told me it was worth waiting for.

Rafi sat down and started to tell me of his dreams to build a better, more ethical society. He was developing a program in Israel to help poor, single-parent families.

After a few minutes, he looked at me and asked, "How are you doing? Really. Sometimes you seem so tired — between the kids, all the Shabbat guests, and those weird guys who live with you. I don't know how you manage." He glanced toward me with concerned warmth. Did I detect admiration?

"It's really hard sometimes," I confessed. I debated whether to tell him honestly how I was feeling, how confused everything seemed. Hesitantly, I mentioned that Efraim's absence at night concerned me.

Should I tell him that Efraim would walk in shortly before the kids awoke, usually bringing some fancy breakfast or lunch items for them? Often, seeing me still in bed, not knowing I was awake after a disturbed night's sleep, Efraim would change into pajamas and lay down on his bed. Minutes later, he would get up to prepare lunches for the kids. *How could he not be exhausted if he hasn't slept all night?*

I wanted to tell him that my husband's nightly daring rescues of kids from spiritually damaging situations was draining my spirit. Rafi was Efraim's closest companion. Maybe he would speak with my husband and tell him I was having a really hard time.

Testing the waters, I mentioned, "Efraim never seems to get enough sleep. He's always trying to help everyone. I wish he'd at least come home some nights of the week. How long can he keep up this kind of schedule?"

Turning an unmistakably sympathetic ear, Rafi nodded.

"I keep telling him he's got to be home, spending more time with you and the kids. I really encourage him, Shifra."

He looked down, shrugging his shoulders and then grinning.

"But I have to admit defeat in light of Efraim's greatness. He just can't rest knowing there are Jewish kids who are so lost. He thinks he has to save every one of them." Rafi looked out the window. "I think you are amazing. You are a real *tzaddeket* for allowing him to bring people to stay in your home. Everyone loves being with your family."

Rafi went on, "Not many families open their homes on Shabbat to everyone. I'm sure Hashem will really bless you and your family for all the kindness you do." Nodding with palpable admiration, he pressed his lips together. "Hmm, I just don't know how you do it. You are truly an *eishet chayil*."

Rafi's kind words, like a soothing balm, calmed and encouraged me to continue endorsing Efraim's rescue missions. After all, we were known as the neighborhood *chessed* family, the Shabbat drop-in home.

Rafi helped me to realize that perhaps this was, after all, God's will.

Thirty-two

A S USUAL, ON SHABBAT afternoon I immersed myself in the Hebrew Torah class. The unassuming Sephardic *rabbanit* had motivated me to learn Hebrew more than any ulpan teacher ever could.

Rabbanit Sabbato once summarized for me, in broken but comprehensible English, the thought-provoking outlook of Rav Dessler's writings. Inspired, I was willing to sit in the back of her class with my bilingual friend Rivka, who translated for me. I was mesmerized as the *rabbanit*'s petite hands gracefully emphasized Rav Dessler's deep thoughts. In a few months, only an occasional translation was necessary.

"Giving is really receiving," she explained. "There is a verse that says, 'The world is built on loving-kindness.' If the purpose of creation is at all accessible to our finite thinking, then one of its most profound thoughts is that God's purpose in creating the world was to bestow loving-kindness on those who inhabit it. He does so moment by moment, continually.

"However, if we would only keep taking from Him, we risk becoming selfish. The Creator doesn't want us to become egocentric, self-centered. Rather, He wants us to do as He does. We should pass along to others from the gifts we have received. By doing so, the individual benefits doubly.

"First, from the close relationship to God that's established when we become partners in His master plan for the world. And second, we experience great joy from the spiritual elevation that accompanies giving."

I was warmed by her words. *It's true. I get so much when I give with my whole heart.*

A strange voice startled me, "When's the last time you did that?"

I almost turned to see who dared interrupt my tranquil thoughts. "Do what?" I tried to clarify.

"Give with all your heart," was the quick, sharp retort. I hesitated, uncertain of when that actually was.

"If you love to give, why are you tripping over your tongue?" rejoined that irritating character.

"Stop intruding!" I snapped back. "Let me escape into these holy thoughts."

A pompous Irish accent inquired, "An' what precisely ar' ye' escapin' from, lassie?"

Imagining a short, red-bearded leprechaun figure, I observed the voice's shadow tilt to the side as someone else answered for me.

"She don' like givin' ev'ry thin' away. She jus' give an' give an' give 'til she drop." The little image in green disappeared as the voices drifted into southern black accents.

"She ain't givin', they's takin.'"

"They's taken everythin' from he'—an' she don' know it."

As this conversation proceeded, I felt like a stranger in my own head.

"She know it."

"She don'."

"She do."

"Don'."

Feeling my eyes becoming moist, I asked them all to stop it. The *rabbanit* discussed the flow of good and kindness from God to the one who receives it and passes it along to others. I was convinced that she was right. It is true. We were born to do kindness, to share with others from all the good we've received.

Uncontrollable tears poured from my tired eyes. A softer, more resolute inner voice comforted me when she promised kindly, "You don't have to keep doing it."

Though my friend Rivka was engrossed by the *rabbanit*'s profound

words, I noticed her glance at me frequently. Seeing me cry, she knowingly handed me a package of tissues.

By the end of the discourse, the uninvited participants swimming
in my brain had faded away. The last one had stirred up an image of a
dignified matriarch wearing a long flowing robe and an elegant white
scarf on her head. With a soft but unwavering tone, she whispered,
"Kindness flows lovingly from the heart; it is not wrenched and torn
painfully away from you." With one more backward glance before she
disappeared, as if to answer my unspoken thought, she promised,
"You are not going crazy, Shifra. You are starting to grasp what is
happening in your life."

After the class, I darted home. I could not explain my strange
thoughts to anyone. Crossing into a side street, I slowed, dragging
my feet. The gap between Rav Dessler's words and the life I was living
startled me. The foundation in Judaism was real, but somehow its
interpretation in my home was damaged.

Visiting Rivka was typically the highlight of my day, so I stopped
in. Rivka was a much-loved neighborhood figure. She welcomed her
Russian neighbors who had little knowledge of Judaism to come by
to learn or just to talk. Known as a woman who was always involved
in some acts of lovingkindness, she also learned Torah with great
enjoyment whenever she could.

Torah books were strewn, as always, on the living room table and
worn couches. The familiar, delicious scent of freshly baked apple cake
that greeted me was comforting. I accepted the steaming mint tea
with honey as we sat together for a few minutes. It had become our
tradition to sip the heartwarming beverage and share our thoughts.

I commented, once again, about Efraim's amazing ability to help
troubled youth.

"He goes 'round the clock, hardly even coming home to sleep
anymore. He'll do anything to save another *Yid*." I had consciously
repeated these words to Rivka more times than I could remember.
I desperately wanted to believe them, but something caught in my

throat this time. Rivka stopped her food preparations and wiped her hands on her familiar, faded apron.

Looking me straight in the eyes, she said quietly, "Shifra, he's still a man."

How often in the past had I devotedly defended his altruistic character? And how many times had she tried to get me to see that something was terribly wrong?

Now, with the speed of a bolt of lightning, I knew she was right. I felt myself floating in a huge, empty space, unhampered by gravity. Grasping for something to hold onto, I found her outstretched hand. My head started pounding and my stomach ached. It was hard to breathe. Rivka had waited patiently, allowing me, finally, to absorb the enormity of this revelation.

For the first time ever, I allowed myself to think, *"He is just a man. He is not a saint. He is just a man."*

And now, returning home from the *shiur*, I saw my home as though for the first time. Strangers were scattered on the couches, talking and laughing, eating the fruit I'd planned to give the kids for their school lunches tomorrow. Efraim was the center of the party. He looked up when I came in but was too engrossed in the conversation even to nod. No one else seemed to notice, or care.

Home, but whose?

THIRTY-THREE

MANY EVENINGS, AFTER GETTING my lively bunch off to bath and bed, I collapsed into the silence. Like many women, my nonstop day started at about 6 a.m. and ran its frantic course until midnight. I was grateful I could doze off almost anywhere.

I usually dropped off on a kitchen chair, head deposited on my arm, which stretched — surrounded by the dinner dishes — along the width of the table. As the adrenalin slowed its raceway rushing, I was aware of becoming groggy, nodding somewhere between consciousness and oblivion. Most evenings, between homework, baths, bedtime stories, phone calls, and the day's calamity, I would find no chance to clear the table, pick up the remarkable array of toys, or wash the dishes.

Tonight exhaustion pulled me into its gravitational force too quickly. Half asleep, I drifted from the hard, wooden chair's surface to the couch. I was aware that the only sound breaking the night's stillness was the clock's steady ticking. Picking a blanket off the floor, I pulled it over my shoulders. Tossing off the mess, I sank into the sofa's spongy comfort.

At the first cry for water, semi-alertness returned. After giving Kayla a drink, I made my weary way to the bedroom, remembering to turn off lights and lock the front door. I had just enough energy to brush my teeth before dropping deep into slumber once more.

When Efraim walked in that night, I was fast asleep. He urged me to get up and go to town for dinner. I blinked at the clock, which read 11:00 p.m. and mumbled sleepily, "I need to know in ... to reserve a babysitter ... plan accordingly." A wide yawn overpowered me. "I'm too tired to go out now." Burrowing under the covers, I tried to get comfortable again.

He insisted, as though this were the opportune time to fulfill some husbandly duty. "We should spend some time together, remember?" It was more of a command than an invitation.

"No problem, I'm in favor," I mumbled. *That is, after all, what I've been begging for.* "But how about when I'm awake? I've already eaten and I'm not hungry, just exhausted." My eyes were still closed and perhaps I was incoherent because a moment later, the ceiling light was on.

Through sheer willpower, I pushed my eyelids open. Efraim was on the phone, asking the local babysitter to come immediately. "An emergency," he said into the receiver. "How quickly can you come?" She agreed to rush right over. Efraim hung up the phone. "It's OK. She was intending to stay up late to finish a book report due tomorrow."

"Great," I yawned repeatedly.

Was he starving? I wondered. "There's some soup and noodles left from tonight's dinner," I offered, hoping he'd change his mind, as I struggled to sit. I was too tired for his icy stares, and I didn't want him to get angry, so I gave in. Straightening the disheveled clothes I was still wearing, I considered changing my outfit to something that looked less like the arts-and-crafts paint project we'd enjoyed in the afternoon, and less slept in.

But Efraim insisted that his driver, who was waiting outside for the last twenty minutes couldn't wait any more. Anticipating the response I heard so often, I asked, "Why do you spend so much money for a taxi driver to sit and wait?"

It was not surprising when he stated flatly, "He owes me. I got his nephew off drugs." Efraim checked the bathroom mirror as he combed his hair back, sliding his first graying wisps over his receding front hairline.

Does everyone "owe" you?

After splashing my face with cold water and adjusting my head covering, I hastily straightened a corner of the living room so the babysitter would have a space to do her homework. Embarrassed by the clutter that would have to be cleared in the morning, I whisked away piles of folded clothes, deposited the dishes from dinner into the sink, and swept all the shoes into a conspicuous pile for the morning rush.

Glancing around for more chaos, I noticed Efraim had changed into a new sky-blue shirt. It smelled expensive and looked like it came from a fashionable men's clothing store. He absentmindedly rolled the perfectly wrinkle-free sleeves haphazardly up to his elbows.

Under the pretext of a last-minute garbage collection, I scooped up the dented pail into which he just tossed the shirt's packaging. Alone in the kitchen, I pulled out the scrunched receipt from one of Jerusalem's most exclusive men's shops. My jaw dropped. The price of this shirt could have paid for a week's groceries!

As he splashed on his cologne, he nonchalantly mentioned that the parents of a kid he saved from a cult had given him several fine shirts and pants to show their gratitude. I bit my lip angrily in an effort not to criticize their way of spending the cash that could have purchased new shoes and other basic necessities for all our kids. His clients always seemed to have money for luxury items. *Why doesn't Efraim insist on being paid normally so he can bring home some cash for his family, and pay the mortgage on time? Do I always have to worry and wonder if we'll have the money to pay the bills?*

Changing my blouse, I threw on a sweater and a warm jacket.

Why can't I ever know how much — or when — money will come in? Why do we pay the electricity and phone bills only under threat that they'll be cut off? Why does he only come home with cash under intimidation? In addition to exhaustion, having no clue about our financial situation left my nerves frayed.

We stepped into the cool night and the waiting taxi. *I'm not hungry. I am exhausted. This outing will make my morning so much harder — and we need the money for so many other things.*

There was no conversation. If I asked him anything, he would drive me crazy with long-winded and disconnected answers. I was just too tired, so I allowed myself to nod off.

As the car hit a speed bump, I was jarred awake. Turning toward

Efraim, I saw he had also been in a deep sleep, his head bouncing against the closed window, his mouth hanging open.

Nice evening out.

My tired thoughts wandered to when I'd first met this charming, good-looking guy. I recalled how his rabbis and everyone who knew him thought he was amazing, a *tzaddik*.

Although he became a *ba'al teshuva* only several years earlier, he was a promising yeshiva student, with a tireless penchant for helping others. I recalled Efraim's enticing yet modest manner of speaking. Tingling with spiritual energy, his esoteric explanations of Jewish fundamentals were inspiring to a recent *ba'alat teshuva*. It was wonderful to be in his charismatic presence. So many memories of Ohel Sarah and ...

My thoughts abruptly returned to the moment, as we pulled in front of the late-night steakhouse. The lights were dim and chairs were piled on the tables. Arab workers splashed buckets of soapy water across the irregular stone floors and pushed the water out the door and down the several steps to the vacant sidewalk.

Aside from an elderly couple walking their large shaggy dog, no one was around. It was long after closing hour. The sidewalks in the center of this neighboring town normally rolled up at 11 p.m. Efraim assessed the situation. Racing up the steps, he pressed a bill into the manager's hand.

In return, he received a comradely slap on the back and an invitation to stay. My problem-solving better-half waved me in. The manager walked us to a table on the side, pulled down the chairs and set out two menus. "We are here for another thirty minutes. Enjoy, *chevra*."

Most of my midnight snack of grilled shish-kebab and fries with the traditional Sephardic assortment of many salads, spiced with hot pepper and minced garlic, returned home with me.

I couldn't even wash for bread. My husband ate like he was starving. The manager, whom Efraim had invited to join us, pulled up a chair. He leaned over its green metal back and enjoyed Efraim's tales of heroism. He invited us to come again, anytime.

Of course, I thought, *he'd probably invite anyone who slapped him with one hundred shekels just for the honor of buying a meal*, but Efraim's ego was soothed.

As the taxi sped on the return journey, Efraim had the driver stop near the apartment where Mona now lived. "I have a chance to meet a kid who's into a Christian group. His parents told me that tonight he's staying at a friend's home in this area. You want to come with me?"

I shook my head. "And will you stop to check on Mona, while you're here?" I asked bluntly.

His icy stare, which was becoming a trademark in our conversations, confirmed my suspicions. "No, but what if I want to see how she's doing? You should be happy that someone is willing to take responsibility for such an underdog."

A migraine headache was starting to hammer behind my right eye. "The babysitter has to go home," I said.

"Right," he was quick to acknowledge. "Thanks for going out. Bye."

With eyes closing, I nodded off. So that was it. He shook the driver's hand, pressing a folded bill into it, no doubt an appreciative acknowledgment for "services owed," and slammed the door.

Before I surrendered to the intense head pain which was coming increasingly more frequently these last few months, the taxi driver emphatically told me what a great man and example of religious virtue Efraim was.

"There's no one like him!"

That's good. I tilted my neck trying to swallow the cold wind that came rushing in through the open window. The pain that detonated in my right eye exploded all over my head. I needed ice, my bed, and sleep, desperately.

I remember walking in the door, apologizing to the babysitter for the late hour and paying her from some grocery money. After a peek in on the blessedly sleeping kids and replacing a blanket, I retreated to my bedroom and collapsed again.

This time, I would probably not be interrupted until morning. I lay down, trying not to think. The only thing that actually helped me through these severe headaches was to clear my mind of all thought. Focusing on my life was very painful.

THIRTY-FOUR

"SHALOM." I PUT DOWN my *siddur* when I finished the morning prayers and answered the ringing phone. It was for Efraim.

"He's not here, but you can leave a message," I offered, searching the cluttered kitchen counter for a pen.

"Rabbanit Baumen, it's uh, Eli from the uh, bank," our neighbor introduced himself in English.

The "bank" was the term for the local black-market office where we usually cashed dollars or dollar checks for shekels. This was a common practice in many Israeli communities, before dealing in foreign currency became officially sanctioned.

"How are you, Eli? Is everything OK?"

The phone remained steady between my shoulder and ear as I placed the breakfast dishes in the sink.

His hesitation was not a good sign.

"Well, uh, I've got these checks that uh, bounced. And they're, uh, for some big amounts. And, well, I uh, need to speak with Efraim uh, about this."

"OK, Eli. How many checks are we talking about? And what amount is large?"

Squeezing the phone in my hand, I sat.

"Well, uh, there's this one for $3,000, and uh, I've got another for, uh, $2,800. Wait a minute, uh, I know there's more." He shuffled through some papers as I felt my eyes pop out.

"Yeah, uh, here Shifra, it's uh, $1,500 and uh, $830."

"Are you telling me they all bounced?" He must have heard the

103

shrill tone in my voice. Could he also hear my pounding heart?

"Well, uh, Shifra, I'm afraid so."

"Who are they from, Eli?" Turning over the supermarket receipt, I prepared to write.

"Well, uh, I'll make copies of them and uh, you can see for yourself. I'm uh, just on my way out, so, uh, can I bring it by now?" he asked.

"Eli, wait, did you give Efraim all that money?"

"Yeah, uh, sure I did. In shekels, as he asked. He said he knows these, uh, people, that he uh, helped get their kids out from some uh, missionary group. So I, uh, gave him the whole amounts.

"One of the checks wasn't even due yet, but he uh, told me it was urgent; that your family needed some of that, uh cash. I uh, don't usually do that, but I uh fronted him the cash, but uh, now that one bounced too."

"Eli, when did you give him all that cash?" My stomach turned to knots and I felt desperate.

"Uh about ten days ago, Shifra. And uh, today they uh, all came back." I knew Eli considered Efraim a *tzaddik*. He was a nice, sweet guy who accepted Efraim's stories without question. "Shifra, it's uh, probably a big mistake. Don't you, uh, worry."

Nearly $10,000 in bounced checks and he's telling me not to worry. It was hard to catch my breath. "Bring them over Eli, I'm home."

Maybe there was a wrong date, or they bounced for some technical error. Either way, where's the money Efraim said we needed for the family? Our mortgage bank was sending threatening letters. Is that what Efraim was thinking of? If so, why didn't he tell me, since I'm the one who has to face them?

The kitchen became a blur of dirty dishes and mess on the table and floor. I gobbled some cookies to boost my energy.

Almost $10,000. If they paid him for helping their kids, we should have received tens of thousands of shekels. So where is it?

The sudden ring of the doorbell shook me.

"Sorry, *rabbanit*, I guess you, uh, didn't hear me, uh knocking. I uh, rapped for a few minutes."

"I'm sorry, Eli, come in. Let's see what this is about." I felt dizzy and leaned against the kitchen table. On each of the four American checks, large black letters stamped across each one read "returned for lack of funds."

Eli took back the checks and handed me a Xeroxed page of them, front and back, plus the page listing the bank fees for bounced checks.

While I just stared, stunned, he said, "So uh, Shifra, please ask the uh, rabbi to call me, so we can uh, straighten this out." His weak smile was meant to be encouraging. "Bye now. Uh, take care."

My head nodded mechanically. "Thanks. Take care, Eli."

Numerous colored lights flashed in my head. The left side of my body felt weak, and I began to sweat. *Was I having a stroke?* My head throbbed violently on one side; the pain, shooting down behind my eyes was excruciating.

I recognized the impending migraine, but it was a much stronger magnitude than ever before. Tilting my head, I tried to inhale slowly and remain calm. Mostly, it hurt to think.

I left the copies of the bounced checks on the table that evening, knowing that Efraim would see them whenever he came home. He woke me about 6:30 a.m., demanding to know how I got them.

"Eli called and asked to bring them over." I felt the need to defend myself.

Before I could ask him what this was about and where the money Eli had fronted him was, he snarled angrily.

"That idiot! His mind works like he speaks!" Crumpling the papers, he shoved them into his bag. "I told him not to cash those checks for another week! Now he'll want me to pay the bank fees, and those people will be livid to have to deal with this nuisance."

"Even if it was a mistake, where's the money?" I needed to know.

"You've really become a selfish woman," he said as he sped out of the room to tell his beloved children good morning and hug them into a wonderful new day. By the time I dressed and entered the kitchen, he was sitting them down to breakfast, asking them about school and their friends. And of course, he needed to walk them out, as a good father should.

I just sat and stared, not knowing what to do.

Thirty-five

MY CONTRACTIONS BEGAN ON *motza'ei Shabbat*. As the last of our company prepared to leave, I called Efraim aside. "They've been coming five minutes apart for about an hour, and they're starting to get stronger," I told him as another wave came over me.

Leaning on the cluttered Shabbat table, I began slowing my breaths and relaxing deeply. When that intense minute passed, I knew we'd have to leave soon. "Let's call the babysitter and straighten up some." But Efraim's eyes were not on me.

His attention was drawn to a small group still lingering at the door. We had about twenty guests. Most were new faces, but a few regulars stopped by to visit as well.

I tried to get Efraim's attention. "I need you to help me get the kids ready for bed and to prepare some things for them for tomorrow." I was not sure if he would walk out with our departing guests, but I wanted his practical assistance now. The kids, the post-Shabbat cleanup...*Oh, I have to do a wash!* I thought of the overfull laundry hamper I hadn't gotten to on Friday. *The kids need clothes for tomorrow.*

Two of the young men standing near the door nodded toward me and wished me a good week as they shouldered their backpacks. The young lady with them might have figured out that I was in labor. She gave me an encouraging grin. "Thanks, Shifra, good luck."

Leaning forward, I tried to return her smile, but my eyes closed. Everything faded to the background as a powerful surge of raw energy drew me in. My breathing slowed. I relaxed my neck and shoulders, allowing my legs to hold me. As the powerful contraction passed, I opened my eyes to glimpse the back of Efraim's head, as he walked out the door.

Will he return? I could not even guess.

Do the laundry. I called the kids to help clear the living room jumble.

"Come in everyone, I have something important to tell you."

Until they arrived, I had time to load the wash, move the utensils from the table to the kitchen sink, roll up the plastic tablecloth with all its disposable contents, and toss it away. I did a quick tally according to the three additional contractions that had come at steady five-minute intervals.

"Kids, I called you fifteen minutes ago." My boisterous bunch was letting loose after their relatively good behavior on Shabbat. I could hear them gleefully jumping on the mattresses and who knows what else.

Dovy rounded them up.

"Kayla, Ima's calling us. *Yalla*, let's go. Come on Yair, move." Playfully shoving Yair, who allowed himself to be pushed along, Dovy gathered my flock. I was on my knees on the floor, leaning onto the couch, head lying on my arms.

A sudden silence prevailed and I felt all eyes on me, even as I concentrated. I was visualizing the image of a large dew-moistened pastel pink rose whose petals were opening, gradually and tenderly. As the intensity receded, I looked up into a sea of compassion.

"Ima, are you OK?" Dovy, suddenly very serious, wanted to know. Kayla ran to bring me a cup of cold water. Two-year-old Yair came to help pull me up. A concerned Kayla helped him.

"Thanks, my sweets, I needed that." My hugs eased their concern.

Rising to my feet, I told them that with God's help we would have our new baby soon. "I need your assistance now, kids. Dovy, call Rena to come and babysit as soon as she can. Her number is on the fridge. Kayla, when the laundry finishes please hang it up outside. Dovy will help you, and I hope it dries by tomorrow. Clean up this room as much as you can. And everyone find your shoes now, so you won't have to look for them in the morning."

I paused, glancing at my watch to see that this contraction came only three minutes from the last. Back at the couch, eyes closed, I sensed that the kids were each doing exactly as I had asked.

Was that only a minute? I checked my watch again. The room was coming to order! *The miracle of birth.* I chuckled.

"Rena can come in fifteen minutes," Dovy reported. *Will Efraim be back by then?* I collected my medical papers, slippers, hot water bottle, and my list of names to pray for. Adding them into the bag that was already packed for the birth, I paused.

"It's time to call a cab." I lifted the receiver, dialed and handed it to Dovy. *I'll bet Efraim has one sitting outside, just waiting for him, if he hasn't left already.*

"Where's Abba?" Dovy asked abruptly, a bewildered gaze in his eyes. "Isn't he going with you?"

By now the contractions were at consistent three-minute intervals. *The taxi should be here by the next one,* I thought optimistically.

"I don't know, Dovy. I love you, kids, all of you," and kissed each precious one. "Please God, tomorrow you'll come to see your new sister or brother. Say *Tehillim* that everything will be OK."

We heard a car honking. "The taxi, *baruch Hashem.*" I smiled.

Kayla pulled at my bag and Dovy helped her lift it as everyone escorted me outside. I leaned on the cab, blowing slowly, awaiting my chance to get inside.

"Here's a drink to take, Ima," Kayla handed me the bottle of cold mineral water she knew I always carried.

As I slid onto the back seat, Efraim sprinted over from the bus stop down the street, where the guests still stood. "Hey kids, we're going to the hospital to bring your new baby brother or sister. Every-one be good. See you later." He got into the front seat with his good friend, even though this time I had called the driver.

"Efraim, we need to get the hospital quickly," I said between contractions.

As we drove the twenty-five-minute ride, the contractions slowed. *That's funny,* I took a long cold drink. When we arrived at the hospital, Efraim pulled out his wallet to pay the driver.

I told Efraim, "We'll just walk around for a while since there are hardly any contractions right now."

He turned to me, muttering, "So, is this a false alarm?" There was a nasty edge in his voice. "Did we *shlep* out here for nothing? You always mess everything up."

"Sometimes, labor slows just from the change of place, or tension." I looked at him and saw a frightening stranger staring back.

Efraim's responses at each birth had changed dramatically.

At Dovy's birth, Efraim was so involved and so talkative that I had to ask him to be quiet so I could relax and breathe when the contractions came on really strong. Now it felt like he was doing me a big favor, leaving his followers and accompanying me, like he was stuck with this boring, wearisome responsibility that he'd rather do without. He did not even pretend that the birth of his next child mattered to him.

For an hour we walked in the fragrant garden area surrounding the hospital. There was a complete lull in the contractions, and the conversation.

Unsure whether to go home or wait nearby, I decided to ascertain what progress I had made. The waiting room was crowded, and it was near midnight when a midwife confirmed that it made sense for me to remain at the hospital.

"I think that when your contractions begin again, you may give birth very quickly."

"I want them to start naturally though, without inducing."

The young midwife was very supportive. "In my opinion, if you will sleep a little, your body and mind will rest, and," she smiled, "you'll give birth naturally."

"That sounds good." Her attitude was already helping me relax.

Efraim decided to go home. "I'll stay with the kids and let Rena go home. Just call me when you want me to come," he said sweetly, within earshot of the young nurse.

The midwife escorted me to the women's ward, introducing me to the nurse on night duty. "No one will bother you here," she winked, "at least not until the morning."

The midwife added, "Just come back to us when you're ready."

Sleep, surprisingly, came easily. About 6:30 a.m., I awoke to nurses switching shifts. One nurse explained each patient's case to the others.

Half an hour later, a light wave rippled gently through me. After washing my hands and face, there was barely time to say the morning blessings when a much stronger surge came on. Soon, intense contractions had me blowing while I envisioned the rose imagery coming into its glory. I found the deep-knee squat to be the most comfortable position. The morning nurse came to check my temperature and blood pressure, but changed her mind and ran quickly to bring a wheelchair.

"I'll walk," I said, and then doubled over the bed, blowing hard, as a colossal wave tried to pull me under.

"OK, let's go," I said in the few seconds that separated the contractions.

The nurse escorted me to the delivery room.

"She looks ready," the nurse suggested to the new midwife on duty. That was quickly confirmed and within twenty minutes I held my very alert, fair-skinned beauty in my arms.

"I love you, I love you, I love you." Unexpected tears of happiness and relief streamed from my eyes. "You're healthy. You're beautiful," I whispered to my cherublike treasure and suddenly realized how anxious I had been.

It was nearly 8 a.m. Thinking the kids might still be home, I called from a phone near the bed. Kayla answered.

"*Mazal tov*, honey! You have a baby sister."

"Ima. *B'emet*? Really? Can we come to see her now?"

I heard her yelling out, "We have a sister. It's a baby girl."

It sounded like everyone was trying to take the phone. "Kids, put it on speaker and listen." The baby was crying her first hello to her siblings. "Do you hear her?"

Everyone excitedly took turns wishing *mazal tov*.

Dovy took the phone last. "Ima, Abba just came home. He's making our lunch now. Do we have to go to school? Can't we come to see you now?"

Just came now? My mind blurred. "Dovy, your baby sister and I need to rest a little. I hope to see you this afternoon when everyone gets home from school. And please help convince the others too. Thanks, Dovy. Can I speak to Abba please?"

Efraim gave a hearty *mazal tov*. "As soon as I take the kids to school, I'll come to see you. Take care," he said, and hung up.

I had hardly begun to nurse when the midwife said she was taking my daughter to the nursery. "The delivery rooms are very crowded, so you'll be moving to the maternity unit very shortly. Don't worry, you'll have her back before long," she assured me.

As I went down the hall, this time gratefully sitting in the wheel-chair, I noticed all of the Jewish couples and Arab *chamulas* (extended families) filling the waiting room and hallways.

The maternity ward and baby nursery were packed. No one was able to bring my daughter to me, and I still felt incapable of getting out of bed. The nurse had told me to call her the first time I got up, but she asked me to try to wait a while since there were so many new patients.

I felt such a craving to hold my sweet baby. Still longing for her, my eyes closed. The next time I looked at my watch, an hour had gone by. *Where is Efraim?*

A nurse came in to do the routine checkups, apologizing that she was unable to come sooner. "We are swamped. This must be a good day to give birth."

"I want to see my baby. I need to nurse her, now. I'll get up and bring her myself." I sat up and started to go down from the bed, but as dizziness overcame me, I remembered I hadn't drunk or eaten anything since Shabbat day. The nurse helped me back onto the bed and went to bring some tea.

Encouragingly, she said that another nurse would bring my baby very soon.

No one had come yet when Efraim arrived an hour later. It was hard to share my joy with him, as his sunglasses reflected back my own image. I would have preferred to look into his eyes and tell him what a blessing we have. I wanted him to appreciate this baby.

But from the second he entered the room, he raced with details of his morning's adventures. "After I packed the kids' lunches and sent them to school, I needed to stop a minute to see a kid in a cult. He was going to Tel Aviv, and this was my last chance to try to convince him..."

My eyelids lowered. The endorphin high was doused and deep exhaustion hit me. My voice felt suddenly as weak as my body. I wanted only one thing. "Bring me the baby. I want her, now." I insisted in a loud whisper. "You have to show them this." I pointed to the tag that allowed him to take our baby from the nursery.

He stopped talking and went quickly.

Please God, help me. Help my family.

When he returned, he kissed her lovingly and said the blessing of *Shehecheyanu*. With new life in my arms, I felt renewed hope. *This baby will bring mazal, good fortune, to our home. I can feel it.*

At the same moment, I knew that her name would be Ariella, from the Hebrew, meaning "lion of God." She would be a lioness. She would grow up unafraid and strong. I watched her nursing peacefully and tried to shut out Efraim's rambling words. I presumed he needed to explain why he took so long to get here, but I couldn't listen and didn't care.

"...he was just starting to listen to me when his friends..."

The words became foggy as I rolled to my side and settled with my new daughter into a deep, peaceful sleep.

Thirty-six

T HE GLISTENING SNOWFLAKES, FALLING steadily in the night's snowstorm, glued themselves to all the visible surfaces. Pulling the delicately flowered linen curtain aside, I pressed my pounding forehead onto the icy window pane.

It offered some relief to the migraine that hammered through my right eye and down the corresponding side of my head. Swirling flecks of pure whiteness found asymmetrical reflection in my downward racing teardrops. The dark night, on the other hand, was a true mirror of the blackness settling into my soul.

Tonight, as on most Friday nights, Efraim ate the meal at home. Soon after, he typically left to participate in some local *simchas*. In our small Galilee community, there was always a *Shalom Zachar*, *kiddush*, *siyum*, or other cause for an *oneg Shabbat*.

The celebrants usually extended open invitations. Occasionally I would attend, bringing some or all of the kids. I loved to feel a part of the community, despite the wall of silence I had erected in my throat, separating me from neighbors and friends.

Tonight, as usual, Efraim ran out as soon as the meal ended. By the time I cleared the table, put away the food, and had the kids bundled and ready, he was long gone. We headed to our neighbors who were celebrating the birth of their first son after four daughters.

But like Eliyahu Hanavi, no one seemed to notice when he came or went or how long he'd been there, if at all. We assumed we had "just missed" him. Kayla and Ariella shyly offered their *mazal tovs*, before joining other girls who'd arrived, while their brothers feasted on the delicacies and then went off to play with the boys.

The small crowd that braved the freezing weather and deep snow was treated to steaming tea and homemade pastries sent from many of the neighbors' kitchens, including my own. As the men sang Shabbat songs in the next room, Tirtza, the happy *ima* of her first blue bundle, described her elated reaction to the midwife's announcement that her baby son was born.

The women chatted amicably until our tired children tugged to go. It was late when we arrived home, and even Dovy was too cold to delay coming inside for long. Eager to change into warm, dry pajamas and get cozy under their quilts, the kids dropped off to sleep.

I don't know how long I stood, forehead against the freezing window, staring into the dark night. I waited for what felt like hours until the migraine headache passed.

Efraim had not shown up by the time I dragged myself to bed.

Shabbat morning, I momentarily daydreamed that I was married to a real man. This *abba* would awaken his sons. He would encourage them to rise for Shabbat services, whispering, "Quietly boys, your *ima* is so tired. Let's not wake her."

Grinning at the lovely thought, I felt a pleasant fleeting release from the tension in my shoulders and neck.

Returning to reality, my weary limbs begged to stay in bed. I would gladly have remained snug beneath the cozy down quilts, but the brief reprieve was over. That *abba* did not live here.

Come on Shifra, you can do this, I insisted, persuading myself to get out of bed. *Quickly, quickly now.* I dressed hastily, layering warm sweaters and slipping leggings under the plush corduroy skirt. The lining in my old black rubber boots provided no warmth, but I hoped they'd keep the puddles from seeping in.

At least the boys could not challenge why they needed to rise and the girls didn't. *One* ima's *presence certainly outweighs two little girls.* Pulling myself out of the early morning fog that filled my head, I tried to recall some of the sage advice I'd heard about patience, raising children to care, and tenderly encouraging small seedlings to grow.

In the end, by tickling Yair, promising hot cocoa to Dovy, and assuring them that we would be among the first to sink our footprints into the deep snow that had fallen overnight, they were lured from under the quilts. *We might get there by* Shemoneh Esrei, I thought, *or at least before the Torah reading.*

"Ten minutes to wash and dress, boys. After that, the cocoa will start to cool off."

I hurried out, choosing to avoid the last "oofs" and "Ima! Why?" kvetches.

"I-I-I-ma, Shabbat!" Yair whined. "I need my Shabbat *menucha.*" I knew he would turn over to the other side and doze off again.

That's it. Make 'em, don't break 'em. Better he sleeps late this Shabbat than to equate Shabbat with forced wakefulness by a nagging, insensitive mother. I was too tired to argue.

Setting the cups of hot cocoa together with some fruits and cookies on the table, I vacillated over whether to return and oversee their progress. Then Dovy hopped in wearing one sock and one shoe. "Ima, these socks don't go together." He held up the obvious mismatch.

"Try another pair, Dovy."

This is not a crucial situation. I sternly warned my ever-vigilant angel of guilt, *Don't even try to make me feel incompetent.* "At least they both look warm," I said aloud.

Dovy hobbled to the bedroom to search for another pair.

"Maybe you'll sock it to your brother and bring him in with you," I said in jest.

"Maybe if their father was here to go to shul with them …" I couldn't help wishing in a low voice, as I warmed my hands on the cup of boiling hot, honey-sweetened, mint tea. I leaned my face near the brim to enjoy the fragrance and benefits of the warm, rising steam.

Dovy's voice returned me to reality.

"OK, I socked it to him."

I turned to see Dovy and Yair wearing socks as mittens and ear warmers. Yair—of course, it would be Yair—also held one over his nose. Chuckling, I asked, "But did you find any pairs?"

"No, but who cares?" Yair sat at his place. "Ima, the cocoa's not hot," he complained.

Dovy shrugged and tied his shoes. "We're really late for shul, Ima." My Dovy functioned best with organization and order. He was embarrassed to arrive anywhere late. "Maybe we should daven at home."

Without answering, I smoothed his tousled sandy hair with my fingers.

"We can build a snow *minyan*," Yair suggested, ducking the punch he saw coming from Dovy. His big brother opened his hand at the last minute, slapping him good-naturedly on the shoulder. "Maybe you'll look like a snowman by the time we get to shul." Then my eldest became serious. "Drink your cocoa and let's go."

"Great idea, Dovy. Here are your coats." I handed one to each boy.

On the way to shul, Dovy asked me why Abba wasn't with us. "Why does he show up when the *tefilla* is over?"

Just then, Yair threw a handful of fresh snow at Dovy's back, while Dovy flung a big heap at Yair's head. Yair bent to scoop his comeback. At least they were running in the direction of the shul while tossing the freezing snowballs. I was relieved not to have to offer any second-rate explanations about Efraim's absences.

It took us less time than usual to get to shul. Brushing the boys off, I heard the *chazzan* reciting passionately "*Shema Yisrael*."

Parting with a nod, we took our seats.

Thirty-seven

I felt unprepared for Benny's birth. The days and months flew. Efraim's routine had not changed, and I lived with nearly constant migraines and occasional chest pains. Ariella was still nursing when I learned that I was expecting another baby.

My life was confusing, like an endless maze with no exit. I did not want to live like this anymore but didn't know what else to do. I went to the hospital alone. And when the midwife stepped out for "just a minute" to get something, Benny appeared.

It made sense to me. I lived alone, raised my kids alone, and now brought this precious baby into the world alone. The midwife was flustered that she had missed attending the birth, but I assured her it was just what I needed and thanked her for giving me this gift.

This child brought a sweet fragrance of hope. Little Benny was born content, and I thanked God for that. He was exactly the baby I would have designed. I wondered if he would be the last baby I would bring into my life. And it allowed me to feel even more grateful for his arrival. I loved him with all my heart.

Little changed in the years to follow. Efraim came home less and less, always with a story of heroism and lifesaving prowess. We had few guests and no live-ins. Each child needed special attention. We were struggling to put food on the table. Bills went unpaid even after the warning notices came. Still, there was one wonderful occasion, and that was Batya's birth.

"She's so cute." Kayla looked closely at the little bundle wrapped in a pink blanket, topped with a yellow cotton hat. She was the first to hold her sleeping baby sister.

"I want to hold her too." Benny sat on the hospital bed, snuggling close to his big sister. "It's my turn," he insisted, but Kayla was not ready to let go. She stroked the baby's angelic, fair skin with the side of her pinky. Her hand glided gently over all that was uncovered, from the infant's forehead to under her chin. "She's so soft," Kayla whispered to no one specific. "I love her."

"Now me hold her," came Benny's pouting voice.

Dovy acted as referee. "Kayla can hold her for a few more minutes, and then you, Benny."

"Benny, you're a big brother now," I encouraged.

I asked Dovy to hand me a bag from the closet. "Here are presents to celebrate your new baby sister." I smiled. "She wants to tell you how much she loves you." Benny pushed it aside. "Baby. Me hold baby."

He climbed onto my bed and Kayla lovingly placed her new sister in Benny's arms.

I hugged my two youngest, as Yair, waiting his turn, told me, "Ima, I built the biggest tower with Lego and then..."

Ariella sat on the edge of the large easy chair, waiting her turn. "Did you have fun with Rena last night?" I asked, as my fingers untangled a knot of hair the brush missed this morning.

"We made a welcome home sign for you and the baby." Her voice was low. "Ima, why didn't she stay with us at night? I don't like to sleep without someone with us," she whined.

Still combing my fingers through her curly brown hair, I explained, "Rena stayed until pretty late. Then Abba came to be with you. And Rena went home. You were probably asleep when he came in. But of course, someone big was with you."

"Give me her," Benny was again insisting, as I went to place the new baby in Ariella's outstretched arms.

"OK, Benny, a few more minutes, OK? Kayla, you keep an eye on both of them," I winked, even as I kept one hand at the baby's side.

Dovy overheard Ariella. "I was up when Abba came home." He

fixed his eyes at the end of the bed, where his Abba had been standing before he walked out to buy something to celebrate their new sister.

"I guess I was too excited and couldn't sleep," he continued. "So I got up to take a drink. It was about four in the morning."

"How do you know that?" seven-year-old Yair wanted to know.

"How do you think, silly? I looked at my watch." His lips wrinkled condescendingly. He looked over at his sister. "You were up too. You were crying, Ariella."

My hand still in place on my newborn, I caught the sweetness of Benny's cooing to his baby.

"Why were you crying, honey?"

Ariella's head lay heavily on my shoulder, and I had to lift her chin so I could see her face. Momentarily moving my hand from the baby, Kayla became alarmed, "Hold her, Ima. Benny might drop the baby."

"Will not," he insisted, even as my hand returned to my new daughter's side.

"Kayla, you can also keep your hand here," I smiled. "Yair, don't wander off," I called out when my prankster went looking for adventure in the hallway.

"So honey, why were you crying?" I shifted positions slightly.

"I kept waking up but didn't want to get out of bed even to go to the bathroom. But then I got up and went to the bathroom. And then I wanted to come to you, but you weren't in your room, and I remembered you went to have the baby. So then I looked for Abba in the whole house and he wasn't anywhere. And then I started to cry," she whimpered.

"And then I came and saw her lying on the couch, crying," Dovy completed the story.

"Why couldn't you find Abba? Maybe he was in the bathroom?"

"He wasn't. Where else should I have looked for him?" She looked up surprised. "Do you want me to go outside at night to look for him?"

"What? You would look for him in the street or in someone's house?" Dovy grimaced.

"Wait a second, kids. Of course Abba was home. Maybe..."

"Ima, I also looked for him. In the bedroom, the kitchen, every..."

His eyes darted again to the doorway. Efraim was just coming in with a bag of drinks and treats. "Hey, *mazal tov* kids. Let's celebrate your new baby sister's birthday."

He began handing out candy bars and cans of juice and soda. Ariella scooped up the baby, and sitting, held her lovingly on her lap. She looked at her baby sister with happiness. Benny gladly accepted his snack but insisted that he'd rather hold the baby.

"Soon, sweetie. First, you can have a snack so you'll have lots of strength to hold her some more." Efraim offered the other guests in the room some treats, blessing everyone with a lot of *nachat* from their newborns.

"Why are you crying Ariella? Aren't you so happy to see your new little sister?" He teased her while playfully tickling her arm.

She and Dovy both turned from him. Dovy refused to take the chocolate bar he offered. "Hey, I got you the biggest one." Efraim held it closer to Dovy's face, but my eldest rejected it.

"She's crying because she didn't see you in the middle of the night." I looked up at him. "Would you tell her where you were so she'll know we didn't leave the kids sleeping alone in the house?" There must be a reasonable explanation, I pondered.

Efarim's grin turned sour, his eyes narrowed, and then he shouted, "Why are you kids bothering your Ima? You know she just gave birth! Why are you upsetting her? I told you to behave yourselves when you come to the hospital. Now let's go so your Ima can get some rest."

He pulled Benny forcefully off the bed spilling his soda on his shirt. The impact of his hard landing on the floor made him cry. *What's going on?* "Easy, Efraim. What are you doing?"

Kayla jumped down before he could grab her.

"They're not disturbing me. We were just talking. And Dovy and Yair didn't get to hold the baby yet. Oh, there you are," Yair returned to the room at that moment wearing a green rabbit on his head.

"Hey everyone, there's a clown downstairs making these great balloon animals for all the kids. Come on."

Yair would find his way to the fun. I laughed, briefly putting out of my mind Efraim's icy look and angry reaction. I wanted to erase it.

"That's a good idea." I stood slowly, picking up my precious newborn from Ariella's arms and holding her close. Touching my lips to her warm, pink cheeks before placing her into her bassinet, I looked closely at the pink index card. I checked that it clearly indicated not to give her a bottle. "I'll bring our new little lady back to the nursery and walk downstairs with you."

Efraim stood squarely in front of me. "I said I'm taking them home. You don't need to have them running wild here. And you don't need to walk us downstairs. You need to get your rest. Now, I said. Just do what I tell you."

"We need to end this visit on a pleasant note," I whispered back, feeling like a wounded lioness trying to protect her cubs. I was powerless to shelter them from the man that should have been their staunchest defender. Somewhere between hormonal imbalance and simple exhaustion, I began to long for my bed, and silence.

"I'll walk you until the clown, and then you can continue on home with them," I insisted. I brought the baby to be kept safely in the nursery until I returned.

Efraim ordered the kids to wait for him. Taking me aside, he said threateningly, "Look, you witch, we're leaving and you are not accompanying us."

I stopped, leaning against the wall to regain my balance and trying to catch my breath. I didn't want to cry here, in the hall, in front of the kids, but it took a lot of willpower to hold it back. *How will I be able to provide a safe haven for my children when I get home?*

I held each of my kids, hoping for the wisdom to know what to do and how.

As I hugged Ariella goodbye, I prayed that the lioness within me would rise to the occasion, soon.

I watched them pass the waiting area where a volunteer entertained all the new "big brothers and sisters." Only Benny wanted a balloon animal. The others seemed too preoccupied with Ephraim's emotionally charged outburst.

Thirty-eight

"Yair, please come for dinner," I asked again. The other kids were already at the table, filling their plates with seconds, quarreling over who had more ketchup.

Benny was happy to hold his hotdog in a roll, wrapped with a napkin, while Ariella cut hers into small pieces, mixing them into the tomato-sauce covered spaghetti. Dovy, downing two, three, four servings of pasta, seemed to need to fill each of his growing limbs. With a hearty appreciation of the meal, he wiped his mouth clean with a napkin. In contrast, Kayla's attitude was more polite, one bite at a time, as she tried to finish her plate. Usually, I was too busy serving and refereeing the sibling antics to notice their individual habits.

Why is dinner quiet? Yair's not here! Why am I so eager for him to come? My sweet-natured, mischievous son had a way of irritating others, mostly me, especially when I was stressed. The ending of a famous old poem came to mind. "When he was good, he was very, very good. But when he was bad, he was horrid." I couldn't help smiling, wondering if the poet had met Yair in a different lifetime.

"Yair, we're almost finished eating, and I'm clearing soon. No more dinner after that." My patience was fading as I walked into the bedroom to see what business was detaining my dear seven-year-old son.

Yair noticed my presence as he continued pouring wheat-germ oil in a circle around himself on the floor. Nonchalantly, he explained that he noticed some ants in the bedroom and was trying to stop them from bothering him.

He had set some crayons, paper, and a hammer inside the circle. If he was another child, I might have handled things differently. I lost control as I saw images of baby Batya slipping and cracking her head on the slippery, oily floor. "Clean this up now! And why did you pour out this expensive oil? Take a rag and wipe it!"

His didn't blink. Yair had recently begun speaking with an exaggerated lisp. The doctor could find no medical cause and suggested we wait and see. He might just grow out of it. His teachers suggested he wanted more attention, or that it added to his clowning. I decided not to pay attention to it. "I'll uthe tithues," he said. "Why thould we wathte a good rag?"

"Why did you waste the *oil*?" I retorted. "I've been calling you for dinner. Why didn't you come?"

Offhandedly tearing off sections of paper from the roll of tissue, he laid them over the oil. Yair said, "I was bithy. I needed to figure out how to thtop the antth, and I didn't finith drawing pictureth of animalth uthing the letterth of their nameth yet."

"What?" Anger gave way to bewilderment.

"Our *rebbe* thaid that Hashem uthed letterth to create everything. I wanted to thee how to create on elephant from itth name."

I looked closely at the swirls of color and noticed the *pei*, the first letter of the Hebrew word *pil*, looked like the large body of an elephant. The *yud* formed its trunk.

"I can use two *lammed*th," he shrugged, "one for each ear."

Yair always had a matter-of-fact explanation for his original behavior. His intriguing inner world was a subject of discussion at teacher's meetings. Other mischievous kids hesitated when caught in the act and at least pretended they were sorry.

My son explained his reasoning with intellectual agility and uncompromising insistence on his clever solutions. I tried to preserve my patience and avoid confrontation. I knew from past experience that it led to tension. *Raise each child according to his own way.* I repeated the mantra that helped me maintain balance.

Tonight it wasn't working. I sympathized with his frustrated *rebbe*, who tried not to crush Yair's resourcefulness. He told me that

Yair walks out of his second grade's very audible prayers, claiming they interfere with his *kavana*.

"I need to pray to Hathem outhide in the yard," he said. "Every-one'th yelling in here." He refused to remain, even with the promise of treats.

"Yair, dinner. Coming?"

"Ima, I'll clean up the oil and finith my picture, firtht. You go and eat. I'll take my own food thoon," he reassured me.

I didn't want to yell at him. I knew it wouldn't change anything. It would only leave me frustrated. In the pit of my stomach was a sense that Yair was sitting on a fence. His dark hair and deep blue eyes were remarkably similar to Efraim's. Perhaps he would become a brilliant *talmid chacham*/writer/artist/inventor. It hurt me to think he might become like his father, a wild anarchist, always appearing the perfect one, with a charismatic smile.

I sensed my acceptance of his special personality might sway him.

And then, I lost it. "Yair, come right now. You come when I call you. Everyone else is finishing their supper. And I want you all in bed soon. Now! Come here now!"

I felt my blood boil in a way I thought was reserved for clichés. *He has to listen to me. I need to maintain order — somewhere in my life* came a stronger voice. The tension welled and I slapped his hand, which was slowly unrolling the tissue paper and gliding it across the oiled floor. "Finish now."

Batya waddled into the room, tomato sauce smeared on her face, hands, and blouse.

Before I could grab her, Yair cautioned, "Bati, don't run in here. The floor ith oily and you might thlip and fall," he said in his best big-brother, concerned voice. "Yairi cleaning it up now, OK?"

As she stopped short, I picked her up and left the room. Running warm water, I undressed her and deposited her in the bathtub.

If I had more time and energy, I would have liked to support Yair's creative style. He would benefit so much from home-schooling with private tutors.

As I bathed my youngest, I recalled a recent meeting at Yair's *talmud Torah.* Even his very conventional school principal had commented that most children would learn best in the old-time tradition of one-on-one learning with a *rebbe* or parent who knew that child very well.

"Each soul has its unique way of developing. It's a monumental task for a teacher with thirty or more students to succeed in encouraging each one to explore his potential. This is where the parents and teachers must work together."

The school principal confided this to me. I felt I needed to defend Yair's personality while ensuring they keep him in the *talmud Torah* when the principal quietly admitted that most kids develop a "flock" mentality.

"Yair's ability to maintain his creative integrity against so many odds is impressive. Yet, if he is to remain in our school, we must come to some kind of understanding."

I waited for the falling ax, knowing all too well how frustrating Yair could be. I had far fewer children at home. They were mine and I sincerely loved each one. I was willing to talk, listen, patiently explain, promise prizes, or occasionally threaten punishment. Usually one of these brought the desired results.

Only Yair maintained, as the dignified educator across from me put it so well, his "creative integrity." I was grateful for this, certain that others would have been less kind.

The principal's fingertips tapped at his desk and I tried to translate the message they conveyed. The *rav's* other hand stroked his long, salt-and-pepper beard. Starting at his chin, his fingers pulled the long whiskers gently forward, as though trying to wring an idea from them. "The boy is good natured. He doesn't try to hurt others, although he is too young to know that some of his antics might be dangerous."

An image of Yair vehemently insisting on entering the house through the windows came to mind. "The eyes are the windows to the soul," his *rebbe* had told him. With a completely straight face, Yair told me, "If I want to thee my *nethsoma,* Ima. I need to know how to go in through the window."

Sitting in his principal's office again, I shook my head, half-smiling and wondering how the Ba'al Shem Tov's mother, had she lived to raise him, would have handled this.

The *rav* was musing aloud, but I sensed he was trying to think of a solution, rather than converse with me.

"Although his eyes are more often glued to a bird at the window or doodling in the margins of his book, he answers readily and knowingly to the *rebbe*'s questions." He looked at me thoughtfully. "Yair has sometimes asked me questions that I would hardly expect from an older boy. He wants to know why his big *neshama* has to be in such a little body. He has asked me how Hashem chose which family he would be a part of. He wonders if it is possible that Hashem could make a mistake."

My tongue ran involuntarily along my lower lip. *What mistake is the* rav *referring to?* My self-confidence slipped. Instead of focusing on my son's idiosyncrasies, the conversation might start revolving to the possible origins of his personality.

"Your husband should come here with you, and together we will attempt to decide on healthy reactions to Yair's innovative style."

"My husband is often away or busy with his work," I hedged. I could tell this experienced educator immediately sensed my discomfort.

"Rabbanit Baumen, your husband's business is to save souls. I'm sure he will find time for his own son," the *rav* nodded persuasively. "I hope to see both of you here within the next few days."

After consulting with Efraim, I made an appointment for us to speak with the principal the following week.

When Efraim didn't appear at home that morning, I considered postponing the meeting but remembered the *rav*'s penchant for punctuality. *Would another day be different? Today we cancel and tomorrow we come late—or cancel again.* Checking myself in the mirror, I decided if I go, at least the *rav* will know there is parental involvement, even if it's lopsided. I prepared to leave with enough time to arrive early. I would make it by 10 a.m.

When the phone rang, I was determined to tell the person on the other end I'd call back.

"Shula, hi. Can I call you..."

She began to cry.

Glancing at my watch, I knew I must go, but my neighbor didn't pause.

"I'll stop by later this morning, Shula," I was finally able to inter- ject. "I want to hear everything. I'll see you soon, my dear." At her hesitant OK, I replaced the receiver before she could begin again.

I was now five minutes late, and the *talmud Torah* was still a seven-minute walk from the house. Grabbing my purse, I ran out. At the bottom step, I realized that I forgot to lock the door. I turned back to do so, then skipped down two stairs at a time. Walking quickly, taking the shortcuts through several parking lots and apartment buildings, I arrived in five minutes. *So I'm only ten minutes late. Not bad.*

Adjusting my headscarf, I hurried to the secretary to let her know I arrived. "My husband is not here yet," I let her know. "I'll wait outside for him."

She nodded as she continued typing on the keyboard.

I looked for Efraim outside. I did not want to explain his absence to the principal. *Should I repeat what he told me on the phone?* Efraim said he'll have to come late, if at all. He was in a heavy debate with a Christian missionary and the outcome was sure to have a fateful effect on all the Jewish kids listening in. I said, "This meeting may be fateful for our son. I think the *rav* is wavering over whether Yair can remain in the *talmud Torah*. Even if he lets our son remain this year, he may not allow him to continue in third grade if he doesn't think we're willing to work with the school."

I knew Efraim was becoming impatient, but added, "You know the educational dictum that Rabbi Mendels advocates — education must include the partnership of the *talmud Torah* and parental guidance."

Efraim was quick to retort, "By the way, it's one of the reasons we chose this school, remember?"

He continued harshly, "If he tosses Yair out, our son won't be on the street looking to worship idols like these guys want to do. We'll find him another school, maybe an even better one. But right now, I can literally save Jews from throwing away their Judaism. I'll get there as soon as I can."

"Efraim —" the phone went dead.

I deliberated about returning home but was afraid that Efraim would not call to tell me when he arrived. I didn't want him to meet alone with Rabbi Mendels. I needed to be there.

The secretary told me the rabbi preferred meeting with us together and to let her know when my husband arrived. "He will shift his schedule as much as possible to be accommodating," she smiled kindly. "Just let me know when you're ready."

I nodded appreciatively. After finishing my morning prayers, I explored the *talmud Torah*'s wide hallway. It was cheerfully decorated with posters and handicrafts prepared by the different classes. One wall offered a display the boys had made depicting verses from *Ethics of the Fathers*.

My attention was caught by a poster that read, "Three things hold up the world: Torah, prayer, and loving-kindness." Below the sign was a shelf, holding art projects depicting this axiom.

Several boys demonstrated this with a table sitting on three legs. Another painted a ball with continents and oceans to represent the earth. One original thinker had used three human leg-like clay forms to hold up a snowman-like figure sporting a black clay hat and sidelocks.

Each person is a world. I was impressed that a child would recognize these traits sustain each of us. Lifting the name tag to see who this creative project belonged to, I was not surprised to see the name Yair Baumen, second grade.

Two hours later, Efraim arrived for our appointment. Running in breathlessly, Efraim called me to come immediately. "There's no time to waste," he told me.

As soon as the *rav* admitted us, I understood that he was displeased with our tardiness. We exchanged greetings and, without being asked, Efraim launched into his speech. "My children's education is at the top of my priorities. We review the *parsha* and I ask Yair to explain to me what he is learning." Efraim sat sideways, his body half off the chair. Maybe he thought it emphasized his words, but to me he appeared contorted, ill at ease.

Having made that point, he sat back, looking more relaxed.

He continued as though he was the rabbinical educator.

"It is a hard task as parents to encourage our children's development. We try to allow each child to fulfill his particular potential, to acquire his destined path." Efraim paraphrased the *rav*'s own very unambiguous position of education. The rabbi set down the pencil he'd been toying with and leaned back. He appeared pleased to hear his own explicit stance being rephrased, albeit with an American accent.

Without waiting for the *rav*'s comments, Efraim continued, "I believe Yair can accomplish great things with the appropriate regimentation from his teachers and our love and dedication, as it mirrors what he is learning here in your exemplary *talmud Torah*." Having declared his opinion, Efraim nodded compellingly.

I was, as usual, at a loss for words. *Should I accuse Efraim of lying?* Then the *rav* would really have a good reason to expel Yair. I waited to hear his response.

The *rav* picked up the pencil and held it upright, twisting it back and forth, as though studying its lead point. "The philosophy is sound. Taking action is the challenge." He laid the pencil on his desk and stroked his beard, once again appearing to find answers among the whiskers. "Yair is a good boy." The *rav* glanced at each of us. "He needs both of you to help him keep his balance. All children do, but especially the more imaginative ones, because it is easier for them to think of alternative concepts and theories. Yair inevitably thinks of a 'better way' to do things." The principal smiled, almost involuntarily raising his bushy eyebrows. "Sometimes they are quite ingenious."

Nodding in agreement, I tried to repress a grin. Over the next half hour, we discussed what and how often we would learn with Yair. We discussed boundaries and how to get him to do what was expected without argument.

The *rav* concluded our session. "His rewards might be private walks with each of you alone. As long as it's reasonable, you might let him choose the location. In this way, you can be more relaxed about his need to express himself individually, without concern that he will influence others."

It all sounded fine, *except for the private time alone with Efraim.* I feared that would cause more harm than good.

Thirty-nine

On the way home, I visited Shula, my widowed neighbor who had called earlier. After her husband passed away, she had married off all but her youngest son, who was frequently in trouble with the police. Distraught, Shula asked me to sit, as she offered me tea.

She sat on the couch, her eyes darting fearfully around the room. "I don't know who to talk to about this. But you've always been very kind Shifra, and a good listener, and I have to talk to someone."

I waited for her to catch her breath.

"My son comes home late, just before dawn most days. I hear him coming in, boiling up some water, opening the fridge." She looked so sad. "I usually just stay in bed. I haven't been sleeping so well since I've been so worried about him. Only when I know he's home safe, I can finally fall asleep."

Sighing several very long sighs, she said, "I think he's using drugs." Her voice went very low. "I found some white powder and needles when I was cleaning his room." She looked scared.

"Shifra, I tried to tell myself it wasn't true, but there's more. He won't talk to me, and he quit work. He spends all his money and borrows a lot of mine." Her eyes darted toward the door, as though afraid he might walk in. "I think he steals my money too."

She stared at the floor.

She looked me in the eye.

"When he started wearing those dark sunglasses all day and all evening, even at night, that's when I knew." Again the heartbreaking sighs, her body rocking back and forth. She finally sipped the lukewarm tea. Staring into the teacup, she murmured almost inaudibly, "I know he's on drugs." As if trying to erase the spoken words, she replaced the mug on the table and waved her hand in the air. Her eyes showed great sadness, as she stood and walked to the door.

"What should I do? What should I do now?" she muttered to herself as much as to me.

Drug users were among our many guests, and I was familiar with some of the questions Efraim used to determine the situation and counsel families.

"First of all, hide your money, wallet, and credit cards. And don't lend him money, knowing what he will do with it." I waited. "If you think he's dangerous to himself or others, including yourself, you have to call the police." Again I paused to allow her to absorb this. "Try to notice other changes in his attitude and interests. Who are his friends? How else does his appearance seem different?"

Shaking her head, her eyebrows shot up as she looked at me. "How did we to come to this? My son, a drug user?"

Empathetic, but having no answer, I shrugged shaking my head.

"You may want to speak to a social worker about drug counseling centers."

Shula took my hand.

"Shifra, thank you. You and your husband help so many people. Maybe Rabbi Baumen would have some time to talk to my son."

"Maybe," I agreed, "but in the meantime, you need to have some basic information to get started. If you want, we'll go together to speak to the social services agency. And please, Shula, you can come by whenever you want to talk."

Returning home, I was clearing off the kitchen table from its last crumbs, pondering her remarks when it struck me. The sunglasses Efraim sported, whether early in the morning or in the middle of the night, might be a sign that he was covering up more than tired, red eyes. His attitude toward me was becoming increasingly nasty—and he and Shula's son shared the night hours. *Was there more they had in common? How had I not thought of it until now?*

Later that day, when I hesitantly suggested the possibility to

Rivka that Efraim might be using drugs, she listened carefully, waiting until I finished.

"What should I do?" I asked, feeling the despondent note in my own voice.

"You're the expert, Shifra," she said. "You know what you need to do."

But I didn't. This wasn't theoretical, or someone else's sordid life. A drug-using husband did not fit into my life's story. Efraim? It didn't make any sense to me.

Before sunrise, I heard the front door squeak open and close quickly, but carefully so it wouldn't bang. It was enough to rouse me from my early morning stupor. Through heavy eyelids, I saw that Efraim's bed was empty, just as it was when I finally fell into bed exhausted only a few hours before. It was after 1 a.m. by the time I offered the last glass of water and comforted the last child from her nearly nightly nightmares.

I heard plastic bags rustling with the treats Efraim had no doubt bought for the kids. His ingredients for breakfast and school lunches cost more than the wholesome dinners I tried to prepare. I decided not to get up, or to confront him for the time being. What would it matter?

There would be a detailed, highly seasoned exploit to explain his nightly absence. This past week he had focused on rescuing Jewish girls from Arab partners. The action was high, and probably, I thought sarcastically, so was he.

Some rescue missions did take place. There were a growing number of organizations and individuals who were successful in returning wayward youth, including some of the thousands of Jewish girls who were deluded or flattered into marrying a Moussa or an Ibrahim. But I no longer believed Efraim was one of those heroes.

I remained under the warm blanket while my thoughts floated in a drowsy fog. Soon enough the alarm clock, or one of my early risers, would insist that I start the day. Efraim tiptoed into the room.

I could hear him clearing a space on the cluttered nightstand next to my bed. Barely opening one eye, I could see him putting down what looked like wad of two-hundred-shekel bills held with a rubber band.

I was furious. Again, he waited until I was fuming at his absence and pressured by late notices to show up with cash. I never knew the amount or the frequency of the money he brought in. I felt bought off and cheap. Yet I thought for the umpteenth time, *How could I support my family alone?*

This payoff lent meaning to the last words of *Modeh Ani*. Even if no one else, including me, believed I was worth anything, God did. He let me wake up alive. I let myself feel His Presence as I faced Efraim's barely concealed gloating expression.

"Where's the money from?" I mumbled derisively, wondering what version of heroic-acts-and-grateful-parents-who-highly-valued-his-benevolent-services-for-saving-their-child-from-a-horrendous-fate-that-awaited-them he'd offer today. Would it be the cult crusade or missionary ministries stealing Jewish souls? Rising at last, I stepped into my worn but loyal slippers, not waiting for, nor really caring for, his answer.

Efraim offered precise details of his nocturnal debates and schemes to win back the minds and hearts of rebellious youths. As I washed my hands, he rattled off at high speed, perhaps word for word, his influential winning arguments against Christianity and immorality. "God does not change His mind. He chose the Jewish people and promised us that..."

I brushed my teeth. The running water muffled the details of his most recent daring rescue of yet another Jewess in distress. I suddenly recalled how deeply I had once admired this modern charismatic Man of La Mancha. Perhaps I had been his Dulcinea. He had surely found many more since then.

"Her parents," he claimed "were so overwhelmed with grateful-ness they gave me this." He pointed to the stack of bills he had now conscientiously brought home. "These parents tried everything to bring their daughter home from the Christian missionary groups pretending to be Jewish. They even kidnapped her away from the missionaries, but the girl escaped at the first opportunity."

As I checked the breakfast options, he assured me that they believed him to be a *tzaddik yesod olam*.

Straight-faced, I nodded. This morning's sermon left my mind spinning. I was looking for the safe center from his verbal tornado when gratefully, my oldest son walked in.

"Good morning," Efraim greeted him. "Look! I bought milk and cereal for breakfast," he announced cheerily, as I noticed the fancy rolls filled with expensive cheese spreads he was packing into sandwich bags together with the fruits, chocolate milk, and snacks.

When had he bought and done all that?

Walking into the bedroom to pull out clothes, I made sure everyone was waking up. Yair, dawdling as usual, sat up in bed and asked his *abba* why he was wearing sunglasses in the house.

Only then did I really look at Efraim's face. I had learned to avoid the painful, blank response that my glance drew. Sunglasses? In the house? In the early morning? I could only guess what lay behind those dark lenses.

Instead of an answer, Efraim let out a hearty, *"Boker tov!* Time to get up and start the day, everyone."

"That seems so normal," I convinced myself, an *abba* getting the kids ready for school, packing their lunches, buying cereal for breakfast. I was tired from another troubled sleep, and he who saved the world through the night was bubbling with energy.

My head spun from the incongruity, but for now I wanted to focus on the kids.

"Ima, I need a white blouse today," Kayla informed me. "It's Rosh Chodesh."

"Me too," chimed in the younger ones.

"Oh, right," I said. A quick search through the overflowing ironing basket resulted in shirts for everyone. They all needed ironing.

"Kids, today you can eat breakfast first while I iron."

I set up the rusty ironing board as I overheard Efraim cheerfully ask each one about school.

"Yair, how was that math test you had yesterday? Did you

remember the multiplication tables I studied with you?" Efraim had indeed come home in the early evening to learn with the kids, but as he nodded off, I was the one who reviewed the math and the rest of their studies.

"Ariella, do you remember how to spell elephant? It's really silly that *ph* should sound like an *f*, but English is just like that. What can you do?"

Without a pause, he added, "Here sweetie, give this to Ima as a Rosh Chodesh present."

Ariella handed me a two-hundred-shekel bill. "It's a present from Abba," she smiled, though her eyes looked sad. Each child handed me an additional bill as they claimed their newly pressed shirts.

Is this normal? Confusion blurred with the steam rising from the iron, as Efraim called out casually, "I'm walking the kids to school now. I love you. Oh, I'll probably be a bit late tonight, so don't wait up."

Peeking from the window, I watched incredulously as my husband packed the kids into a car I'd never seen, got in the driver's seat, and drove them in the direction of the school. Before I could adjust my head-covering and pull on a sweater to go out and ask where the car came from, he sped off. I stood on the stairs, my chest tightening.

Minutes later, I counted the hundreds of shekels in my hands, wondering how far away I could get. The thought of leaving gave me a moment of peace. I would leave Efraim and his madness in a second, but not without my kids. And this would not sustain our family for very long.

I took out the pile of bills and began to make an accounting.

FORTY

I T WAS ALREADY 10 a.m., and I had barely begun the day. I was thinking myself into a dither, sinking into repetitive thoughts. I was reminded of quicksand that I'd seen in old western films. The unfortunate soul that stepped recklessly into that cannibal-like mud could try to twist and turn, but rather than escape, he would find himself sinking deeper into danger.

I finished smoothing the pillowcases and replacing the last blanket. I filled a basket with dirty laundry. Poking under the beds with the end of a broom, I came up with additional socks to match the ones already stored in the overflowing single socks' bag. Throwing the dirty laundry into the washing machine, I added detergent and angrily slammed the cover.

Grabbing the broom again, I vigorously swept the floor in the girls' room.

This can't be normal. Two hours since the kids left and I'm still straightening blankets! I haven't even gotten dressed yet! Where did the day go? Snapping myself back into real time, I tried to stop the words from turning into another mind-numbing assault and instead to prepare my thoughts for this evening's meeting.

As I tackled the kitchen sink, I reviewed our counseling history. There were many who tried, and with one exception, none who recognized the depths of our dilemma.

Nearly two years ago, when Efraim had first agreed to humor me and enter marriage counseling, I had first gone alone to meet Dr. Menachem Gershon. A large bear of a man, this psychiatrist and

professor of psychiatry was the only one in the long succession of
lesser qualified counselors we met who could see through manipulative, rambling Efraim. A local psychologist had highly recommended
him as a tough talker who could "pierce brick walls."

There was no need to explain. After briefly describing Efraim's
habits and my hell, he knew exactly what I was talking about. He
gave me a complete profile: manipulative, abusive, egomaniac, liar,
addictive personality, narcissist. Then he summed it up in a word:
sociopath. Did I hear him add psychopath in an undertone?

I remember that I rapidly swallowed air. *So I'm not insane* was my
first reflection and relief flooded my entire being.

This doctor didn't mince words. "Get a divorce," he told me. "He
won't change." The momentary respite dissipated and I trembled,
splintered into tiny fragments, as though parts of me were in the
room while some elements were soaring away.

"He can't change. You must divorce him."

I felt paralyzed, unable to respond, and I could barely hear him.

Had he sensed my apprehension and panic?

Shaking my head, I stopped washing the dishes and narrowed
my eyes, attempting to recall his exact words.

"You believe he'll change if you wait long enough. You are willing
to be a martyr for the sake of your religious system, or for the sake
of your children. You think divorce is the worst thing."

He was reading my mind.

"You're wrong, though I don't think you can believe me now. You
think he'll do *teshuva* out of his love for the kids, or belief in God, but
all he believes in is his sick, very sick, imagination. He only accepts
his own fabrications as true."

I recalled the grim look on his face as he looked at me with concern. "Shifra," he said, "If you're not with him, he believes you're
against him. And he cannot tolerate anyone who opposes his ideas.
You'll continue to suffer, without a doubt, and the kids will suffer."
He lowered his eyes. I sensed he was deep in deliberation. "You have
no idea what all this is doing to your children. No idea at all."

"I want to save our marriage," I pleaded. "He's really a good man.

He just made some mistakes. I can live with that — if he'll start acting differently."

Dr. Gershon rubbed his large hands together. "I know that's what you want. But you're wrong. You should get a divorce."

Silence.

"I'm not ready for a divorce. I don't even know what's going on. Maybe he is helping a lot of people. I just need him to be nicer to me, to spend more time with the kids, to have some normal boundaries."

"You're asking him to change his entire personality, his entire belief system." Pausing, Dr. Gershon explained, "That's something he cannot do and will not do. It's not one little technical point like coming home at night. It's about what drives him to stay out: his need to be surrounded by 'yes' people who are drawn to his charismatic, rescue charade, his need for power, his use of drugs, his excessive and manically disorganized spending habits, and extreme desire for extra-marital relations."

He allowed me a few moments to absorb his words. I heard it, but could not process anything. Dense walls appeared, blockading all semblance of rational thinking. A heavy fog settled in my brain.

"What does that make me?" I mustered, hoping his tone would soften. I sensed he was now analyzing my speeding palpitations and fearful retreat.

"Your childhood home was dysfunctional, abusive. It left you feeling powerless and codependent, waiting for someone to rescue you. In your favor, you are not afraid to face the truth. But change is another thing. To modify one's personality is a Herculean task."

"How can you know all this?" I became suddenly defensive. "I've hardly told you anything about me yet. And you've never even met Efraim."

"I did my doctorate in the sociopathic personality. For many years I studied, investigated, and personally interviewed those suffering from such disorders." He went to his massive, brimming bookshelves and pulled down a heavy, worn volume. Wiping off some dust with his finger, he handed it to me. I stared at the cover: *Sociopaths and Psychopaths*, written and compiled by Dr. Menachem Gershon, Ph.D.

I opened to the index. "Narcissists, Sociopaths. Psychopaths. Compulsive liars. Addictive personalities..."

I became extremely confused, feeling like a terrified child. "What are we talking about?"

We made eye contact.

"Try to hear this." He slowed his speech and softened the tone. "He won't change. Whether he doesn't want to or he can't — may be argued. But in my vast experience, over several decades, he will only get worse. You and your children will suffer. He will lie compulsively and betray you in every way." He paused, taking a deep breath. "I would say he already has been unfaithful, perhaps with many more than one woman."

As a university lecturer, he could probably have gone on for hours. But feeling emotionally flooded, I was grateful when he stopped talking. He handed me a wad of tissues to wipe away the cascading tears. My life was hard, but I didn't expect to hear this. Shifting awkwardly in the one-seat sofa, trying to connect my thoughts, I asked when I could come with Efraim.

Dr. Gershon was tall, even while seated. He rested his hands behind his head.

"He will come once, and after we speak he will comprehend that he can't sway me, that I don't fall for his myths, and he will find a reason not to return. He will say I'm not religious, or I said something erroneous. Your husband will say my fee is high. He'll claim you have no capital for this charlatan and insist you go to a mediocre counselor — one who will not discern your husband's illness."

I nodded, sensing his accuracy, but was paralyzed by a life of dysfunctional solutions to legitimate problems.

"I'll try to get him to come," I insisted optimistically, almost as though I hadn't heard. It was buoyant confidence born of deficiency. I had no one else and nothing on which to depend.

He shrugged. Did he know that he could not convince me? He said softly, "A codependent, needy person does not abruptly rise like a lion and bellow out signs of autonomy. It will take you time, but don't give up. You *can* get out of this tragic dilemma and save your children. Do it for their sake." After a pause, he added kindly, "I believe, in time, you will be able to overcome your fears and uncertainties, and make the correct choices to rescue your family."

I filed his encouragement into my memory, hoping and praying I would one day be capable of it. I wrote out a check that should have gone for part of our mortgage. Hoping it would clear, I asked to postdate it.

"Will that make such a difference?" he asked, even as he agreed.

"Probably not," I was forced to admit. *But maybe.*

Glancing at the empty, yellowed sink, I felt a peculiar calm, knowing the answer to my problems was now obvious.

There's so much to do. It's about time I get started.

Tonight Efraim and I would be at another round of counseling with yet another therapist, who would no doubt fail to diagnose the situation. At the counseling session, I maintained that I needed a husband who would come home at normal hours to sleep in his own bed, and spend time with me and our family. His returning near dawn most days of the week was unacceptable. I wanted him to stop counseling girls and women in general, and specifically to stop visiting Mona.

I wanted a semblance of financial stability, to know when and approximately how much we could budget each month. I accepted that considering my husband's skills it would not be precise, but his being paid with fancy clothes for himself, the use of cars for his work, and the keys to occasionally "vacated apartments in order to have a convenient place to meet the youth" was unacceptable. He overstepped too many boundaries. I was unable to get Lori's story out of my mind, though Efraim insisted she was a lying, starry-eyed teen.

"Why don't you tell them that while you're saving their kids, you are unable to work at other jobs? Tell them you still have to support your family." I turned to the solemn-faced counselor. "Isn't that obvious?"

"And I will not start again to open our home to every unfortunate who comes within Efraim's sight. It is no longer OK for our kids, or for me." I surprised myself by feeling no remorse.

In an exasperated response to Efraim's persistent interruptions to comment on my past history, I nearly shouted, "Yes, I come from a dysfunctional family."

And here Efraim took up the discussion.

"She never received much attention or love from her troubled family," he said, shaking his head with palpable concern. "And that, I believe is the source of my wife's extraordinary needs today."

"Are these 'extraordinary needs?'" I snapped back. "Isn't this what 'normal' means?"

In his captivating voice, raised just above a whisper, so the listener had to lean in to pay attention, Efraim elucidated, "We both developed dynamic outer lives with some dysfunctional inner turbulence. When we met, Shifra wanted everything I did: an open home, lots of Shabbat guests, and active involvement in the community. Now she's different. She reneged on our agreements."

He grimaced.

Drained from the waste of time and expense involved, I surveyed the office. Alongside a painting of a bouquet of pink cyclamens in a mosaic style lavender vase, several prominently framed diplomas were hanging over the desk. I read, "David Linkson, therapeutic counselor." The certificate was dated two years ago. *This is the expert Efraim said would help us rebuild our* shalom bayit.

Inexperience was etched on the young man's face.

That is why my husband insisted we see him. Efraim rejected every one of the recommended authoritative therapists. He found fault with each one: the first had not been religious enough, while the next followed a different *rav*. Another's interpretation of Adler did not suit Efraim's fancy, and so on.

Efraim was clearly receiving this counselor's endorsement. My husband would have continued talking anyway, but compliance fed his ego.

"I am trying to respond to her needs, given my own limitations. I am making a strong attempt to be home early. Last night I was home."

My eyebrows shot up. "Coming in at 2 a.m. is not my idea of coming home early." My rising tenor no doubt revealed emerging anger and frustration.

He was ready with a comeback. "I came in before that, but sat in the living room, learning for a while. I must have dozed off."

He described in fine detail his evening's rescue escapade to explain his weariness. This time it involved a fifteen-year-old who was involved in a satanic cult. The child came to Israel for a few weeks and Efraim worked selflessly to save her.

I grimaced, and my fingernails dug irately into the armchair's tapestry. *Are we paying for story hour?*

The young counselor made a note and was, as I'd come to expect, drawn in.

"And I still took great effort to return home before midnight," Efraim concluded his narration.

"It was 2 a.m. Do I need video cameras to prove my point?" I asked, ignoring the highly dramatic presentation.

"Do I?" Efraim retorted, casting an aspersion on my point of defense as he glanced at the bewildered adviser for approval.

Touché, I thought. *You've put another idiot into your back pocket.*

FORTY-ONE

THIS WEEK, EFRAIM NOTIFIED me that a few guests, mostly non-religious tourists and a few new *ba'alei teshuva*, would join us for Shabbat.

As usual, after *Havdala*, Efraim spoke to them, thanking them for joining us.

"You have enriched our family and our Shabbat experience with your presence."

I could see that he was sparking their imaginations as he spoke of the Shabbat Queen's departure and the longing of our souls for her return. "Try to stretch out the holiness of the seventh day by making *Havdala* later whenever possible, and by lighting additional candles from the flames of the braided ceremonial light. Try to refrain from going immediately into your regular weekday routine. Hold onto your elevated souls by singing, dancing, and attending a *melaveh malka*, the fourth meal of the Sabbath." To accentuate his animated speech, he pulled his *kippa* forward.

I leaned against the wall, too tired to join the next step of his customery ritual. Clapping his hands together, he sang a tune that drew everyone into a dance around the messy tables. A frenzied quarter of an hour later, he signaled the laughing youngsters to stop. "It's time to go back to the homes of our neighbors where you slept last night to gather your things. The first bus out is in half an hour, so let's try to make it folks!"

A few thanked me for hosting them. "Cool," "Wow," "Can I come again?" and "Thanks for a really nice weekend" were some of the usual comments. A few complimented me on the food, and some praised my wonderful kids.

A young woman standing alone and off to the side, as she had throughout Shabbat, nodded timidly in my direction. I approached her to tell her how much I enjoyed her company. *There are so many sad, searching youths, so unfocused as to what life is about,* I pondered remembering my own teenage years. I wished I felt my old joy at hosting weekly Shabbatot. *Perhaps if Efraim and I trusted each other and united together as real partners...*

As though leading a football team to a touchdown, or perhaps like Moshe Rabbeinu herding his tender flock toward the promised land, Efraim escorted his guests to the bus stop. Sometimes I wondered if they would lift him onto their shoulders, like some tribute to royalty. As the house emptied of all the guests, leaving just me and the kids, I realized that once again no one stayed to help. I'm sure that had Efraim just suggested they gather the dishes, stack the chairs, or return the serving trays, they would have heeded eagerly.

"Can you help me straighten up?" I asked when he returned from the bus stop

"I'm going to learn with our *tzaddik* tonight," he said, winking at ten-year-old Yair, our fun-loving, mischievous son. "You're always saying we should review his studies, so that's what we're doing to-night. Come on, son."

For months, even years, I'd been asking and encouraging Efraim to spend time with Yair learning Torah and helping him catch up to his class. Recently he acquiesced, taking him for evenings of *abba*-son reviews. *How could I argue now?*

Yair grabbed his coat and book and was running to the door.

"Be home early, tomorrow's school," I reminded them uneasily.

"See you soon. *Shavua tov* kids!"

Efraim and Yair walked out, leaving the others in a foul mood. I could see that Ariella pretended to read while she daydreamed. Dovy angrily packed his schoolbag for yeshiva. His Sunday morning bus left at 6:30 a.m., and I sensed he was glad to be getting out of the house.

I knew it would take a lot of argumentative persuasions to get their help now. And Kayla was so tired from helping out with so many guests over Shabbat that she went to bed early. I scraped and stacked plates, looking forward to a long evening, bedding down the kids, and cleaning up — if I remained awake long enough.

Tomorrow I sweep.

"Get in the taxi, Yair," Efraim ordered as he hailed the driver. With a good-natured slap on the back and a hearty *shavua tov*, Efraim whispered the address. The driver nodded, speeding along the familiar route.

"So, Abba, what's on for tonight?" Yair was anticipating their evening out "learning." Throwing the brown-and-blue covered *mishnayot* onto the seat, he grinned.

"Cool. Hey, I could do this every night." A fleeting thought of Ima's face, always so concerned about him, faded quickly as he looked out the partially curtained window into the black night. He already guessed where they were going to learn. *TV hour is now! Yes!* He clenched his fist and pulled it toward his chest. "*Yalla,*" he buzzed softly.

The second the taxi slid near the curb, Yair pushed the door open and jumped out, remembering to grab his book. He successfully shut out his father's endless monologue to the gullible driver and wasn't going to stick around for the grand finale. It was boring already. Abba either told the same story to different drivers or different stories to the same driver. "Come on, Abba, it's cold out here," Yair yelled through his chattering teeth. "Let's go on up."

Yair watched his *abba* pass a large shekel bill to his audience, telling him to keep the change. *Thanks for listening, doc. I feel better now.* Shivering in the biting cold air, he turned to enter the predictable destination.

"Come on, son, I have to spend some time with these messed up people. She's out of work now, and they hardly have food to eat."

Yeah, tell me about it, Yair mused. The last time they came here, they brought a month's worth of groceries.

As they trudged up the dark stairs with the graffiti scribbled in every possible place, Yair played his father's game by volunteering to cheer up Shmueli.

The TV was blaring when they entered Mona's apartment without knocking. Mona, dressed in a mini skirt and a lacy blouse, screamed out obscenities, saying that she could have killed him, taking him for a thief. Then she complained about her lousy Shabbat because Shmueli had made her leave the TV off even when he was at shul praying.

"Ever since you got him into that stupid yeshiva, he keeps telling me what to do and what not to do."

Yair and Shmueli slapped a high five. "What's happening, man?"

"*Hakol b'seder*. Everything's great," Shmueli returned.

"Cool. Me too. What's on TV?" Yair was ready for his night out.

"Not much," Shmueli shrugged, preferring to read. Since this was Yair's only opportunity for prime-time viewing, he was not about to pass it up. "Go ahead, read if you want."

As Yair settled into a comfortable position on the couch, he noticed from the corner of his eye, his *abba* handing a wad of bills to Mona. Momentarily, he cringed. Ima said he couldn't take the martial arts course because they couldn't afford it right now. *That looks like it would pay for private lessons.*

"That's just enough for rent, you liar. How am I supposed to pay for electricity and food?" She yelped like a wounded dog. "You're holding out on us."

Yair sat frozen, trying to stay focused on the remote control as he flipped from the sports game to some really cool sitcoms. Efraim was yelling back at Mona, who was cursing and screaming, telling her to shut her disgusting mouth.

Yair avoided looking at Shmueli.

Shmueli scrutinized his latest library book, using all his power of concentration to shut out the ugly mood that always came on the heels of Efraim's visits.

The voices trailed off as they walked, still arguing, into the back room.

Slumping low on the couch, Yair's eyes were glued to the screen. He had the TV all to himself. "I wish we had a TV at home," he said out loud.

"Hey, take this one. Your *abba* bought it for us anyway." Yair shot up in his seat, his eyes widening.

"What?"

Shmueli shrugged. "Your *abba*'s always buying us stuff."

Yair had been here a few times before since they had begun their new "learning program," but he was always glued to the screen. Now he looked around. "That's a cool aquarium. The grass looks amazingly real."

Shmueli lifted his eyebrows. "Yep, that too," he grinned.

Yair twisted to glance around the room, wondering why his *abba* bought them all these gifts. His searching eyes spotted his own bow and arrow set. He shot up and darted over to check it out more closely.

"Hey, this is mine," he blurted out. "I couldn't find it anywhere."

"No, it's not. This is mine," Shmueli became defensive. "I even took lessons to learn how to shoot it."

"What?" Yair resentfully remembered searching their whole house several weeks ago, looking for his prize bow and arrows that Abba had bought him. He and some friends wanted to go shooting in an empty field near home, but it was missing, *until now*, he thought. He ran his fingers over the bow. It was scratched in the same place. Examining the arrow case, he found his initials carved into it. "Look," he pointed out the prominent "*yud, beit.*" "These are my initials, Yair Baumen."

Shmueli shrugged.

"If it was yours, it would be in your house," he said defensively, gripping it tightly. "This is mine."

Most of the junk Efraim brought didn't really interest him. But Shmueli spent hours training with a private instructor Efraim had hired, and he wasn't going to let this go.

"Abba," Yair called out impatiently. "Abba, where are you?"

Shmueli relaxed his defensive pose. "Forget it. When they finish arguing, they'll come out. They can scream for hours."

Yair sat hard onto the couch. "Oof!" He finished off the half-full carton of ice cream that Shmueli offered him.

"Your dad will probably buy us more tomorrow. He usually brings us lots of stuff on Sundays."

Angrily, Yair flipped through stations, trying to find a high-action movie. Almost everything was immodest — according to his Ima's opinion.

So what? No one's here to tell me not to watch it.

"Lucky me," he smirked, letting go of some of his anger over his embezzled bow and arrow. Slumping down further in the couch, he waited for his *abba*.

Yair could not tear his eyes from the screen. Shmueli, on the other hand, tried to stay focused on the autobiography of a teenage Holocaust survivor. He turned the chair so it faced away from the distracting scenes.

Mona's screeching pulled them both back to the dreary, undecorated apartment. In the intermittent silences, Yair noted that Mona had not hung up any pictures or curtains like in his home.

If they hate each other so much, why does Abba help her? She's crazy. How does Shmueli deal with her every day? He peered at Shmueli, who appeared to be concentrating totally on his book.

A few minutes later, Abba appeared and commanded, "Get your coat, Yair."

Efraim bent over Shmueli and pushed up the cover of the book to read the title.

"Smart kid," he nodded, his jaw jutting out proudly.

Glaring at the TV, he paused. In his peripheral vision, he noticed Yair's focused interest. "Turn that trash off. It's a waste of time," he snarled.

"How's the learning going, Shmueli? Your *rebbe* told me you could be a *talmid chacham* if you keep going like you are now." Shmueli kept his eyes on the page.

As Yair stood, he again noticed Mona's sheer lacy blouse. *Why doesn't Abba yell at her to dress modestly?*

"Where's your *mishnayot*?" Abba asked, and Yair searched the room. He'd thrown it somewhere.

Shmueli looked up, pointing his finger toward the messy kitchen. "On the table."

"Thanks."

"Open it to where you're learning," Efraim said, and Yair tried to remember what he was studying in school.

He flipped it open to a familiar page. "Here." Efraim took the *mishnayot* and started reading and explaining. Shmueli looked up, listening. He repeated the commentary he'd learned.

After about five minutes, Efraim stood up. "It's late and you have school tomorrow. When we go home, you can tell Ima some of what we just learned, OK?" His eyes narrowed toward Yair meaningfully.

"Sure, Abba, no problem." Yair understood. He shifted his weight self-consciously. He had learned, hadn't he? He could tell Ima truthfully that he learned. Yeah, he could. And he shifted back to the other leg.

Efraim called his driver while Mona muttered at the TV or to herself.

Tousling Shmueli's hair, Efraim said, "Good night, kid. Keep up your learning. Make me proud."

When they settled into the heated cab, Yair leaned forward and whispered, "Abba, why was my bow-and-arrow set in Shmueli's house?" Turning his head to the right, as though to look out the window, Efraim corrected him. "That's not yours. Didn't you say you couldn't find yours? I bought the same kind of set for Shmueli."

"But it had my initials on the arrow case. And the bow..."

"I said it's not yours," Efraim answered with finality. "After you lost the bow and arrows I gave you, I bought that case for him to use."

"Abba it's scratched in the —" Yair persisted.

"You're wrong, Yair." Efraim kept his voice low. "You're scatter-brained. You lose everything. Don't go blaming others."

Yair sat back, the wind taken out of him. He put his clenched fists into his coat pockets. One was torn, and through the hole he angrily scratched onto his pants leg. *It is mine!*

Yair shut his ears against his father's monologue of daring exploits to the driver. By the time they arrived home, he'd firmly determined that his father was a liar. *And he stole my bow and arrow set.*

Now he was in a quandary. *If I tell Ima, she'll know I wasn't learning.* Momentarily, he reddened as he did a quick review of this evening's prime time. *I actually learned a lot. And Abba will kill me for revealing our secret.* He closed his eyes in complete frustration.

"We're home, Yair. Wake up." Efraim opened the taxi's back door. You have the *mishnayot*?" he asked abruptly.

"What?" Yair shook as the cold night's air slapped him through the open door.

"What? Did I take it?" He couldn't remember. "Maybe I left it there." He was sleepy and confused.

"You what?" Efraim forcefully pulled Yair up from the seat and out of the car. He put his knee onto the seat and lurched forward to search the floor and rear window shelf.

"Don't worry, *chabibi*, my friend," the sympathetic driver assured him. "We'll pick it up next time we go. It will be another opportunity to help those unfortunate folks."

Efraim took no comfort in that. "Here it is." He picked it up from the floor where it had fallen, and backing out of the car, handed it to his weary son. Thrusting his arm back in to shake the driver's hand, he blessed him with good health and peace in his home. "That's the basis for everything, my friend."

"*Toda rabba*, rabbi. Thank you. May there be many more like you in *Am Yisrael.*"

"Abba," Yair said. He noticed the dark, empty street. With his teeth chattering from the biting cold, he asked, "What time is it?"

"Late enough for you to go to sleep."

The door was unlocked. Efraim switched on the light. The wall clock ticked loudly in the silence. In the kitchen, piles of dishes soaked and leftovers were out on the counters.

It was 10:30 p.m. They had been gone for four hours. Efraim pulled off his winter jacket and turned on the electric space heater.

"Good night, Yair. Go right to bed. Now."

"Yeah," Yair said, walking slowly into the bedroom. He wished his *ima* would wake up, and he hoped she wouldn't. Tossing his coat onto a pile of toys, he surveyed the room. Dovy and Benny were asleep.

He peeked into his sisters' room. Ima was still wearing her Shabbat dress. She was lying on Batya's bed, with her arms wrapped around her. Flipping on the nightlight, he saw she was still wearing her stained apron. The girls were sleeping head to toe in the same bed. Yair shut the door. Quickly, he dressed in his pajamas.

He was too tired to brush his teeth, and he didn't care. "Good night, Abba," he called softly. Under his breath, he muttered *Thanks for learning with me, Dad*. He muttered the first line of *Shema* as his head hit the pillow. Before he fell asleep, he heard the front door click and bang shut quickly. The key turning in the lock was the last sound he heard before falling asleep.

FORTY-TWO

DOVY WAS UNABLE TO fall asleep. He pulled the frayed quilt up until it covered his head. When he felt the need to breathe more air, he shoved it impatiently off his face, preferring the cold air in the room to the stuffiness. Flipping to his back, he lashed out at an imaginary foe.

As the inner rage intensified, he punched his tightly clenched fist into the pillow. He was trying to fight off the self-incrimination that once again disturbed his sleep. He was frustrated with himself for feeling so angry toward his *ima*, yet he could not stand up to his father. The inner struggle intensified.

He tried to calm himself by reviewing his *Gemara* by heart. It used to be easy for him, but now it didn't last more than a few minutes. His normally razor-sharp thoughts were easily blurred these days.

Dovy knew his decision not to go to Mona's house anymore was the right one. Although several months had passed, he remembered every detail of that last visit. The despicable scenes kept replaying in his memory, causing tension in his jaw. As though watching a movie in his mind, he saw Abba telling Ima, "I'm happy I'm able to spend some quality, private time with the kids." His voice was the epitome of sincerity. "Come on Dovy, let's go learn tonight," Abba had said, handing him the *Gemara*. "Ready?"

By now Dovy knew the strategy. "Yeah, I'm ready. Let's go." The tone of his voice sounded vague.

Dovy reviewed the carbon copy scenes. The cab waits outside. Abba tells his stories. The impressed driver nods. Dovy imagined the driver's thoughts: *A tzaddik and a good fare. I get a good story and the patron tips well.* The driver knows the address. Father and son walk upstairs. Abba enters the apartment as though he owns the place. Inevitably, he hands some money to Mona. She begins to get angry or curse. She's always angry. Nothing is ever enough.

Dovy sat with Shmueli to learn *Gemara*. Although Dovy was older, the boys studied well together. *Shmueli has a really brilliant, searching mind*, Dovy had thought on many occasions. *Too bad he's got such a messed-up mother.*

The TV drowns out the adult's strained shouts. Shmueli and Dovy had better things to do than watch the trash that Mona enjoyed. On that night, Shmueli couldn't take the racket anymore and he flipped it off.

Dovy recalled how he tried not to listen to his Abba's outbursts or Mona's endless criticisms of Abba, of the Orthodox yeshiva he had insisted on sending Shmueli to, and something about her pitiful life.

Dovy didn't want to know any of it. He just wanted to learn Torah. He had realized then that his visits were good for Shmueli. Dovy also knew that none of Shmueli's friends were ever allowed go there.

"You don't appreciate anything I do," Efraim bellowed. They walked toward the back room, sounding like they would slit each other's throats if they could.

Why does he come here if she's so ungrateful?

The silence when Efraim closed the door was a relief.

Shmueli offered cake and drinks, which he poured into disposable cups. "Want some?"

They ate in silence. *Is he as embarrassed as I am that they act so stupid?*

It was not so long before the two emerged, somewhat calmer. Mona was talking about her seemingly futile search for a job, sounding less dramatic. Efraim appeared to be listening, and he gave her some suggestions. Dovy stared hard into his *Gemara*, fuming. *Something is really wrong here.*

Shmueli looked up briefly and then forced his concentration back onto the page

Dovy's peripheral vision was drawn to Mona's disarrayed clothing. Following a fleeting look at her, he dropped his eyes swiftly. Efraim whispered something into her ear, and she shook her head childishly, refusing. "Now!" he yelled. Sulking, she turned back into the room, returning minutes later wearing a bright yellow pullover sweatshirt and pants under her mini skirt.

Efraim sat with the boys and asked them about their learning. He put his arm around Shmueli, telling him he could be a *talmid chacham* one day if he kept up his learning. Shmueli nodded respectfully. "Yeah, maybe."

Dovy was sure that the yeshiva was the only stable reality in Shmueli's life. He knew his father had worked ceaselessly to obtain a trial period for Shmueli at a well-known and respected *talmud Torah*. He also knew they had made a major exception for this kid. No other student's family had a TV.

All the families were keeping Shabbat and *mitzvot*, with many following a strict path of Torah law. It seems that Shmueli's outstanding character and his brilliant mind shone through the trial. They were not in the same yeshiva, but on several occasions, Dovy overheard the rabbis claim that the boy might be especially gifted, an *illuy*. Shmueli clung to his rabbi and the yeshiva's ideology.

The rabbis often complimented Efraim's extraordinary dedication to the boy "You are just like a father to him." Shmueli was grateful to Dovy's father for that. In addition, the long hours of yeshiva no doubt gave him respite from his sick mother — and her toxic TV.

Soon, Dovy and Efraim were outside waiting for the taxi. Efraim explained again about the great hardship those two had. "If I can help just a little, I don't care about her persistent ingratitude. She's not normal and she can't keep a job, but Shmueli deserves a chance to succeed in life." Compassion trickled from Efraim's words.

"Stop Abba, I got it. You've told me a thousand times," he replied.

"Well, I just want to make sure you remember why we come here. No one else really cares about them. And Shmueli could just become a bum on the streets if good people don't get involved with him. That's why I worked so hard to get him into this great yeshiva. Even your *ima* doesn't want to help them anymore. She doesn't understand what a *mitzva* it is."

"So maybe I'll tell her," Dovy half-teased, half-threatened. "I'll tell her how much you're helping Mona to get the money she needs, how well Shmueli is do —"

Efraim snapped to attention. "Don't you tell her anything! Do you hear me? Nothing. I told you she's jealous that I want to help others." Efraim trembled furiously. With a sudden move, he grabbed a hold of Dovy's jacket, squeezing the front of the collar together, nearly choking him. Startled, Dovy pulled his face back defensively. He feared his father's unexpected violence.

"Don't be such a wise guy," Efraim ordered, lowering his voice. "You don't have to come here at all." Efraim thrust him away, and Dovy struggled to keep his balance.

"I don't want to!" Dovy retorted, equally furious as he tried to control his fear. With an undefined but strong sense of betrayal, he burst out, "Why was Mona's blouse —"

"What? What blouse? She was wearing a sweatshirt." It was stated effortlessly as the pure and unadulterated truth. A moment later, just before their ride appeared, Efraim grinned and winked as though his barely adolescent son was a close confidant, "Keep your teenage thoughts to yourself, kid." Dovy felt sick to his stomach.

That was the last time Abba took him out "to learn." Yair was sacrificed to the special outings instead. Burrowing under the blankets, Dovy kept shaking his head, trying to find relief from his guilt.

Dovy considered painfully, *Yair is such a mischievous kid. Left alone with the TV and the goings on in that rathole, he could easily be influenced to follow in Abba's deceptive ways.*

Dovy was confounded. He was afraid to tell his *ima* — afraid to hurt her, afraid of his father, afraid he might destroy his family. His *abba*'s secrets were too heavy a burden to carry alone. He felt like they might suffocate or break him. But with whom could he share them?

Shifting positions for what seemed like infinity, he thought about how he waited for his little brother to come home. Dovy's sense of responsibility for Yair's fate weighed heavily on him. Each time his younger sibling left with their father, Dovy had an overwhelming need to see that Yair would survive the ordeal.

Because of Abba's rule to keep secrets, accompanied by veiled threats of retaliation, Dovy was unable to speak to Yair. And with every excursion, it was only when Dovy heard the door open and Yair said good night to their father that Dovy was finally able to let go, close his eyes, and drift off to troubled sleep.

FORTY-THREE

AKING A SHORTCUT THROUGH *the back streets will get me there faster and less noticed.* I hurriedly crossed the street. I had left the kids alone and wanted to get this over with quickly.

The streetlights on this road were unlit, as usual. I tripped over a tree root that jutted dangerously out of the ground. *What the municipality saves on electricity, they may have to spend on hospital bills.*

I looked at the moon and stars, which offered a hint of illumination. I chanted softly, "I lift up my eyes to the hills from where my help comes."

With the new month, the moon was forming a sliver of gray in a banana contour. At Creation, the lesser light wanted to be equally as great as its daytime counterpart. I learned that when Mashiach comes, the sun and moon will be the same size. *But until then, they can have mutual respect for each other, can't they? I don't ask for much, but why should I be so humiliated?*

The next words of the psalm vibrated through me: "My help comes from Hashem, Who made the heavens and the earth." Repeating the words soothed me, even when I saw the fence-enclosed building with many windows.

My last conversation with the community rabbi came to mind. He told me that until I decided to get a divorce, I must act as a wife, otherwise, I would be considered "rebellious" in the eyes of the *beit din* and God. As long as counseling was an option, every opportunity should be found to heal the rift.

"Rift?" I responded to him. "Is this a chink in the relationship?"

I remember my voice cracking. "God help me! This is an earthquake, nineteen on the Richter scale." How I broke down then, right there, completely against my will. I didn't want to. But maybe it helped. He said I should try, and if I really couldn't, then maybe the time to open the *tik*, to file for divorce, had come.

So there I was, proving my strength, "acting like a wife." *I can keep going, I can do this.* Does it really matter to anyone why I'm not ready to divorce yet? I reviewed, for the ten thousandth time, my reasons to wait, to want to believe in the advice givers and soothsayers.

I have nowhere to go, no family support, no savings, no money-earning skills, a house full of kids, and I'm afraid of him.

Inhaling the sweet rose scent from the bushes near the front door, I rang the bell. I dried my eyes before the attendant could open the door. *This place should be the threshold to an enchanted secret garden. For me, it has become a chamber of affliction.*

The *rabbanit*, wearing her customary dark hair-covering and re-assuring smile, greeted me, "*Shalom*, how are you?" I felt welcomed into the softly lit waiting area with lovely, pastel paintings decorating the walls.

Reflecting her smile, I nodded hello. "*Baruch Hashem. Hakol b'seder*, everything is fine." When I sat, I opened a book of *Tehillim*, but rather than reading the familiar verses, a melody and words floated toward me. "My help comes from Hashem, Who made the heavens and the earth." That's all I needed.

I picked up a booklet from the side table. It offered spiritual insights to the Jewish woman for her special *mitzva*. "*Similar to the lunar cycle, a woman's body and psyche are remarkably altered each month. There is a time of oneness and of being capable of conceiving life. This is an opportunity for complete unity, and perhaps for providing a home for a soul to descend into this world.*

When biologically this possibility passes, we enter a time of sepa-ration. Being apart physically allows us to consider the significance and wholeness of our marital relationship. It is a time to increase the aspect of our relationship that goes beyond the corporeal. This space is a gift, to develop verbal and other nonphysical communication and connection

And when those weeks end, the mikveh *waters, representing the elemental source of life, reminding us once again that we are returning to the Oneness."*

I had known that once. It was still a precious thought, but it was not my reality.

"You can go in now," the *rabbanit* said in her soft voice, calming me like the fragrant scent of lavender.

The *rabbanit* whispered to me as I walked to the steps. "There are three partners in marriage: God, the wife, and the husband."

Had she perceived my distress? I wondered, even as I was sadly aware that only two were involved in mine. Descending to the inner, watery womb of the *mikveh*, a longing for renewal washed over me.

My bond with Hashem strengthened powerfully in this place, at this moment. Submerged in prayer, I rose to the surface to return to the infinite closeness I felt with God's Presence. Seven times, seven prayers, seven levels of longing. Seven times, seven years and the slaves are meant to go free. *God, set me free,* I begged before ascending the stairs.

"Kosher," the *rabbanit* called quietly. And I knew she was. And this place was. And my prayers were. All were kosher, except for him. *Was I?*

The *rabbanit* blessed me with a long and happy life. And when her eyes met mine, I felt that she took some of my pain. *Why did I never consider talking to her? Does she know? How many secrets is she privy to?*

Lowering my eyes, I blurted, "It's so hard."

"Do your best for *shalom bayit*," she smiled, nodding encouragingly. "Hashem will surely help."

"May the one who blesses also be blessed," I returned, deflated of hope and eternally optimistic, all at once.

On the walk home, it was darker than before. Traversing the same back streets, I watched carefully so as not to trip. The kids waited for me. I hummed, "I placed God before me always," to accompany my steps. *How would I survive without Him?*

I walked in to find that our neighbor and frequent babysitter had stopped by to say hello. She was reading with Batya. Dovy and

Benny did their homework while Kayla and Ariella sat at the small side table engrossed in a five-hundred-piece puzzle. Yair was absorbed in his comics. School books and shoes were scattered everywhere, and small bowls of pretzel crumbs and salt attested to the fact that they had not starved.

"*Shalom*, my wonderful family," I called, receiving immediate responses.

"Ima, Batya colored all over my math notebook, and now I can't do the homework," Yair popped up from his supine position on the couch, not looking too upset. "And we have a class trip tomorrow. I need three sandwiches and a bottle of water and lots of nosh. And we have to be in school on time."

"That will be a switch," Dovy called out from his well-lit corner. "Think you can manage that?" he teased.

"Watch me!" Yair retorted. "I'll be the first one there." *When he wanted, he could. If only he wanted to more often....*

Dovy handed me a list of phone calls for me, mostly "wannabe" Shabbat guests. I stuck it onto the fridge with a magnet, as I eyed the mess on the kitchen table. Scattered strings of spaghetti dripping in tomato sauce were proof that the hungry had eaten

After much urging, the table was cleared, some dishes washed, and some of the floor swept. Books were replaced into the school bags and mostly put into their places. The bedtime event passed with its usual tempest in a *kum-kum*, the Israeli teapot.

When it was quiet enough, Rena told me how much she loved her national service, working at a special school for kids at risk. After helping to wash the dishes, she said she was tired and ready for bed too. "I also want to get to school on time," she said eagerly. "There's so much to learn and do."

I nodded approvingly.

"Thanks for reading with Batya and helping to straighten up." *She's such a nice girl.*

Connecting pairs of shoes, tucking one sock into its mate for tossing into the laundry, and wiping the milky spills, I circled the kitchen and living room. Exhausted, I could not wait any longer to sleep.

It was after 1 a.m. when I finally locked the door. *If I leave the key in the keyhole, he can't come in*, I considered. But I tried that before and it never stopped him. In the past, he pried open windows or somehow picked the backdoor lock. I replaced the key on its hook.

It was still dark when Efraim returned. Unlike his usual homecomings before dawn, tonight he made enough noise to ensure that I would wake up. He knew that as a good, religious woman, I had to.

FORTY-FOUR

THE COMMUNITY'S WOMEN'S COMMITTEE successfully completed their fourth annual pre-Shavuot fundraiser for the local girls' school. Some women had collected various prizes for the Chinese auction, while capable cooks offered specialties for an elegant dinner. The bakers in the community created a feast for both the eyes and palate.

After the large crowd left, Mindy refilled her plate. "Everything was delicious! Shifra, I want the recipe for that cheese and onion quiche. This is my third piece." Raising her eyebrows, she warned with a playful wink, "Don't tell anyone."

"You should start a catering service," Dana encouraged. "You create one amazing desert and quiche after another. Really," she went on," if you ever want to earn some money, you can cater *simchas*. Start small, like with *sheva berachot* or a *b'rit*."

"Hey, I'll help," Mindy offered. "I know how to peel a mean potato. We'll work our way up to bar mitzvahs and weddings."

The cleanup crew noshed their way through the job.

"Right," Estie agreed amiably, winking at me as she licked whipped cream from her fingers, "in her spare time." Estie and everyone else knew about the twenty-four-hour open home of the Baumen family.

"Thank you, ladies." There was some good-natured chuckling, "but I stayed to collect my things, not to start a new project." I laughed at their kind encouragement as I gathered my pans and trays in my shopping cart. I couldn't help smiling as I commented, "But if I ever need a recommendation..."

As the ladies rolled up the last of the disposable tablecloths, Dana found an untouched plate of my whole-wheat cinnamon-raisin-apple cake. "Look, I won the grand prize," she teased. "Thanks for your kind donation, Shif."

Declining the offers of a ride home, I insisted, "I brought my 'everything wagon.' It'll be easier for me to walk. Anyway, I need some fresh air. Thanks, everyone. *Yishar ko'ach* and goodnight."

Outside in the clear spring night, I spotted a shooting star.

"*Ribbono Shel Olam*, that's a pretty prize. Thank you for the special light show." Drinking in the cool fresh air, I briefly reviewed the successful evening's event.

Deciding it would be better to freeze leftovers than run out of food, I stayed up half the night to bake extra cakes and pies. In the end, many more women than were expected had come and there was next to nothing left. The prizes were great. *That complete kitchen mixer/blender set would have been so useful.*

It was past midnight when I arrived home, exhausted.

"How was everything, Rena?" I asked the babysitter.

She yawned. "Batya fell asleep in the carriage around seven. Kayla and Benny fell asleep about nine."

I assumed that playful Yair would stay up horsing around and Ariella would read until they both conked out, and I was right.

"Dovy studied until about 10:30. He finally fell asleep on the couch."

"OK, that all sounds normal, *baruch Hashem*." I pulled money from my wallet to pay her. "Any calls?"

"Oh, yeah. Here." Rena handed over a list of some ten messages. Most were duplicates. I read, "Can I come for Shabbat?" or alternatively, "I am coming for Shabbat." Some included a name or phone number, but most did not. *If ten called,* I sighed aloud, *I can expect at least double for Shabbat.*

"Wow, big Shabbat," said Rena who occasionally dropped by on Fridays to lend a hand.

Walking her toward the door with half-closed eyes, I mumbled, "I think it's time to say goodnight, Rena."

"Laila tov."

Rena declined my offer to see her home. In our rural community, walking alone even at night was considered safe.

Lifting Batya onto her bed, I gently kissed her forehead. A quick check on the others, a few replaced blankets, and it was time to crash. Changing my clothes and robotically brushing my teeth, I considered tonight's compliments.

They were an enormous emotional boost. Great baker... catering...earn some money... Staring into space, the kernel of an idea was planted. Walking very slowly into my lonely bedroom, it began to sprout. As I crawled under the quilt blankets, the thought of a baking business began to take shape. Mumbling *Shema* somewhat incoherently, and barely able to lift my hand to my eyes, I sensed something positive was about to happen.

FORTY-FIVE

Journal Entry — A Letter to Efraim (unsent)

Why doesn't Efraim just talk to me?

I consulted with him about some important things I'm doing. I told him I respect his judgment and insights, that I look up to him. I told him I am so proud to have such a wise husband, who is also so good and caring to me and our family. In one of those fleeting moments, I had an image of what a happy family we are.

Together we would accomplish so much. As we sat together over a quiet late evening snack, Efraim confided, in a straightforward and quiet way, about his day and the people he met. And he asked about my day. We discussed our challenges and even touched on feelings about how hard it is sometimes. We were open and enjoyed good communications.

Am I hallucinating?

I can no longer listen well, or at all, to Efraim's dizzying run of ideas, capers, and schemes. So ridiculous as to be unbelievable, I ignore him. I go deaf. Is this how peaceful, ordinary people dismiss threatening political tyrants? We live in denial.

I'm angry, and it's making me depressed. Everything went so wrong. Perhaps I am as much to blame as he is for going along silently for so long. I encouraged him to work hard for Am Yisrael. I wanted an open home.

"Bring home guests," I told him, but I can't keep up with the dizzying pace of our home and kids and the endless, needy guests. If I were smarter, or more capable, this might be OK. Maybe. Other families have guests.

I'm really angry at his deceptions. How can I try to be so nice when he's ignoring me, sleeping in a separate room, if he sleeps at home at all? It's not real. When I lose my temper, then he talks nicely, brings money to pay bills. It's a good strategy. The more there is to cover up, the more it's worth acting, because the more he has to lose.

I am really angry — how often can he get away with his *tzaddik* act? Take your show back on the road. I've seen it too often to believe it's real. Disgusting coward!

Dear Efraim, with the ever-present sunglasses,

You're so sweet, but if I argue or disagree, you become Mr. Loud, obnoxious, screaming, staring, demanding, verbally abusive. When I'm silent, I'm the best Ima, woman, wife. If I disagree, I become crazy and can't see straight. You don't stop judging me — you find me guilty of everything. I won't live half-dead, paralyzed by your reactions. Thanks for the good there was, once. Maybe. God help you. God help me. God help my family.

Forty-six

I BEGAN CHOKING EVERY TIME Efraim wandered into the bedroom at dawn, timing his entrance to precede the kids' awakening.

I thought of locking my door but was worried the kids might need me.

Stripping the sheet, pillow, and blanket from his bed, I hoped he would grasp how unwanted his company was. Indifferent, he laid on the bare mattress. Humiliated, I detested his unwanted intrusion into my personal space.

On several occasions, I caught him reading my private notebooks. He lacked any regret when I took them back. In response to his flagrant intrusion into my privacy, I hid my personal journals. He took any cash he could, even taking back what he gave me. I hid any money I put aside together with my writings, out of his reach in a hidden storage space.

The phone's insistent ringing interrupted my mental ordeal. Kayla's teacher Miri was calling, her voice filled with concern. After inquiring how I was feeling, she said softly, "I thought we might meet in person, but this is such a busy time before Chanukah, and I know you really have your hands full." She paused, "Would you mind if we spoke a few minutes on the phone until we can arrange to get together?"

I was more than happy not to meet Kayla's sweet and perceptive teacher face to face.

"I see Kayla's concentration slipping away. She seems so sad and so silent."

"She's always been quiet," I suggested too quickly.

"...She's not participating in class at all. She stopped bringing in her homework. At recess, she sits alone. I feel like something is troubling her." Miri waited respectfully, finally asking, "Can you think of what that might be?"

Her pause allowed me to absorb what I should have known. "There's been some..." I searched for the right word, "a little stress at home, I guess."

Who hadn't heard of the incredible Baumen *chessed* family in our community? Miri, like so many others, probably believed we were incessantly involved with outreach and soul-saving.

"Sometimes you can get spread too thin," she offered sympathetically. "You know, my *abba* has also been involved in community work for many years. Maybe you would like to speak with him." She paused and her voice softened even more. "He really respects your family and all the *kiruv* work your husband is involved with."

When my legs became wobbly, I steadied myself at the edge of the kitchen table. She waited as I coughed suddenly, covering the speaker on the phone.

Clearing my throat, I whispered, "Yes," in response to her concerned "Are you OK?"

"We're preparing a Chanukah play and classroom project," Miri informed me. Since Kayla would never agree to go on stage, I asked her to be in charge of decorating the class bulletin board."

"She enjoys arts and crafts," I agreed. I let my back slide down the wall behind me until I sat on the floor. My arms shaking, I grabbed my knees close to my chest.

Miri suggested, "In the meantime, do you think you might be able to spend some special private time with..."

I covered the phone speaker again and held it away from my mouth. I didn't want her to hear me sobbing. When I could no longer unscramble her words, I inhaled deeply and told her I must hang up. "Thank you," I managed as I replaced the receiver. My forehead smacked onto my knees and my body shook, threatening to overwhelm me.

Trapped! T-r-a-p-p-e-d. How do I help Kayla and the others? I caved into my isolation. There was no family support, no money, and not a crumb of self-confidence. How much more will my kids have to suffer in this disgusting, dysfunctional home? I screamed silently to the ends of the earth until my mouth hurt from being stretched so far. I swallowed the shriek, holding it down until my stomach hurt.

Very gradually, as the fog began to lift, I remembered that Miri's father, Rav Scheiner, was steeped in Kabbalistic teachings and well respected throughout the country. Maybe I should see him. Short of breath, but no longer crying, I pushed myself from the floor, and walked to the sink, still full of dishes from last night's dinner, to splash water on my face.

FORTY-SEVEN

KAYLA WALKED IN SLUGGISHLY, letting her book bag slide from her shoulders and fall. She looked like she'd been crying. Passive in response to my welcoming hug, I gestured rather than asked what happened. Her knees buckled and she fell onto the couch, just missing piles of folded laundry.

"I can't do it. I don't understand any of it." She pulled her math book from the bag and threw it on the floor. I'm stupid." She slumped farther into the spongy sofa. "Why do I have to go to school if I'm stupid and can't learn anything?"

I plopped down beside her. "You are not stupid. And every day we learn together. It's getting easier for you to understand. You..."

"No! No! No!" she yelled. "I'm stupid, stupid. The kids know it. The teacher knows it. And," she looked at me for the first time since she was home, "you know it too."

Shaking from her outburst, she allowed me to sit close to her, with my arm around her shoulders. I could feel her melting into me, when she began to cry, heaving, like her heart was breaking. Our tears mingled, as we sat, mourning our losses.

I dug a wad of tissues from my pocket and offered her one, while I blew my nose and wiped the moistness from my own cheeks.

"Kayla, I know that you are a smart girl. It takes a little longer for some kids to catch on, but there's nothing wrong with that. You'll know it just as well as the others." I tried to sound reassuring. "You are smart, and together, you and I are a winning team, Kayla." My fingers passed through her long, black hair, gently massaging her scalp. *How ironic and how good that she can't read my mind to know what a failure I believe myself to be.*

I picked up her math book from the floor and opened it to the last page we had learned.

"Some nosh, and then let's get to work," I invited. I knew this was only a symptom of the crisis, but I didn't know how to broach that yet. She helped herself to a juicy orange, sharpened her pencil slowly, and dispiritedly pulled out her worksheet.

By the time the others arrived, we were halfway through the page. Kayla was explaining the multiplication examples to me when they bounced through the door.

Efraim happened to appear for dinner that evening. He was in a good mood.

"Yes, let's go to Rav Scheiner. Maybe he can help us enhance our *shalom bayit*," Efraim agreed when I suggested the meeting. "I'll make an appointment right now." Walking out of the room he hastily dialed the *rav*, as though peace in our home was of utmost importance to him. I felt jittery. *Why is he so eager? Something's not right with this.* My hands shook as I scraped the carrots for the soup, adding them to the split peas and barley. I chopped tomatoes for the salad.

"Ariella, can you please set the table?" I called out, hoping to avoid an argument.

"Ima, I'll finish reading this page and then I'll come. OK?"

True to her word, she appeared and took the mismatched plates from the cracked plastic dish stand to set them for dinner.

A few minutes later, Efraim returned to the kitchen wearing a broad grin. "He's very sympathetic and really wants to help. He'll see us this evening at 10 p.m."

I added eggs to the soup. Together with the salad, we had a full meal. *What did he tell the* rav? I was suspicious of his enthusiasm.

"Why don't you rest?"

I turned my head at the novel thought.

"Go lay down," he insisted warmly. "It's only 6:15 p.m. and we have to go out later."

My apprehensions were overcome by my weariness. "Just for a quick nap," I told him. "I want to finish Kayla's homework with her after dinner, so wake me up in twenty minutes."

"Sure, no problem," he assured me.

As my head touched the pillow, I fell into a dream-laced sleep.

A cat's shrieking woke me into confusion. *Was it day or night? Was it time to get the kids up — or* I thought suddenly — *time to put them to bed?*

I opened the shades and flipped on the light. 8 p.m.! Frustrated, I shook off the last residue of sleep. Washing, I straightened my wrinkled clothes. *It's too quiet; where are the kids?*

"Better yet, where is Efraim with the kids?" I asked aloud.

In the kitchen, the still-boiling soup had turned to a dark paste and was starting to burn. The salad sat untouched.

I saw school books lying on the table and floor. Kayla's was open to the last page we had worked on together. *No advancement here.* "He sabotaged our hard work!" escaped my lips.

I looked outside, walked to the local playground, and asked a couple of neighbors if they'd seen my crew. No one had.

The kitchen clock ticked in at 8:30 p.m. as I ladled some of the overcooked mush into a bowl, picked out a cracked browned egg and sat alone to eat.

It was bedtime for the younger ones, and the others would not be far behind. Reaching for the phone, I wondered whether to call the babysitter. I dialed her number, asking her to come in forty-five minutes. We still had an appointment.

At 9:15 p.m., the door flew open and everyone walked in, talking and laughing.

"Abba took us for pizza," Dovy reported.

"And ice cream," Yair added.

"I had a good dinner ready right here," I protested.

"The kids all said they wanted pizza, and anyway I didn't want them to wake you. You looked so tired." He said that for the babysitter's benefit. Rena had walked in with them.

I did a quick tally. With two slices each, drinks and ice cream, it cost over one hundred shekels plus the taxi.

As they walked in, the children scattered in different directions. Dovy sat stiffly at his English homework. I noticed Kayla sigh as she closed her unfinished math workbook, packed up her book bag, and go to her bedroom. Yair put on a musical adventure story-tape and got comfortable on the couch, where Ariella sat, her sad eyes lowered. She didn't respond to my hug and wouldn't say a word. No one said much of anything.

"How was the pizza, Yair?"

"Good," he answered tersely.

"Ariella, did you like the ice cream?"

Efraim interjected, "I think she has a fever. She feels a little warm to me.

I pressed my lips to her forehead, ascertaining she was not feverish. She ducked away from my kiss and hug, running to her room.

"What happened?" I asked, but everyone turned into themselves, each in a separate corner.

"We have to leave soon," Efraim prompted.

The kids looked at me.

"Where are you going?" Kayla asked, as she came back to take her pencil case. I knew she wanted me to stay.

"Abba and I have a meeting tonight. Rena will stay here with you."

I saw Kayla and Benny's fleeting looks at each other.

"I'm sorry that I dozed off, Kayla. I really wanted to do your homework with you. Maybe Dovy or Rena will help you finish if you're not too tired now."

"Forget it, Ima, it doesn't matter," Kayla shrugged.

"And Yair, we also missed our studying time."

"No problem, Ima, I'm good," he grinned light-heartedly, though he was not doing well.

Tugging at my sleeve, ever so delicately, Kayla whispered, "Ima, please stay with us."

I took her aside, "What happened, Kayla? Are you OK?" I asked. "Maybe you want to tell me something."

She looked past me, then down, remaining silent.

"Kayla?" I waited.

I hugged her close and told her we'd be home soon.

"Remember to say *Shema* and brush your teeth, kids," I called as we left Rena in charge.

The taxi driver warmly greeted his dear friend Efraim as we got into the car. "*Erev tov, Mrs.*" Now that the kids weren't in earshot, I lashed out.

"They could have eaten at home. The food was ready. Even the table was set. I asked you to wake me up. They needed help with their homework. Yair and Kayla are falling so far behind. I'm really upset. Why did you take them out for pizza?"

"Why can't you just appreciate that I gave you some time off?" he shot back in a hushed voice. "I took the kids out so you could get some sleep. And why are you talking so loudly? Does everyone have to hear you complain?" He tried to end the conversation with the downturned mouth, threatening grimace, and accompanying icy stare I'd come to know so well.

Efraim could probably slice through steel with that stare. His piercing look slashed my heart to ribbons. My tongue became paralyzed. It was more than a look. Even though he held back from vocalizing threats of violence, I caved into fear.

FORTY-EIGHT

THE DRIVER DROPPED US off in front of Rav Scheiner's home, which also served as a yeshiva for *baalei teshuva*.

The elderly *rav* answered our knock. He shook Efraim's hand and smiled kindly at me, warmly inviting us into his study. I glanced at the comfortable library. Torah books in English, Russian, and Hebrew were strewn on the table. There were pamphlets decrying the missionary threats and others explaining the incompatibility of Far Eastern religions to Judaism.

Black-and-white photographs of great *rabbanim* lined the soft rose-colored walls. I scrutinized the *rav*'s dignified appearance. His large, black-felt *kippa* sat atop the scholar's high forehead. A long, white beard covered much of his suit jacket. I sensed compassion and realized I wanted to believe that.

Rav Scheiner waved his hand toward some chairs, welcoming us. The compassionate rabbi passed up his own plush, leather seat near his desk to sit closer to us.

Offering us hot drinks from the steaming teapot, Rav Scheiner adjusted the space heater so that it faced me.

"You must be cold," he commented with a kind, fatherly look. Then he inquired about the children.

"I think they are having a hard time," I ventured. "There is a lot of tension in our home and it is affecting them badly." I sensed my husband's resentment, but could not stop.

Rav Scheiner said, "Yes? What do you think is wrong?"

"They need their father's attention." My eyes darted toward Efraim.

"He's hardly home, except in the morning, when they leave for school," I whispered. "And he's never home in the evening — or at night."

Efraim began his scripted response, but Rav Scheiner signaled for him to stop.

He held one of Efraim's powerfully built hands between his two light, frail ones. Leaning forward and speaking in a captivating whisper, he reminded me of my husband.

"You've known me for many years, Efraim. I will tell you something that I do not usually say to anyone."

He seemed to be deliberating carefully about his next words.

"I do not say these things for honor, but sometimes we must risk sounding proud in order to share our experiences and to help each other."

Rav Scheiner's eyes did not leave Efraim's face. "Like you, I have helped many young people return to their Jewish roots from many of the evils of this world. There were many sleepless nights and exhausting days," he sighed. "I give my life for *Am Yisrael*.

"It has not been easy for my family. My wife and my children sacrificed a great deal. They suffered from my absence from their daily routine, Efraim, but they encouraged me." He turned toward me. "Shifra?"

I suddenly thought he might try to convince me to be patient, that the sacrifice would be worth it. I bit my lower lip hard between my teeth, restraining myself from leaving the room.

Betrayed again? I wouldn't be able to cope if the *rav* condoned Efraim's actions. I tasted blood on my inner lip.

The *rav* seemed to notice every nuance.

"Shifra, it's important that you hear this too."

Still chewing on the injured lip, I nodded respectfully. Inwardly I wanted to lie in the dark street and die. In a disconcerting moment, thoughts of suicide darted through my mind. Pills, a gun, jumping off... But an equally lucid picture of my kids' anguish and abandonment stopped me short.

Leave them alone? With him? And the frightening ideas departed. Teary-eyed, I resolved to listen to the caring but probably ineffective *rav*. At that moment, as if the sun's rays were penetrating the heavy fog in my brain, I knew. If I can't trust them to his influence, then he can't live in our home. *I will file for divorce. I'm ready.*

"Efraim," he continued, slightly elevating his voice, "all of my success is due to my wife's support and blessing."

I looked to see if Efraim was paying attention.

"But if my wife would say it is too much for her or that it is affecting my family poorly, and she would ask me to stop," he waited to allow his next words to sink in. Not wanting to miss a syllable, I leaned forward. He continued, "I would have to stop. Everything."

This time, it was Efraim who was startled. His shoulders stiffened nearly imperceptibly, but I knew he was offended. A faint shadow darkened his cheeks.

The *rav* continued, "It would not be appropriate to knowingly cause one Jew to suffer while attempting to help another." He maintained unflinching eye contact.

"Yes, of course." Efraim agreed, as he focused his blue eyes, deep as the ocean and clear as a cloudless spring day, on the *rav*'s. I might have been moved if I hadn't heard it before.

The good *rav* continued, "Especially when that Jew should be the most important person in your life, your wife."

It was a clean cut.

I knew he would never return to confer with this man. The respected Rav Scheiner dared to disagree. No words were needed. With an almost indiscernible mannerism, Efraim rejected Rav Scheiner.

Feeling supported, I knew Dr. Gershon was right. I wasn't ready for a divorce then, but I was now.

"Thank you, Rav Scheiner," I said as we stood to go. I meant it sincerely. He had lifted the final residue of confusion in my path.

Rav Scheiner, still speaking like a loving father, urged Efraim, not me, to do all he could to keep our family whole. "Come home by midnight. You can be home by then, yes?"

Efraim wore his frozen smile. He hugged and good-naturedly patted the *rav*'s back. "You're a good man, *tzaddik*," he said. "I can learn a lot from you, Rabbi."

The *rav* was not drawn in by the sham. "Yes, you can learn a lot from me." His concerned look in my direction was the validation I needed. It was the first I had received since Dr. Gershon's vote of confidence that one day I could make the necessary transition.

"Or," he turned his gaze to Efraim, stroking his long, white beard sadly, "you can learn the hard way, and lose everything."

With a couple of long strides, the paper dragon reached the door. All in one breath, Efraim said, "Thanks, Rabbi. We need to go. Our babysitter needs to get home. Good night." And he stepped outside.

I sensed that Efraim could not hold his pose much longer. His deflated ego needed space. I saw the explosion coming, but for the first time, I wasn't afraid or I didn't care. A gaping hole in my heart felt like it was beginning to heal. I had the confirmation I desperately sought. Is this what emancipation from slavery felt like?

I turned to see the *rav*'s troubled expression.

"Shifra, let us know if my wife or I can help in any way. Maybe I can speak with him again." Then he held his hand several inches above my head and blessed me as a father would his child. He understood. "Wait a moment, please."

I stepped back inside, wondering what the rav would say or do. He returned with a small velvety pouch. Enclosed within was a *kemei'a*, a small, handwritten Kabbalistic amulet.

"This has a special blessing for courage and peace. Keep it with you, Shifra. And may God guide your path."

I nodded gratefully, knowing I wouldn't ask him to speak to Efraim again. The *rav* used beautiful, encouraging words that a listener had to desire. My husband needed a harsh drill sergeant whose words pierced like a bayonet. But I was glad he offered. Like a deer thirsts for cool water, I craved support and validation. *I might call just to hear his respectful words.* It would make me feel less lonely.

In the cool night air, we waited for the taxi. The congenial smile that was pasted on Efraim's lips for most of the evening was gone. He assured me in his most convincing manner, "The Rav doesn't have the energy to be involved in serious *kiruv* anymore. He's getting too old."

Rain fell as we waited.

As the taxi arrived, Efraim mumbled he will come later.

"It's almost midnight. You promised," I said as a simple statement of fact.

"You promised," he snorted, throwing his head from side to side. "Grow up, you stupid woman. I'll tell you when it's time for me to come home." Lowering his voice, he sneered again. "And you were supposed to go to the *mikveh*." His accusation was accompanied by daggered eyes.

"What would that matter if you're not home anyway?" I asked.

It was hard to believe he wanted or expected me to comply with the *halacha* he so blatantly disregarded. The droplets became a torrential rain that caused me to shiver as I faced him squarely.

"You know what? Don't come home. It's not your home anymore. I am filing for a divorce." I said it. No tears. No fear of anything he might throw at me. I had moved away emotionally and swelled with the ecstasy of freedom.

He handed some bills to the driver and whispered into his ear as they shook hands.

The driver pulled out, setting the blinker for the turn as he glanced into the rearview mirror.

"*Aizeh ba'al*, what a good husband you have. A good man!" he rambled on as he increased the heat in the car. "No one expected this storm tonight. But even on a night like tonight, Reb Efraim helps Jews. A *tzaddik* that man is."

A bolt of lightning illuminated the skies. In that flash, I realized I would gather more information by agreeing than by sulking.

"He is amazing," I nodded. "How did you get to meet him?"

"Months ago, he flagged me for the first time. Yes," he settled into his memories as he increased the speed of the waving windshield wipers. "Your husband was picking up that sweet, little boy he takes care of."

He inched forward into the heavy rain. Straining to see barely a car length ahead, we crawled.

"*Aizeh laila, aizeh laila*, what a night!" muttering under his breath, he managed to skillfully control the steering wheel on the slippery streets. The street lights barely made a difference. Only the periodic lightening allowed him to observe the road.

"What's his name?" he continued, snapping his thumb against his middle finger rapidly. Maybe the clapping thunder jolted his memory. "Shmueli. Yes, a very sweet little boy, *motek*. But his mother, I don't like her. She's nasty. Sometimes she's nice to your husband, but they argue a lot. It's always in English, which I don't understand, so I don't really know what's going on. No manners." He made a clicking sound with his tongue. Barely pausing, he continued to drive slowly. "But your husband comes faithfully. And he told me how you encourage him to take care of that sweet, little boy."

I could sense his glow of approval. "You must be a *tzaddeket*. He showed me the packages of food you're always sending for them, and small gifts. *Madhim!* Amazing."

I restrained myself.

"I myself take him to that apartment three or four times a week."

I tried to keep my voice nonchalant, "He does try to help her."

This driver thinks he's praising his hero. I wished for a tape recorder. As the heavens opened, he continued, "And to educate your children to do such kindness. It's a big *mitzva* for you to encourage him to bring them along. The rabbi told me how you bake *challot* for her for every Shabbat. You are also a real *tzaddeket*, *rabbanit*," he repeated to himself, "a real *tzaddeket*."

I strained to hear over the thunder.

"Did you know," he boasted, "that I was the one who took your family to meet the boy and," he snapped his fingers again, "Ah yes, Mona — that's her name — at the pizza shop earlier this evening? They looked like they were having fun together, *kef*."

He glanced at the mirror. "I guess you don't like her company so much, huh?" he sympathized. "I can't blame you for not joining them. But why should the boy be an outcast just because his mother's an idiot?" he pondered aloud. "It's easy to understand why the boyfriend abandoned her."

My neck and shoulders tightened as I fumed in silence.

"Don't worry, Mrs." He must have assumed my hushed reaction was due to the daunting driving conditions. "You'll be home soon."

Forty-nine

IRST THE VAGUENESS AND then the increasing revelations about Efraim's life and its effect on my kids threatened to overwhelm me. Extremely embarrassed, I decided to consult with our personal *rav*, Rabbi Kaufman the next morning.

How often had I come to seek the good *rav*'s advice about some issue of Jewish law or some other quandary? Why had I never brought up Efraim's behavior or asked for marital counseling? Walking hesitantly up the narrow stairwell to his small, familiar apartment, I realized this was too painful, too inconceivable. Even now, as I took slow deep breaths, I was unsure what, or how, to ask.

Religious Jews are ingrained with the concept that speaking badly of others, *lashon hara*, even when it's the honest truth, is unacceptable. Since I became observant, I learned that we are meant to look for the positive whenever possible, even when we might suspect wrongdoing.

"Laws are laws," I told myself. Was I asking him to bend them to my liking? Would this go against the principles I tried so hard to learn and to teach my family? What was I going to say to the rav *anyway? "You see, Rabbi, something is terribly wrong in our home. So I'd like your advice on how to get to the bottom of it. Can we speak some* lashon hara, *just for a while, till things clear up? I just want to share the lowdown on my rotten spouse with my kids."*

Nervously rubbing my hands on the sides of my skirt, I considered turning and going downstairs. I looked at the worn welcome mat and wondered how many had come before me to ask for advice or comfort.

Maybe just from my nervous appearance, the *rav* would know what I wanted to ask. Noticing the sign to knock loudly, I considered that he might not be home as I rapped on the door.

Was I relieved or chagrined when the door opened so quickly? Were they peeking through the peephole for someone else?

The *rabbanit*, wearing her welcoming smile and a grandmotherly floral house robe, invited me in.

"Shifra, it's so nice to see you. How about a cup of tea?" she asked as though she'd been expecting me indeed.

"Rabbi," she called into the study room, "we have some lovely company. Shifra Baumen is here."

The old-fashioned furniture reminded me of my grandparents' home. For reassurance, I looked at the large framed black-and-white photo of the happy young rabbinical couple with their smiling babies. It sent a quiver of longing through me.

Walking slowly and stopping to catch his breath — *just like me*, I thought curiously, the rabbi emerged from his study. Rolling down his white shirt sleeves as he came into the living room, he greeted me.

"Good to see you, Mrs. Baumen, good to see you. How are you, and how is your family?"

There's nothing like a nervous habit to get intuitive people to wonder if there's a problem. I nodded, biting my lower lip,

"*Baruch Hashem*, everyone's OK." I chose to speak without my usual, well-orchestrated shiny eyes and broad smile.

When the rabbi and I seated ourselves at their living room table, Rabbanit Kaufman went to the kitchen.

"Tell me, please," the *rav* encouraged, "how can I help? Perhaps you'd like the *rabbanit* to listen too. She's very wise."

When she returned with her familiar tray of tea and homemade cookies, I was grateful she wanted to stay. Part of me wanted to protect them both from my sad state of affairs. I knew it would bring them sorrow, but my mouth refused to remain silent. I tried to condense the stressful saga, to spare the nasty details, but they sat, listening deeply, nodding for me to continue.

The *rabbanit* frequently dabbed her flowered cotton handkerchief at her moist eyes. Finally, as I slowed my outpouring of despair, the *rav* pounded the mahogany table with his thin, wrinkled fist. He spoke as though he were addressing a large gathering. I sensed that he echoed the revered Chafetz Chaim himself. Piercingly he proclaimed, "The laws of proper speech were never meant to protect the guilty while causing the innocent to suffer! Your family must heal, and to do so, all of you may discuss this topic in any manner necessary. You must discover the truth and draw closer together."

As I stood, grateful and teary-eyed, he asked me to wait a moment. Retreating to his library, he returned with haste this time. He held a paperback book on marital abuse in the Jewish community, *The Shame Borne in Silence: Spouse Abuse in the Jewish Community* written by the famous Jewish psychiatrist, Rabbi Dr. Abraham J. Twerski.

"Read this, Shifra," he said softly. "Unfortunately, you're not alone."

I took it from his shaking hands, wondering why I'd vacillated about speaking of my predicament with this compassionate, great rabbi. The *rabbanit* drew me close, whispering, "Come to visit any time. You know you are always welcome here." The wrinkles around her mouth and eyes smiled her invitation.

The *rav* sat, sighing and shaking his head. "I've got to talk to the men. They are so thick-headed. They *must* respect their wives, the mothers of their children!" He closed his eyes as his long, pale fingers drummed the table.

As she walked me to the door, the *rabbanit* assured me that her husband was likely thinking out this week's Shabbat discourse already. "I know that look so well. He can't tolerate abuse in any form." She assured me the issue of abuse in the community would be addressed. "If you need anything at all, this is the place, Shifra." When she embraced me warmly, I felt like a cherished daughter, in a way I'd only dreamed of.

The short walk home gave me a few minutes to think. I felt the kids would sense I had reached a breaking point. *There's no turning back. We cannot live like this anymore. No more denial. No more acting as though you don't get it. No more covering up for him.*

FIFTY

THE NEXT MORNING, AFTER the kids left for school, I locked my bedroom door and pulled out a box of assorted papers from under my bed. It included newspaper articles or ads that I kept as references. I searched among the recipes, medical breakthroughs, and general information for the newspaper clipping I'd cut months ago. I was so nervous, I had to flip through the contents twice, slowing down the second time, so I wouldn't pass it again.

"Here it is," I said to myself, trying to keep my voice calm. "New in Jerusalem. Divorce counseling available for English-speakers. Call for free consultation and referrals. Anonymity respected."

I felt myself quivering as I dialed the number. The woman who answered the phone did not ask my name. I asked her what steps I needed to take to start divorce proceedings.

"How do I open a *tik*?" I wanted to know. "And I need a rabbinical court representative, preferably a woman."

When she asked what I was looking for, I had no idea.

"I guess she needs to know what she's doing." Then I added, "She has to be tough, really tough. She can't be easily swayed or taken in by charismatic *tzaddikim*." I paused. "Or liars."

The woman on the line did not hesitate. "I think you want Suri. Yes, I've heard a lot of good things about her. She cannot be swayed easily. Yes," the woman was convinced, "I suggest she's the one to call. She's tough, really tough." She read me Suri's phone number and said to call again if there's anything else I need.

"Thank you," I said, quietly praying for salvation.

My hand trembled as I recorded the number. I felt my stomach knot into a ball and my throat tightened painfully. But there was no going back, and I dialed the number.

Suri and I spoke for a short time before we set a date to meet and then to open the divorce file. She, like Dr. Gershon, understood immediately what was happening. And she warned me that it probably would not be easy, or fast. She told me it might get worse before it got better. And then Suri told me something that really took my breath away. She said, "I won't leave your side until you have your *get*, come what may!"

FIFTY-ONE

THE PHONE RANG INCESSANTLY and I didn't want to know the latest crisis. When I finally lifted the receiver, my neighbor and friend Dana sounded relieved.

"Is everything OK?" she asked with concern.

"*Baruch Hashem*, everything's fine. Why were you worried?" I responded, wondering what she had heard.

"Listen Shif, I need your help." Dana sounded anxious.

"OK, my friend, how can I lend a hand?" I wanted to know.

"So it's my parents' sixtieth wedding anniversary in two weeks. My family is coming from the States and we're planning an amazing evening. We're preparing songs, skits, a slide slow, and an elegant meal. We've been working on this for months." She was breathless.

"Sounds beautiful, Dana. How special that your parents live here and everyone is flying in."

"I agree. But my dad just went into the hospital, and it looks like I'll be there with him for at least a week, maybe more."

"He should have a complete and speedy recovery. Oy, Dana. How can I help?" I assumed she might want me to watch her little ones.

"Remember I recommended you go into catering?" she asked, reminding me of the pre-Shavuot celebration at shul.

"OK, I remember."

"So I'm hiring you for your first catering job!" She went on quickly. "Can you help me with this? Listen, I checked out some other local caterers, but then thought—if you can do it, I'd rather pay you. And I already know what a great chef you are." After a pause she went on, "We'll be about fifty people — that's nothing for you." I heard her smile. "You can prepare an assortment of your amazing meat dishes, quiches, hot veggies, cakes, and pies. We'll do the fresh salads. My girls and their cousins want to decorate and set up. And the boys will be in charge of cleaning up. So that just leaves the food."

At first, I thought she'd heard about our financial situation and was just being nice. Then I remembered that evening, the compliments, and the thought that this might be a way for me to support my family. *This is my chance to try.* I asked for more details, expectations, and costs. When she told me how much others had asked in payment, I was surprised.

"Shifra, that's what they charge. And that's what I'll pay you. Will you do it? Please, please, please with a cherry on top!"

I started laughing. "Dana, it was your idea then. And it makes sense that you'll be my test case now. Yes," I said.

I didn't hesitate. It was a gift. And if her family enjoys the meal, she will give me fantastic public relations. I knew they would. *Thank you, Hashem, for this heavenly hug.*

FIFTY-TWO

YAIR SWUNG HIS FEET onto the low table in front of him. "Hey, bring that over here." His hand stretched out to the beer Moish had just popped open, saying, "Hold on, man, I gotta check it out first. Don't want you to get sick if it's no good." Yitzy grabbed at the tall can, grinning mischievously. With a garbled blessing, he gulped down the brew.

"Yeah, right. Just hand it over and I'll check it out myself." Yair flipped himself up from the sofa chair, reaching toward the drink, and punching good-naturedly at his friend's shoulder.

"Hey, did we come to see a movie or what?" Moish yelled impatiently, trying to set up his mother's work computer. She needed it for the translation and editing services she offered, and he was rarely allowed to use it. Today she was attending an all-day professional conference for translators and would not be home till the evening. Moish grinned, happy that she was away and that it was available just when the boys decided they needed a day off.

"We're trying to create a mood," Yair said, guzzling the alcoholic drink.

"Mood shmood," Moish muttered to himself. "If my *abba* finds out we skipped yeshiva today, I'm in big trouble."

"Yeah, well if my parents find out I checked out for the day, I'm grounded for a year," Yitzy responded. "They think learning is the biggest *mitzva* ever."

Gulping more beer, Yair felt vaguely bothered that his father was the one who introduced him to movies and TV. His mother opposed

189

the "brainless media trash," but his shoulders went up involuntarily to shrug off her disapproval. *Like Abba said, just don't tell Ima. She doesn't get it.* He twisted himself into a more comfortable position, not wanting to think about her now.

"As if I can ever concentrate enough to know what *rebbe* is saying," Yair tossed out. "It's all a blur of Hillel said and Shamai disagrees." He slumped on the sofa. "Those rabbis spent all their time arguing. It's amazing they were able to come up with stuff that people still learn two thousand years later."

While Moish struggled with the computer, trying to get the screen size right, the boys bragged about how they had accomplished their day off. Yitzy began enthusiastically, "That was a smart idea bringing our schoolbags with us when we left home this morning."

They met a couple of blocks from the yeshiva and after a brief hesitation decided, for the first time, that they'd cut school and go to hang out together at Moish's house. "My father usually gets home from *kollel* late in the evening, but today," his eyebrows shot up, "Ima will also be away till late." They decided to stop at the supermarket to pick up snacks. It was Yair's idea to buy beer. They each dug into their pockets. Counting the money they found down to the ten *agura* pieces, Yitzy discovered happily, "I've got four shekels."

Moshe found a five-shekel coin.

"Wait a minute. I almost forgot." Yair's eyes lit up, as he smiled mischievously. He pulled a crumpled twenty-shekel bill from his front pants pocket.

"Where'd you get that?" both friends demanded.

"My Abba," Yair snickered, raising his eyebrows roguishly. He muttered mostly to himself, "He likes to give presents to the people he trusts to keep his secrets."

A raucous sound coming from the computer screen brought him back to his surroundings.

"Turn that down," Yair yelled out.

Yitzy pushed off one sneaker with the other and stretched out near the bowl of popcorn. Stretching his elbows to get comfortable, he nearly knocked it over.

"Don't make a mess. We gotta leave this place clean," Moish insisted, already wondering if this was a good idea. "Maybe we should forget this and go back to yeshiva. We could walk in during recess. Maybe *rebbe* won't even notice."

"Yeah, right. Our *rebbe* has X-ray eyes. He doesn't miss anything." Yair said with a touch of pride. This teacher really liked Yair; he spent time talking with him about other things, not just Torah. With a faint grimace at his lips, Yair shrugged that thought away too. He was really getting to like movies, especially fast-paced action ones. The screen lit up with a fiery explosion. Those nights at Mona's whetted his appetite for them.

Later that evening, Yair was in a great mood. His mother hardly had to repeat her requests that he prepare for bed.

Nine-year-old Yair whistled as he strutted off to brush his teeth. *Take it easy, everyone. What's the big deal? Everything's great. What's all the huffin' and puffin'?*

He crawled under the blankets and turned on his back, linking his fingers under his head. Remembering to say *Shema*, he sat, swung one hand over his open eyes, and rattled off the prescribed prayer. He shut out the tension mounting all around him by reviewing his day. *What a day!*

FIFTY-THREE

THE NEXT DAY, AFTER helping a young neighbor with her newborn, colicky baby, I returned home to find my six-year-old son Benny sitting cross-legged in front of a bonfire in our backyard.

He was flicking unlit matches onto the burning, dried-out twigs and some old wicker garden chairs. Gazing silently into the flames, he was indifferent to my presence. My young son didn't even look up when I asked, "What on earth are you doing?"

After dowsing the small fire with a garden hose, I prodded him into the house. Benny was a serious kid, the responsible, quiet type. I could not imagine him acting delinquent.

"Stay right here in the living room. I'll be right back," I told him sternly. His only response was to stare past me, still not saying a word. I felt myself shuddering, needing a few minutes to collect my thoughts.

Peeking in on Kayla, my eyes went directly to a half-full bottle of blue-colored alcohol in front of her on the desk. There was a lingering trace of smoke in the room. At its source, I spotted the remnant of a cigarette. Glancing at her sideways, I lifted the stub and sniffed. The smell was not from the regular store-bought kind. *Where had my eleven-year-old daughter found, let alone acquired, marijuana?*

"What is this?" I demanded. With her head bowed, my generally meek Kayla described an apartment outside of our neighborhood, where a lot of people hung out.

With great hesitation, she let me know in a broken, barely audible voice, "If you take this away, I can get more."

Shocked beyond belief, I couldn't speak. *What happened to my*

Kayla? My mind raced in a thousand directions. Returning to Benny, who sat sullenly on the couch, I stared vacantly.

Once again people in pain came before straightening up my own home. But my kids? Two of them falling apart at the same time?

Then I spotted a note on the table among the leftover lunches and spilled milk. Written on a small, smudged piece of paper, it was left leaning onto the milk container.

Ariella had scribbled in her difficult-to-read handwriting, "I went to a frend. I'm not comeing home tonite."

No explanation, no hearts-and-smiles sign-off that often adorned her name. Her scratchy signature appeared shaky and undersized. It looked as though it was falling off a cliff. Holding it tightly, I tried to think where she might have gone. Turning to Yair, I asked, "Did Ariella say where she was going?"

Dovy breezed into the kitchen. As the oldest, he was often the family spokesman. I had barely opened my mouth to ask him what was going on, when he announced, without any customary greeting, "We got together and decided that you should not mess up our family by getting divorced. Abba wants *shalom bayit*, so why are you doing this terrible thing to us? We can't take it anymore. If you don't stop..." and here he paused for only a moment before the next blow, "I'm going to start hanging out with girls."

My tall and lean, teenaged son watched my reaction. His clear blue eyes, like his father's, were unflinching. Shaking my head in disbelief, I noticed his white shirt, dark pants, and large *kippa*. I couldn't picture my young yeshiva boy with a girl.

"What? What is going on here?" No one answered, but the silence echoed as thoughts tumbled in my head. I was trying to be mother and father to them, spending all my evenings studying with each child as needed, sitting with them at bedtime, telling endless stories, and singing softly to comfort the younger ones to sleep.

I told them little about my struggle for our freedom. I thought I was protecting them, thinking they don't need to hear too many gory details. Now I felt driven to explain our need to escape from their father's madness.

My head pounded like a drum. I was aware of the blood draining from my light complexion. My heart racing, I sat down hard on a chair. I felt the terror of an animal ensnared in a deceptive trap.

The kids appeared to be of one united, indignant, angry mind. Dovy lashed out again, "You are betraying the family. Why are you doing this to us?" He spun on his heels and walked out, slamming his bedroom door to emphasize his fury. That was the first time, and I prayed the last, that he would ever do so.

Where do I begin? I must locate Ariella. I called neighbors and classmates. She did not have many friends, and there was no one I could think of that she would stay with. Her siblings' lips remained sealed regarding her absence, but it was only an hour later that my missing eight-year-old daughter, frightened by her own bold escapade, decided to return home. She refused to say where she had been, or why. *What is this foreboding silence? Why isn't anyone talking to me?*

All of my questions that evening went unanswered, met only with sullen faces and frowns. Aside from Dovy's outburst, everyone remained eerily aloof, moving away if I even came near. The evening passed in frightening surrealism. Aside from arguing over everything, no one talked or smiled.

Only Batya held onto me, as though clinging for dear life. I could tell she felt afraid of all the tension. I let her stay in the bath longer than usual. We played with her yellow chicks and she playfully spilled soapy water from cup to cup. I tried to disguise my cascading tears by dripping water onto my face and making comical motions.

That night, I stumbled from bed to bed. Kayla was stiff and unnatural, her eyes wide open. She turned when I sat on her bed. When I put my hand on her shoulder, she began to heave and cry. Trying to gauge the pain and frustration, I asked quietly, "Do you want to tell me what happened?"

Kayla sucked in her bottom lip. Her lips and eyebrows turned down. Weakly, she shook her head. I hugged her. "We can work this out. And we will be OK." She pulled the blanket higher. I sensed her sadness and bent over to hold her. She did not resist, but did not respond either.

Benny pulled away from my goodnight kiss. That had never happened before. I told him we would talk tomorrow and that I loved him. "We will be OK, Benny."

Lying in bed, Dovy thought back to this evening's burst of anger when he irately yelled at his mother.

My God, I threatened her!

Once again, his father had manipulated him, and his mother was hurt. Dovy groaned before turning in bed once again. It took hours for the knots in his stomach to loosen up until exhausted, he finally fell asleep.

How could I contend with each one's reaction and fight Efraim as well? Unable to sleep, I needed desperately to get some objective advice. At dawn, I sat cross-legged on the couch, my hands holding up my tired head. I was entrenched in weighty thoughts when I heard the squeaking door once again broadcasting Efraim's return. Their loving father had returned just before they awoke, with bags of treats and tasty sandwiches that had become the expected fare.

I pulled the blanket over me on the couch.

Removing his shoes, he tiptoed past me, no doubt hopeful that I was asleep. Catching myself in a sarcastic giggle, I wondered why, if he was so smart, he didn't oil the daily announcement to his surreptitious entrance.

Shortly afterward, when Batya came waddling out of the bedroom crying for me, Efraim emerged from the bathroom, wearing new pajamas and slippers. He picked up my crying toddler with a hearty, "Hi, sweetie." Swinging her airplane style, Efraim had her laughing, ready to wash her hands without the cajoling I often needed. One by one everyone awoke. Efraim's hair looked more mussed up now than when he entered. It looked as if he'd just woken up. *Hmm. Reverse brushing.*

He called out to me, "Shifra, what beautiful children we have. And what good *middot* they have." Each one was complimented in some personal way, as Efraim urged them to get dressed and ready for school. I was still sitting on the couch when Dovy came in for breakfast. From this angle, I watched Dovy lower his head as his father whispered in his ear. He looked up. I could see he was troubled. When he raised his shoulders and dropped them, I wondered if he'd been convinced of something against his will by his dad.

I suddenly noticed Benny standing next to them. Efraim handed something to him. Benny started walking toward me.

"Ima," he said as he gave me a stack of one-hundred-shekel bills, "this is from Abba. Ima," he tried to sound convincing, "Abba loves you."

The banknotes felt disgusting in my hands. I didn't want to touch them. Swallowing the scream that was erupting from deep inside my guts, I kissed my sad-eyed son. Quietly, I told him, "Love is not about money, honey." Putting down the dirty piles of bills, I hugged him close. "You, I love."

As soon as they were all ready, Efraim herded them out the door, cheerfully calling out that he'd be home for dinner, if he could.

FIFTY-FOUR

A FTER EVERYONE LEFT FOR school, I found Efraim's gun under Benny's pillow. I was straightening up the bedroom, trying to transform a nightmare into a home and a safe place.

Mentally, I replayed the scene of my younger son lighting fires and I felt his pain. *How can he protect himself — and how can I protect him — from the alternating fierce arguments and sullen silences that fill his childhood home?* The despair that caused my stomach to twist in pain abruptly sank to rock bottom as my hand touched the cold, hard metal firearm.

In a flash, I remembered Efraim insisted we buy it because we sometimes traveled to areas in Israel considered dangerous. Efraim also accumulated a large supply of ammunition from who knows where, as well as a large collection of knives from camping stores, which he kept in his closet.

I didn't pay it much attention at the time, but I was concerned about the kids' finding the gun. I had heard about a workshop for kids whose parents owned weapons, which is not uncommon in Israel. It stressed that firearms are dangerous and kids should never think about touching one.

We contacted the guide, Jack, an old-time immigrant from Texas who drove us to the appointed open field. Tall and heavily built, Jack easily maneuvered a large barrel filled with red colored liquid into the shooting range. With his deep, twangy southern accent, he warned the kids, "Y'all don't ever touch a gun or even pick up a bullet if ya see it lyin' on the ground. Y'all understand?" Jack's theory was that

197

if a kid actually felt the powerful discharge and explosive impact firsthand, he would never touch the dangerous weapon.

After his somewhat intimidating speech, which seemed appropriate considering the topic, he protected their eardrums from the gun blast with earplugs.

Dovy was first, and he took his place behind the dirt line that our guide drew with the toe of his leather boots. Jack stood to his side, helping him hold and aim an old-fashioned revolver at the liquid-filled target.

As Dovy prepared to fire, my youngest and I stood far off. She clung to my leg, daring to sneak a look, but holding on for dear life.

Benny stood with his older siblings, but after the first thunderous explosion, he shied toward me. I told him, "It's enough that you watched. You and Batya don't need to go closer or pull the trigger," but both of my younger crew insisted on taking their turns.

Each of the older ones, placed their fingers on the trigger. Using all their strength, they were able to fire, probably with help from Jack. Each one was thrown back by the powerful discharge. I knew that Benny could not squeeze the trigger, but Jack made it appear that he had hit the center target.

Three-year-old Batya put her tiny hand on Jack's as the cowboy held her steady, talking to her all the while. He made a loud popping sound and shook Batya a bit, so she'd get the idea without the fright.

Bringing everyone together, Jack explained, "If someone plays with a gun and shoots someone, even by accident, the red water, which was now squirting from several holes in the barrel, would really be someone's blood." Watching their innocent eyes grow, I was sure they'd never touch the gun.

On the way home, everyone bravely talked about firing the weapon and how far back they had been thrown. I heard Benny's hoarsely whispered promise, "I'll never touch this gun, ever."

But this morning here it is, loaded, under his pillow.

I called my best friend, and confidant, Rivka, and told her everything in vivid detail. As though describing the gory parts of a bad dream, I told her about the fires, the drugs and alcohol, the threat of starting to hang out with girls, and an eight-year-old runaway. I slowed down dramatically for the finale.

"And Benny took the gun to his room. What on earth was he planning to do with it? How can I do this to my family?" I demanded of her, unfairly. "Look how much pain I'm causing them!"

I breathed heavily into the phone, completely emptied. I tried to hear some voice of wisdom but instead sensed a deafening silence.

I was ready to be locked away.

And then came Rivka's calming voice. "Shifra," she said. She paused for what seemed like a very long time. Maybe she was waiting for my breathing to slow so that I could hear her. "Shifra, is it possible that Efraim set the whole thing up, so you won't want to proceed with the divorce?" Even as she said those simple words, my rattling brain calmed down.

Of course! My kids didn't think of these ideas. They don't know where to buy drugs. And Kayla doesn't even sip wine on Shabbat, only grape juice. And how would Benny reach so high in the closet to get the gun?

In my lioness' desire to protect my cubs, I overlooked the obvious. "I stopped thinking," I confessed. Feeling stupid and enlightened all at once, I promised Rivka, "I'll talk to them. Somehow we will get to the truth. Thank you, my dear friend."

Some shaky minutes later, I dialed Suri's number and told her briefly what had happened. The intense emotional upheaval had leveled out, the mystery resolved. She was not surprised.

"This is the classic case of the abusive husband confusing the issues and using the kids against his already battered wife's emotions. Shifra, I know you're tough. And I warned you it would get harder before it gets easier. Some women never seem to get it. As one mom to another," she added, "Shifra, you have really good, smart kids. Give them more credit."

Tough-talking Suri and deep, wise Rivka were my two angels. I somehow felt with them supporting me, I might survive this journey through Gehinom.

I needed to find the courage to discuss tough issues with my kids. I was not protecting them by keeping the details to myself. We needed to uncork bottled-up emotions and actions that were separating and dividing us. More quickly than I could have guessed, the uncorking ceremony began.

FIFTY-FIVE

"DOVY! WHERE ARE YOU, Dovy?" Peering over his *Gemara*, Chaim snapped his fingers in the direction of his learning partner. "Planet Earth to Dovy, do you read me?" Chaim teased good-naturedly. "Ahh, maybe we're coming up with an earth-shaking new idea, Rabbi Baumen, yes?"

Dovy, his forehead wrinkled in concentration, shook his head. Staring blankly past his best friend since they were little and now his *chavruta* of three years, Dovy's thoughts were clearly not on the open *Gemara* he held. He could not shake off the excruciating conclusions that were emerging. Sinking into heavily focused contemplation, Dovy appeared to be hypnotized.

Both boys were considered by the rabbis and many of the older students to be "top learners." Each one could potentially become an outstanding scholar. In the crowded *beit midrash*, the other yeshiva students, sitting in pairs, were learning loudly. Learning *Gemara* this way taught the boys how to reveal the finest details of a complex situation in order to comprehend how the Jewish laws were established. It always engendered much debate, as these young men were honing their ability to ponder concepts both broadly and deeply.

Dovy grimaced, his lips pursed together. The muscles in his shoulders tightened. Chaim, no longer laughing, leaned forward, reaching out with his right hand to touch his friend's arm. Chaim had never seen Dovy so agitated.

With burning indignation, Dovy slammed his clenched fist into the white laminated table. "How stupid am I?"

Chaim studied his friend silently for a full minute before asking.
"Nu? What is it?"

Dovy looked down. "I can't talk about it."

"That's Abaye's opinion," one boy was saying. "But look at this." A
steady loud exchange of ideas racing through the study hall brought
Dovy back to the present.

Chaim felt his back relax as the zombie look in Dovy's eyes returned to the familiar appearance he'd known since childhood.

"You can't tell me?" Chaim asked.

Surprise filled Chaim's voice as he leaned back in the chair, calling
to mind that they had shared everything for as long as he could
remember, from kids' toys to the day Chaim's father had collapsed
and was rushed to the emergency room. Dovy came every day during
shiva, becoming Chaim's lifeline to the world and encouraged him to
talk. Dovy made sure that Chaim had someone to cry with and was
there to help him begin to hope again.

He drummed his fingers on the table softly. "You can't tell me,"
he repeated softly, looking away. "We're closer than brothers," he
said. Lowering his voice, he said, "You shouldn't have to tell me. I
should know."

Dovy shrugged. "You don't want to know." Turning to stare at a
boisterous *bachur* whose manifest enthusiasm was attracting others
into its center, he sighed audibly. "That's where I want to be."

Chaim stood and stretched his hefty six-foot-tall frame. He walked
to the end of the table and around to the other side, where his closest
friend slumped in his chair. Dovy crossed and uncrossed his legs, the
front of his shoes knocking against each other. Chaim turned a chair
backward and slung one leg over the seat, sitting down. Deliberately,
he rolled up his shirt sleeves and crossed his arms.

"The angels accompany you," he started to say with the hint of a
sly smile, "to where you want to be."

"What?"

"Stand up, Dovy," Chaim ordered his friend, as he quickly rose
from the chair. Without thinking, Dovy stood. Chaim put his arm
around his *chavruta*'s shoulders and walked him into the heart of

the animated learning. Engaging in heated scholarly debate, Dovy was able to temporarily emerge from the raging waves of guilt and confusion that threatened to drown him.

Later that evening, the boys pulled their thick jackets over their bulky sweaters, preparing to go for a walk in the night's biting cold.

Dovy began. "Thanks for shaking me out of my stupor this afternoon."

"Talk," Chaim said tersely. "What's going on?"

"I thought you knew," Dovy answered with a touch of sarcasm.

"I think I do," Chaim responded. Even with the bright light of a street lamp, they could barely see each other's eyes between the knit hats and scarves covering the lower half of their faces. Yet Dovy sensed that Chaim's eyes reflected the hurt in his own. "Do you remember how you forced me to talk after my father died? You refused to let me drown in silent misery."

Dovy looked down. "That was different. It was an act of God. As painful as it was, we could not question it. You needed to strengthen your belief and ask 'What now?' 'Why' was not an option."

Dovy added, "I learned, mostly from you by the way, that when our faith is strong and we feel His presence, we don't get have to get lost in asking 'why?'."

In the rare, light Galilee snowfall that was beginning to fall, the boys left tracks. At first, they showed dragging feet. Gradually, the even prints of a steady walk emerged, as Dovy poured out his heart.

"Everything I am telling you now is for therapeutic purposes, Chaim. I feel I may collapse under this burden if I cannot share it with someone." So saying, Dovy ensured that his words would not constitute *lashon hara*.

Dovy recanted the "learning" evenings at Mona's, the uncensored TV shows, the money he often saw exchange hands so freely, his Abba's low-life drug addict "clients" who were really his cohorts, his concern for Yair and all his siblings. He felt like he couldn't stop talking.

"No matter what, he tells us not to tell my *ima*, even if we're just buying some extra nosh at the grocery store. This incessant mission of keeping his secrets is choking me. Something is really wrong, but I couldn't figure it out, until today."

Chaim nodded, listening closely as he flexed his near-frozen fingers to stimulate circulation.

Dovy explained. "Today we were discussing the laws of being a witness. It's really complicated. We learned that in most instances you need a minimum of two witnesses, and they must testify separately."

When he paused, watching the mist appear as his warm breath hit into the icy wind, Chaim waited.

Dovy wiped a splash of snow from his reddened nose. "I don't even know how much my *ima* knows. She seems upset at him a lot and they don't talk much — at least not in front of us kids. And now they're talking about getting a divorce. But what does she really know?" He paused. "He always lies to her. He says he's taking us to learn or on a *tiyul* or something like that — like he's going to spend some time with us. And she's always asking us where we went and how it was — and we always lie to her." Dovy could not believe what he just said. "Chaim, that's it. Do you get it? We've been conditioned to always lie to her." He stopped, agitated. "Is she supposed to be a private investigator?"

Chilled, but willing to keep on, Chaim stuffed his ungloved hands deeper into his pockets. "Yeah. Maybe she's suspicious, but she has no witnesses. And everyone's covering up for your dad."

Chaim pulled one hand out of its cozy place and packed some snow off a bush into a snowball. He threw it angrily across the empty park. He really respected Mrs. Baumen. Aside from all her neighborhood *chessed*, she was like his second mom, especially when his own became a widow.

Dovy spoke slowly. "I think that it would make me crazy if everyone I loved and cared about was lying to me." He felt a hot flush across his face. "This has been going on for years, Chaim. I can't believe it. What an idiot I am."

"Dovy, you're a kid. Kids do what their parents tell them, at least most of the time," he said trying to sound funny.

"At least until we become teens."

"Yeah, right."

"But I'm the oldest. Chaim, if I don't stop the charade, no one else can defy my *abba*. Will this just keep getting worse? And how is it affecting everyone else?"

"This is a good sign, Dovy my boy. You're growing up. On one hand, even considering defying your dad can be really scary. On the other hand, you're willing to take responsibility to make things right, and that's scary too."

"Maybe if I told Ima, even a part of what's happening, just clue her in, it would make a difference." Dovy imagined his dad's vicious look striking him dead. He shivered sharply at that moment more than from the slushy snow that was beginning to seep in somewhere between his pants legs and shoes.

Pulling a damp tissue out of his pocket to wipe his nose, Dovy pushed up his jacket sleeve to check the time. "Oh man, we've been out here freezing and circling the neighborhood for almost two hours."

They both turned at the same time in the direction of the dormitory, taking long strides.

"I heard they found a cure for frostbite," Chaim chuckled, bowing his head into the wind. "Do you think there's a pharmacy open now?" he asked jokingly.

As they pushed open the large metal doors to the dorm and stomped the snow off their boots on the thick rubber welcome mat, Dovy pulled the snow-soaked scarf off his face. "Chaim, I'm scared. What if I tell her and she confronts him with it? He'll know I squealed." He paused as he jerked the zipper to open his coat.

"And what if —" now he stopped short, his voice permeated with sadness. "What if I tell her and she doesn't do anything?"

FIFTY-SIX

AT HOME, I DECIDED to gather the kids right away. Efraim was not there, and I could still feel the vibration of Rav Kaufman's fist on the table.

I pondered my toxic situation.

For a start, some nut cases suggest a return to concubines. Does he justify his actions with some questionable halachic loopholes? How does it lessen the pain to me or the kids? What's the difference if it's random nights of unfaithfulness or a second home with a girlfriend renamed as a second wife, who I am not supposed to know about? Either way, he hasn't enough love and concern for one woman's feelings or for his children from that marriage. How can he propose that he will care for and support a parallel family?

Apparently, he can't. Mona is always angry with him that he doesn't spend enough time or money on her and Shmueli.

And what is he doing with the kids? I can't trust him with them. He lies all the time.

The sign of a fool is that he thinks he's fooling everyone when he is really fooling only himself. We're all onto him!

Mamzer, *idiot,* mamzer! *He'll lose everything!*

"He already has," I whispered to myself. "Help me, Hashem, get him away from me and the kids. I call to You, begging You, Hashem. Save us from his madness. It is a rope around my neck."

"Come in now. I need to talk to you. All of you." They must have felt the gravity in my voice. I had never seen them move so quickly. Dovy and Yair noisily tried to push each other out of the single couch seat, while Kayla silently took her place opposite me. Ariella sat next to me, and Benny brought a low bench to sit on. Thoughtfully, he moved to one side and asked if I wanted to put my feet up.

"Yair and Dovy, can you figure out how to calm down?" I frowned. They finally sat somewhat sideways into the chair, punching playfully at one another.

Quietly, I told them what Rav Kaufman said and that it was time for us to talk.

That's when the earth quaked. Dovy, who had become increasingly straightforward, broke the ice. It was as though he had been waiting for a signal. He described how their father often took him aside to explain what was going on with me.

"Abba told me you're going through some stage in life where most women want to be free of their responsibilities, including taking care of the kids. He said you just want to have a good time. He kept telling me that after a while, you'd realize the mistake you were making. It was up to me..."

Dovy paused. "Abba said I could stop you from doing something crazy, like destroying our family, by making you feel threatened. You'd be so scared that I'd do something stupid like hanging out with girls that you'd snap back to your senses. He said all your friends who are helping you are crazy too. I was supposed to keep it a secret from the others because they're too little to understand."

It was obvious from his wrinkled forehead and narrowed eyes that he was weighing his next words.

My Kayla, so quiet and shy, kept looking down, away from my searching eyes. Ariella, snuggled into my shoulder and started to cry. "I didn't want to go away. I was too embarrassed to ask anyone to stay at their house, but Abba told me to write the note anyway."

Sobbing, she accepted the tissue I offered. "He told me, 'Ima's acting crazy' and that I can help you start to feel better if I just don't come home at least until after dark." Innocently, she did her best to listen to her *abba*. "I didn't know how that would do any good, but Abba sounded so sure. So I started to walk, but it got dark and I was scared."

She put her head in my lap. I felt her shake. "I didn't want to go

anywhere, Ima, and I knew you'd be worried, but Abba said I can't
come home until after it got dark."

I didn't respond. I just hugged her and caressed her hair and face.

Kayla was now staring straight ahead, unable to face me.

My eyes swept the room, wondering who else would come forth.
Dovy, glancing at the others and me apprehensively, abandoned his
place on the couch. He paced the carpet, nearly tripping over Yair's
book bag. He was still mulling over his next words. My anguish increased as I observed gentle Kayla's inability to say what seemed to be
choking her. Benny's expression was wrinkled in apparent confusion.
I could tell from his lips, which he squeezed together, and how he
rocked from side to side as he squirmed in his place, that he was
itching to speak.

"Benny," I prompted, "whose idea was it to light the fire? And why
was the gun under your pillow?" He pressed his lips harder. Thinking
he was afraid to say *lashon hara*, I reminded him of the *rav*'s words. I
was really surprised when he confronted me, disappointed.

"Ima, did you really think I took the gun?" My accusation had
hurt him deeply. "I promised you I wouldn't touch it."

Even as he spoke, it dawned on me how unfair my initial reaction
was. What proof was there to suspect him of wrongdoing?

"I never even touched it. Abba put it there. He wanted me to tell
you that I would shoot someone because you want a divorce."

Benny shivered at the thought. I now understood that he was
more shocked than I was at finding the loaded gun within reach.
Releasing Ariella from my arms for the moment, I encircled my little
man and apologized for ever doubting him.

"I know you're a good boy. And I know you tell the truth. Ima
got very confused when so many things happened all at once. I'm so
sorry, honey, that I even thought you would do something like that."
I held him close, sensing that we were forging a covenant of trust.

"Ima," he continued slowly, "Abba burned most of the wood. When
we heard you coming, he made me sit in the yard holding the matches.
I didn't want to do it and I was too scared to tell you right away,
'cause Abba seemed s-s-s-so..." Benny had never stammered before.

"...crazy." We all turned to Dovy, who completed the sentence for his little brother. "He kept talking about how crazy you are," Dovy went on with a bitter tone, "but he's the one who looked really crazy."

Kayla shuddered. Now that she was looking straight at me, the fright in her sky-blue eyes was evident. Benny went to sit next to Kayla; Ariella pulled my arms back around herself and cuddled into me.

Kayla could not restrain herself any longer. In her soft voice, she said, "Abba told me that when women are in their forties, they go crazy and don't know what they want, so they make up stories about how mean everyone is to them — especially their husbands. Lots of women leave their children and just want to go out and have a good time. He said that after a while they forget about it and stop being so wild — and then they feel bad."

She sobbed, "Ima, I didn't want you to leave us." Her small body shook violently at the thought. Benny put his hand tenderly on her shoulder as she went on. "Abba said I could stop you. First, he told me not to tell anyone." Kayla's eyes darted around the room. *Was she afraid that Efraim was hearing her now or watching for her siblings' reactions?*

In that charged moment, Dovy burst out angrily, "Secrets. Abba and his secrets. He tells everyone not to tell anyone, but he already told everybody — except Ima. All the time he says, 'Don't tell Ima'." Everyone nodded in agreement.

"We'll come back to the secrets." I tried to keep some semblance of order as I felt the impact of everyone's escalating emotions. Forcing myself to remain calm, I asked Kayla what happened next.

"Abba took me to the supermarket and bought that bottle of blue drink. He told me that if I said I drank from it, you would be upset." Then, her voice lowered, "He took me to someone's house and gave him money and bought that cigarette." She lowered her voice, "He bought a few. This man showed me how he put something into a piece of paper and rolled it up. I didn't like him. He had ugly brown teeth and yellow, broken fingernails. And his house smelled disgusting. I kept asking to leave, but Abba kept on talking to him until, finally, I started crying and we left."

Now Kayla paused, her fingers twisting ringlets into her straight black hair. She turned to glance at Benny, who in such a grown-up manner remained supportive at her side. Taking a deep breath, she went on. "Abba told me that if I want to save our family and stop you from leaving us kids, I should tell you I'll take drugs. When we came home, he spilled out most of the blue drink. He told me I should tell you I drank from it. Ima," again she looked me straight in the eyes, "I didn't even taste it. It looked so disgusting."

Kayla was not a big talker, and I could see how very hard this was for her. Now Ariella voluntarily slid away from me as her big sister approached. I held Kayla close as she gasped, "Ima, I was so scared of that man. And I don't think you're crazy." She peered at me with her beautiful, trusting eyes.

"Would you leave us, Ima?" Benny asked soberly.

I focused on each one of my kids, trying to absorb the drama that was playing out. The irony and absurdity of all that I was hearing forced a smile to my lips.

"I'm not crazy," I promised, "and this is not a stage I'm going through. I don't want your *abba* to say or to do things to hurt you or me anymore, so I'm looking for a way to help us. But I'll never leave you, my precious children. I love you all so much."

Sighs of relief mixed with anger and confusion forced our emotional floodgates open. There seemed to be no end to the stories, the forced secrets, the whopping lies, the threats. The common thread through all was, "Don't tell Ima. Ima's crazy and selfish. She doesn't want me to help other people." They were consistently sworn to secrecy about some scheme or meeting with someone.

"But Abba said he's only telling me and I shouldn't tell the others," was frequently repeated. In reality, each lived with a "dark secret" that everyone else knew. There was still a lot of confusion when the exhausted little ones finally drifted off to sleep, long after their usual bedtimes.

The older ones held out longer, but soon after midnight, even Dovy could no longer keep his eyes open. This was the first of many family gatherings, all of them designated—in Rav Kaufman's words—to break the barriers between the family members, to heal, and to unite us.

Efraim had woven a massive spider's web of secrets and lies. Gradually, in the weeks that followed, we spewed out much of the spider's vile poison with which he intended to destroy us all.

Alone in my room, reviewing each child's testimony, I staggered. *I think I am protecting my innocent kids by revealing so little of what I suspect, when in reality they actually know firsthand much more than I was ever aware of. They kept the secrets that were imposed on them by Efraim's veiled threats. He forced them with his warped way of demonstrating his love for them.* I slapped my open hand against the side of my aching head. *They* were protecting *me* from being hurt by the things they knew.

Realizing that I would be unable to remember everything that was said or who said what, I began keeping a journal. Every night, if I could keep my eyes open, I recorded their testimonies. If I fell asleep, I might write for hours the following morning. I had a great drive to document every detail, the way they said it, the tears, anger, or fear that accompanied the "confessions," and even the silences that occasionally interrupted the outpouring of pain.

In the weeks that followed, Efraim never came home in time to hear or interrupt our gatherings. He was so ensconced in his own world that he didn't notice the transformation that was gradually taking place, until he had no power to do anything about it.

At our next family gathering, Dovy again spoke up first. He seemed unable to contain the pain and anger that was harder for the others to put into words.

Kayla sat alone quietly. Ariella was lost in a stare that frightened me. Benny was crying, shamefaced. Yair appeared distant, uninvolved. He was folding papers into small airplanes and shooting them at Batya, who was clinging to me.

"Hi, Batya," he cooed mischievously, but she tucked her face into my shoulder and refused to look at him.

I could hardly believe the bizarre, unfolding scene. It was

shattering, like prisoners of conscience being unchained, the hanging rope removed from their necks at the last minute.

It became clear that each one of my children had been exposed to Efraim's raving chants for a period of several years. I hugged Batya, determined to protect her from his sickness.

Dovy fumed, "Abba told me, 'Don't tell Ima!' every time we went anywhere. It didn't matter if we were on the way to school or to my friends."

Dovy exhaled some of the tension. Trying to imitate his father's soft-spoken manner, Dovy listed the accusations against me. "She's crazy, she refuses to understand. She doesn't appreciate anything I do for others. She's jealous, she gets angry over nothing. If you tell Ima, she'll try to make trouble. She'll tell all her crazy friends that I'm not nice to her."

My jaw dropped down as the list went on and on. They had been indoctrinated. What did he do to force them to keep his secrets?

Rocking his head from side to side, Yair burst out in a chant, his voice rising with each repetition. "Don't tell Ima, don't tell Ima, don't tell Ima."

Kayla, putting her head down, cried in a heart-wrenching manner as Dovy's outpouring picked up speed.

"Your mother is a *meshugeneh*. She thinks only about herself. She doesn't like that I save lives or rescue so many people." Dovy's face was beet-red and his eyes were glaring. He banged a clenched fist vindictively onto the table, walls, and anything he passed, as he paced the room. Shaking, livid with anger, he spouted the poison out of his system.

Mimicking Efraim's hideous sneer, he went on. "She doesn't want me to be faithful to *Am Yisrael*. She thinks she's so religious, so pure. She thinks she knows everything, but she's stupid."

He paused to breathe and suddenly looked up to check my reaction, as though he abruptly remembered that this might be very painful for me. My mind raced to words Efraim had said to me directly.

"*You always say, 'NO, you can't do that.' You go crazy about everything. You never want me or the kids to have any fun.*"

Benny jumped up suddenly and dashed to the bathroom. Moments later, I heard him vomiting. Setting Batya onto the couch, I stood up to go to him. Dovy was muttering under his breath and I strained to listen, as I left the room.

"She messes up everything. I just married her because I was trying to help her, but she doesn't appreciate anything."

"You ugly witch," I recalled Efraim repeating to me on numerous occasions. "You only *pretend* to want to help people."

I shuddered as I ran to Benny. His head was perched over the toilet as he threw up his dinner. Rubbing his back, and handing him tissues did little to alleviate his crying, heaving, and shaking.

I thought of Efraim's spiteful comments. Absorbed in my own pain, I didn't consider that he was brainwashing my kids with the same hideous lies. More than once, he had suggested, "You should be on drugs." Occasionally I had even wondered if he was right.

Now, it became staggeringly apparent who was crazy.

When Benny finally finished throwing up his guts, he splashed cold water on his face. I brought him a drink to wash out the disgusting taste in his mouth. In my mind, I heard Efraim's agitated voice. His accusations didn't stop.

"You always try to stop me from doing *chessed* or getting kids out of cults or off drugs. You don't want me to help deserted women who are really desperate. You act insane. You just want money."

It took a long time, but finally, I could imagine him speaking similarly to the kids.

"Don't listen to what she says. Just listen to me.

"You see how dedicated I am to saving Jewish souls.

"Don't be stupid and crazy like your Ima. Your Ima had a crazy childhood and now she's crazy. Some doctors said she's schizophrenic and should be on drugs, but she refuses to take them. Listen, kids, do whatever you want, spend the money I give you. You can have more, whatever you want. You don't need to save it. I can always get you more. Just *don't tell Ima*."

Back in the living room, some of the tension seemed to have been diffused. It was time to really talk.

Fifty-seven

A
S THE HAZE OF confusion lifted, I looked at the faces of each of my beloved children, almost as though for the first time. I was with all of them daily, involved in every aspect of their lives: their friends, their homework, school, and afternoon activities. I knew where they were twenty-four hours a day, or so I believed.

Now I learned of their double life: spiritually sensitive, modest and sheltered at home, while they were learning and experiencing firsthand—from their own father—base and immoral elements of the world. *Oh, my God!*

We had our meetings nearly every evening for weeks, unless the kids had some school activity or I had to attend a meeting or a wedding or to prepare for the growing number of *simchas* I now catered.

Once we got started, it was hard to stop. This evening, as usual, hours after we began, the frequent multiple yawns signaled it was time to finish. Only sleep allowed them to end this powerful catharsis. The nightmare of their days was ending. They did not have to crawl any more into separate corners, careful not to repeat a secret that was actually known to all, except me. We are lost in time and space. How much time has passed?

When nearly everyone but Dovy was sleeping, he looked at me with such sad, sunken eyes. "Ima." I waited. "Ima, did you know...? I mean, do you remember Tomas?" I nodded.

Dovy looked away. "Oh." In the silence, I heard my heart pounding like a hammer.

"Abba...he...he...takes us to see him sometimes. He, he showed

214

us pictures." Lowering his eyes, Dovy sank lower into the couch.

"Pictures?" *What is he telling me now?*

As if gathering the strength of Samson, he said it out. "Pictures of ladies." He hesitated for a very long minute. "Without clothes." Dovy was squirming, his cheeks were flushed and his head was shaking anxiously. "Tomas has magazines, a lot of magazines." Dovy was unable to sit still. "He showed them to us." Dovy's face burned like a bush fire. "Abba looked too." He slouched further on the couch. "And Abba started laughing."

Dovy shook his head, almost in disbelief of what he had just said, but a look of great relief seemed to slowly replace the tortured expression. Then he gave into the weariness of the hour and the warped content and curled up on the couch. I watched his breathing deepen, and wondered if my shattered heart, or theirs, would ever be whole again.

It struck me that they were trying to act heroically. Aside from their fear of their father's threats, much of what they didn't say was an attempt to protect me. They didn't want *me* to be hurt by the way their father insulted *me*.

Outraged, I screamed under my breath, "I'm supposed to be protecting them!" I turned my palms upwards, fingers taut. I sat up straight and clenched my fists. "No. No, no. No! No!" I remonstrated angrily. "I'm not giving up. No more! No More! No, No More!"

Shaking my head, I tried to pull the revelations together, to concentrate on the notes I scribbled during the night's intense dialogues.

Reading through the jumbled scratches on the paper in front of me, I gasped, as one idea repeated itself over and over again.

With intense effort, crying all the while, I sat at the computer and typed them onto one page. It came out a bit chaotic, but now I could no longer deceive myself. There was no vague chance for reconciliation. I could not pretend I didn't know the truth.

Bone weary, my fingers flew over the keyboard, tying together the wild strands of the "Don't tell Ima" saga.

I released torrents of tears for the torment my kids endured. I can't say how much I cried over my children's suffering. After I don't know how long came tears of gratefulness for their validation. I realized that for years I thought *I* might really be wrong, hallucinating or even psychotic. And if I wasn't then, I might be in the future.

This is what emerged.

Journal entry

Since we began our almost nightly family meetings, massive segments of the vast web of lies and secrecy have been exposed. In a deafening waterfall of words, I learned from the kids more of their secret visits to places I said were off-limits or hadn't known about: Efraim's "co-counselors," many of whom I distrusted, and the rescuees, who still had a long way to go to stabilize.

My kids gave countless details of their father's escapades to which they were eyewitnesses: watching videos, talking privately with girls often in a separate room, cursing, smoking what they had learned was marijuana.

Often he sat them down in someone's home in front of a TV. Since we did not have one at home, it was a fascination that ensnared them. Even so, they were aware of the drama playing itself out around them as much as the one on the screen.

Sometimes he took only one child, who was expected not to tell the others. At other times, several went together. Either way, he told each one to lie to me, with precision scripting.

"Tell Ima we went for pizza or ice cream."

"Tell Ima we were learning in the beit midrash," the boys were warned.

"We were studying for a test," Kayla felt threatened enough to repeat.

"Abba walked me home from school today, and we stopped for a snack and to talk," Ariella had parroted.

I was deeply concerned for all of them, but Ariella really worried me. At some point, she had lapsed into silence and I could see her great longing for her father's love. I sensed she was having an especially hard time coming to terms with the reality that her *abba* had not spent private, quality time with her because he loved her. She seemed to be sinking into an alarming melancholy.

FIFTY-EIGHT

WHENEVER WE PASSED EACH other in the street, before he became confined to his home and then his bed, Rabbi Kaufman asked me to visit. Knowing he was seriously ill, I was reluctant. Occasionally I telephoned to ask about his health, and he inevitably offered me words of strength.

My parents had both passed away years ago, but I could not help contrasting the rabbi with my siblings, who never showed concern or offered to help. My brother had kept his silence, and my sister made it clear that I need not inform her of my situation.

This elderly couple, relative strangers, was visibly distressed by my situation. The Rabbi had suggested someone whom he thought was most competent and compassionate to turn to for halachic rulings. He was agitated that because of his illness he could not be more helpful.

This afternoon it was the *rabbanit* who called, asking—actually insisting that I come. "The *rav* is asking about your family. His is very upset that he was unable to assist you more. It will alleviate his pain to speak with you."

She overcame my resistance to intrude during his illness when she added softly, "Please come, for his sake. He cannot tolerate leaving things unfinished."

Her meaning appeared obvious, and I finally agreed to come in the early evening.

I was rushing toward their familiar building when the fiery red sun dipped low toward the horizon. The burning glow dimmed, leaving a

darkened, almost melancholy sky. The sun's setting took only minutes.
I must hurry.

I rushed through the large metal-framed door but strained to
climb the stairs. My hesitation to disturb him now was much greater
than when I first revealed my sorrows.

The living room had become a hospice. The special electric bed on
which the rabbi rested was elevated to ease his laborious breathing.
The soft pastel sheets indicated his preference to be home with his
family rather than hospitalized. The lights were dimmed and he appeared to be asleep. Two of his sons learned in barely audible voices
near him, by the light of a small lamp. They frequently looked toward
their dying father. Occasionally, with his eyes still closed, the rabbi
nodded his head, perhaps agreeing with their scholarly comments.

*Why did I come? This holy man is surrounded by his loving family. Why
am I imposing on their precious time together?* Feeling my face flush, I
wanted to run away.

His body shook as he gasped for air and began to cough. His
eldest son came quickly to his side and held a cup to his mouth
for him to spit into. I turned to see the *rabbanit* coming from the
kitchen, where I glimpsed some of their other adult children and
grandchildren saying *Tehillim*. She approached her weakened husband
with a cup of warm tea and began to spoon-feed him. He blinked
his appreciation.

When his coughing fit stopped, the *rabbanit* motioned to me to
come close.

"Shifra," he began, and then coughed again.

"Please," I said, "I only came to see you and thank you for all your
kindness to me. Please save your strength."

His loyal wife of sixty-three years closed her red, swollen eyes
briefly. "He did save it, to tell you something important. Allow him."

Involuntarily, I bit into my lip.

Very softly, so that I was forced to lean close, the rabbi whispered.
"Well-meaning rabbis will tell you to remain in your marriage for the
sake of your children." The sentence was punctuated with racking
coughs. His eldest son, blinking back his tears, lovingly washed his

father's face. "They will say the sacrificial altar in the Temple cries when a man divorces his wife." He paused to gasp for air, for life itself, and I moved away, alarmed that his last breath might be expended on me, rather than his wife and children.

"Please, I understand. May Hashem bless you and give you strength," I said. This was too painful. I drew back.

He insisted, "The children will find role models among kind Jews to fill the void. But vile scenes of abuse and infidelity are almost impossible to erase. You must leave this tragic marriage. May Hashem give you the wisdom and courage to go forward." His hacking cough increased and tears escaped his closing eyes.

"He never cries for his own suffering," his faithful wife whispered, lowering her head, "only for others."

The muffled sounds in the other room increased, as the words of *Tehillim* mingled with crying.

I could barely speak, let alone express my gratitude for his extraordinary concern. "Thank you. Thank you from my heart, Rabbi Kaufman." I whispered back hoarsely and rose to leave. I walked to the front door, anxious to allow the family their privacy with their beloved patriarch.

The *rabbanit*'s loving arms embraced me. I wanted to comfort her at this heartrending time. But even in her great sorrow, her compassion toward me was staggering. With a reminder that I was always welcome, she said, "Hashem prepares each step we take. *Hameichin mitzadei gever.* He will make the way known to you."

"And may you also see His revealed loving-kindness," I offered, as she steadied herself to return to her husband.

Tearfully, I nodded with immeasurable appreciation. Glancing once more toward the *rav*, whose sons had come to fix his pillow and wash his face from the spittle that formed at his lips, I closed the door behind me.

With sudden dizziness of overwhelming gratitude, I stopped on the first step. *The rabbi, in his last moments, could have literally saved his breath. The* rabbanit *didn't have to call me. Or if she was committed to doing her husband's bidding, she could have been less insistent that I come.* Lightheaded with sudden clarity, the thought hit me. *This must be the way of angels.*

Leaning against the wall, allowing my feet to scrape down one step and then another, I felt entirely unworthy of this level of self-sacrifice. My thoughts flew to my immediate family who had discarded me, like a dirty rag. These two elderly people, strangers until a few years ago, proved to me that love exists. They were offering it to me unconditionally. It was a powerfully humbling thought, causing me to cringe. The words of psalm 27, which were ingrained into my consciousness, emerged. "Though my father and mother have forsaken me, Hashem will gather me in."

The fading image of Efraim as a pious man crumbled. He was a damaged, unlit match next to this rabbi's pure, heavenly fire.

Descending the dark stairwell, forcing one foot to follow another, I recited psalm 23. "Though I walk through the valley of the shadow of death, I will fear no evil, for You are with me…"

An unexpected sense of affection and blessing that I had never known in my life, settled over me, sending shivers through me as I tried to absorb the magnitude of their love and compassion.

As I returned to my kids, the rabbi's words accompanied me. "The children will find role models among kind Jews to fill the void. But vile scenes of abuse and infidelity are almost impossible to erase." If there was any lingering inner turmoil about what I must do, the *tzaddik* had succeeded in erasing them with his dying words.

Walking slowly into the darkness, I said softly, "Hashem, I know You will show me the way. Please give me the courage to walk on Your path."

I decided to take the kids away for a few days' retreat to give us all a vacation from Efraim's influence and hopefully a fun and relaxing change of scenery. I did not tell him in advance so that he would not decide to join us.

I made arrangements to stay in a youth hostel in the south, which would include meals for Shabbat. After that, we would buy our food supplies in the grocery store. After Efraim left the house on Friday morning, I quickly packed our clothing and some games and books for the long bus ride. This time, I was the one who was taking the kids from school early, and we began our journey. We were all very excited.

I left Efraim a note, telling him we would not be home for Shabbat, and included my divorce terms. We would split the sale of the house when the youngest child turned eighteen. In the meantime, they would live with me. And he should pay child support that would keep them fed, clothed, and educated properly. The court would decide on visitation rights (although I would insist on some form of supervision, or at least several children visiting at once, and not one at a time). To prevent unnecessary additional trauma to the children, he should give me the *get* quickly.

In the end, we stayed for a week, taking day trips through the beautiful Negev, into racing river beds, and to the beautiful swimming areas of luscious Gush Katif. We laughed and played for hours. I felt the tensions releasing, as the sun and clean water purified us. The therapeutic qualities of these days — the tree climbing, the good-natured water wars, the racing and rolling down sandy hills — left us relaxed and happy in a way I could only have dreamed about.

We would have loved to stay, but the money was running out, as were changes of clothes. And they were missing school, some more than others. And so we returned with an assurance that we would go away again, as soon as possible.

We returned to an empty house. No Efraim and no guests were there to greet us. Only this letter:

Dear Shifra,

Couldn't you have given me the letter without taking off with the kids on Erev Shabbat? Why did you abandon me, just before Shabbat? You deserted me just when I was under extreme pressure with several mitzvot on the verge of completion. May Hashem cause merit to be gathered for my dad, may he rest in peace.

So what if for a while I push myself to the brink? It is for you, my beloved wife, Shifra, and our precious children. Hashem, may He be blessed, will give us extra protection because of the monumental Godly work that He is allowing me to accomplish.

But if you must see it this way, that you don't want me to struggle for Am Yisrael, and you are hinting that our future is in jeopardy, then I am forced to basically give up my commanding position against cults, missionaries, and Arab drug dealers. You are asking me to end my work for the homeless and fatherless, along with other emergency rescue missions.

To those who curse me, let my soul be silent and let my soul be like dust to everyone. Yehoshua ben Perachya said, "Judge everyone with favor." There are incredulous, lying slanders against me. I am and always have been faithful to you and to b'rit Avraham, and have not in any way messed around!

Please, God, we will be together 120 years, plus forever in the next world. And that means we will be together in Gan Eden.

So if this is what it takes to keep our family together, I agree to your requests that I discontinue my Holy work.

I love you,
Efraim

FIFTY-NINE

THE STORIES THAT EMERGED from our now routine gushing evenings were complex and startling, even terrifying. Sometimes the details came in order, and sometimes the child became confused, unsure of what happened first and what came later, as if in a dream. Often, the story of one child tied into the tale of another one, and they were able to complete each other's missing pieces. I tried to record their stories, trying to make sense of the confusing details the same night, after the last one, usually Dovy, finally gave into sleep.

There was much hesitation at first, but as they realized no punishments or judgments were being made, each one began to open up. Each one listened to the other, shaking or nodding their head, often interrupting with a different or opposite version. High tensions were dispersed or enhanced with occasional laughter, crying or angry outbursts, or sullen silences.

Sometimes, I sat privately with Ariella or Kayla, who had a much harder time speaking with everyone around, and just listened. I tried not to show my fury at their father, whom they occasionally tried to protect. *We have such amazingly loyal kids.* I wished they had parents who were worthy of them.

I often cried myself to sleep and awoke in a sweat, wondering if this pain would ever go away. I prayed I would be able to protect them from him.

When I shared just a bit of their harrowing tales with Suri, she immediately recommended Gisella, a gifted psychologist who counsels families suffering from traumatic situations. "They can all go to meet her together. She's calm, nonjudgmental, and extremely insightful. Afterward, you'll decide whether to continue as a group or individually."

Gisella turned out to be my third angel. When I first spoke with her briefly, she immediately understood our predicament. When I ended the conversation by telling her I was unable to pay her fees now but would pay them over time, she dismissed it as a non-issue. "Whenever you can, you will." And with that she ended the discussion.

Ariella told her story, in parts over time. She told some to Gisella and some to me, with additional details filled in by Yair and Dovy. When Gisella asked Ariella's permission to tell me some of this story, Ariella agreed and even seemed relieved. Merging what I knew with comments from Dovy and Yair, who heard it from Shmueli, this is what I later learned happened one evening, and afterwards, several months ago.

"Ariella, please come to eat." We were looking forward to Leah's engagement party. Ariella really liked Leah, a family friend who lived in a neighboring town. She always had something kind to say to Ariella. "We have to leave soon." The kids urged her to hurry.

"Come on, Ariella, it's not school," Yair teased. "It'll be fun."

Benny, my sensitive one, walked over to ask what was bothering her, but she wouldn't even look at him. He even asked if she wanted to sit next to him on the bus. I was moved by his reaching out to her, but she just shook her head.

"Ariella, we'll all be late if you don't get a move on," Dovy said practically.

"I don't want to go." My sad daughter buried her head into her arms and sulked. She looked unusually distressed.

"I don't want to leave you here alone, honey. Please join us." Thinking fast, I offered, "Look, I'll just take a sandwich for you, or you can just fill up on the cakes and fruits. Ariella, please, we've all been looking forward to this for days."

"I'm not going," she insisted. Her face was beginning to turn an angry beet red. "And I can stay by myself. I don't need a babysitter!"

Efraim telephoned just then. "I'll be home soon to pick up some papers that I need for a meeting this evening."

"OK, but we're going out. Remember, tonight's Leah's engagement party."

"Right, I almost forgot. Well, have fun," he said.

"Ariella's really upset about something and now she doesn't want to come." Without meaning to, I thought out loud, "Should I just leave her home?"

"Well, I'll be home soon," he responded quickly, "and I'll stay with her."

"I thought you have to go somewhere."

"That can wait," he offered generously. "Don't worry. Take the others and have a good time."

Everyone was waiting impatiently at the door, I felt torn wondering what was bothering her so much and concerned about whether Efraim would really come home right away. And if so, would he stay? Would he leave her or take her with him? *Which was worse?* I did a quick calculation. *We'd be gone about three hours, and she would probably fall asleep soon.*

"Ima, we'll be late if we don't go now. The bus is coming in two minutes." Dovy impatiently checked his watch.

"Everyone have your sweaters? It's chilly out." I called out as I grabbed mine, making a firm mental note to talk with Ariella tomorrow.

"Yes, Ima," Dovy answered after making a quick visual check. "Please hurry."

"I'm sorry Ariella, that you're not coming," I said. "You can still change your mind."

But as she burrowed deeper into the chair, avoiding my kiss on her cheek, the others marched out the door. "See you later, honey," I said. I flashed her a smile as I ambivalently followed them out.

When Efraim walked in two hours later, carrying pizza and soda, he found her curled up and weeping. "Hi, sweetie," he chimed.

Ariella didn't want to look at him.

"Hey, you're my special girl. Abba loves you more than anyone." Pushing her gently to the side of the chair, he squeezed himself in next to her. "Maybe no one else will ever appreciate you enough," Efraim said softly, "but I always will."

Ten-year-old Ariella peered through her tears at her father.

"Why didn't you take me with you today like you sometimes do?" she pouted.

"I wanted to, sweetie, but I couldn't today. I had to talk to some people who were in big trouble, and they don't have an *abba* or anyone else to help them."

"Like Mona?" she whimpered.

"What?" Tensing, he turned toward Ariella.

"I saw you were going back to Mona's house. Why do you always have to help her?"

Efraim answered smoothly, "Mona is also a *bat Yisrael* who needs help. Hashem wants your *abba* to help a lot of people that no one else can."

When Ariella glanced into his soft blue eyes, she knew she had the best *abba* any girl could ever have. Gradually, she stopped crying.

"Hey, you must be hungry." Efraim opened the box of cold pizza. There were two slices left. He warmed them up in the toaster oven and gave them to her on a plate.

"Did you eat, Abba?" Ariella asked considerately.

"Yeah, I ate earlier. Where do you think all the pizza went?" he grinned.

She gobbled her late dinner. After wiping her lips and *bentching*, Abba called her again to sit with him. "How about if I tell you a story?"

He dimmed the lights, and she cuddled close to him. He put his arm around her shoulders, so she felt safe and protected. As he spoke in his soft voice, the day's tensions dissolved, together with her anger at him for not coming home earlier. She began to get drowsy.

"Sweetie, you know how much I love you," he said. He paused, lowering his voice even more. "And honey, if you see me going to help people, Mona or anyone else, you don't have to tell anyone. It will just upset Ima if you tell her. Lots of people, even Ima, can't understand how important my work is."

Standing, he brought his face close to hers, while gently running his fingers over her hair, and whispered, "And I'll take you with me more often, so we can spend lots more time together." He hesitated for a moment. "But Ima won't like that I'm letting you miss school. Hmm," he chuckled, "so I guess we won't tell her that either. It will be our secret." He patted her warm cheeks, as she began to doze off. "Deal?"

For Ariella, it was an injection of pure happiness. She was Abba's favorite after all. "I love you, Abba. I won't tell anyone." *They'd be so jealous if they knew Abba loved me most.* He covered her with a warm blanket and shut off the telephone ringer.

Ariella finished her story here, but Shmueli mentioned the rest of it to Dovy.

That evening, after they'd gone for pizza, Mona and Shmueli waited for Efraim at their apartment. They were celebrating Shmueli's birthday. Efraim slipped out to bring the gift-wrapped professional basketball he had hidden in the back of his closet, the birthday present he had forgotten.

Since they couldn't continue the party without him, Efraim had to return as soon as possible. Abba told them his lateness was because one of the kids was sick, and of course, he had to be there for her.

Ariella continued to spill her guts, sometimes defiant, sometimes crying, as she described their arrangement.

After Abba accompanied the younger kids, he would leave Ariella and Kayla at the gate of their schoolyard. As soon as he turned to leave, the two sisters continued in together. Ariella would dawdle and soon fell behind Kayla, who walked slowly to where her classmates jumped rope or chatted in small groups. Kayla did not notice Ariella was no longer with her.

When Kayla met her classmates, Ariella returned to her father, who waited in a taxi. She checked to see she wasn't being watched and slipped into the backseat wearing a broad grin. She felt happy beyond words.

Abba is taking me with him. He really loves me the most. She melted into the seat as they sped off; it didn't matter to where. *They were walking along a stream bordered by colorful wildflowers. Ariella skipped along, without a worry or a care in the world. She was free. Bending to pick up a beautiful pink cyclamen she felt like a princess. "Abba, come see," she called out. Her tall, loving dad walked quickly toward her. As she held up her find, he lifted her up in his powerful arms and spun around with her. She giggled and giggled...*

"Ariella!"

"Yes, Abba," she answered dreamily.

"Ariella, let's go. We're here." Abba was opening the door. She didn't remember that they had driven anywhere at all.

"Where are we?" She hoped to see a park, maybe a picnic bench. She hoped he would take her to some pretty area, where they could just be together. Looking up at the tall building with laundry hanging outside each window, she repeated, "Where are we?"

"Come on, sweetie, you're going to meet some people I help." Leaning into the open passenger side window, he paid the taxi driver as he quickly finished his story. "That girl that I got away from her Arab boyfriend is now married to a Jewish guy. They have two kids and they're religious."

The driver nodded enthusiastically, "*Gever, tzaddik.* May there be many more like you among the Jewish nation." The driver thrust out his hand to shake the hand of this amazing man.

Ariella tingled with pride that her *abba* was such a hero to so many people. She stood on the sidewalk, waiting. Hurrying up the front steps of the old tenement building, they stopped at the elevator. Efraim pushed hard on the metallic button, but there was no response. "This elevator never works," he muttered. "Come on."

They walked up six flights of littered, stinking steps. *It smells like someone went to the bathroom here,* Ariella thought, as she held her nose. Large black graffiti jumped into her view.

"Abba, where are you?" she called, panting as she raced up the steps to keep up with his long strides.

She ran frantically, afraid to lose him. As they passed the fourth floor, she heard a woman screaming, "*Tafsik, tafsik,* stop it!" Ariella's eyes widened as she heard something crashing, like a large, heavy glass. *"Tafsik!"* came the angry scream again. But "it" didn't stop. Resounding slapping sounds, like a hand slamming onto flesh, were followed by louder screams, this time without words. "Aiyyyyy! Aiyyyyy!"

Ariella shivered, "Abba, wait for me. Abba!" she heard herself screaming. Efraim came back toward her with a smirk, "That's nothing. Soon someone will call the police and then you'll hear even more yelling."

Now a man's husky voice bellowed, "I'll teach you to respect me!"

As they reached the sixth floor, Ariella became more frightened. The stink here was worse. A man lying on the landing at the top of the stairs rolled over holding his stomach. He was moaning and groaning and appeared to be in a lot of pain.

As Ariella ended her harrowing epic saga at our family gathering, she seemed to be reliving it.

"Ima, I was so scared." Her silence gave way to heavy sobbing. "I thought Abba was taking me to someplace fun, but it was ugly and stinky. Everyone there was crazy and screaming." She stopped to catch her breath.

Thoughtfully, Benny ran to bring a roll of tissues.

"I think that man was beating up that lady," she said. Her eyes narrowed, unbelieving.

"Yeah, but I'll bet our brave Abba didn't try to save her," Dovy said. He sat across from me, his fists clenched. I had never seen him so livid. He looked like he could kill. "I know exactly where he took you. He used to take me to this drug addict's disgusting apartment." Dovy tensed. "When I told him we should call a social worker or the police, he screamed at me. 'They only want to arrest him. I'm the only one who can help! You keep your mouth shut!'"

I suddenly felt excruciating pain in my stomach and shoulder. My throat felt like it was closing. *Did Efraim have to bring this innocent, sensitive eight-year-old and a young yeshiva boy to such despicable places to meet his drug-dealing partners? In his sick imagination, did he really think they would applaud his "heroic" counseling?*

"Abba wanted to spend time with me. Abba loves me," Ariella insisted, but her protests slowly turned to grief.

He tormented her beautiful spirit!

I wanted to hold her, but her rigid body refused comfort. She looked so fragile. I was afraid she might break if I pulled her into my arms. *Really a daddy's little girl. She would thrive with a healthy, loving father. Where does one find a substitute for an abba's love,* I sighed, *or a replacement for a broken heart?*

SIXTY

OVY SEEMED DESTINED TO be a *talmid chacham*. He was our logical, well-organized, clear-minded first born. Years ago, the plans for his bar mitzvah fell into place naturally. He knew exactly with whom he wanted to prepare his Torah portion and he wrote and edited his own speech until it was perfect — down to the thank-you segment. His rabbi recommended a scribe who wrote the *tefillin* parchments with fear of God and great accuracy.

Six months before his bar mitzvah, Dovy insisted his father accompany him order *tefillin*. It took two months of unswerving perseverance, but it was worth it. Efraim gave the down payment and then the process of writing his *tefillin* began. According to Dovy's *rav*, a bar mitzvah is not a wedding. He encouraged the boys to make a modest party with the emphasis on "the *mitzva* and not the bar."

I rented the local shul hall, and Dovy invited his rabbis and classmates, plus a few neighborhood friends. I prepared the celebration feast, as effortlessly as I prepared for Shabbat each week. It had gone so smoothly that I was caught by surprise when it came time to organize Yair's big day.

It was important that Yair's bar mitzvah leave a positive impression. He flitted around *talmud Torahs* like a butterfly among the wildflowers. He could taste and enjoy, but he couldn't stay at one for more than a fleeting visit.

I wanted this celebration of his manhood to leave a sweet taste. I didn't see how dinner in a standard *simcha* hall, even an elaborate one, would leave any long-lasting desire to strengthen his *Yiddishkeit*.

We needed to create memories that will have meaning for him one day — if he ever decides to transform from an immature child to a responsible adult.

At thirteen, the spirit of conscientiousness is supposed to descend. I tried to think where we could observe his big day that would enrich the meaning for him. In my imagination, I visualized a giant soccer field. Instead of dirt and grass, I saw a huge magnet covering the ground with angels of consciousness sticking fast, even as Yair wished them away.

"Where do they have fields like that?" I laughed aloud.

The next moment, in a spark of inspiration, the *Me'arat Hamachpeila*, the Tomb of the Patriarchs in Chevron, came to mind. After several phone calls, it was confirmed that the room of Avraham and Sarah was available for the Torah reading on Yair's bar mitzvah day, and the *simcha* hall next door was available for the celebration meal.

Over the next few days, I made an effort to get everyone excited. "Just imagine, all the *Avot* and *Imahot* will be present at Yair's bar mitzvah in Chevron!" Efraim didn't seem to care either way, but at least he didn't negate the idea. Yair was unconvinced, but he was willing to go along with me.

Now I had to deal with my incongruent feelings. I very much wanted Yair to know that he was much more important than the discrepancies that divided our family. Yet part of me was furious that Efraim did not offer to share the preparations for our son's landmark day. I would have to tend to all the arrangements, including Yair's Torah reading lessons, acquiring the *tefillin*, invitations, *benchers*, and preparing the food.

I had ordered the *tefillin* months ago. Since I could not know whether Efraim would pay for them, I saved every shekel and borrowed money from a neighborhood *gemach* to buy a good set. Surprisingly, the day before Yair would wear them for the first time, Efraim handed me the full amount in cash.

I supposed I should be grateful, so why am I fuming that he waited for the last minute? Couldn't he have said he'd arrange the payments before I raced around anxiously trying to scrounge the money?

My exasperation peaked when Efraim secretly took the precious *tefillin* from my drawer. With many tears and a heartfelt prayer, I had enclosed them in the blue velvet bag embroidered with outlines of Jerusalem's classic arched homes. *Yair had chosen well.* In addition, I had bought him a new *siddur* with his name engraved in gold letters.

Please, son, let these become your closest treasures. When you wear the tefillin *and* daven *from this* siddur, *may you always sense Hashem's Presence and compassion.*

When Yair was little, I thought he might become like the Ba'al Shem Tov. Now I just prayed he would keep his own name good. And I hoped he would know that I believed in him.

As I walked into Yair's room, folded clothes piled high in my arms, Efraim was holding the familiar package in his hands.

"*B'ni*, my son, I'm giving you your first *tefillin*, which are the key to your becoming a man. Treat them like gold, or," he quipped, "at least like your most prized soccer equipment." Without a glance or a word to me, Efraim dramatically handed Yair the wrapped treasure.

"What? What just happened?" My jaw dropped. The look, the hug, the words I had wanted to offer my mischievous son when we would present him with his *tefillin* blanked out.

Another betrayal. *How can I spoil this moment for my son? Was he not already challenged by the learning and requirements of a Torah life? And by our dysfunctional family? Should I turn this moment of awarding the* tefillin, *which should have been a joyful family occasion, into a furious attack on his father?*

Struggling to hold back angry tears, I placed the clothes on the desk and hugged him, wordlessly, hoping he would write the emotions off to sentimentality about his bar mitzvah.

"Thanks Abba, Ima, I'll try to make you proud." With raised eyebrows and a mischievous smile, he held the *tefillin* thoughtfully for a moment, before tossing them lightly on the bed. "Really, I will," he nodded his head, trying to appear serious.

I had a vague awareness of being watched. Without ever speaking to me directly, Efraim seemed to know my plans exactly. In his short visits home, he would take each child aside for a personal "heart to heart" talk. *A kid wants to tell his dad what's happening in his life.* He seemed to be wringing the information from them, bypassing any need to confer with me. Shrugging my shoulders, numbly, I realized he's been doing that for most of our married life. Why should I expect anything different now?

⁙

Looking out the window at the black winter clouds that had been accumilating for days, I gathered my checkbook, keys, and the draft I'd written for the invitations. All week, Yair had been excited, knowing we'd be choosing the cards soon — and today was the day.

Unable to take all of the kids and concentrate properly, I suggested that Yair ask one sibling to join us. Ariella was the lucky one. As we hurried to get ready to leave, the clouds delivered their promised rains at last.

Of all days to traipse around looking for the invitations. "The bus to Jerusalem is coming in seven minutes, kids. Get your boots and hats."

"I'm glad you'll all stay dry," I said to the remaining gang. They were disappointed they would not be coming to choose invitations.

Watching the downpour increase its fury, I reconsidered my plans. Suddenly a taxi, windshield wipers flapping furiously, pulled up. The passenger side window rolled down and Efraim motioned that we get into the cab. "Come on," he mouthed, his voice drowned out by the thunderous claps.

That morning, he knew we were going shopping for the invitations but said nothing of joining us. Why is everything so frustrating?

"We were going to take the bus," I yelled back inaudibly, "but I changed my..."

Observing the heavy raindrops, Yair took one look at his *abba* waving his arms and bounced out the door and into the car. Ariella must have assumed that Yair had received my approval and dashed into the storm to join him in the back seat. *If I don't go, he might go and formulate something foolish. Who knows what will happen?*

Defeated, I pulled on my warmest scarf and crawled into the car next to Ariella.

"So, where are we going?" Efraim asked jovially. "Did you decide the best place to have the invitations made for our bar mitzvah boy's big day?"

The taxi driver, Shlomo, was tensely wiping the mist from the inside of the window, even as the defogger worked full blast.

"Meah She'arim," I answered flatly, "but I'd rather not go in this weather. It's not an emergency that it has to be done today."

Efraim was nodding to the driver, "Let's go."

"The invitations can wait for another day. The printer may even close early in this kind of storm," I repeated, waving my hand to indicate to the kids that they should follow me out of the car. I leaned forward, to make sure my voice could be heard,

"Driver, *rak rega*, wait a minute, we're..."

"*Ya'ala*, let's go," Efraim finished the sentence.

"I said it's not..." I began again.

"And I said we're going." Efraim turned in the direction of the driver. In an exaggeratedly patient voice Efraim explained the predicament to him in Hebrew, "Shlomo, I postponed some important meetings to help organize our son's bar mitzvah preparations. Let's go!"

Twisting around to face me directly, with a stare icier than the hefty hailstones now hammering on the car, he screwed up his mouth, signaling that I shut mine.

Slinking down into the seat, searing humiliation numbed me. I knew everything, yet it still paralyzed me. Inwardly I convinced myself — *not in front of the kids, hold it in. Don't turn this into an outing of despair.* Staring silently at the frosted windows, I begged God to stop the tears in their ducts. *It's enough that the heavens have opened wide. Please leave me some remnant of pride.*

"Hey, that rhymes," commented the internal joker who arrived just in time to push me back from the towering precipice I imagined jumping from.

I rise, I fall, I rise, I fall. Every attempt to face him leaves me weaker.

Yair was animatedly describing a new soccer play to his attentive father. They bantered about some big game.

"Do you really think you'll know the *parsha* by your bar mitzvah?"

Ariella teased Yair, giggling. "Why don't you read out the names of famous soccer players instead of the Torah portion?"

Digging into my purse, I searched for some tissues to wipe the tears now escaping onto my cheeks. Facing the rain-stained window, I saw a mirror image, minus the face.

The normally two-hour ride into Jerusalem took much longer. We passed cars sliding without control. There were several accidents. A few cars stopped with their blinking emergency lights barely discernible. Visibility was almost nil, and I worried whether the taxi's brakes would hold.

As we slowly climbed the hill toward Jerusalem, I berated myself mercilessly. *Again, you gave in, you idiot. Can't you ever just say no? We may get killed for your cowardice.*

"Is it any wonder he kicks you like a dog? You let him do it," blasted the dragon in my head. His flames seared my nerves to ashes.

Navigating the narrow and now flooded one-way street into Meah She'arim was a nightmare. One of the few pedestrians who dared venture out darted in front of the taxi just as it pulled up meters away from the small print shop.

Blowing out in relief, I reminded the kids to pull their coats closed. In the few minutes it took to exit the cab and enter the print shop, they got drenched anyway.

Apparently, we were the only actual clients, although several locals had entered the small shop to escape the storm.

Shlomo, the driver, entered soon after we did. Several small coil wire heaters took the chill out of the air, but the bitter cold was seeping into my bones. I wondered if the kids would get sick. *I hope he does!* I couldn't help thinking, glaring at Efraim who was zealously writing something on a sheet of smudged paper he had picked up from the floor.

Removing our wet coats, we stood drying our hands near the heater for a few minutes, exchanging comments about the weather with refugees from the storm. The owner was only too happy to show us the bar mitzvah invitation designs. He had no doubt despaired of having any clients today.

Yair and Ariella playfully commented on the pros and cons of the pages they flipped through as I placed markers on the ones I preferred. We discussed the colors of the paper and text and chose a symbolic picture of *tefillin*. I glared at Efraim, who appeared oblivious. He was concentrating on writing on the dirty page and speaking on the phone.

The moment I pulled a sheet out of my pocketbook, he closed the phone, folded the paper and joined us.

As I showed the page to the graphic artist with the names and wording I selected, Efraim leaned over, scooping it from my hand. He closely scrutinized the draft, comparing it to the sheet he was holding in his hand — and the mystery was solved.

He's making sure I wrote our names as "Rabbi Efraim and Shifra Baumen" on the same line, and not separately, as a divorced couple would. He needed to see the word Rabbi. That is what he was worried about. First, he does nothing, leaving everything up to me. Then, instead of asking me or discussing it, he orchestrated this wild and reckless trip to find out what I would write. He's sick. He can never ask, only control.

Shaking my head in frustration, I fantasized about the day we would separate our names and our lives. It pained me that it hadn't hapened yet.

After rereading it thoroughly, he grinned, handing it to the graphic artist. To me he said, "Hurry up, the driver's still waiting," as he pointed to the man who sat cozily in front of the heater, getting paid to warm his hands.

"Let him wait," I remarked dully, as I finished signing the checks and handed them to the secretary. The rain was letting up, and those who sought shelter began to disperse. Yair and Ariella kept themselves occupied watching the printing presses roll off a variety of posters and invitations.

When we were finally finished, we walked into a light shower. Efraim kissed the kids and complimented Yair. "You chose a really cool card. I can't wait to get one," he winked good-naturedly.

Dear fun Dad. Too bad I didn't do anything worth complimenting.

Efraim walked with the driver. At the car, they shook hands heartily. Pressing a folded bill into his hand, Efraim slapped Shlomo on the back. "*Achi,* my brother," he said, "get them home safe and sound."

Efraim called out to me, "I'll try to be home early. Bye."

I lifted my head but could not complete the nod. He would not be home early. *Hopefully, he won't come at all.* A chill went through me as I sneezed in rapid succession.

Shlomo praised Efraim as he drove, "There aren't a lot of men like your husband. He gives all his life for the good of *Am Yisrael.*"

"Just get us home," I muttered, mostly to myself. "*Dai!* Enough!" I just wanted to drink some hot tea with lemon and honey and crawl into bed.

Sixty-one

THE FAMILY SAT ALONE, sullenly, around the Shabbat table. There were no guests.

With his hands waving dramatically, Efraim talked incessantly about the Jewish youth he was saving. In repetitive detail, he described cult and drug subcultures he infiltrated during his recent rescue operations. He left no spaces for comment or discussion.

Sweet Batya pulled up a chair next to me and wearily laid her head on my lap. Was she exhausted by this whirlwind, or did she just seem to know when it was a good time to nap? I ran my hand slowly through her wavy hair. My fingers kissed her soft cheeks. She soon closed her eyes, sighing herself to sleep.

"Stop now, please. We've heard all of this, many times." I don't know why I bothered; I knew he'd continue.

He persisted. "I literally pulled this guy off the ledge." Efraim's voice rose dramatically as he continued, "Stupid kid, taking drugs. He really believed no one appreciated him or would care if he lived or died." He glanced at the kids, to see that all eyes were on him. His reenactment of the scene became more dramatic as he left the table and moved toward the window. "He wouldn't listen to me."

Efraim, catching his breath, opened our window and thrust his hands out of it. "I grabbed him by the pants and shirt and pulled him inside. We both fell on the floor," he said as he dropped down onto the rug next to the table and rolled to his back and then turned onto his knees. "I kept him pinned down until some of my guys who were with me came to hold him down. I told him he's my brother."

239

Standing, he bent and moved right into Ariella's face, forcing eye contact. "I said 'I love you. You're an important part of my life.'" He quoted himself, with my frightened daughter now the object of the emotional barrage. He rolled his shoulders back impressively, as if to add height to his swelled ego, and clenched his fist victoriously.

He knows exactly what she's longing to hear. You cruel mamzer! *Why can't you just tell your daughter that you love her — without your sick theatrics?* Ariella quickly laid her head on her folded hands.

The names, locations, and reasons for the suicide attempts changed, but Efraim's heroics and the positive outcome always remained the same.

I grimaced, unable to tolerate another self-aggrandizing exaggeration. "Enough! Move away from her!" I shrieked, feeling all sense of self-control slipping away from me. "Stop talking about this — and stop lying. And stop telling the kids to lie to me!"

It was clearly another fabrication. I looked at the startled faces of Ariella and Benny. He had leaned forward protectively to put his arm on hers as she tried to pull back from her father's wild stare.

Dovy focused his eyes sharply on mine, clenching his fists. I could see he was struggling like a warrior to restrain himself. Kayla began to cry. I held Batya close, hoping she wouldn't awaken just yet. Efraim took a quick look around trying to regain his audience. He turned to Yair, who remained unusually silent.

"Listen to this." In a moment he turned the intrigue and thrills of his rescue activities into a *d'var Torah*. "When Avraham Avinu learned that Lot had been kidnapped," he continued as though this was his main point, "he gathered his guys, all the souls he had made, to rescue Lot."

I felt my skin crawl. *What was wrong here? Would he never stop?*

"I don't want to hear anymore."

I began to shake, feeling I might burst.

His retort came rapidly, "So now I can't even say a *d'var Torah* at the Shabbat table. What other evil decrees are you planning? Why don't you just tell us now?" He sat back haughtily in his chair, assuming he'd silence me as he always had. He apparently could not believe the circumstances were changing.

My insides were searing hot and I suffered as though I were being torn apart. For so long, almost a decade, I gallantly, or cowardly perhaps, struggled not to shout in front of the kids. Most of our ruthless confrontations, until this year, had taken place while they were in school or asleep. *What does it matter? They knew most of the disgusting details anyway. They were my sources for much of it!*

"I don't want to hear any more of your fantasies. I don't want to hear your voice at all. You can go now, go to all the places you go after the kids are asleep, or all the warped places you take them to. Just go there now. Go and find yourself a wife who won't make evil decrees for you."

I sat forward, unable to control my shouting. "How much can you hurt all of us — and not care?" For a moment I wondered if my yelling would bring the neighbors or the police, but no one came.

Jumping up again, he was quick to retort, "You're trying to destroy our family's unity. Our good children have a loving father, and you only think about yourself."

How had I ever taken those words to heart and castigated myself for selfish inclinations?

He lowered his voice. *There are clearly too many witnesses around. Efraim destroys his victims best in private encounters.*

As he paused before the next verbal assault, Ariella blurted out, "Give Ima a *get*! Give it to her now!" She was shaking and crying. Benny moved closer to her, as if to shield her.

Efraim lowered his voice again, patiently explaining his legal rights to seek *shalom bayit*. "Maybe *Ima* wants to destroy this family, but I want you to grow up with two parents — not like all the messed-up kids from divorced homes that I have to go around saving. Divorce makes your life a mess. All those kids grow up confused and suicidal."

He seemed to believe every word he uttered. The absurd contradictions made me shiver. He was creating a script for the theater of the irrational and bizarre. Efraim exhibited no fatherly anxiety for his tender daughter who was begging him to divorce her mother.

Benny, in his innocence, asked, "Abba, why don't you save us? Why are you only saving other kids?" My son's sweet purity evoked a suppressed giggle from his father, as if to imply, "What a cute suggestion."

But Efraim displayed no recognition of his son's distress. He offered no affectionate comfort to this young child's very real pain. There was neither an outward compassionate gesture nor a minimal acknowledgment of his internal crisis. I witnessed no rallying attempt to rescue these distressed Jewish children.

I wanted to scream, "You are incapable of loving anyone, even your own offspring," but I was unsure how much of the rug should be pulled out from under such young, tender feet. Certainly, it should not be whisked from beneath them all at once.

I was too exhausted to keep this heated dispute going and worried about its effect on the kids. Was this my old cowardly element? Either way, I decided one parent should maintain a semblance of dignity. That would have to be me.

As if he suddenly realized he stood alone, Efraim raised his voice dramatically, "I would die for my children," he declared. "If anyone tried to hurt you, I would kill them." His incensed stare bore into me. This was not an empty threat.

Dovy, whose newly gained height brought him almost eye to eye with his father, stood up. "Abba, *you* are hurting us." He confronted his father's menacing posture with steady, cool eyes. "All you have to offer is a fantasy world of rescue missions. You either disappear from our lives, or you bring us with you to your corrupt places." His intent gaze remained firm as he hit his fist furiously into his open hand.

Efraim's eyes narrowed. He appeared alarmed that Dovy might go into details.

It was a dare that Dovy, ordinarily so respectful, did not back down from.

"Why do you take us to visit Mona and Shmueli all the time? And then you warn us not to tell Ima. You buy him fancier clothes and games than you ever bought us. Why do you threaten us that if Ima finds out she'll be angry? Why do you bring us there at all?"

Ariella's face was red. "Why does she wear a short nightgown when we're visiting? And then you yell at us to dress modestly, but you don't tell her to do that."

Yair looked hesitantly at me and then turned to his father. "Why did you tell Ima you're taking us to shul and then you bring us to Ilana's house?"

This was a new one. I'd never seen Yair take anything seriously, as he was now. "Ima told you she doesn't want us to go there because Ilana and her friends take drugs." Yair's voice was accusing, angry.

Kayla cringed and shrunk back, the palm of her hand covering part of her face.

Efraim's eyes were now narrowing in Yair's direction. This was clearly a revolution. Yair continued, "And then you tell us, 'Don't tell Ima. Don't tell Ima!' Everywhere you take us, you tell us, 'Don't tell Ima.'" I never heard him so bitter. He was always hiding his emotions behind his mischievous smile.

"You don't want to live with us or for us," I yelled. "Go away and give us some peace. If your concern is really for the kids, then stop teaching them to lie to me, and stop taking them to the homes of your low life, drug-addict friends."

"I won't let you destroy this family," he blasted back. "You'll never see a *get*, even if you turn the kids against me. I have the legal right to be here!"

With his last retort, he must have realized there was nothing to remain for. "There are people who need my help. I have to go...." Eyeing his unfinished dinner, he threw his shoulders back and walked to the door, never ceasing to defend his right to keep the family whole. Almost as a unit, our eyes followed him. He opened the front door, wishing everyone a good Shabbat. "I'll be home late," he reminded me, leaving me trembling in disbelief.

"Don't bother," I retorted.

Benny stammered tearfully, "You forgot to say the blessings after the meal, Abba."

As the door swallowed Efraim's back, a familial sigh of relief was released. Batya chose then to open her eyes. Groggily looking around she asked, "Where's Abba?"

None of us could answer her question, and I didn't care.

Sixty-two

FRAIM OBSTINATELY REFUSED TO give me a writ of divorce. As the monthly trials in *beit din* dragged on, each day became an eternity of unremitting anguish.

During those years, Shabbat prayers, my life-giving reprieve, brought me great peace of mind.

Breathing deeply, slowing down my racing heart, I invited sweet prayers to replace thundering torment. Meditating allowed me to focus on the small voice within. Its reassurance was nearly my sole source of support — that voice and my dear friend Rivka. Her friendship, like a looming light tower in a black night's storm, accompanied me and I clung to her, too much.

Typically, we were the last ones to leave shul after the Shabbat prayers. One morning though, she didn't look up as I left my seat, walking past her. No smile, no supportive nod of her radiant face. She appeared immersed in heartfelt prayer. I waited, but her eyes remained fastened to the *siddur* until I sensed that she was purposefully disregarding me, and I left.

I assumed she might call during the week, as she usually did. When I called, she was atypically rushing and unable to speak.

This became the new ritual. She didn't look up in shul or call me at home. She gave no explanation, and I was too wretched to question, assuming I had no right to expect more. My isolation was complete. The light tower and the life raft disappeared. Only the darkness remained. I felt I would drown.

Inside a black, cavernous hole in my heart that threatened to fill me entirely, there was no one now, except God Himself. *Ain od milvado.*

"God, help me, for Your sake," I cried, "for the beautiful children You gave me. Not because I am worthy, but because You want good, You are kind." Tears streamed freely, and immense heaviness filled my head, arms, and legs. I bowed involuntarily until I fell to my knees. "God, please get out me of this living hell. Please, please help me. Don't leave me like this, please, please God, for the sake of Your Name, for my children, please..." I felt my prayers soaring on the wings of tears. And I began to sense His Presence would stay with me and protect my family and me. I was grateful for this gift and felt humbled by the overwhelming relief I felt in His Presence.

Another year passed without compassionate Rivka to offer her tea and warm, loving hugs. I realized I had unloaded too much of the burden onto her shoulders. Years later, when she would confess her weariness, she told of the details that troubled her sleep, haunting her dreams.

"I was ashamed to tell you, so I lowered my eyes. It was a cowardly escape," she admitted sadly. "Please forgive me," she said, "I didn't want to abandon you. I just didn't know what else I could do."

It really was too much to ask from even so lofty a soul. I comforted her, paraphrasing the words of the biblical Yosef when he was sold by his brothers and went on to become second to Pharaoh in Egypt. He told them, and I repeated to Rivka, "It was not you that sent me away. This was the Hand of God."

I told her, "My prayers changed when I could no longer turn to you." Looking away, I heard the small voice that accompanied me. "You learned to rely on Him, to really know there is no one else but God."

"Mine also did," she admitted, her eyes filling with tears, and we were both silent.

When our eyes met again, for a long, steady moment, I knew she had been an angel for me, even in her pulling back.

SIXTY-THREE

Y BIOLOGICAL CLOCK FORCES my eyes open at the faintest glow of the dawn. I'm grateful for this semi-conscious time, borrowed from sleep hours. I use it to stretch my body and mind, reflecting on my thoughts before the regular daily tasks began. After another humiliating day in the *beit din* yesterday, I brimmed with tension.

Deeply inhaling a supply of strength and confidence, I decisively exhaled anger and fear. In doing so I prepared myself to face another day of life with an abusive, spiteful husband.

Efraim walked in at 6:30 a.m. *He's early today. I didn't suppose he'd show up till closer to seven.* No words were necessary, or exchanged. Ignoring his arrival, I continued the exercise routine. *If the kids don't wake up, I'll still have time to make an entry into my journal.*

These therapeutic morning pages gave direction to the tumultuous thoughts that allowed me no peace. I did not plan the flow; the words directed themselves. As the pen touched the page, my hand wrote automatically. It was amazing what these scribbled sentences described. Even the size, shape, and spacing of the letters and words changed with my emotions.

In the still-reigning silence, I felt that I'd scrawled on the paper for hours, but a glance at the clock showed that only fifteen minutes had passed. I heard the first rumbling sound of children waking but knew that dad would be looking in on the early birds. Feeling spoiled by the thought, I decided to curl up and read what my stream of consciousness had recorded. I read:

Rise up. Rise up. Court's a bad place. Rise up, rise up! Court's a bad place, bad place. They don't move. I'll go to aguna court. Court's a bad place. They are lethargic. They could rule and rule not. What will happen to them in 120 years? They could speak and speak not. Anger, rage, anger, red rage! They sit. They have ears but do not hear. They have no sense. They are confused. They make no sense. I will pray, and God will help me. They give into confusion. Another opening, another chance to stop him hurting my family. They let it pass. They could take his rights, make it hard, keep him away... But Nothing, Nothing.

The large size of the letters was accompanied by heavier, angry-looking lines. Almost a whole page was filled with the word, "Nothing." It was written again and again, each time the pressure on the pen went harder into the paper, here and there almost tearing through the page.

They will be punished — for the mockery of justice. Protect me from contemptuous corruption and courtroom crimes.

Turning toward the door, I checked through blurred vision that I was still alone. Shaking my head to clear my sight, I noticed my cheeks were moist. That's when I realized for the first time that I was crying. The ink on the lined paper was smeared from tears. My nightgown was damp.

My first thought was that Efraim should not gain pleasure from my torment. Throwing the blankets off, they fell to the floor as I rose to lock the door. But just then my sweet Batya entered hastily.

"Ima, I can't find my shoes anywhere." She looked frustrated. "I looked in all the places already." She stopped short when she saw my red eyes. "Ima," she calmed down, "did you lose something too?"

Such sympathetic, brown eyes looked up at me that a smile burst from within. "I'm OK, sweetheart." Laughing now, in the light of her concern, I joked, "I can't find my shoes, either."

Batya took me seriously. Picking up the bulky quilt from the floor, she giggled as she chided me, "Ima, they're right here, under your blanket."

"OK, Batya, you helped me find my shoes. Now I'll help you find yours." Then in sing-song rhythm, I chanted, "My shoes, your shoes, first let's find tissues." Wiping both our noses and drying both our eyes, I was grateful that the day had begun. The loves of my life were already bringing in the sunshine.

Sixty-four

THE ENVELOPE THAT I held in my hand was addressed to "Mr. Dovy and Miss Kayla Baumen." Along with the usual assortment of bills and a notification of termination of electricity because of nonpayment, this piece of mail bore the return address of one of Efraim's closest cronies.

Oren was a self-acclaimed physics genius. His scratchy, erratic handwriting resembled an unsolved mathematical equation. Walking slowly up the few steps to the house, I recalled having read the beginning of one of his books on physics. Titled *Physics in the Light of Creation: Directional Proof of God's Existence*, it was long-winded, grammatically disjointed, and cumbersome. Twelve pages into the introduction, I gave up on the text.

The endorsement on this complex physics discourse was none other than Efraim. This is the man who struggled with the kids' "new math" and elementary algebra. Efraim had put together an impressive essay. I wondered whom he plagiarized in his authoritative physics analysis as a key to the spiritual realm.

I shuddered to remember Oren's slovenly dress and manner and monotonic boorish style of speech. He overstepped personal boundaries consistently in the course of conversations. On more than one occasion, I found myself stepping back as his face came within inches of mine.

Oren was divorced from his wife, who was raising their four young children alone. The thought of his trying to manipulate my kids gave me the creeps. *What on earth... Why is he writing to my kids?* I intercepted this piece of correspondence.

"Dear Dovy and Kayla," it began, "Because you are the two oldest, I am writing to you. I think you might have the most influence on the others..."

In the course of several typewritten paragraphs, he repeatedly excused himself for writing to them, and he repetitiously explained why he was doing so. With an asterisk marking the beginning of each sentence he listed his relationship with various extended members of Efraim's family and with Efraim's closest friend, Rafi. He even mentioned that he had "known and respected" me for a long time. *How endearing.*

He continued, "In this letter, I will try to tell you why I think your parents' divorce would be a bad thing, how I know the false rumors spoken about your father are untrue, why your father is a good man, and why you should respect him."

A wave of nausea overcame me.

Oren claimed that "everything" in his double-spaced, large-font, typewritten pages was "absolutely true" and he'd be willing to go to court to testify so. *Who's asking him to be a witness?*

The telephone's loud ringing brought me back to the open front door of my living room where I stood, holding the papers and mailbox keys. Pushing the door shut with my foot, I lifted the receiver.

The local representative of the women's *chessed* committee was calling to request that I prepare a meal for a family with a new baby. Jotting down the pertinent information on my calendar, I thanked her. She laughed, saying, "It's a mutual appreciation society" before we hung up.

Mutual appreciation can be for good ... I thought of Efraim's scheming relationships with his comrades... *or not.*

Settling at the kitchen table, I poured all the leftover cereal and milk into one bowl, absentmindedly picked up the closest spoon, and continued reading about Oren's divorce. "Unlike my own situation," he added, "your father and mother get along in most things, as far as I know. They seem to fit together. They have similar beliefs and lifestyles. If you can influence them to stay together, then you should do so."

"What chutzpa!" I dropped the spoon, screaming, "Did he ever once ask me?" My thoughts raced. *What right does he have to butt in? How dare he try to persuade my kids!* I was furious.

"When people get divorced, the father often has less contact with the kids, or he loses it altogether," the letter went on.

How dare he? my thoughts echoed. *Efraim's lack of connection with his family is compelling this divorce.*

I could imagine Efraim, Oren, and probably Rafi as well, brainstorming on how to best influence the kids.

Oren wrote, "When good people do great things, someone inevitably finds fault and says bad things about them." He gave a number of examples that were so vague, he may as well have not written them. "The same thing happened to me," he concluded.

Of course, two peas in a tzaddik's pod.

Over the course of two pages, he quoted the Jewish laws of respecting and obeying one's parents. He listed the laws of caution concerning *lashon hara*, especially toward a father.

The lengthy composition ended with, "The Torah does not want a man to get divorced from his wife. It wants the family to stay together. We should keep the Torah. It is better for your parents to stay together. You should do whatever you can to help them to do so."

Angrily I threw the pages on the floor, and stamped on them, digging the heels of my shoes into them. I considered ripping them to shreds but decided to consult with Suri. Perhaps this could be useful to my case.

Pulling Oren's unread book off the shelf where it had gathered much dust, I turned to the phone number that he had stamped into it. My fingers raced over the face of the phone, pressing the wrong numbers. I tried to control the volcanic anger erupting in my brain. At last, I demanded that my shaking hand obey and press the numbers correctly. I tried to concentrate.

As the phone rang, the voice of cowardice asked, *What will you say? Anyway, he won't listen to you!* I slammed down hard on the table with the back of the tablespoon I was pressing into my palm.

"Shut up!" I shrieked to that unacceptable voice of pessimism just as someone lifted the receiver.

"Oren here," he answered.

"This is Shifra," I began.

"Shif-ra." He pronounced it slowly, phonetically, as though deciding what to say next. "How — are — you?" he drawled his concern.

"Don't write to my kids, don't talk to them, and don't bother them. Don't try to manipulate them. And don't ever try to contact them again. Do you understand me?" The words rushed angrily on their own.

Suddenly I imagined him, on the other end of the line, looking at Efraim, confused. I could almost see him shrugging his shoulders, as if asking silently, *what should I say now?*

In that moment of his hesitation, imagining his helplessness made me feel a fragment less impotent. Despite my bitterness and distress, I grinned. *Idiot. Just like Efraim.*

SIXTY-FIVE

EFRAIM'S REPEATED APPEAL FOR *shalom bayit* was finally referred to the higher court of the *beit din*. The Chief Rabbi of Israel appeared at its head.

After skimming the voluminous file, he asked Efraim to explain what he wanted.

Efraim explained how his poor children suffered from the tragic court battle their mother insisted on.

"I am trying," he said with a well-controlled voice pattern, "to be a better husband and a better father." He straightened his jacket collar, patting down the front of his white shirt, and checked that his worn black hat sat correctly.

"It's not right that our family should be destroyed by divorce. I ask the revered rabbis to encourage my wife to continue our counseling, which I believe was starting to help us clarify our differences. Your honor, I want her to give *shalom bayit* one more chance." His voice lingered between a whine and a plea.

It was hard to read their straight unexpressive faces. The rabbinical judges must have heard those same words many thousands of times. At least they did not appear to be taken in by the sad, puppy dog appearance with which he tried to gain their empathy.

I shuddered. Now they would have to give me an opportunity to respond.

The Chief Rabbi beckoned me to rise. "Do you believe your husband wants *shalom bayit*?"

"Yes, your honor. I believe he does." Suri was visibly taken aback by my response.

Efraim nodded knowingly, the smirk of victory playing at his lips.

"But not with me," I spoke slowly, allowing the significance of the words to penetrate. "If he divorces me, Efraim's girlfriend will expect him to marry her."

I watched their jaws drop, one by one. Now they were responding. And I was ready to be heard.

"Mona is the mother of his son, who's almost the same age as our fourth child."

Efraim held himself stiffly, staring straight ahead. The tension lines around his mouth deepened.

"It is obvious that this divorce will create a dreadful dilemma for him, because she is not a nice person, and there seem to be other women he would prefer to continue his present relationships with."

I paused, not wanting to break the spell.

"Of course, he's desperate for *shalom bayit*, but I am not willing to help him out of his predicament. I don't want his *shalom bayit*!" I choked out. It was suddenly hard to breathe. I was shaking. *This has to be sinking in! They have to realize what this means!*

I heard my voice become weighty and deliberate. My fingers stretched out tensely, as I pleaded. "I want a *get*. I want this madness to end!" Frantically swallowing some air, I begged them. "Please, Your Honors, I have been waiting for four years. Make him give me the *get*!"

With a fleeting look in his direction, I saw the color drain from Efraim's face and his eyes darken with rage.

With his vicious, razor-sharp stare, he attempted to slash away my courage. The daggers that had repeatedly endangered my existence for so long now fell short. They had no effect on me.

As if choreographed in advance, the three *dayanim* of the Superior Court turned as one to Efraim, who was now ashen-faced. The Chief Rabbi sternly told him to go back to the local *beit din* and follow the rabbis' decree, which was to give me a *get*. They were clearly angry and disgusted with him for having even made an appeal to appear before them.

This was the first crack in the fortified wall of Efraim's humongous ego. He stammered something in self-defense as he picked up his large *Gemara* and checked the tilt of his courtroom black hat. As the rabbis turned to leave the courtroom, he stopped sputtering. Instead, he shot daggers from his eyes in my direction. Again they fell short. I shrugged my shoulders at his sorry threats, which no longer rattled or confused me.

Making one last attempt to antagonize, he warned Suri, "She'll never get the kids, the house, or any money. You're wasting your time because I'm not going to give her a divorce. I'll fight for *shalom bayit.*"

"Right," she retorted sarcastically, "you're doing everything you can to make a wonderful marriage."

As he walked to the door, he smiled derisively at me, "See you at home, Shifra, and stop trying to destroy our family." Neither of us commented on his dramatic exit. There was no sense wasting a breath on a response that would not pierce his thick ego.

After four years in court, I hoped the rabbis of the Superior Court would put more pressure on him, twisting his arms, or his neck.

"They didn't push me into another useless round of counseling, but they stuck me back into the holding pen. Nothing really happened." I protested to Suri as we left the courtroom.

"Shifra," Suri answered rationally, "they shattered his monstrous ego. He's used to getting away with everything — and it was obvious that they didn't believe a word he said."

Logically she was correct, but my patience was worn out. "I'm getting tired of these meetings that lead nowhere, and I'm taking your time for which I can't even pay."

She interjected, "You may as well stop here, Shifra. You're not getting rid of me, not until you have your *get*. We'll come back as long as it's necessary." She twirled her pen thoughtfully. "Soon, you should qualify for the *aguna* court that's just being established and should be up and running in another year or two.

Historically, the term *aguna* referred to a woman whose husband disappeared. Without proof of his death, she might assume he was deceased, but she remained technically married. This state of limbo once described the *aguna*, who was unable to remarry until witnesses or evidence became accessible. Such situations frequently occurred during wars or long journeys, often by sea.

Today the term includes many husbands whose whereabouts are known, but they refuse to give their wives the letter of divorce. Sometimes they want to cruelly punish or threaten their spouses. Or they may like the showcase look of "being proper family men," even as their actions are anything but appropriate. Occasionally the men are mentally ill.

In response to the hundreds of women in Israel waiting five or more years for a get, a new rabbinical court for these suffering women was being established. This *beit din* would be empowered to use harsher measures to compel the recalcitrant husband to grant his wife the writ of divorce. These judges would freeze bank accounts, checks, and credit cards. They could confiscate driver's licenses and gun permits. They would be able to prohibit the husband from going into his home or contacting his children. He could be jailed, where he could be prohibited from having his *tallit*, *tefillin*, *siddur*, or any religious study books.

Suri reminded me that there are also many women who refuse to accept a writ of divorce from their husbands. "There are also many abusive wives in the world."

I looked at her. "How is that relevant to me?"

"It's not, and no implication meant. I just thought of this guy I'm trying to help, whose wife reminds me a lot of Efraim." She grimaced. "Maybe we should set them up."

"Right, that would be true justice," I shot back. "So, only another year or two for the *aguna* courts to get set up, huh? I'm moving up a notch. You really know how to comfort the forlorn, thanks."

But I refused to give in to the all too familiar despair. *I will not return to that mindset.* At that moment I was rewarded with a fresh idea.

"Next time, after the judges do nothing—and tell us to go out and come back again in a month, I'm not leaving. I'll sit there until they force him to give me that coveted piece of paper, or they can call the cops and throw me out. Listen, Suri, you leave. I don't want you losing your license," I said, grinning solicitously.

"You can't do that because I need you!"

Her face contorted into something between a scowl and a sour smile.

"OK, so I'm being selfish," I agreed. "But really, you leave and I'm going for a showdown."

My rabbinical court representative looked thoughtful and then nodded roguishly, "If you're up to it, go right ahead."

Weeks passed, and sure enough, at the next legal encounter, the plot and its last scene remained the same.

"OK, I'll give her a divorce," he was saying, "even though I really want *shalom bayit*."

He's destroyed the majestic beauty inherent in that phrase.

"But if that's what she really wants…" he continued according to the familiar script.

"Of course, our children will remain with me, in the house," he was saying as the judge on the right rolled his eyes heavenward. Today only two rabbinical judges of the required three were present so they could not render a legal decision even if Efraim agreed.

They encouraged him to reconsider, insisting that small children need to be with their mother. Efraim claimed he could take much better care of them. Whether they thought it futile, had no patience, or didn't care was unclear.

Either way, they didn't refute his statements or insist that he cooperate. Once again, they ordered us to return in six weeks. Efraim picked up his familiar large *Gemara* and bowing his broad-brimmed hat to their elevated seats, walked out. He had paid his monthly dues and was off on his latest adventures.

Nodding goodbye to Suri as she unhurriedly left the room, I remained seated, though the judge repeated that I was dismissed. The male secretary taking notes echoed the judge's words. He added sternly, "If you don't leave, a security guard will be called to escort you from the room."

"I'm not leaving without a proper judgment forcing him to grant me the divorce," I spoke up surprisingly calm. The taller of the judges explained that with only two present there was little they could do.

"Even when there are three judges in court nothing is done. So what's the purpose of meeting with only two?" I snapped back disrespectfully.

In response, the judges rose and left. *Great timing, Shifra. They're going for lunch and you'll be warming the chair while missing your own midday meal.* As I considered what might happen next, the door of the judge's chambers opened. The taller one whom I thought had occasionally displayed a bit more empathy, though I could not tell how much, returned to collect some files. He appeared slightly less formidable now. "We already issued a ruling, *chayav get*, that he should give you a divorce. Be patient, he'll give it to you," was all he offered. As he turned to leave, he insisted again that I vacate the courtroom.

"The ruling was not properly recorded," I told him, which got his attention.

More than occasionally, words or sentences were omitted. After careful perusal, Suri had been stunned to verify just a few days ago that the issuance of "*chayav get*" was not written clearly and therefore was never properly recorded. I think she wanted to wait until the full court of three judges were present to make the announcement. I also wondered if anyone took the protocols seriously.

Still in his long, black judge's robe, his typically stern appearance altered to a baffled look. He replaced my thick file on the plenum, flipping it open to the page of the court's ruling as recorded in the protocols. After following his finger down the page, he looked at me with furrowed brows over the top of his reading glasses.

"Is your legal representative still present?" he asked briskly.

"I assume she's gone by now, but I will check." I wondered sarcastically if the door would lock as I exited. Suri was sitting in the outer chamber with a cup of coffee, chatting with a colleague.

"What are you doing here?" I whispered with pretend contempt, wagging my finger at her. "I'm so relieved you're still here, thank God." I waved her to come. "The *rav* wants to see you." Both rabbinical representatives raised their eyebrows. I guess they were surprised that a judge would agree to speak with the legal advisor after he dismissed the litigants. *And it's lunchtime.*

I whispered, "He realizes that the judgment was never properly recorded."

On the way in, Suri flipped expertly through the substantial folder that she lugged around with her. During too many years of handling, the name was fading. *Hopefully, it won't be in use much longer.* Suri nodded encouragingly, winking conspiratorially as she approached the bench. Together with the judge, they examined the legal records together. He shook his head, agreeing that this was a terrible omission. "It will be fixed," he promised. "But there is nothing more I can do now. Please go."

"I want more than a *p'sak din* now." Enunciating each word slowly, surprising myself, I said, "Force him. Make him give me a *get*." I hadn't planned to be *so* dramatic, but the crying flew of its own accord. "I can't do this anymore."

Poor judge. I stood to speak to the judge presiding over my case, but in my heart, a prayer was emerging. I shouted to the Heavens, "You have the power to protect the victims and to force a recalcitrant husband to give a get. Use it! For God's sake, force him to give me a divorce!"

Sixty-six

From my journal

For nearly six years, I have been awaiting my divorce.

Two weeks ago, I took a brief break. The specialist I was referred to by my family doctor confirmed my assessment. Something that felt like a baseball had attached itself to my kidney. I knew that serious illnesses were often psychosomatic. Was this the physical outcome of my emotional suffering?

I didn't tell anyone apart from Suri so that she could postpone the court date until I received the medical diagnosis.

For two tense weeks, I took care of the kids, did homework, and prepared meals while I waited for the results of a series of tests. My sense of floating in time and space became exaggerated. For years I have been anxiously anticipating my fate in the courts; now the medical laboratory would also have its say.

What does Hashem want from me? I asked myself over and over again. Surviving and waiting, hoping and praying, I filled my days and penetrated my dreams at night as I tossed restlessly, wondering what else I could do.

Miraculously, despite the surgeon's solemn anticipation, the results verified the baseball's benign intentions. It was a fluid-filled cyst that took up space but was not at all life-threatening.

Deep relief filled me, and I sensed it was a sign.

Hashem wants me to live. He will get me through this.

I called Suri. She was relieved for me and told me we have a new date. "You survived this," she said, "and you're going to go from strength to strength."

For some reason, this time I believed her.

SIXTY-SEVEN

I TOLD VERY FEW PEOPLE about the prolonged battle to receive my *get*. Although we were no longer the renowned *chessed* family inviting lots of guests for Shabbat meals, let alone live-ins, no one seemed to want to break the silence. Maybe they were afraid of what they would find out.

From concerned comments, I gathered that some assumed I was simply burned out from the constant activity. "You look really tired, Shifra," I heard more than once. Maybe they just followed my lead, which was to maintain silence and to get the kids and myself through each day with a semblance of normalcy.

There might have been other speculations, but the laws of guarding their tongues seemed to be strictly enforced by the neighbors. To some extent, I appreciated the privacy, but the loneliness weighed heavily. Together with the responsibility of holding my family together, it froze my shoulders into place — no matter how often I rotated them or stretched. My neck could barely turn left or right, forcing me to only look ahead. I began to feel the cervical vertebrae squeezing out of place. I could massage away the pain for moments at a time, but it always returned.

My friend Simmy was one of the few who knew how profound the chasm ran between Efraim and me. She came by occasionally to cheer me up, usually bringing one or more of her kids.

"How is Lori?" I asked as we sat on the floor next to her newest baby. He was trying to crawl, and she helped push his knees into position.

"She's actually doing quite well," the spark in Simmy's eyes was as bright as ever. "And guess what?"

"She's engaged?" I ventured.

"Almost as good," she teased, giving me a sly wink.

"I need a clue." Trying to sound good-natured, it took too much energy these days to retain a light moment for too long. Involuntarily, I bit down hard on my lip, a habit that seemed impossible for me to break.

Simmy picked up her triumphant baby as he finally managed to crawl toward the toys a few centimeters away from his chubby, groping fingers. "*Yofi*, baby, you did it," she encouraged him with juicy kisses and her natural, hearty laugh.

Almost as an afterthought, she turned to me as she picked herself up to the couch. "She's coming to Israel in three weeks, please God."

I felt embarrassed. *What would I say to her?* Piercing my heavy silence, Simmy went on, "She really wants to see you."

I couldn't answer.

"She knows you didn't know, Shifra. And she wants to know if there is some way she can help." The baby was gurgling happily in his Ima's arms, pulling playfully at her pearl stud earring.

What would I ask her to do? I wondered to myself. *Wash the dishes? Right.*

Absentmindedly I walked into the kitchen and squeezed out a soapy wet sponge into the sink and began to wipe off the breakfast leftovers on the kitchen table.

I calculated quickly. *She must be in her mid-twenties now.* I felt myself shake with resentment. My empty hand rubbed hard at my cheek when I thought of the sweet young girl who had come to learn about Shabbat and Torah. *It's not fair that she was hurt and humiliated like that.*

There was no controlling the tears. I didn't even try. *Anyway, it was only Simmy.*

Sixty-eight

AFTER TALKING OVER THE events of the last *beit din* fiasco and the general events of this past month, I slumped down in the austere black sofa in Suri's office. My teeth sank into my lower lip between the words. "If I don't get the *get* soon, they can just lock me away. Suri, it's been nearly six years. I can't keep doing this. I'm losing it. And I can't keep accepting your help. There's no way I'll ever be able to pay you...."

"Oh, don't get started, Shifra. We have more important things to talk about." She was pacing the room, stopping at the large window as if some answers were there, just outside the pane.

My head pounded and boiling blood raced to my face in response to her offensive comment. *You too, Suri? Do I do something to attract nasty comments?* I felt like digging a hole into her expensive designer couch with my fingers, but didn't. In the silence, I wanted revenge, bloody and final — against my brother, my parents, Efraim, Oren, even Rivka, everyone who had ever hurt or humiliated me. I felt a tsunami of self-pity wash over me, followed by raging anger. It was true. You could "see red."

Was it a few seconds or a few minutes later that I blinked myself out of that semi-trancelike state?

Suri was staring at a dove on the outer windowsill. She probably didn't notice my exit from or my reentry into the present.

Snapping her fingers, she spun toward me. "What did you just tell me? This Lori is coming to Israel?" She nodded her head, and I watched the dangling amethyst-beaded, silver earrings brush her neck. "Yes! That may be it. That may be what breaks him."

I waited for the fog to lift from my mind. "Spell it out, Suri."

"We'll subpoena her to appear as a witness. Until now, he's brought character references that testify to his saintly character." She grimaced and paused, rubbing her slender fingers against each other. "Lori will paint a very different picture—one Efraim won't want anyone to see."

"I hate to bring her into this mess."

"Shifra, it will probably be a healing closure for her. And she said she wants to help." She added with her characteristic touch of sarcasm. "Did you think she meant washing the dishes?"

How did you know? I sat up on the couch. "Would Efraim know in advance that she's coming?"

"Yes, it will appear in the summons to *beit din.*"

"I'd love to see his face." For the first time in years, I felt a sweet smile settle on my lips. I watched the dove pacing the windowsill, almost comically, as the bird of hope crooned its song into my heart.

Suri started nodding her head. "I wouldn't be surprised if he gave you the *get* before she's called in, anything to keep her from talking."

I leaned into the soft cushions. "I could live with that, Suri. I could really handle that just fine." I dreamily conjured up a picture of Efraim seeing Lori, a confident, self-assured young woman, in the courthouse as my witness. The color draining from his face, the broad-brimmed, black hat falling from his trembling hands, his mouth trying not to hang open...

"When did you say she'll be here?" Suri asked as she sat at the keyboard to type up the request for a witness' appearance.

SIXTY-NINE

THE MORNING AFTER THE court invitations were received, Efraim walked into the house after the kids left. I no longer cared and continued clearing the breakfast table when he came up behind me.

Wearing his large dark sunglasses, which I no longer doubted hid his drug-induced, dilated pupils, Efraim raged. Clenching his mouth tightly, he seethed with anger. I spun around to see him clench his hand into a tight fist.

Without pausing to think, I hoped, prayed, that he'd assault me. Physical violence, though not the worst kind of abuse, is easier to prove. I stared at my own reflection in the lenses that shielded his state of mind. Time slowed down into microseconds when I saw it coming. I felt myself leaving my body as he unleashed his fury.

Just as abruptly, as I felt the hairs of his fingers brush my cheek, he stopped. We both stared at each other. He would not give me the satisfaction. For six years, Efraim had played his role of the misunderstood saint seeking peace with the woman he truly loved.

In the rabbinical courts, he wore the wide-brimmed black hat he reserved for special performances and carried a large edition of a *Gemara* that he hadn't opened in years. He would not now imprudently give me the black-and-blue proof that might force their hand.

He sneered and turned angrily. When he walked out, he slammed the door, ending the surreal episode.

Time switched gears. Together with my racing heart, it gradually returned to a more normal rhythm. I replayed the scene that had just taken place as though it was captured in a series of still pictures. He had not struck me, but the intention of violence was crystal clear.

When I could move, my first thought was to call Suri.

"Suri, thank you for answering the phone." I attempted to project calm and self-control, but she inquired right away if I was OK. "He tried to punch me in the face, but stopped at the last minute," I reported.

Oddly, instead of the anxiety I anticipated, a wave of validation rolled over me. Years of never-ending verbal abuse and unconfirmed suspicions had gnawed away at the last remnants of self-worth or confidence. I had begun to believe that I was insane, maybe hallucinating. *How close would I come to that precipice? Would I plunge into that deadly black abyss?*

"Go to the police right away. Tell them exactly what happened and tell it hard," Suri directed. "Look, Lori's coming to testify has increased the tension."

Two years ago, when Suri decided to receive her law degree in addition to being a rabbinical-court advocate, she distributed every one of her cases to other rabbinical court legal representatives, but she kept mine. She had possibly become even more determined than me to have him give me the *get*.

She continued, "Remind them about his gun, the stock of ammunition, and the knives he carries. Make sure you tell them that you're scared."

As she spoke, I went to the files I had hidden in the back of the closet and gathered the pictures of his weapons, excessive numbers of bullets, and assortment of knives. For years now, his hobby, as he flippantly labeled it, had not impressed the rabbinical court. It seemed to play in his favor. I could only assume they feared him.

"I'm here for you, Shifra," my lifeline to reality was saying. "I'm waiting to hear what happens."

The policewoman asked endless questions, taking her time to write the detailed deposition. She instructed me, "You have to call and tell us when he's home. Police officers will come immediately to bring him in for questioning. He'll be warned. And he'll be unable to return home for seven days."

Her job was finished when I signed the charges. But the tall Sephardi woman, with the fringes of her blonde hair tinted pink and a gold ring on almost every finger, leaned forward.

"Go immediately to the family courts. They will give him a restraining order for a month." I heard the deep concern in her voice. The dangerous pattern of escalation of violence was not new to her. She quickly wrote out and handed me the phone number and address.

Nodding gratefully, I left the police station. *Seven days seemed like heaven, thirty would be entering* Olam Haba. This would be the first time in six years of court procedures that someone would help me keep him out of the house. Now that the verbal abuse had escalated to a near physical assault, I could go to the state's court with my *rav*'s approval.

I called Suri to update her.

She was quick to tell me, "Speak only to Judge Steiner. He's good. And he knows a rat when he smells one. I'll call you right back to tell you when he's presiding." Hanging up the phone, I waited for her to call back. I felt hot, then cold chills going up my spine. Grabbing the phone before the first ring finished, I paid attention to her directive. "He'll be there this afternoon at four. Be there before that, so you'll be sure to get in."

My adrenalin had peaked and was diminishing. "He didn't hit me," I said meekly.

I guess Suri knew I had no self-esteem and a devastated ego. My self-worth was bound up in a ludicrous penchant for telling the truth.

"It doesn't matter, Shifra. He displayed violent behavior and you're frightened for yourself and the kids. This is an escalation, and once it starts, we cannot know how far he will go." Suri paused to make the point. "And the chances are, Shifra, that it will get worse, probably a lot worse. And that could mean for the kids too."

"There's no turning back now," whispered the spirit of hope. Suri, typically, reminded me to call her after the hearing.

"Yes," I answered softly to both of them, "I know."

As soon as the kids were home, I called to tell them I would be home later.

I was the first to arrive at the family court for the afternoon session. Exactly at four o'clock, I was beckoned into the courtroom. The *kippa*-clad, South African judge listened patiently. He even urged me to speak in English when, anxious and quivering, I failed to remember my Hebrew. He questioned me about my kids, when the abuse had begun, what I had done until now. It was obvious that he had a lot of experience dealing with headstrong husbands.

After I gave him the revealing pictures of Efraim's weapons collection, he asked the court secretary to hand him a form from which he read aloud a range of restrictions. I watched him mark off one after another:

"1) Cannot come home for 30 days." Check.

"2) Cannot approach within 300 meters of home for 30 days." Again he moved the pen sharply.

"3) Cannot come within 300 meters of kids' schools for 30 days." Here he paused to ask the address of each child's school.

He continued, "The police will take his gun into custody. He cannot carry cold weapons." Imagining his massive ego bristling at being denied his favorite knives, I grinned.

"Tomorrow," the judge continued, "he'll have to appear in court and show just cause why I should not extend this restraining order for 90 days." He told the secretary to stop typing, as he peered at me kindly over the edge of his reading glasses. In a low but audible voice, he confided, "I doubt he'll be able to convince me."

I sat stone-still in disbelief, holding back a flood of tears. Overwhelmed with relief, I heard the judge's last words echoing in my mind. *I doubt he'll be able to convince me. 90 days, 90 days, 90 days.*

It was hearing of this three-month span that crushed his ego.

SEVENTY

WHEN LORI WALKED INTO my home with Simmy, I dropped a
dish. It didn't break, but I shook. A very pretty, self-confident
young woman walked over and gave me a warm and loving
hug. I held her at arms' length. No braids were bouncing, but there
were the same sparkling, beautiful eyes.

"Shifra, I am really happy to see you."

Simmy called out, "I'll make the tea, and you two can just relax."

I didn't argue. Lori wanted to know all about the kids, and I was
happy to tell her, delaying *the* conversation.

"Tell me what you've been doing. Simmy fills me in here and
there, but—"

With deep emotion I blurted, "Lori I am so happy to see you, and
looking so well. Tell me about your life now."

Lori was open and honest. "It took me a while to work out what
had happened here. I think if I didn't have my amazing parents, I
might have become really depressed." She looked at me thoughtfully.
"But I do have amazing parents," she smiled. "After I was finally able
to open up to my mom, I also agreed to go for counseling."

We took the steaming tea Simmy had prepared, and she joined us.

"My dad was ready to fly to Israel, but Mom said we need him
here with us. She said, 'That guy will get what's coming to him. Right
now our daughter needs us.' And so he didn't buy the plane ticket."
She smiled, sipping the tea slowly.

I nodded, glad he was there for Lori, but wondering to myself if
he couldn't have hired someone else to take care of Efraim.

Lori continued, "You know, Shifra, after a few months I was able to separate Efraim from Israel, from Judaism..." she turned slightly away from me, "and from you."

My eyes filled with tears as she continued.

"I realized that I didn't need to throw out the beautiful concepts with the dirty water, to rephrase an old saying. My parents even suggested I go to the local rabbi and ask him my questions."

I continued listening closely.

"So I asked him if I had done something wrong that this happened. And how could someone be a rabbi, married with kids, and do what he did to me?" She looked down and said in a softer voice, "And probably to others as well.

"This rabbi asked his wife to join us, which I appreciated. We spoke for quite a while, on several occasions. They told me I should not see this as a punishment." Lori stopped for a moment to sip her tea. "With, or without wanting to do bad, an individual can stop following the healthy and authentic way of Judaism and start doing his own thing. As he steers off course, he can often no longer discern between good and bad, truth and lies, right and wrong. And," again Lori turned slightly away, "some people have emotional problems that emerge."

Right, like narcissism and sociopathic behaviors.

"The *rabbanit* and I discussed their open home. She told me she really wanted it, but she realized the kids also need just a mommy and daddy without the crowds, so they set guidelines. Once a month, they have no guests. Sometimes they even go away in case anyone might show up unannounced." Lori tapped her fingers on her skirt. "And she and her husband agreed that he would only counsel girls if she was present. Mostly, he talks with boys or couples." We all nodded. *How obvious.*

"I began going to them for Shabbat. They also have guests, singing and dancing. And they have some cute kids too." I nodded, so grateful she was willing to replay the scene with a healthier outcome.

"I really enjoyed it. My parents agreed to come as well." Lori was nodding her head happily. "We began going to shul, and gradually, many questions and considerations later, we are all keeping Shabbat, kosher, and adding other mitzvot all the time."

I wished that I had something to do with her returning to a traditional life. As if she was reading my mind, she continued, "Shifra, when I saw how gracious you were to everyone, how patient you were with your kids and others, and how unselfish you were, it really made an impact on me."

I looked down, trying to hide my wet eyes.

"I saw the beauty of tradition in your home and spirituality in your kind eyes, Shifra, that I had been looking for. That had a lot to do with why I was able to give it another try."

Simmy was nodding vigorously.

"For all of Efraim's tours and Torah talks, Shif, it was you that I wanted to emulate," Lori concluded.

I looked at them both sheepishly, "With some modifications, of course." We laughed, and the tension in the room disappeared.

SEVENTY-ONE

A SOMEWHAT CONFUSED EFRAIM WALKED into the waiting room of the rabbinical court. As soon as he spotted Lori, he ambled over to her, with only a remnant of his usual bravado, as if he had to remind himself to appear charismatic. There was a slight quiver in his once flamboyant smile as he looked at Lori.

I sensed that this moment might foretell whether I would receive the *get* today.

Lori's eyes narrowed as she pressed her lips together. Her hardened facial features were defiant and determined as she stared back. An unseen battle was being fought. As I rose to do I don't know what, Suri motioned for me to wait.

Efraim blinked first. He surveyed the room as if to see if anyone else had noticed. We all had. His defeat obvious, the great hero slinked away.

Suri quickly covered up a most unprofessional smirk with her hand. I winked at her concealed thumbs up, and suddenly it seemed very possible that my wretched ordeal might end.

Squeezing Lori's hand, I nodded my heartfelt gratefulness. Could we have asked Lori to come sooner? Would she have had the kind of inner strength she had demonstrated today? Would Efraim have been this crushed before the Higher Rabbinical court refused his plea for *shalom bayit* or before the family court removed him physically from my home?

These decisive events were sharp slaps across his psyche. Among the many remorseful thoughts, one increasingly familiar voice whispered gently, "Shifra, you're doing your best. Let it go."

I looked up, expecting to see Suri or Lori, but they were each lost in their own thoughts.

As we waited for the scribe and two witnesses to appear, Efraim walked into the hall. Rising quickly to see where he was going, I spotted him walking through the exit. I ran after him to tell him that Lori was prepared to testify under oath and that it would be publicized. I would make sure of that.

Uncharacteristically, he followed me back inside. The door to the courtroom opened. "Are you ready?" asked the rabbinical court attendant, as the two witnesses walked in. Efraim lowered his head.

"I'm ready," I said quietly, and walked through the door. *This is the gate to freedom.* As I held out my hands to accept the coveted piece of paper, I sensed I was getting my life back.

In the blink of an eye, it was finished. He gave me the *get*, even before Lori was called to testify. But until I exited the courtroom with the *get* in hand, she refused to leave the waiting room, just in case.

Seventy-two

Two years after the get

YAIR RAN THROUGH THE door and breathlessly called for a family
meeting — right away.

"What's the big deal?" Dovy asked impatiently, as he pulled
himself from his *Gemara*.

It was unusual for Yair to call for a family gathering. Usually, he
would have to be strongly persuaded to attend. Wiping my hands on
my apron, I settled onto the couch. I didn't mind resting.

"Come on everyone," I called. "I'm really curious to hear what
your brother has to say."

It took a few minutes for everyone to settle. "You better make
this good," Dovy said. He scowled his displeasure. He didn't like his
Torah learning disturbed.

"I just wanted to read to you this letter I received from a former
classmate." Yair looked around mischievously, making sure everyone
was present.

Dinner will wait. I adjusted my scarf, wondering what could be
so imperative for the whole family in a letter from his old friend.

"It's from Shmueli," he explained importantly, immediately drawing everyone's attention. Everyone remembered Shmueli, Mona's son,
who was a few months younger than Yair.

"Kobi, one of my classmates is his neighbor." Yair stretched his
arms wide and yawned.

"OK, Yair," Dovy pressed impatiently, "we're waiting."

Yair would not rush. "Shmueli gave it to him months ago to hand deliver. Today, Kobi finally brought it to class." Yair waved the letter teasingly. "He apologized that he kept forgetting it." Yair looked up impishly, "Maybe he thinks I'm getting ready to switch schools, so he got nervous and brought it."

Free-spirited Yair seemed to flourish by changing schools every couple of years. His present yeshiva, like others before, was unable to keep his attention for very long. I had learned to be satisfied that he remained a fun-loving mischief-maker and never got into serious trouble, as far as I knew. He honored *Shabbat* and respected Jewish law. He'd explained to me that he just needed to "take it easy."

Kayla asked with a half-smile, "And who gave him that idea, Yair?"

At the mention of Shmueli's name, I sat straight, catching my breath. Sliding to the edge of the chair, I made a great effort to focus my attention fully.

I felt my tongue racing along my lower lip, as Batya took her place next to Benny. Dovy leaned over from the couch, trying to scan the closely protected sheet of paper. The others scattered on the floor around the coffee table.

Sitting at center stage, Yair tested our patience as his eyes skimmed the letter that he'd obviously already read. "Listen to this! Wow!" His eyebrows pushed up to their fullest height and his lips stretched open and he repeated "Wow!"

"Stop joking around, Yair, and read the letter. I'm in the middle of learning," Dovy balked. Feigning apathy, he pretended to leave. I wasn't so sure I wanted him to read it, but Dovy's intimidation settled it.

"Get ready. This is big."

My son read, "Dear Yair, it's been a long time since we've seen each other. How are you doing in your new school? I hope you plan to stay there."

Yair paused, adding a teasing "not likely" before he continued.

"I really wanted to talk with you when we were in yeshiva together, but I didn't know how to start. Well, years have passed and, somehow, this morning I just decided to write to you and say what needs to be said. I hope you realize how much nerve it takes for me to do this.

But my rabbis taught me that Jews have to have a lot of guts."

I swallowed hard. After receiving the *get* two years earlier, I was struggling hard to rebuild. Shmueli's name was mentioned occasionally, but the kids did not seem to think too much about him. Personally, I was left with an aching lack of closure.

The letter continued: "Remember when your *abba* came to school to take us out for pizza? He's been doing that for years, long before you ever dropped in. He's been coming to buy me lunch two or three times a week since I can remember. Did you know that?" Yair shook his head. We were all taken by surprise.

"When you came, he often invited you too, which is cool, but I could tell that he wasn't happy about it. I guessed you weren't supposed to know about our visits."

"Now it starts to get interesting," Yair added his commentary.

"Do you remember when we were little? He used to bring you and some of your brothers and sisters to visit me and my mother? He was always bringing us food and giving us money. Lots of times when we were alone, he told me he was my *abba*. But I have my *ima's* last name.

"In school, he told everyone, including the *rebbe*, that he has known and taken care of my *ima* and me since I was born, so I'm like his son. He always quotes the famous *mishna*, 'Anyone who teaches someone Torah, is considered like their spiritual parent.' Anyway, I'm really confused if he's my real father. My mother says he is, but that your mother is such a witch she'll make our lives unbearable if we talk about it. She always told me it's our secret.

"I remember your *ima* came to the yeshiva a few times to visit you. She saw me too, and she smiled. She didn't seem like a nasty person. Well, I'm trying to figure out who my father is and if I really have any brothers or sisters.

"Remember all those times you used to come to visit when we were little? Abba — if he is my *abba* — always bought me toys and clothes. And remember that aquarium? And by the way, Yair, now I think it really is your bow and arrow that I have, and I am willing to return it to you if you want them. Anyway, I used to pretend that you were my brothers and sisters.

"Yair, do you remember you once asked Abba why I had so many more games than you did? Even as a little kid, I thought, 'You have an *abba* and brothers and sisters.' I would have given you all the toys in the world in exchange."

Ariella interrupted, "I remember sitting in their apartment, watching TV, while Abba went to talk with Mona in the other room. Then Abba told us not to tell you we went there." Although it had all been said before, she hung her head, shamefully. Being told to lie to me by her *abba* still troubled her.

Still bearing a heavy grudge, Dovy faced me, reminiscing, "Abba used to take me there, and he always said 'Don't tell Ima.'" The cynicism in Dovy's voice was clear. "You would be angry that he was helping a poor, single mother instead of being home. He stopped bringing me when I threatened to tell you." I nodded, remembering that my oldest son had not even mentioned those visits until the great emotional gushing took place in the midst of the divorce process. *In his way, he had tried to protect me from being hurt.* I tried to concentrate on the letter, even as the memories replayed themselves.

Yair continued reading, "Anyway, we're not little kids now, and a guy wants to know his last name and his roots. Do you know what I mean? You know who your dad is, even if he's really messed up. I'm confused and it's taking a lot of effort for me to write all this. I hope you'll write me back. Do you think you'll tell your family I wrote? I guess I'll understand if you don't write me back, because this could be pretty messy. So if I don't hear from you, I'll just keep playing the guessing game and I won't bother you again.

"It was fun having you in my class for a while. Try to learn some Torah. It'll be good for you. ☺.

"Do you want to meet and talk?

"Your friend, (hopefully a brother), Shmueli."

Collective sighs of "whew" and "wow" passed through the room. *That was unbelievably mature for a fellow just several months younger than my seventeen-year-old son.* As the startling words sank in, a heated debate raged. Is he or isn't he?

⟊

"What real proof is there?" Benny insisted. Since the time he'd been unfairly suspected of taking the gun and hiding it in his room, he had developed a powerful inclination for hearing all the facts and evidence before judging a situation.

I wondered if the youngest ones could fully understand the implications of Shmueli's letter and his questions, but they certainly felt something was out of place.

Batya was clearly confused. "How can we have a brother who doesn't live in the house with us? And how could Ima not know it? She would be his mother! Right?"

"What?" Ariella piped up angrily, with a twinge of jealousy. "Abba took you out for pizza?"

All eyes were on Yair. "How come we hardly ever got pizza?" Batya complained.

"Why didn't I know that?" I asked Yair. After our endless "gushing gatherings," I thought there were no more secrets. Suddenly I sensed it might take a lifetime of small comments and innocent remarks until we achieved full disclosure.

Dovy turned referee. "Hey guys, this is not about pizza. We're trying to figure out if Shmueli is related to us."

Typical of our family gatherings, the kids took turns rapid-firing questions or comments which were simultaneously answered by another sibling. This was a conversational feat I could never figure out. *Definitely from their father's side.* I could barely follow the quick Hebrew, let alone comment. Kayla hardly entered the fray, while Batya tried her best to decipher all the clamor.

As the decibel levels increased, I struggled to decide whether this conversation was appropriate for the younger ones. In our religious circle, it was considered virtuous not to discuss the "facts of life" until the kids were older teens.

I considered briefly that Batya, and even Benny, might be too young to hear some details. On the other hand, the days of the "great gushings" formed a solid unity among the kids. Rabbi Kaufman, of blessed memory, was absolutely right. Being clear and upfront — without secrets, cover-ups, or lies—had greatly encouraged our healing process.

As I waited for the steamy debates to reach a crescendo, I recalled once trying to clarify with Yair, privately, what he had watched on TV when his *abba* brought them to Mona's apartment. Soon after, I noticed that Benny and Ariella were commenting to me on the shows they'd seen on their visits to that apartment. Then there was the time I asked Dovy confidentially how Mona dressed when they were there. A little while later, Kayla came to me to ask why it was OK for Mona to dress in a see-through short blouse in front of Abba.

It was obvious that secrets about their father's "other life" had become anathema to our family. Sighing, I realized that the younger ones would stay. And I hoped I would be wise enough to respond fittingly.

Long ago, I learned that if I insisted on speaking first, they would interrupt endlessly. Patience was far more productive. After emptying out their stockpile of insights and theories, one of them, probably Dovy, would turn to me for guidance.

As they spoke animatedly, I watched Batya's confused eyes, trying to understand the gush of ideas. Dovy and Yair sat a hands-breadth apart, shouting loudly and concurrently. Kayla leaned in to listen.

I returned to my own thoughts, grateful that I already extensively considered all the details I could gather about Shmueli. Everything fit: Efraim's dedicated care for Shmueli's *b'rit* and bar mitzvah, and everything in between and beyond. He had bought toys, games, and food, and paid for Mona's everyday needs. Searching through Efraim's bewildering heaps of papers, I found crumpled receipts for her apartment's rent payment, Shmueli's school tuition, and private lessons.

Soon after I filed for divorce, I learned he had always shopped for two households, leaving Mona's things under our stairs until he could deliver them. I shuddered, remembering the day Dovy pointed out the convenient hiding space—right under my nose, under the stairs outside our front door.

"Are you OK, Ima?" asked sensitive Kayla.

"I'm OK, sweetheart," I answered. "This is a real mess, isn't it?" She smiled at what I hoped would look like a playful wink.

Registering that the whirlwind of debate still raged, I returned to my deliberations.

Closing my eyes, my thoughts returned to a conversation I had with Suri about Shmueli's birth. I was feeling confused and frustrated after another depressing day in the rabbinical court. Suri again asked the *beit din* to demand a DNA test from Shmueli. Mona had obstinately refused, claiming that her son did not need to have needles stuck into him to prove my conspiracy theory.

"Suri, how can I prove to the rabbis that Shmueli is Efraim's son if she refuses to do the DNA test? Can't the *beit din* force them?"

"Maybe they can," Suri with her characteristic cynicism, "but they're obviously not."

I sank into silence.

"Shifra, let's do a quick review of what we know."

Suri waited, but I had no energy to talk.

"You are not giving up, my friend. Let's make sure this is clear in your mind. Efraim heard about an Ashkenazi rabbi who called for a return to concubines, claiming that it would offer family status and stability to women who would otherwise remain alone, essentially ostracized from society. This is another form of kindness that this doer of kindnesses considered to espouse, no pun intended. Some time later, he claims that Mona is a homeless young woman, whom he met on the street." Suri interrupted herself. "As an aside, I tend to think she made her livelihood from the streets, but no matter. She lived with you for several months spending a lot of time with her hero, who was the light of her life. You left for the States when your dad was seriously ill and Mona was supposed to stay elsewhere, but according to our star witness, four-year-old Dovy, she remained in your home."

"Right," I grimaced. "Let's call in the witness."

"Tomas, your illegal South American questionable convert said he was in your home for most of the two weeks that you were absent. Remember he remarked how often he and Mona argued over their rights to the phone, the bathroom..."

"And the kitchen," I reminded her, starting to perk up at the absurdity of it all.

"And your husband's time," she finished. "Didn't Tomas tell you that Steve and Mona had competitions for who could act more depressed? Everyone wanted Efraim's attention. She was there alright."

"Yeah, so he said."

"Let's move on," Suri talked fast, sticking to facts. "Exactly nine months after you returned, she has a baby. Now she won't talk to you at all, only Efraim. Yeah, she's angry that you'll make her feel guilty. Remember what she said when she showed up pregnant? 'You're not angry?' And when you went to visit her in the hospital, she said, 'Don't take my baby. You already have one.' What's the connection? Why would she think you're coming to take her baby? Maybe it's because Efraim was the baby's father." Suri spelled it all out.

How stupid could I be?

Suri continued. "So Efraim decides that pregnant Mona should live elsewhere and asked you to help her find a place. In other words, you should be involved with her, as a good co-wife should."

"I can't believe I helped her find a place."

"Shifra, you didn't even imagine how low he could get at that point," she tried to comfort me. "You had little kids, you were pregnant, and you had just lost your dad. You had a lot on your mind."

"A lot on my mind, OK, but how gullible is gullible?" A cloud lifted. "I just believed everything my hero said, and could not imagine there was an option for a different narrative."

A dull headache was beginning to develop.

"Even though you were hardly in touch with her, except for that unexpected visit when you found out she was pregnant, Efraim insisted you go together with him to visit her in the hospital."

"Right. But, according to the nurse, he had stayed with her during her labor and saw her following the Caesarian. Why would he want me to intrude on their cozy relationship?" I asked aloud, not expecting an answer.

"I think I know," Suri said. "He knows you're a loving, considerate, good-hearted person. He wanted you to see this very newly born baby, to let your heart melt for him. He gambled that you would be less angry with the child if, or when, you found out." The fog in my brain lightened. That made sense.

Suri went on, "And maybe that's why he brought the kids to visit Shmueli. They would already have a relationship when the truth became known. But we're jumping ahead.

"So Efraim arranged the *b'rit* and acted as the *sandak*, an honor often reserved for a close relative. He hired the *mohel* and announced the baby's name.

"Efraim was adamant that you not only attend the *b'rit* but prepare the meal for it as well." She stopped to catch her breath. "Listen, Shifra, those who knew you were in the States and yet saw Mona around might have started wondering. So Efraim brought in two guys, chaperones as it were." Suri sniggered. "That was good thinking on his part. Then when the community would learn, and Efraim would make sure that everyone knew, that you were personally involved in this grand *b'rit* affair, it would make it less likely that someone who can add two plus two might accuse Efraim of foul play."

I was getting the idea. "And that's why he told his personal taxi drivers I was sending the food, baking *challot*, encouraging the kids to visit — which I heard from the taxi drivers' own mouths."

Suri excused herself to take a phone call and my thoughts wandered to Dr. Gershon's conclusion. Efraim embodied all the characteristics of the narcissistic, sociopathic personality. He said he would need to speak with Efraim about his childhood to know whether to add psychopath to the list. And that wasn't going to happen.

"Sorry, Shifra, let's keep going." She continued recreating my life story. "All along, Efraim arranged and paid for Shmueli's needs and schooling. He bought him toys and clothing and arranged private tutors. He acted as guarantor to the yeshiva and attended the parent-teacher's meetings in lieu of the boy's mother."

"He paid for the kid's tuition, their food, and rent..." I mumbled.

"And his rabbi confirmed to you in an innocent comment that Efraim, the *tzaddik*, was really in every way, the boy's *abba*. And then we get to the bar mitzvah ..."

I didn't want to talk about this anymore.

"...over which he presided and paid for, as you discovered in the receipts you found in those piles of discarded papers."

I found receipts made out to Efraim for their rent, the yeshiva, the bar mitzvah caterer and more from his disorganized papers. I was surprised that the clarity hurt less than the raging suspicions that had nearly driven me mad.

"And, of course, there's Shmueli," she said. "The kids confirmed that he was urged by Efraim to call him Abba, at least in private."

"Yes, the kids."

Suri's voice interrupted my short reverie. "Do we need to go on? I'm sold."

"I think the *beit din* is too, Shifra, even without the DNA test. He invested too much time, money, and effort into a singular relationship with a nasty, selfish —" Suri paused, clearing her throat, "woman for this to be just a gesture of reaching out to the destitute."

"Needing to support two separate households, he needed twice as much money, but possibly could no longer concentrate on his professional work," Suri added.

I recalled that his sunglasses had become daily wear after he stopped working at the architectural firm. "And drug dealing is an easy way to make fast money.

"It's hard to know what came first. According to Dr. Gershon, he was already sunk in his insanity, and that's what led him to think he could do anything, with anyone, and get away with it, even if he had to sell his soul to do it." I lowered my eyes. "What a waste of a life." I shuddered. "He hurt our beautiful kids who have so much potential."

"Listen, Shifra, narcissists don't take the blame for anything, ever. It will forever be your fault." I felt her scrutinizing me. "You know it's not."

Then why did I feel that I let everyone down? And how will I pull my disjointed family back together? I couldn't fathom it, but I had confronted Efraim without fear, so anything was possible.

Suri was coming to the finish, "We may not know every detail or be able to trace his downfall completely accurately, but we don't need to. We don't need to know about his other female relationships, which drugs he used or sold. All we need now is to find a way for you to receive your *get*."

"Do you think he really helped anyone?" I still could not help wondering.

"Possibly. There's Ohel Sarah, individuals who credit him with helping them with personal problems or becoming religious. But how many did he hurt? How many did he introduce to drugs and then try to save them? Shifra, he displays all the traits of the caustic narcissist."

She read a passage from Dr. Gershon's book that he had kindly given me. "Grandiose sense of self-importance... Lives in a fantasy world that supports his delusions of grandeur... Needs constant praise and admiration... Sense of entitlement... Exploits others without guilt or shame... Frequently demeans, intimidates, bullies, or belittles others."

That conversation ended with Suri's reminder that we would meet in court again in a few weeks, and I should keep my eyes and ears open for any further concrete corroboration of the facts.

The concise review restored my confidence that the truth would win, even if they continued to refuse the DNA test.

When I had left her office, I had reflected on the possible dilemmas that might arise from having an anonymous half-brother.

Returning momentarily to the buzzing conversations among my kids, I knew the time had come to set the record straight. I continued my review of the facts.

Efraim had exerted much more time and effort to get Mona's son into a yeshiva with a good reputation than he'd ever done for our boys. He had worked day and night to ensure Shmueli's acceptance.

Efraim spent hours insisting that although the boy's unwed mom had problems, he himself would ensure a kosher home, no TV, and good attendance. He pulled every string. These lunchtime visits to the yeshiva fleshed out the picture. He told the *rebbes* he was like Shmueli's father, but *not because Efraim "taught him Torah."* I grimaced at the irony of Efraim's non-Torah lifestyle.

I looked up to see Batya's sad face. "Come here, honey." I put my arms around her as she sat on the couch next to me. "We'll try to make this less confusing soon."

But there was something else. *I had long ago decided that one day I would have to tell the kids about Shmueli.*

Years ago, after months of pondering the convoluted details, I came to the unanticipated conclusion that Shmueli, their half-brother, had done no wrong. He too was a victim of his father's delusional lifestyle.

He had no "known" family to turn to on his father's side, and crazy Mona insisted she had no close family. Shmueli could easily have become a wild person, a drug addict, a drunk, or worse. Yet, when I visited the yeshiva to check up on my own mischievous, nonstudent Yair and asked about Shmueli, the *rebbes* praised him.

They gave a glowing report. "He is self-disciplined, studious, and reliable. His personality traits are exceptional. Perhaps, if he would be unrelenting in his Torah learning, he could become a true *talmid chacham.*" So he was bright, responsible, and had good *middot.* I winced to think that he also looked very much like his father. It was hard to tell them apart in their baby pictures.

Biblical stories of Yehudah and Tamar, Ruth and Boaz, came to mind. From ambiguous beginnings, Mashiach would be born. "Ours is a generation of vague foundations," an inner, wise voice whispered. Hashem created a blessed branch out of a rotten root. It was clear that Shmueli should not be punished or hurt any more than he already had been.

More than that, in the cosmic surprises that abound, I could envision someone introducing him to Ariella, only a couple of years younger, or Batya, four years younger. Surely, someone traveling between his life and ours could easily pick up a sense of a bond between them, and not knowing better, attribute it to the soul that is seeking its roots in its other half.

As the kids' verbal torrents diminished to a trickle, Dovy looked at me with his father's piercing blue eyes. "Ima?" At his cue, the others turned in my direction.

I guess this time was as good as any to make the point.

I prayed for Hashem to help me put my thoughts into simple words. I told them almost everything, omitting some facts they would doubtless realize in the future.

SEVENTY-THREE

IN THE MIDST OF cleaning the house and planning for Pesach, I realized that the hardest crumbs to scrub away are those scattered thoughts that taunt and trouble our hearts. I learned to use deep breathing and guided imagery whenever I found myself sinking into despondency.

As Dovy and Kayla took my place scrubbing the stove and kitchen cabinets, I took a short break. I sat in a comfortable chair and chose a guided imagery that read: "Go beneath the surface of the sea and enter a room. See what you need from the room and take it out with you." Closing my eyes, I exhaled slowly to reach deep relaxation.

My thoughts floated to a room just under the waves. It looked dark, gloomy, and foreboding, and I was unable to enter into it. I tried, but I could not push myself to enter. Turning my head to the side, I spotted a lit doorway leading to an illuminated larger room.

Curiously, I entered, recognizing my children and friends who had been supportive throughout the years. Rivka, Suri, my dear Rabbi and Rabbanit Kaufman, who had passed away, were all there dressed for a *simcha*. They appeared to be anticipating my arrival, cheering me on as I entered. In the therapeutic silence, I "heard" them encouraging me, expressing belief in me and my potential.

My inner voice clarified, "This is the right room. That dingy place is a storage area filled with scraps of bad memories. You don't have go there anymore." Spontaneous tears climbed up from deep wells of emotion and fell out of the imagery onto my cheeks.

In the imagery, I set fire to the disturbing dungeon-like chamber.

"You no longer need those bad memories floating through your mind. You have permission to get rid of the unwelcoming, self-defeating ruins."

The fierce, fire-breathing dragon that threatened me for so long was pulled into the conflagration. I saw him frantically blowing his deadly flames even as he was consumed by the fire, which finally overpowered him.

Keeping my eyes shut, I shed one more tear. Never before had the sea looked so calm and beautiful as it did right then. This year, Pesach would be special for me. My *biyur chametz*, destroying the unacceptable, would be complete.

SEVENTY-FOUR

SHMUELI AND BATSHEVA WERE making their firstborn son's *b'rit* at home in their cramped two-room Jerusalem apartment. Along with the traditional baby gifts, each of their closest friends brought along cakes, salad platters, and the famous Israeli potato-filled *burekas*.

A large bowl of egg salad sprinkled liberally with paprika, surrounded with a colorful array of vegetables, was placed at the center. The only food they ordered was rolls and pitas. That was the basis of a *mitzva* meal and apparently all they could afford.

I saw Efraim shaking hands with Batsheva's father, Chaim. Efraim was congratulating the bareheaded gentleman, who was wearing jeans and a T-shirt. Filling my plate at the narrow side table, I found myself standing behind Efraim. I could just barely hear Chaim's response. "And *mazal tov* to you, Efraim, on your new grandson. He's a beauty, huh. Not surprised. My daughter is very good-looking, if I say so myself." His hands stretched and flexed in front of him.

They shared an eyebrow-raising chuckle as Efraim replied, "Hey, they call me Abu Shmueli, you know. He's a chip off the old block, if you know what I mean."

I couldn't see his face but envisioned a repulsive smirk. Dovy walked by just as Efraim said the words "Abu Shmueli." He stopped short, a cloud darkening his face. It was hard to read all the emotions, but the pressed lips and suddenly sunken reddened cheeks spoke volumes.

The kids were grown up. Dovy was married with a child of his own. Today was the first time that this admission had come first-hand from his father's sealed lips. Until now, it was an assumption of guilt, confirmed by my conviction that Shmueli was their father's son. When our eyes met, I saw a brief disorientation, and a lot of anger.

"He tells strangers what he never told us!" he mumbled as he squeezed past his *abba*, who appeared oblivious to Dovy's presence. He joined me at the salad table. Since I had long ago acknowledged what seemed obvious, I was now well past my own sorrow. I regretted that Dovy might start to grieve more deeply following this verification. "Don't worry, Ima, I guess I knew it all along. But why couldn't he just be straight with us?"

"I don't think he can be straight with anyone." I surprisingly felt distanced from negative emotions. "He's gone too far off the edge. He would have to devote himself to wanting to change. He'd have to make confessions, apologies, admit his mistakes — and promise never to go there again."

I shook my head with sadness. "Neither his personality, his ego, nor his heart can go on a path of *teshuva*."

Dovy stacked *burekas* onto his plate.

"He would have to want to come clean more than anything else in the world to make things right. And apparently, he's incapable."

Efraim's four-year-old son from his new wife, who was about Kayla's age, moved past us, pushing through the crowd. He played innocently with my grandchildren, who accepted him as "one of the cousins."

Although I had no contact with him, I had come to accept that, like Shmueli, he was not the guilty one. I wondered what future dynamics could come into play. What if in the future the "cousins" became close friends and insisted that Efraim's son join them for family events? I let the thoughts go for now.

Dovy nodded. "Take it easy, Ima."

"You too, my son. You too." I eyed his plate piled high with *burekas*.

"It's not all for me. Don't worry, I'm not on an eating binge." He smiled. "You were right that I should speak to someone. It's helping me clear the cobwebs from my brain."

It was hard to convince him or the others to go for counseling, but seeing how much it helped me, I encouraged them. At least Dovy agreed, and I hoped the others would also one day.

Balancing the pastries in one hand, Dovy lifted his crying baby and grinned. "What do you always say, Ima? 'Life is so interesting, better than a movie.' I guess it's true. Who would believe this scene?"

"Oh, hi Shifra." Efraim turned as if he only now saw me.

"Hi, and *mazal tov* on your new grandson," slipped out.

He looked away. "Yeah, uh, *mazal tov, mazal tov*."

As he stepped away, I sensed a validation I no longer needed. How many years had I banged my head against bricks to figure out if I was delusional? How many endless nights had I tossed in my lonely bedroom, apprehensive and overwrought? Could I have done it differently? Could I have just said appearances and my intuition are sufficient? Should I have hired a private investigator? Hmmph. I shrugged involuntarily — with what money?

Let it go Shifra. It's done. You're in a healing process. Guilt trips are unacceptable. It's enough to glean lessons for the future. Let go and learn this: An impending crisis may be reduced to the ease of pulling a hair out of a bowl of milk if we recognize that we are not in control.

The elderly Sephardi *mohel* was calling for the baby for the circumcision ceremony.

Following Jewish custom, several married women passed the newborn on the pristine white pillow from one to the next. In this tiny room, each woman merely had to turn to reach the expecting arms. Each one silently prayed for the miracle her family needed. Often it was the blessing of conception or bearing a child to term. The last woman handed the treasure to her husband who placed the baby into the *sandek*'s welcoming arms. This was Batsheva's father, flagrantly bareheaded even for the ceremony when other family members had respectfully put some manner of *kippa* on their heads.

The *mohel* began yelling unexpectedly. "It cannot be that a non-religious man, who does not abide by the laws of Shabbat will usher this baby into the Jewish traditions." The *mohel*'s face was flushed; he was adamant that a righteous replacement be found. The father, shrugging his shoulders, submitted. He handed the baby to Shmueli's *chavruta*, who stepped forward to fill the gap. Shmueli indicated that his friend hand the baby to Efraim.

One's blasphemy was blatant, the other's hidden. The *mohel* only noticed the obvious. *So he's not a prophet.*

The greater truth was that these two young people could have sunk to the depths of despair and malfunction. I heard Batsheva was an abuse survivor. And Shmueli, never knowing a normal parent or sibling relationship, clung fervently to God. He was an outstanding Torah scholar and a sincere seeker of truth. This baby would be raised by two people deeply committed to creating a real home and a healthy family. And I was sure they would have many difficult challenges.

Yet my children, his brothers and sisters, and I were proud of them. They had overcome a lot of instability.

If Shmueli wanted the child's grandfather to hold his son, let him have this moment. Nothing more need be said.

EPILOGUE

H AVING RELIVED MY STORY, I prayed for wisdom and that Ariella would recognize the signs that I saw in the man she wanted to marry. It took a few months, but eventually he revealed his true nature. She came home in tears, unable to speak.

"Ima, I can't tell him. I can't tell him I won't marry him. I can't do it alone." We cried together, and she asked me to come with her to speak with him.

"I feel like he controls me. He tells me to lie to you, to tell you I really want to marry him. I feel like I can't resist what he says." The fear in her eyes looked so familiar. And I understood all too clearly the pain she was feeling. We decided to go together to speak to his parents. I already understood that we could not speak to the Efraim look-alike alone.

When he asked her step outside with him, I asked her to stay. She was a frightened, little girl who must listen to him, and I was afraid he would take control. The lioness in me was fierce. "Ariella, please stay with me." She looked down, and I saw his icy stare, first in her direction, and then in mine. Did his parents know?

The conversation was short, and we left quickly.

For many days, she cried in her room, unable to believe she had nearly fallen into a parallel drama. We became closer, and she agreed to go for counseling.

After a couple of years, my pretty Ariella met a young man who was good and kind. Wondering if she could really trust herself, it took her a while to feel at peace with him. She brought him to meet me before she became too deeply involved. I liked him and felt he fit beautifully into our family.

Soon after Ariella and Eitan's engagement party, I asked Efraim if he could participate in the wedding expenses. After he agreed to split the amount each set of parents would provide, I confirmed our commitment to Eitan's parents. That was the last time my ex-husband and I spoke, until a few days before the wedding.

Efraim didn't return my frequent calls or messages asking him to confirm that he would have his share of the celebration expenses ready. A week before the wedding, I began to feel stressed, though I tried to be optimistic. He had participated in the other weddings. Yet recently, he had been calling the kids, commenting that things were really hard now and he didn't have any money. When that remark leaked into a conversation with me, I finally called my *rav* for advice.

The *rav* questioned me about many details: my expectations, his responses at previously weddings, and his financial ability.

"I'll think it over and we'll speak again," he said after assuring me that I did not have to carry this burden alone. "It is not your responsibility. He agreed to pay. Although you relayed the message to the *chattan*'s parents that Efraim would be accountable for a certain amount, you are not liable for his commitments."

Although it did not solve the problem, I felt deep relief. Until we spoke, I had actually contemplated taking yet another *gemach*, which I would have been hard put to repay. The newlyweds could pay from the wedding gifts, but I really wanted them to keep that.

How many times had he promised and not come through in the past? Did I fall for his line again?

The next day, the *rav* called to say I should speak to the *chattan*'s parents and explain the situation. "Just tell them the facts. You are not responsible for his debts. Just share with them what is happening. Perhaps the *chattan*'s father should try to reach him."

I hesitated making the call. About four days before the grand celebration, Efraim called to say he had no money. "Nothing. Not even for the bus."

I grimaced, thinking of the enormous amounts of money he

squandered over the years while I tried to feed our family on a tight budget.

With the *rav*'s words fresh in my thoughts, I remained focused. "What will you tell the *chattan*'s parents when you speak to them?" I kept my voice calm. "What will you tell Ariella?"

"Yeah," he said, "it's pretty bad."

In all the years, I never heard that much remorse. He wasn't blaming me this time.

"It's not my responsibility, you know," I told him, shedding what felt like the last shred of codependent addiction. I had told myself I'd find the money to save Ariella from disgrace and humiliation. Now I sensed that this was a remaining fragment of my compulsion to fix what Efraim broke.

As I said the words, "I'm not responsible," I knew it was true. And a lingering heaviness lifted.

I asked him to call Eitan's parents but decided that in our next conversation I would also explain the situation to my new in-laws. I resisted apologetics, stating the realities. "I just wanted you to be aware," I told my daughter's soon to be father-in-law. He passed the test with flying colors.

With equanimity, he agreed that after the wedding we'd figure it out, and we both decided there was no reason to tell the happy, young couple.

Two days later, Efraim called again. "I have it," he stated flatly.

"What?" I asked. I wanted him to be specific.

"The money."

"How much?"

"The amount we agreed on."

I wanted more reassurance. "Checks or cash?"

"Both," he said. Then with a snicker, he added, "and don't worry, they're not my checks. They're good checks."

"Good."

Under the *chuppah*, I observed teary-eyed, as the last of my progeny circled her beloved. Ariella was not the youngest, but she was the last to marry. After the *ketuba* was read, the wine sipped, and

Eitan placed his ring on Ariella's extended finger, my quiet, inner voice spoke to me in a soothing tone, "You can hold your head up high and know you have done your best." I sensed a pleased tinkle and an approving smile. "You have done very well. You can be proud."

At the end of the evening's lively festivities, all my children and my precious grandchildren came to the women's side to participate in the *mezinke*, a dance reserved to celebrate the marriage of the last child.

To the band's lively tune, my adult brood encircled me, dancing and laughingly pulling at my skirt, just like they had many years ago. As I sat, surrounded by the people I loved most, they teased each other and me playfully, even as their own inquisitive little ones crawled or pranced around with them.

When *sabba* Efraim heard the band announce the *mezinke*, he hesitantly approached. He stood just behind the circle unobtrusively. He wanted to share our family's moving occasion.

Kayla placed her hand on his and the *kalla* came to his side. For a moment, the circle was complete. And I surprised myself by not minding. The glass broke under the *chuppah*, but it felt for one moment that our world was whole.

Lightheaded, I felt the next generation was taking its rightful place in the flow of time. When the music stopped, everyone was still in high spirits, but I could see that Efraim felt excluded in the place of our pure, joyful harmony. He turned to leave. No one tried to stop him. He looked like someone who had suddenly aged in front of our eyes.

My family remained, embraced in a circle of dedication and love.

Our close bond exemplified Rabbi Kaufman's sagacious words, "In exposing the truth, you will become a resilient and unified family."

Thank God, I lived to see this day.

Glossary

aguna: woman who is "chained" to her husband, who cannot or refuses to give her a divorce

agura: small Israeli coin

Ain od milvado: there is no one but God

aizeh ba'al: what a (great) husband

aizeh laila: what a night

aleph: first letter of Hebrew alphabet

Am Yisrael: Nation of Israel

Avot: Forefathers — Abraham, Isaac, and Jacob

Avraham Avinu: our father Abraham

b'emet: in truth

b'li neder: without taking a vow

b'ni: my son

b'rit: convenant, as circumcision

ba'al tefilla: leader in the prayers

ba'al teshuva, ba'alat teshuva, ba'alei teshuva: person/people who are newly religious

bachur: young man

baruch Hashem: Blessed is God

bashert: destined spouse

bat Yisrael: daughter of Israel

beit: second letter of Hebrew alphabet

beit din: rabbinical court

beit midrash: study hall

bentching: saying blessing after a meal

biyur chametz: burning of leavened food prior to Passover

boker tov: good morning

burekas: filled pastry

chabibi: my buddy (slang)

challot: braided breads
chattan: groom
chavruta: learning partner
chayav: obligated
chessed: kindness
chevra: friends
chuppa: wedding canopy

d'var Torah, Divrei Torah: word(s) of Torah
daven: pray (Yiddish)
derech: path

eishet chayil: woman of valor
erev tov: good evening

gan: pre-school
Gan Eden: garden of Eden
Gehinom: hell, purgatory
gemach: free loan society
Gemara: talmud
get: divorce
grushim: small coin used under Turkish rule
gutte: good (Yiddish)

hakol b'seder: everything's OK
halacha: Torah law
Hameichin mitzadei gever: He Who prepares the person's path
Hashem: God

illuy: genius
Imahot: Matriarchs — Sarah, Rebecca, Rachel, and Leah

kalla: engaged woman or bride
kavana: intention
kef: fun (slang)

ketuba: wedding contract
Kever Rachel: tomb of Rachel
kiddush: small party after Sabbath day services
Kiddush: recitation over cup of wine at the beginning of Sabbath or holiday meal
kippa: yarmulka
kiruv: to bring closer (to Judaism)
kollel: Jewish study program for married men
Kotel: Western Wall in Jerusalem
kum-kum: tea kettle
kvetch, kvetches: whine(s)

lammed: letter of the Hebrew alphabet
lashon hara: forbidden negative speech
leben: mid-eastern version of yoghurt
lehitraot: goodbye (literally, until we meet again)

madhim: amazing
mamzer: bastard
mazal tov: congratulations
Me'arat Hamachpeila: Cave of the Patriarchs and Matriarchs
Meah She'arim: very religious neighborhood in Jerusalem
melavah malka: light meal after Sabbath
meshugeneh: crazy
mezinke: traditional dance with parents who marry off their last child (Yiddish)
minyan: prayer group of at least ten men
mishna, mishnayot: Jewish law, basis of the Talmud
mitzva, mitzvot: commandment(s)
Modeh Ani: prayer thanking God upon awakening
motek: sweetie
motzaei Shabbat: night following the Sabbath

nachat: pleasure
neshama, neshamot: soul(s)

nu: so? (Yiddish)

Olam Haba: the World to Come
oneg Shabbat: Sabbath pleasure

p'sak din: legal rabbinical ruling
parsha: portion of the Torah
pei: letter of the Hebrew alphabet
pil: elephant

rak rega: just a second
rebbe: rabbi
rebbetzin: rabbi's wife
rega: second
Ribbono Shel Olam: Master of the world
Rosh Chodesh: first day of a new month
Rosh Hashana: Jewish New Year

sabba: grandfather
sandak: godfather
semicha: rabbinical ordination
Sephardi: of Arabic or mid-eastern descent
seudat mitzva: meal celebrating a religious event
Shabbat: Sabbath
Shabbaton: special program on the Sabbath
Shalom Zachar: Friday evening celebration of newborn baby boy
Shalom: peace, hello, goodbye
shalom bayit: peace in the home, usually meaning between
    husband and wife
shavua tov: good week
Shema, Shema Yisrael: Hear o' Israel...
Shemoneh Esrei: central Jewish prayer
sheva berachot: seven blessings given to bride and groom or the
    week after marriage
shidduch: match

shiur: lesson, class
shiva: seven days of mourning after death of a close relative
shlep: carry (Yiddish)
shmatte: rag (Yiddish)
shul: synagogue (Yiddish)
siddur: prayer book
simcha, simchat: happy, joyful
siyum: completion of learning, usually a tractate of Talmud
sponje: Israeli mop

tafsik: stop
talmid chacham: scholarly man
talmud Torah, talmud Torahs: boy's school
techina: sesame spread
tefilla: prayer
tefillin: phylacteries
Tehillim: Psalms
tik: bag, satchel
tikkun: fix
Tisha B'Av: ninth day of the Hebrew month of Av, day of mourning for the two Temples that were destroyed on this date
tiyul: hike, tour
toda rabba: thank you very much
Torah: Bible
tzaddik yesod olam: a person so righteous he sustains the world
tzaddik, tzaddeket: righteous person
tzedaka: charity

ulpan: studio, place to learn Hebrew

ya'ala: come on (Arabic)
yeshiva, yeshivas: high-school and college level institutions of Jewish education
Yiddishkeit: Judaism (Yiddish)

yishar ko'ach: more power to you
yud: letter of Hebrew alphabet

Recommended reading

I Thought It Would Be Different: Strategies for Self-Esteem and Survival, by Dr. Miriam Adahan and T. E. Klein, Feldheim Publishers, 2013.

Abuse in the Jewish Community: Religious and Communal Factors that Undermine the Apprehension of Offenders and the Treatment of Victims, by Michael J. Salamon, Urim Publications, 2014.

The Shame Borne in Silence: Spouse Abuse in the Jewish Community, by Rabbi Dr. Abraham J. Twerski, Mirkov Publications, 1996.

I'm So Confused, Am I Being Abused? Guidance for the Orthodox Jewish Spouse and Those Who Want to Help, by Lisa Twersky, Israel Bookshop Publications, 2011.

Where to turn for help

The following are a few of the organizations offering assistance to people suffering from domestic abuse. Their inclusion here is not a recommendation or approval by the author. Each person should check carefully to verify whether it is an appropriate resource for them.

ISRAEL
TAHEL CRISIS CENTER
Web: www.crisiscenter.org.il
Email: tahel@crisiscenter.org.il
Office: (02) 672-6847
Hotline: (02) 673-0002

BAT MELECH SHELTER
Web: www.batmelech.org.il
Email: batmelech.office@gmail.com
Office: (02) 633-8929
Hotline: (800) 292-333

USA
SHALOM TASK FORCE
Web: www.shalomtaskforce.org
Email: info@shalomtaskforce.org
Office: (212) 742-1478
Hotlines: (718) 337-3700,
    (888) 883-2323

CANADA
JEWISH FAMILY AND CHILD
Web: www.jfandcs.com
Email: info@jfandcs.com
Office: (416) 638-7800
Hotline (after hours):
    (416) 863-0511

ENGLAND
JEWISH WOMEN'S AID
Web: www.jwa.org.uk
Email: info@jwa.org.uk
Offices:
    London: (020) 8445 8060
    Manchester: (0161) 772 4878
Helpline: (0808) 801 0500

9 789657 041031